Kurt Nickle-Dickle of Whiskers

D1722715

Kurt Nickle-Dickle of Whiskers

N. J. McLagan

REDEMPTION PRESS

Published by Redemption Press, PO Box 427, Enumclaw, WA 98022.
Toll-Free (844) 2REDEEM (273-3336)

Redemption Press is honored to present this title in partnership with the author. The views expressed or implied in this work are those of the author. Redemption Press provides our imprint seal representing design excellence, creative content, and high-quality production.

The author has tried to recreate events, locales, and conversations from memories of them. In order to maintain their anonymity, in some instances the names of individuals, some identifying characteristics, and some details may have been changed, such as physical properties, occupations, and places of residence.

Author photo by Leighton Photography & Imaging Studio
Cover illustration by Ken Weigand

ISBN 13: 978-1-64645-521-8 (Paperback)
978-1-64645-472-3 (ePub)
978-1-64645-523-2 (Mobi)

Library of Congress Catalog Card Number: 2021914723

CONTENTS

ༀཆ

PROLOGUE

It was not by chance on that gray, humid day, when the sky was full of rum-tum-grumblings, I stumbled upon *The Book* in the woods near the lake. There it lay in shadow upon the sullied ground, entombed like some lost antiquity beneath a mound of decaying oak leaves—leaves hastily and cunningly laid by the gusty breath of a long-past thunderstorm—leaves sent to conceal for all eternity the wealth of secrets penned upon the volume's primordial pages.

As I bent down and brushed the leaves from the book, my fingers struck the raised edges of an engraving, and when I pried the volume loose from the earth and withdrew it from the shadows, I was able to see the engraving in its entirety, a skillful rendering of a mountain carved in relief into the thickness of the book's rich brown leather cover. I marveled that, despite the entombment beneath the moldering leaves, the leather had not one mark defacing it.

How rare and wondrous was *The Book!*—ancient by all indications—its weathered bindings smelling of antiquitous tombs; its parchment pages brittle and timeworn; its frontispiece, like its cover, masterfully rendered, reflecting a time long-past when artistry and workmanship were valued above worldly treasures.

As I gazed at the book's frontispiece, I somehow felt as one with its subject, a pastoral scene of an animal kingdom laid at the foot of a great cloud-tipped mountain. So resplendent was the scene with scrollwork and fine embellishment that at once I was reminded of the family crests of houses blessed with great fortune. It struck me as odd that I, an ordinary man, should feel such kinship to it.

Curious to know the book's content, and seeing no title, I began turning the parchment pages one by one. To my astonishment, not a single word did I find to suggest the volume's purpose. Surely such a finely crafted book should have some content. Disappointed, I moved to close the cover, but hesitated when my eye detected, deep within the volume's bindings, a light, dim and barely perceptible. Bemused by the faint and fragile spark, wondering who or what could have bound it within the dark and lifeless volume, I watched it grow in brightness until its burgeoning rays flooded the parchment pages, causing them to gleam like sheets of polished silver.

The light began to shimmer; the pages fluttered; and out from the book there burst a silver fountain that consumed the book and soared toward the heavens, then showered down like gentle rain to pool beneath the darkening clouds. Despite the grayness of the day, the great body of gathered light sparkled as does the surface of a wind-tossed lake when sunlight striking its myriad caplets turns it to a field of diamonds.

As I stood transfixed, my gaze locked upon the marvelous sight in the sky, there fell upon my ear a faraway sound like rushing wind. And I saw, cast darkly against the light, a shadow of bird-like proportion that soared and dove in great spirals, disappearing within the light, reappearing, transforming itself as it flew, turning shadow to substance, becoming, at length, the Great Winged Creature—the Nimbus! Though the pages I had held in my hands were void of script, I sensed words I could neither see nor hear had risen from the brittle parchment and summoned the creature forth.

Then earthward he plunged—this union of light and shadow—this Nimbus—downward, downward—riding the tail of a mighty wind whose gusty voice heralded his coming and called great billows of dust to rise about me.

I covered my eyes to shield them from the sting of wind and blowing dust, but managed still to see dimly the dark raptor as he stretched his blade-like talons toward earth. When the Nimbus touched ground, the wind, as if to humble itself before the creature, diminished to a gentle breeze, whispered syllables I could not discern, and fell still and silent.

And I saw, within the shroud of settling dust, the dark silhouette whose wings, still spread, spanned the length of east to west. When the dust came fully to rest I beheld the colossal creature himself, looming above me, folding his massive wings as he peered into my eyes.

I opened my mouth to speak, but no sound came forth. Perhaps the Nimbus spoke, or perhaps I merely sensed his words, but before I could attempt again to utter a syllable, I heard the first of a wondrous tale and found myself transported into the tale itself—to the very place—to the very moment the story began. Feeling no more tangible than air, yet fully possessed of my senses, I watched and listened as the whole of the story unfolded.

Permit me now to tell the tale from the beginning, just as it was told to me by the Nimbus.

CHAPTER 1

THE GATHERING GLOOM

There is no need to fear the dark—the dark of night that does no ill—the dark that calls when light withdraws and sleep is cast upon the land and quiet voices bid creatures of day, "Come. Dream your dreams until the light sends us away."

This darkness cools the summer day at its end and often yields a part of itself to the moon, inviting that great light of evening to spread a blanket of silver upon the land. *This* darkness watches lazily as the moon tucks its shimmering blanket into folds of hills and gently pulls it over tops of trees, and rolls it out in soft, downy billows across lakes and fields and meadows. No, there is nothing to fear in *this* darkness.

But there is a dark that's ever black, and blacker still, that longs to cross our window sills—the dark whose name is Ancient, Death, and Legion—the dark whose name, when whispered, summons evil from the tomb—the dark that chills the evening's shade—the dark they call the *Gloom*. In this, there is much to fear:

> Beware the Gloom, dear child, that gathers on nights ill-begotten; that crouches in shadow and creeps within shade; that, cloaked in black, steals on goat's feet through foggy glades, entrenching itself in crack and cranny, filling rock and rift with evil intentions, appearing to be what it is not.

15

Beware the Gloom, dear child—that thickety cloud of watchity widgits—that rickety crowd of kratchits and kridgits that creeps and crawls into caverns musty within the earth, dark and crusty, seeking its master, the gnomish nib, asleep within his earthen crib.

Beware the Gloom, dear child—that mutable menace that slips from out shadow and slides from out shade, then flees to distant dreary places, there to gather strength to sound the knell—strength to wield with cloven claw the wand that strikes the leaden bell.

Who can say what wisp of a hand stirred the boy from his sleep that night? Perhaps it was no hand at all. Perhaps it was the dismal croak of a deep-voiced bullfrog, who, while calling night creatures to wake, mistook Kurt for one of its own.

Or perhaps it was the sepulchral stillness that fell upon the air when the crickets stopped their chirping—when something cold at the west end of the valley dropped the temperature to such a degree it hushed the perpetual chorus that nightly lamented the long day's demise.

Certainly it could not have been the voice of the old grandfather clock in the hall. Certainly not the steady *tick-tock-tick* so familiar to the boy. For every night the ancient oak timepiece thus ticked. And every night Kurt fell asleep to the beloved clock's whispering, "Good night, sleep tight, sleep tight, sleep tight."

But if one had listened closely, one might have heard within the steady ticking a message, muffled and only faintly discernable, like words escaping a hand clasped over a mouth—a hand that sought that night to silence the old clock as it tried to warn, "Awake! Awake! Awake! The midnight nears! Awake!"

Perhaps the circumstance of Kurt's waking was no more peculiar than the fact he slept at all. The late-August day had been disagreeably hot, and now the stale, humid air trapped within the bedroom hung over the boy's bed like a thick, gray canopy poised to drop and smother him at the least stirring. Even the open window near the foot of the bed dared not draw a breeze or offer so much as a fresh breath.

Nevertheless, Kurt did waken, and with a start, for a piercing chill ran the length of his body, and the bed so familiar to him—the old feather bed that from his earliest youth had cradled him to sleep—at once felt cold and discomforting. Lit by the blanket of wan moonlight filtering dimly through the window, it resembled hard, gray granite—a rigid slab into which the soft folds of bed linens had been skillfully and deceitfully carved.

Turning his thoughts from the bed, Kurt sat up and perused the shadows and darkish objects in the room, searching for something that might have fallen from a shelf or otherwise wakened him. But he found nothing amiss—unless one considered the grim, gray light itself a thing amiss. For unlike the silver moonlight of other nights, this drab imposter washed all traces of color from the bedroom walls and drained life-giving hues from curtains and furnishings and all else in the room.

Bong!—Bong—Bong! When the clock in the hall began to strike, Kurt counted the ten clear, ambient chimes, taking comfort in the picture they spawned of the clock's great silver pendulum swinging back and forth and back and forth, its movement perpetual, never faltering, always mathematically correct.

Bong!—Bong!—Bong! As he counted, he was surprised at what seemed a slight hesitation before each stroke. Was it his imagination, or was the tone growing deeper as well?

The last chime faded and Kurt allowed himself to fall back to sleep. But when the clock struck eleven, he found himself awake again, for now the chime sounded heavy and belabored, as though the aged timekeeper wished not to mark the hour at all.

Though troubled at first by the faltering chime, Kurt soon set his mind at ease, blaming the burdensome air through which the sound had to pass. Or perhaps there was a weariness within the clock, he reasoned—a weariness brought on by too many years of steadfastly marking seconds and minutes and hours.

When at half past eleven the clock struck once, a cold shudder passed through the boy's body, for now the old timekeeper spoke in a voice no longer its own—the voice of a soul dreary, dark, and dreadful. The low and ominous tone echoed through the hall less like a chime and more like the toll of a ponderous bell.

Gathering the bed sheets up tight around his neck, Kurt lay quiet, listening, certain if he listened intently enough his ear would detect within the knell's fading remnant some telltale element. But the tone trailed away, leaving only the clock's perfectly metered *tick-tock-tick*—ticking that echoed the steady swinging of the great silver pendulum back and forth and back and forth in time with the pulsating chirp of the crickets, who again lamented outside the window, and the metered croak of bullfrogs, who now called unceasingly to the night creatures. The nocturnal rhythms, as delicately balanced as a fine orchestra, filled the air with night music, and once more Kurt drifted off to sleep as thoughts of the dim, gray light and the bell disappeared somewhere within the folds of the bedcovers.

All at once the ticking of the clock slowed to a languorous pace, and like an orchestra robbed of its conductor, the night rhythms fell to clamorous disarray! It was as if a cymbal had crashed to the floor! And again Kurt awoke with a start.

Perhaps the grandfatherly clock, in slowing the swing of its pendulum, wished to draw the child's attention—to roust him from a stupor. Or perhaps it sought to stall time—to delay the inevitable countdown to some terrible catastrophe.

But time waits neither for boy, nor man, nor beast, nor keepers of time. Already, shadows stole across the wall opposite the window in Kurt's bedroom—dark shadows that drew the boy's attention and sent him rushing to the window seeking the shadows' source. Peering out, he saw that scattered nimbus clouds had formed above the valley and were drifting slowly across the moon. "Cloud shadows," he told himself. "Only cloud shadows."

When he grabbed the window sash to pull it down, he noticed a darkness building toward the west. Billows, black and churning, were tumbling down the hillsides, gathering thickly on the valley floor. "Fog," he told himself. "Only fog." But gazing longer, he found himself unable to move, as though by casting his eyes upon the mysterious fog he had unleashed the binding spell of an ancient sorcerer. It was not until a gust of cold air rushed in through the window and whipped the white lace curtains around his shoulders that he was able to free himself and slam the sash shut.

The frigid gust of musty air disappeared in the space of the room, leaving behind a remnant of staleness, a trace of rancidity. The burdensome air already present pressed against Kurt's chest as though now it were imbued with some viscous, unbreathable substance.

Kurt jumped into bed and pulled up Grandmother's quilt that lay folded across the footboard. The clock's ticking grew louder and the boy's eyes turned again to the shadows on the wall—shadows now hard-edged, black, and serpentine—shadows that swayed sinuously to and fro to a muted melody Kurt had no wish to hear. The darkly piped strains twisted around the boy like strong black tendrils, holding him spellbound, locking his gaze upon the shadows on the wall.

As the melody faded, the shadows slowed, entwining themselves into a misshapen specter. Kurt watched the grim apparition slip sideward along the wall and halt at the window's edge. Ever so slowly, as though a hand—or many hands—had reached out to draw a deadly shade, a veil of fog descended the window glass, and the ashen light within the room dimmed to deepest gray and darkened to blackest black.

No distinction was there now between the world beyond the glass and the world inside the room. All without and all within lay in cold, abysmal darkness.

Kurt could discern neither up from down, nor forward from back. He felt as though he would have fallen through the poleless darkness for all eternity had it not been for the fine thread to which he clung—the silver thread—the relentless *tock-tick-tock* of the old grandfather clock.

From deep within the darkness came the cold clash of hammer striking metal—the first stroke of midnight—the casting of a spell.

Kurt fumbled for the edge of the quilt, and finding it, quickly drew the cover up over his head. Again came the clash of hammer striking metal as the clock struck the deuce.

How the old clock struggled against the hour! Belaboredly it struck, as one who is forced to wield a hammer greater than himself.

> *Twelve times it struck,*
> *marking the hour—*
> *Twelve times it fought*
> *to quell the dark power—*
> *Twelve times it stood*
> *for the terrible fight—*
> *Till at last it fell still*
> *with the twelfth stroke of midnight . . .*

Midnight!

Kurt held his breath, afraid to breathe.

From the depths of the darkness came a tramping of feet—a multitude of feet—muffled at first and off at a great distance. The tramping grew louder, and soon Kurt heard it clearly. An army! Its myriad legions thundering toward him!

The boy gasped for air. He thought to run but could not move from the bed. Surely he would be trampled—he, his bed, his house, and all in it! But to his surprise, the grim army passed overhead. Legion upon legion it passed, tramping above him in the dark until the last remnants, having followed their vanguard far to the west, faded to a faint rumble and disappeared altogether in the distance.

For some time after, no sound broke the silence. But the marching called to Kurt's mind a tale his grandfather once told him—a tale about a bell of dark countenance—a tale within whose dismal tapestry was woven a sullen warning. Now he remembered it as one remembers the dreadful shadow of a bad dream:

Well away from Whiskers' gate,
Watchity widgits lie in wait.
Hiding far from human view,
Kratchits and kridgits are lurking too.

They call to join them ghoulish cronies,
Darkish things and terrible bonies,
Hear them marching from the tomb,
The cloven feet of the Gathering Gloom.

Watchity widgits wield the wand—
They strike the bell and seal the bond.
Kratchits and kridgits echo the knell—
With gadgets and gidgits they strike the bell.

While ghoulish cronies howl and moan
And terrible bonies growl and groan,
The darkish things that lurk and loom
Blather and bleat to stir the Gloom.

Staring and glaring and sneaking and peeking
Down through the clouds, their sunken eyes seeking,
They wickedly watch the earthen crib,
Awaiting the stir of the gnomish nib,

Till out he rolls, the nebulous nob!
Thundering forth, the horrible hob!
And calls to arms the Gathering Gloom
That summoned him forth from out his tomb.

Now begins the terrible march,
The thunderous tramp toward the arch,
Stomping and tromping mid roar and rumble,
Stamping and tramping mid rum-tum-grumble.

21

Hear the thumping, bumping, clumping,
Stumping feet of the Gathering Gloom;
Moaning, groaning, scowling, growling,
Howling bleat of the Gathering Gloom.

Marching feet!
Howling bleat!
Hideous fleet!
The Gathering Gloom!

When the grandfather clock struck half past midnight, Kurt peeked out from beneath the bed covers and breathed in cool, fresh air. The black veil had lifted from the window glass and the fog had rolled away. The moon, able again to spread a shimmering light across the sill, covered all it touched with a delicate blanket of fine silver. Shadows on the wall, now pale and diffused, were merely those of scattered nimbus clouds—soft, vaporous nimbus clouds—the kind that promise gentle, cleansing rain.

As the silver moonlight erased all traces of dread from the room, Kurt dismissed the nightmarish sights and sounds as having been childish imaginings. He knew nothing of the darkness that lay high and away, far to the west, waiting to call at dawn its master, waiting to wake the ancient Troll, waiting to summon the thunder to roll. For it cloaked itself well, this Gathering Gloom, waiting to call the Troll from his tomb.

CHAPTER 2

THE FALL

With the Gloom gathered high and away, the dark that does no ill reclaimed the night and bestowed sleep upon creatures of light. As one such creature, Kurt fell to dreaming under the canopy of clouds that formed above the valley.

By sunrise, the clouds, fully plumped and ripe with rain, could no longer hold their precious bounty. Coaxed by the light of approaching dawn, they burst and spilled a gentle, cleansing rain upon all things living and nonliving. From the frailest grasses to the mightiest boulders, the rain touched all and washed away the last vestiges of midnight's dreary spell.

> *The valley slept neath nimbus clouds,*
> *Misty, vaporous, veiling shrouds*
> *That held within their wombs that night*
> *A magic rain and silver light.*
>
> *And just before the dawn's first glow,*
> *They sifted on the earth below*
> *The precious pearls, the silver grain,*
> *The soft, the silent, silver rain.*
>
> *And elfin voices on the breeze*
> *Whispered through the swaying trees*

And dried the drops and left behind
A fairy dust of silver shine.

And morning's warm and gentle hand
Spilled silver light on all the land
So all upon the earth could bask
In sunlight poured from sterling flasks.

Never had the valley seen
Such sparkling light of silver sheen—
A crystal light with rainbows drifting
In its midst, their colors sifting

Through the quiet morning air
To color all the earth so fair
With laughing pinks and greens and blues
And yellow, orange, and violet hues.

Sunbeams dancing in the light
In silken gowns of purest white,
With rainbows shining in their hair,
Spun and twirled upon the air.

One playful beam, a radiant child,
Laughing, giggling all the while,
Tripped atop the highest trees,
And tumbled down upon the breeze.

This spectral spirit, this light-laden sprite,
This blithe, bedazzling celestial sight,
Bounced upon the puffy pillows
Of dandelion down and pussy willows.

She laughed and teased, this mischievous child,
Sparkling, shimmering all the while
She wrestled and rollicked and frolicked mid chases
That rousted raindrops from resting places.

Then slipping and sliding down rain-polished leaves,
This innocence shimmered and glimmered and gleamed
Her way into places better left sleeping—
Places in shadow burdened with weeping.

Tasting the staleness of dungeons decayed,
Her appetite whetted by games unplayed—
By questions unanswered, by questions unasked—
She set about the forbidden task

Of searching and seeking in shadows below,
In rooms where sunbeams dare not go,
For secrets locked in deepest tombs
Within the shadow's wretched womb.

Down yet deeper and darker she crawled,
Heeding not the pleading call
Of spirits above, of voices slight,
That tried to warn the falling sprite.

Onward she stumbled through darkened lairs,
Winding her way down shadowed stairs,
Till reaching the depths of blackness below,
Her innocence waned, her gleam dimmed to glow.

This fading fairy, this dying star,
Plunged into chasms blacker than tar
And rolled and tumbled ever so far
From Nickledown and light . . . .

Then on her elfish ears there fell
The distant toll of the leaden bell
That summons forth from deepest Sheol
The dark and dreaded Thunder Troll.

Her thoughts unleashed by the tolling call,
She remembered the fate that must befall

The beam whose elfin eyes behold
The hideous face of the ancient Troll.

Within her fragile skin she shook.
She dared not peek, she dared not look.
She dared not face the loathsome Troll
Whose stare could steal her tiny soul.

So, crouched inside a craggy niche—
A thin and narrow shadowy ditch—
She listened for the closing knell,
The final call of the leaden bell,

Knowing, once the Troll had passed,
Her lot would be to flee at last;
For the Troll would be in distant regions,
Leading forth his gathered legions.

When, at length, the silence came,
She crawled from out her earthen frame,
Certain stealth had aptly saved
Her hapless soul from a sullen grave.

But masters of deceit work thusly:
Cloaked in lies, mid spirits fusty,
Stealing close on silent feet,
They work their deeds of dark deceit.

From up behind the Troll appeared!
And as the sunbeam pled and teared,
His burning eyes of molten coal
Devoured the light from her tiny soul.

There he left her, pale and low,
A twisted beam, a faded glow,
A fallen flower, a wilted bloom,
Alone and dying in the tomb.

Yet, still the call to light pervaded;
Beyond the tomb, its voice persuaded,
"Gather in thy weakish light!
Upward flee in winding flight!"

Till death this serpentine sprig resisted—
Till toiling and straining and groping she twisted
Her dim-lit spirit up from the shade
And, lamenting, flickered through meadow and glade,

Seeking the boy to tell him her story
Of darkness and shadow and faded glory;
To whisper the words, to tell of her strife
And beg him to aid in saving her life.

With all her fading strength she fought
To find the boy, the child she sought,
To warn him quickly, lest he fall
Through darkness, too, and miss the call—

The call that beckons all who grieve;
Who, lost in shadow, still conceive
One glint of hope, and so believe
In Nickledown and light . . . .

Then before her stood the goal—
Her only hope of outwitting the Troll.
She'd found the house where Kurt and his mother
And Charlie, the dog, dwelled with each other.

The weakened, waning, rainbow light
Of the wizened, woeful, diminished sprite
Entered the house through the crack in the door,
Through loose-fitting sashes and holes in the floor,

And filled the room with narrow streams
Of faintly colored pastel beams

That weakly danced behind the door
And lightly played upon the floor,

Giving the air an aged patina—
A luminous glow that eyes much keener
Than Kurt's may have noticed—that Kurt may have seen
Were he fully awake, his senses keen.

The sprite whispered softly and tugged at Kurt's sleeve,
Fearing her destiny ever to grieve
Should he heed not the call, should he fail to leave
For Nickledown and light . . . .

Thus it happened, the start of it all,
With raindrops and sunbeams, creatures so small,
Lighting the way, sending the call
To Nickledown and light . . . .

But Kurt neither heard the whisper nor felt the tug.

Chapter 3

Rumblings

The boy's given name was Kurtis Francis Nickle-Dickle, but everyone, save a few who preferred to mock him, called him Kurt.

The form of address was of little importance to others but was a matter of great consequence to the boy, for the Creator had bestowed the least of embellishments upon the child, endowing him with fiery red hair and copper-colored freckles in good measure—curses to Kurt's way of thinking. And without apparent forethought, the same Creator had perpetuated a woeful legacy, afflicting the child with a noticeable infirmity that set him apart from other nine-year-olds and made him the object of jeering and jest. Like his father, Kurt was lame from birth and nothing could be done about it.

But something *could* be done about the name—that terrible, too-many-syllabled, ridicule-provoking name whose first was stuffy, middle was cross-gendered, and last lent itself to petty prittle-prattle, such as, "Let us tickle the Nickle-Dickle with a pickle."

With brevity and bullishness in mind—and the desire for a long-overdue measure of blessing—the boy shortened his name, in part, to Kurt. A brusque, no-nonsense name such as Kurt, he reasoned, would ward off mockery. It might even start him on the road to endless good fortune.

But fortune, if it lies in names at all, lies in names given, not contrived—names, by birthright, unalterable. Whether Kurt or

Kurtis, the boy was a Nickle-Dickle, and therein lay the key to cursing or blessing.

The trailing remains of emptied clouds had long-since dissolved in the eastern sky by the time Kurt awoke that fateful morning. Had he wakened earlier, he might have noticed the shimmer of life within the fallen raindrops clinging to the window near his bed, and he might have heard the call to Nickledown. The tiny beads tripped and skipped in zigzag dance down the window glass as though water nymphs, too miniscule for eyes to see, laughed and frolicked within. From time to time, they stopped mid dance to gather rays, as one would gather a spring bouquet, and sent them streaming through the window glass and across Kurt's bed, covering the boy with a rainbow blanket as he slept.

Kurt lay dreaming of a flute whose music sweetly called to him from a distant summit high above the clouds. But the night of his dreams grew cold when the flute was hushed by the din of dark ones calling feverishly to their master.

The sense of foreboding that overwhelmed the boy as he stirred from his sleep seemed unfounded when at last he was fully awake. In the twilight of waking, he had half expected to open his eyes to meet the gaze of some wizened creature glaring at him from a dim-lit corner. Instead, he found a room that welcomed morning—a room quiet except for the muffled *drip, drip, drip* of raindrops falling from the roof to puddles beneath the window.

To convince himself all was well, Kurt counted, as he did every morning, the familiar chimes as the clock in the hall struck seven. But this day the sound sent a torrent of grim recollections pouring over him, and he sprang from the bed, rushed to the window, and threw open the sash. Leaning far out over the sill, he listened. The fresh morning air was full of birdsong. The sun felt warm and comforting on his face. There was no bell, no fog, no thunderous army aloft.

"It was all a dream," he told himself, reaching for the window sash. "Only a dream."

A breeze ruffled the white lace curtains near his shoulders, and he thought for a moment he heard the faintest trace of a knell. But the sound faded like the wisp of a dream that can almost be remembered but too soon drifts away to hide wherever dreams come from. As if to mock him, raindrops dripping from the roof echoed, "noth-ing, noth-ing, noth-ing," and he slammed the sash shut, feeling foolish.

"Watchity widgits and kratchits and kridgits!" he grumbled, pulling off his pajamas on the way to the clothes closet. "Who ever heard of such things!" Throwing the pajamas on the floor, he searched for his lucky plaid fishing shirt and old blue jeans he had hidden in the back of the closet, far from his mother's washing machine.

As he dressed himself on that warm, late summer morning, he let pass the thought of unusual happenings in the air about him. Indeed, he should have, for such things are not meant for the minds of mere humans, except at times of particular enchantment, and Kurt had no way of knowing such an enchantment had begun.

> *A secret lay locked away*
> *Where otherworldly ones abide:*
> *Within a strange, enchanted land*
> *Where whiskered ones and sunbeams hide.*

Kurt's footsteps fell unevenly upon the wood plank floor of the old farmhouse as he made his way barefooted toward the kitchen. Halfway down the hall he paused to listen to a faint rumble, the precursor to a storm building in the west. Having studied weather in school, Kurt knew storms approached from the west in his part of the country, so he walked to the window at the end of the hall and looked out in that direction. Much to his relief, he found a vast meadow of blue spread above the valley as far as he could see. When he gazed across the fallow field that marked the west boundary of the farm, a sadness overtook him, and he reached into his shirtfront and withdrew a key that hung from a chain around his neck. Grandfather had passed the key to Kurt's father, and Kurt's father was to pass it to Kurt on the boy's ninth birthday. A legacy—that's what Father had called it. He was to explain the key's significance on Kurt's birthday too. But Father disappeared long before Kurt turned nine, so the boy had no idea what the key was for. He wore it only because it made him feel close to his father.

The key was by no means ordinary, being medieval in style, heavy, and embellished at one end with the finely sculpted bust of a bird—a vulture by all appearances—whose head was ornately adorned with scrollwork resembling a crown. Though the key was solid silver, one would not have perceived it as so from its outward appearance, for its surface was black with tarnish. Indeed, some might have described it as blacker than black, a shade Kurt's grandfather would have called "the color of darkness below purple."

Despite the key's apparent lack of care, Kurt's father had refused to polish it. By way of explanation he had said only that its true "mettle" would show at the proper time.

After studying the key for a moment Kurt tucked it back into his shirt. He was about to turn from the window but hesitated when he thought he detected movement beyond the glass. Stepping closer to the window, he stared intently across the valley's sunlit landscape.

Perhaps it was the antique glass in the windowpane, with its bent toward distortion, that all at once made the whole outside appear to wave at the boy. Or perhaps Kurt's vision had somehow stumbled upon the imperceptible—something alive within the sparkling light, dancing, beckoning, urging him to hurry along. Whatever the explanation, Kurt longed all the more to be outdoors at his secret place by the lake, to spend this last fragile day of summer vacation with his dog and his thoughts and his favorite book before school began again with its annual bevy of troubles.

"Good morning, dear," Mother said when Kurt stepped into the kitchen. The petite woman wearing a checkered blue housedress and a starched apron was standing in front of a large cast-iron cookstove with her back toward Kurt. She was stirring a thick paste of steamy oatmeal that bubbled just below the rim of the pot.

Hoping she had not heard the thunder amid all the burbling and gurgling, Kurt slipped past her and made his way to the broom closet. There he quietly climbed onto a footstool and removed an old blue backpack from a top shelf.

"I won't be having breakfast with you this morning," Mother said, glancing over her shoulder. "I promised to take Mrs. Abercrombe to the train station."

Kurt could see his mother's face was ghostly pale, but he said nothing. Instead, he unfastened the center pouch on the backpack, looked inside, and sniffed the slight odor of fish left in the pack from previous trips. To Kurt, the smell was a fine perfume, an intoxicating scent that conjured images of warm sunshine, blue water, and carefree summer days. Anticipating one more such day, he took stock of his fishing line and fishhooks. When thunder rumbled faintly, he stopped to listen. Before he could determine the thunder's distance, the sound was obscured by a familiar scratching on the screened door. Charlie, Kurt's lanky vagabond dog, stood peering anxiously through the screen, panting as though he had just finished a frantic run.

Mother stopped stirring the oatmeal and held the door open for Charlie. "A storm is coming, dear." Charlie zoomed past her and plopped down beneath the kitchen table. "I know you want to go to the lake today, but I'll be gone for several hours, and I need to know you're safe at home. It was just such a day—"

"I know," Kurt snapped. "It was just such a day when Father disappeared."

"I'm sorry, dear, but I don't want to lose you too."

"But Mother, school starts tomorrow, and all the trouble will start—the names and all that. Just because a person likes to read, that doesn't make him a bookworm. And I'm not a fraidy-cat either. I just can't do certain things with my bad leg."

Mother removed the steaming pot from the hot burner and set it aside. "Kurt, dear, names can't harm you. They're only words."

"Words can hurt," Kurt said, and he dropped the backpack on the floor and slumped into the big oak armchair at the end of the table—a chair that had been his father's—and set his face with a most determined frown.

"And that bully, Duff Skruggs . . . He said I stunk, just because I wore my lucky fishing shirt to school. Everyone knows a fishing shirt isn't lucky if it doesn't have a good fish smell. I should have told on him, but I don't tattle."

Mother drew up a chair and sat down close to her son and reached out and touched his hand. "Remember what your father said, Kurt. 'It's not what you're *called*; it's what you *are* that counts.'"

With a frown that was now even more disagreeable, Kurt snatched his hand away and slumped farther down into the oversized chair.

Mother looked at him sternly. "You must promise me you'll stay at home. There *will* be a storm. Look at Charlie. He knows. Dogs always know."

Kurt lifted the edge of the tablecloth and peeked at Charlie, whose soft brown eyes peered back at him beneath furrowed brows. The dog was quivering noticeably.

"Promise me," Mother repeated.

"I promise," Kurt mumbled, letting the tablecloth fall back into place. A minute later, he found himself staring blankly at a bowl of steaming oatmeal Mother had placed on the table in front of him. Placed there, too, were a plate of crisp toast and a freshly laundered white linen napkin—a family custom.

Having no interest in eating, Kurt watched his mother hurry over to the copper coat rack by the back door, where she removed her apron and donned an odd-looking raincoat made of piebald pink-and-yellow patches—a coat that had been a gift from Kurt's father. After tying a matching kerchief snugly beneath her chin, she returned to where Kurt was sitting and leaned down to kiss him, but Kurt quickly turned his head so that her kiss barely brushed his cheek.

"You must remember your promise," Mother said when thunder rumbled again. Touching her son's cheek, she repeated, "I couldn't bear to lose you," and she left, letting the screened door flap behind her.

A sudden breeze caught the door and banged it several times.

"Perfect day for watchity widgits," Kurt said to Charlie as he hurried to secure the latch. Glancing behind him, he saw the big brown mutt with one ear up and one ear down peek out from under the tablecloth and cock his head to the side.

"It's nothing, Charlie. I was just thinking about a tale Grandfather told me."

Kurt watched his mother climb into her faded gray sedan. He watched until the car disappeared down the long, dirt driveway. After staring a moment at the sky toward the west, he scrunched his face into a grotesque snarl, hunched his shoulders like a fiendish villain he had read about in a book, and turned toward Charlie, drawing his hands up like stiff claws in front of him. "I'm a watchity widgit named Igor," he growled, chasing Charlie out from under the table. "Tha-rum-rum-rum!" he roared, stalking the animal around the kitchen.

Charlie slinked one step ahead of the boy, and at the first opportunity, slipped beneath the wooden bench in the corner. Peering up from under the bench, he stared at Kurt curiously, and little white crescents showed beneath the warm brown of his eyes.

Kurt squatted and stroked the dog's muzzle. "Sorry, boy. I didn't mean to scare you. I've told you over and over, Charlie. Thunder won't hurt you. 'A giant's footsteps on the floor of the sky'—that's what Grandfather said thunder was. And we both know there are no giants."

Kurt tugged at Charlie's tattered brown collar but let go when the dog refused to budge.

"You see, Charlie, everything Grandfather said was just imagination—giants, and watchity widgits, and kratchits and kridgits—all that stuff. It was just an old man telling tales."

Kurt sat down at the table and resigned himself to eating the oatmeal and toast, and soon Charlie crawled out from under the bench and sprawled on the floor beside him.

As Kurt listened to the ticking of the clock in the hall, he wondered how many times the great silver pendulum would swing before the start of school the next day. "Charlie," he said, tossing a piece of toast to the dog, "what if we go to the lake anyway? Mother won't be back for hours. She said so herself."

Charlie whined and crinkled his eyebrows into a point between his eyes.

"Don't look at me that way, Charlie. What Mother doesn't know won't hurt her."

Kurt quickly made four peanut butter and jelly sandwiches (three for himself and one for Charlie) and stuffed them into his backpack along with two cans of soda and two large handfuls of Chunkie Chewies, Charlie's favorite dog biscuits. When he had checked to see that his library book was in the pack and was satisfied all was in order, he hurried to the garage, with Charlie trailing close behind, and fetched his bamboo fishing pole and can of worms.

As he headed across the open field toward the winding road that would take him to the lake, he took no notice of the cowering way in which the dog was following him, his head held low, the worried stare, the crinkled brow. Had he noticed, he might have reconsidered and wisely heeded his mother's warning: "There *will* be a storm. Look at Charlie. He knows. Dogs always know."

CHAPTER 4

THUNDER

The day that appeared warm and inviting when Kurt peered through the hall window proved to be hot and unbearably humid as the boy and his dog trudged along the dirt road to the lake. August's searing sun had swallowed the little moisture laid down by the early morning rain, leaving the road parched and hot to the touch and covered in a thick layer of fine, red dust that, step by step, painted Kurt's feet the color of burnished copper.

Slowly the long road wended its way across the valley floor through a landscape wrought with signs of summer's end. Like a bereaved mother tending her dying children, it passed through flowerless fields and sun-parched meadows, drew near the edges of dry creek beds, touched lightly upon the banks of dust-laden ponds, all the while able to do no more than take quiet notice of the inescapable legacy left by fading summer.

Not long ago, Summer, the Bright Enchantress, still young and full of magic, had adorned the land in queenly array, turning emerald springtime's pale and tender leaves, gold its fragile grasses. Convinced of her immortality, she, without care, had strewn wildflowers like spilled jewels upon the land, lavishing field and meadow with the rich red of garnet, the deep purple of amethyst, the fiery gold of topaz. Now Summer lay on her downward side, slipping toward that little sleep that wraps each season, for a time, in mortalness. Her magic waning, her powers diminished, her rich golden palette sullied by grays and earth-tones, she turned quietly toward autumn, leaving behind a land brown and burnished, blanched and barren—a land bereft of jewel and fine raiment—a land soon to be dressed only in dried weeds and sharp thistles.

Already encroaching autumn had pressed its maleficent mark upon the first of its unsuspecting messengers—leaves, prematurely fallen, hastily arrayed in borrowed tones of ochre and burnt sienna—leaves that, vainly seeking to rush the summer's end, had hurled upon themselves the very end they wished upon the fading summer. A dozen or so such ill-fated ones, rustled by a sudden breeze, danced in brittle merriment across the road in front of Kurt, waving goodbye to the Season of Light. Had no one told them this was the morning of clinging hope that always dawns at August's end—the moment in nether time when Summer breathes once more upon the land before settling to her autumn and winter sleep? Perhaps something more menacing than autumn itself—something deceitful and coldly sinister, well-hidden within the air—whispered to the leaves of an early winter; spoke to them with icy voice, coaxing them to don, too soon, the ruinous red-and-yellow cloak of autumn.

Surprised by the sudden appearance of the breeze, and the equally sudden appearance of a small whirlwind a few yards up the road, Kurt stopped to watch. He was watching still when the whirlwind tousled some leaves by the wayside, drew them into a tight circle, and sent them rushing headlong toward him. Before the tempest reached him, Kurt ducked to the right and the whirlwind veered to his left and swooshed past him. An evil omen—that's what Grandfather would have called it. The hiss of the ill-tempered wind was still resounding in his ears when a second gust struck him full in the face. A moment later, another, having shifted direction, pushed at his back and blew past him. The latter bore in its wake the muffled sound of faraway thunder:

A rumble it was—a thundery rumble;
Nothing more than a thundery grumble.

38

Nothing more; no great surprise—
Except for the other—the STARING EYES!

Kurt felt the eyes peering at him—a multitude of eyes watching so intently he was sure they saw his heart pounding in his chest. Drawing a breath, he whirled around. And that's when he saw them! Thunderheads—the biggest he had ever seen—looming tall and purple-gray above the mountaintops to the west. Kurt was sure these were no ordinary thunderheads. They boiled like the brackish brew in a witch's cauldron.

Billowing, burbling, belching they boiled,
As in them a tumultuous tempest toiled.

At first they appeared as terrible tombstones—granite-like apparitions, rolling and churning within their chiseled boundaries. Then upward they billowed—twisting and turning—molding themselves into tortuous towers.

From tower to tombstone, tombstone to tower,
They changed, rearranged, befitting the hour.

From tower to tombstone, tombstone and back,
They changed, rearranged, growing blacker than black.

For a moment, Kurt thought his eyes were playing tricks on him, as on a summer day when cloud shapes suggest things not there. But when the nebulous thunderheads transformed themselves into full-fledged fortresses, he knew he was seeing more than his imagination could have conjured. There, in fact, they stood: drear castles with deep, grisly dungeons; bleak bastions on whose fog-shrouded parapets grim soldiers marched; tall, twisted towers, whose sharp-nailed spires cast long-fingered shadows across the necks of gargoyles hunched grotesquely atop cold, stone battlements—gargoyles gray-faced, goat-horned, and bat-winged, whose eyes flashed blue-bladed lightning; whose steel-toothed jaws devoured light the way hungry wolves devour a lamb.

They rumbled and tumbled and churned as they fed,
As they sucked the light in and swallowed it dead.
To billowed and burgeoned size they grew,
These tempests of turmoil, towers of dread,
Till high above the horizon they loomed—
Unquenchable fortresses—bearers of GLOOM!

"Hurry, Charlie!" Kurt shouted, stumbling as fast as he could up the road.

The shifting breeze, growing stronger now, followed Kurt and his dog like a wild animal stalking its prey. Time after time, it rushed the treetops, stirring leaves to a frenzy before releasing them to stillness—appearing, disappearing, in a cruel game of hide-and-seek. The moist air it carried smelled of rain and bore an unearthly chill, and when the air grew colder still, Kurt was certain icy fingers stroked the back of his neck. "Faster, Charlie!" he shouted, pulling his shirt collar tight around his neck.

After rounding a sharp bend, the two arrived at the place where the road becomes a narrow footpath leading into the woods. Kurt felt a great sense of relief when he and Charlie stepped into the dense forest. The thick stand of pine and oak held in check the harrowing breeze, and the dense foliage hid from view the dark thunderheads. Snippets of blue, and dancing sunlight were all Kurt could see through the overhead branches—sunlight spilling from the vast blue sky-meadow above, flickering through the rich-green canopy overhead, leaping from needle to needle and leaf to leaf, beckoning Kurt on to his secret place.

Kurt's secret place was a large clearing at the water's edge. To the west of it lay the lake, deep and blue and sparkling—the sea in Kurt's imagination, a place of sunken pirate ships and bountiful lost treasures. To the east, towering above the clearing, stood a steep, gray wall of solid rock—a mighty fortress it seemed to Kurt—staunch and impenetrable like castles of old. Thick pine forests flanked the north and south of the clearing, and several low thickets, dense and dark green, grew in the open space between. Near the pines at the north end, not far from the water's edge, an old, gnarled, scrub oak tree stood like a ragged, twisted umbrella.

Kurt and Charlie headed directly for the shady bit of ground beneath the scrub oak, where Kurt wiggled out of the backpack. Rummaging through the pack, he found his fishhooks and can of worms, baited a hook, and set his pole for fishing, placing the handle into a small crevice in a rock at the water's edge. Charlie sniffed out a suitable place to leave the can of worms—a sheltered place in the cool of the rock's shadow—after which the two strolled along the shore, Kurt letting his imagination drift out over the water in pursuit of pirates and phantom sailing ships, Charlie pondering those things known only to dogs.

While gazing out over the lake, Kurt happened to glance at the sky, where he noticed a singular cloud, high and to the west. It was a small, gray, rather insipid cloud, stationary, drifting neither north nor south, east nor west; just hovering—the way an intruder might do before invading unfamiliar territory.

Again Kurt felt the bone-chilling stare of invisible eyes. A moment later, a breeze swept across his face, and the small gray cloud began to move. When it drifted over the sun, Kurt found himself standing in the coolness of cloud shadow listening to the faint rumble of faraway thunder.

Soon other clouds drifted in—thin, wispy ones—and the faint rumble became a distinct grumble.

Charlie began to shiver; his knees began to shake. He whined and pressed himself tight against Kurt's leg. Leaning down and stroking the dog's head, Kurt tried to reason with the animal. "I told you, Charlie, thunder won't hurt you. Everybody knows it's just something to do with positive and negative particles. You know, science stuff. We studied it in school."

The breeze, growing stronger now, began whistling eerily through the treetops, pulling darker, rain-laden clouds in from the west. Kurt watched for a time as, piece by piece, the gathering darkness devoured the rich blue canopy above his secret place. Hoping a good adventure story would take his mind off the weather, he tramped over to the scrub oak tree and plopped down amid a shower of debris loosed from the tree's overhead branches. After sweeping leaves and twigs and bits of dirt from his pant legs, he removed the library book from the pack, placed it on his lap, and opened the cover. Much to his surprise, the book fell open precisely to the page he had last been reading.

Kurt managed to read a few pages, but his thoughts ever returned to the growing darkness. Determined if he could not master the weather, he could at least master his own thoughts, he closed the book and made an idle attempt to engage his dog in pleasantries.

"Books go well with fishing, don't you think, Charlie? You can put the line in the water and let the fish catch themselves while you go off to visit Tom or Huck or somebody else in the story . . ."

The dog, lying close to Kurt with his chin pressed to the ground and his ears locked tight against his head, stared up at Kurt intently, and the familiar white crescents appeared beneath the soft brown of his eyes.

"Don't look at me that way," Kurt said, glancing sideward at the dog. "We're *not* going home!"

Charlie drew a quivering breath and breathed a long, pleading sigh.

Avoiding Charlie's gaze, Kurt peered at the sky through the oak's twisted limbs. Against the blanket of clouds, the gnarled branches appeared as long, fleshless fingers—bony claws poised to reach down and snatch him up. He looked away and opened the book again. Again it fell open to the page he had last been reading.

With the lake and the ground and all else around him growing gray under the darkening sky, Kurt was surprised to see a faint glimmer of light play across the page. It was a pale, pastel light—a tiny beam that weakly played upon the page, as though dancing on a paper stage. The light flickered dimly for a moment then disappeared.

Looking up to see where the light had come from, Kurt found only the impenetrable cover of clouds. Nowhere was there gap or gape, or breach or break, or crack or crevice or cleft to allow such a light. No knothole, keyhole, pinhole, pigeonhole, porthole, rift, or rent. Nothing whatsoever but staunch, unyielding clouds.

The boy felt something graze the back of his neck. "Who's there?" he said, turning to look behind him.

No one was there, but the slight burst of fright had honed his senses, and he listened intently as, from deep within his memory, the tired old voice of his grandfather whispered a warning spoken years before:

> *You must sometimes see what is not there*
> *And temper the tune of what you hear,*
> *For gnomish nibs and watchity widgits,*
> *Secret, invisible kratchits and kridgits*
> *Live within the air.*
> *When the leaden bell tolls*
> *And the thunder rolls,*
> *Beware—*
> *Take care,*
> *Take care.*

All at once the breeze caught the pages of the book and ruffled them loudly. Kurt tossed the book on the ground as a light flashed deep within the clouds above the lake. Charlie sprang to his feet and whined pathetically, nudging Kurt with his nose.

The breeze began to swell. Faster and faster it blew, feeding on itself like a ravenous beast as it puffed and huffed and swirled and hissed. Taking aim at the scrub oak, it bore down with all its might upon the tree.

Kurt struggled to stand, but icy gust after icy gust knocked him to the ground. "Something's happening, Charlie," he shouted. "Something awful is happening!"

No sooner had he spoken than the wind drew a deep and final breath. As if some hidden force had demanded a complete and sudden hush, it surrendered itself to stillness. Leaves and bits of debris set adrift in the brief tempest settled quietly to the ground, and when the last of them came to rest, there was a heaviness about the air.

Nothing moved—neither limb, nor leaf, nor grass upon the ground, nor crawling creature beneath the grasses. It was as though a harbinger of doom had descended upon the land.

Charlie stood motionless. He appeared to be listening, for his stand-up ear stood stiff and alert. But there was nothing to be heard—nothing, that is, within Kurt's ability to hear. All that was earthbound lay still and quiet.

Only the clouds continued to move. Unceasingly they moved, their ranks unbroken. Legion upon legion they gathered, drawing to a halt above the lake, and above the clearing that was Kurt's secret place:

> *ABOVE, the vaporous canopy grew*
> *Till dark it stood, its gathering done;*
>
> *BELOW, the depth of shadow grew*
> *Till land and lake and sky were one.*

Kurt was afraid to move a muscle, afraid even to draw a breath. A single phrase filled his thoughts, and now he comprehended its meaning with deepest understanding. This was that traitorous pause—that moment before a catastrophe when all appears well, but the soul, in its greater wisdom, trembles in fearful anticipation. This was the ill-disguised *calm before the storm.*

An eternity passed, it seemed, and still nothing stirred. Until . . .

> *A FLASH!*
> *A CRASH!*
> *Another! Another! And yet one other!*
> *Twelve times without ceasing the lightning FLASHED!*
> *Ever increasing, the thunder CRASHED!*
> *As trumpeting fanfares before a king!*
> *A king—or some dark and terrible THING!*

A bell began to toll. Its heavy knell fell upon the air like lead.

Charlie's knees began to quiver. His body began to shake. Kurt tried to reach for his dog but he could not bring his muscles to move. He felt as he had the night before when dark music played, and shadows danced upon the wall, and strong black tendrils held him bound and motionless.

All at once, as when a thundering army led by a royal personage of treacherous fame crests a hill—

Swords drawn and armor flashing,
Drums a rumbling, rams a-bashing,
Down it came, the blinding FLASH!
The thunder's ROAR! The mighty CRASH!

THA—RUM—RUM—RUM!
Roared the Father of Rumbling, Grumbling Roll.

THA—RUM—RUM—RUM!
Roared the voice of the Dark One—the THUNDER TROLL!

Charlie leaped into Kurt's lap and pressed his head tight under the boy's chin. Kurt's stubbornness served him well, as summoning all the strength he could, he threw his arms around Charlie's neck and held him fast.

The breeze reappeared. With a vengeance, it swelled to a mighty wind that whipped through the twisted branches of the scrub oak, tearing leaves and twigs and jagged splinters from their underpinnings, hurling them like arrows toward Kurt. Pushing Charlie aside, Kurt rose to his knees and used his arms to shield his face.

The wind began to howl—and so did Charlie! Like a banshee, the gusty tempest howled, as if summoning kindred spirits to strengthen its battlements.

Kurt grabbed his dog and pulled him close. He felt Charlie shivering uncontrollably in his arms.

The clouds above the lake began to churn. Like a witch's brew in a bubbling cauldron, they simmered and deepened to black-cat black. Within the churning clouds there appeared a form, hunched and dark, whose ashen face lingered a second longer than the rest of its body before dissolving into the mist.

"Let's get out of here!" Kurt shouted above the wind. Pushing Charlie aside, he struggled to his feet.

Charlie tucked his tail between his legs and scrunched against the tree trunk, making himself small.

Throwing the backpack over his shoulders, Kurt rushed to the water's edge and angrily jerked the fishing pole from the rock. "One more day!" he cried out. "That's all I wanted! Just one more day without those awful kids at that awful school!"

The lake at once changed from gray to coal-tar black. The water began to churn. From deep within the clouded cauldron above the lake, a light flashed—and another as a jagged bolt ripped the clouds with a crackle and tear. The bolt struck near the center of the clearing and a deafening thunderclap reverberated off the wall of rock.

Charlie dashed headlong toward Kurt, howling in terror. Another bolt narrowly missed the dog and shot toward the scrub oak tree.

When the lightning struck the tree, it was as though the whetted edge of Excalibur had found its mark. The ground quaked from the thunderous *BOOM!* And with an ear-shattering *CR-R-A-A-CK!* the aged oak's trunk split jaggedly down its crooked middle.

The tree began to topple. Its time-honored roots sprang from the soil. *BOOM!* The earth shook again as the mighty oak hit the ground.

Charlie let out a blood-curdling howl and changed direction, heading straight for the wall of rock.

"Charlie, come back!" Kurt dropped the fishing pole and stumbled frantically after his dog. He saw the animal disappear over the top of a large boulder at the base of the wall.

At the boulder, Kurt pulled himself up its rounded surface, and lying on his stomach, peered down into a space where the concave back of the boulder stood out some distance from the wall of rock. There he found Charlie, crouched in front of a small, dark opening in the wall.

"It's okay, Charlie," he said. "It's only a storm."

He was about to reach down and pat Charlie's head, but paused when a steely blade of blue-hot lightning struck with a blinding flash near the water's edge. The resulting thunderclap shook the ground sending a deep tremor rumbling beneath the boulder.

As Kurt struggled to hold his place on the rock, the sky over the clearing split wide open. Rain poured down in wind-driven sheets obscuring every trace of landscape round about. No longer could Kurt see the lake, the shore, or even the fallen oak through the terrible deluge.

"Let's go home!" he shouted above the roar of wind and rain.

When he turned to reach for his dog, Charlie was gone.

Chapter 5

Through the Passage

Lowering himself down the back of the rain-soaked boulder, Kurt called frantically, "Charlie! Charlie, where are you?" Once on the ground, he fell to his knees, turned an ear toward the black hole, and listened. Sheltered from the wind and rain by the formidable boulder, he was able to hear the familiar voice when it spoke to him—when it answered his call with a single bark that, by its solitude, begged him to follow.

A warning flashed through his mind. "In a cave it's so black you can't see your hand in front of your face," his grandfather once told him. "One wrong turn and you might never come out again."

"I can't come in, Charlie! Please come out!" he called, and he reached as far as he could through the dark opening and groped wildly, but Charlie was beyond his reach.

Just then, a violent wind burst from the hole and pinned the boy against the boulder. A second later, something cold passed between him and the opening, and with it came a most god-awful stench—a musty, rancid, rotten odor, as of something long decayed. It smelled the way Kurt imagined mummies must smell when they're dragged from their tombs.

With as great a speed as it had come, the stench subsided, and the wind, having been momentarily impeded by the cold thing, began blowing from the hole again. Wildly it blew now, howling like a beastly sentinel set to guard the entrance to a great stone fortress. Using its gusty might like a shield, it repelled every attempt Kurt made to draw near the opening, pushing him time and again back against the boulder.

Kurt's thoughts flashed to the cold thing. Though it had seemed but a rush of air, he sensed there was substance to it, and he wondered how a thing of substance could hide itself within a rush of air. Concluding it could not, he decided the only explanation was the cold thing had passed too quickly to be seen and had disappeared just as quickly into the hole.

The hole! Charlie was in the hole, and the cold thing was in there with him!

"I'm coming in!" Kurt cried, his heart pounding; and pressing with all his strength, he pushed toward the wall of rock.

Somehow, perhaps by mere stubbornness, or perhaps by drawing on the secret storehouse of will-inspired might that avails itself at times of desperation, he mustered strength to take one faltering step into the wind. A deep breath, a blood-curdling cry, a push forward, a stumble, and he found himself dropped to his knees again, pressing headlong into the hole.

The wind, fierce and unyielding, tore at his clothes and lashed his wet shirttail angrily against his back. It whipped his red hair in tongues of fire across his face. But still Kurt managed to push forward until his head and shoulders passed through the small, black opening. A moment later, he pulled the rest of his body through, felt a swell of panic when there seemed no ground beneath him, and landed full on his face several feet below on the cold, stone floor of a cave. For several seconds he lay there, making no attempt to move, engulfed in a darkness too thick to yield even one small fragment of itself to the dim, gray light filtering through the opening above.

The wind, blowing downward across his back now, seemed bent on pinning him to the floor. With his purpose fixed on finding his dog, he pushed himself up onto his hands and knees, and waving one arm blindly in front of him, called, "Charlie! I'm here! Where are you, boy?"

The moment his hand touched the top of Charlie's head, the wind roared. Bracing himself as best he could, he held his ground, but Charlie turned and began moving away. Kurt could feel his hand sliding down the back of the dog's neck. "Stop! Please!" he begged, but Charlie continued to move.

Kurt's hand traveled the length of Charlie's back, all the way to his hindquarters. A second before the dog escaped his grasp, Kurt grabbed the animal's tail, stumbled to his feet, and allowed himself to be pulled deeper into the darkness.

The wind turned now and whirled about the boy, pushing, pulling, tearing at him, intent upon separating him from his dog. Kurt felt as though he were at the center of a tornado with Charlie safe on the other side. Charlie pulled, and the three of them—Kurt, Charlie, and the tornado—moved deeper into the cave—deeper and deeper into the pitch-black darkness until reality to Kurt seemed nothing more than howling wind, eternal night, and the touch of a dog's tail.

Though he fought with all his strength to hold on to Charlie's tail, Kurt's fingers soon tired, and his grasp began to weaken, and he felt his hand slip. When he feared he might lose his hold altogether, Charlie began to run.

"No!" Kurt shouted.

"Free him," replied a voice within the wind—a voice soft, yet somehow perceptible above the tempest. "Give way, give way," it urged, in a manner that spoke directly to the deepest recesses of Kurt's heart.

Wearied by the pace, certain his weakened leg would fail him at any moment, he was tempted to heed the voice. At the thought of losing Charlie, tears swelled inside him and hopelessness overwhelmed him. But anger replaced the hopelessness, and determination replaced the anger, and he felt his fingers tighten again around Charlie's tail. "I won't let go, Charlie!" he yelled above the wind. "I won't let go!"

As though a mere utterance had tamed a savage beast—as though a few heartfelt syllables had accomplished what Kurt in all his physical struggling had been unable to do—the wind slowed. With a long and final sigh, it relinquished its hold on the boy. Its temper quelled, its purpose seemingly redefined, it softened to a gentle breeze and kindly blew alongside the child, as though now it wished to guide him on his way. In like manner, its voice, till then a deafening roar, fell to a faint, airy whisper. Kurt was certain he heard words within the whisper; but the words, though nearly discernible, remained a wisp away from Kurt's ability to comprehend them. Like feathers caught in an evening breeze, they floated just out of reach, drifting toward the farthest recesses of the dark, fathomless void.

In the calm, Kurt heard for the first time Charlie's panting, which exactly coincided with the steady pounding of the dog's paws against the ground. Charlie's paw steps seemed sure and directed, as though the animal were bound upon a set course. Kurt realized he and Charlie had turned neither left nor right; had climbed neither up nor down. Rather, they had been moving steadily forward on an even course. Surely no cave would be so formed as to have no twists or turns or ups or downs. Kurt realized what he thought was a cave might not be a cave at all.

Again the breeze drew his attention as the breathy whisper, having broken into measured fragments, now mimicked the *whish—whish— whish* of a small drum played lightly with brushes. The sound joined the others—Charlie's panting and paw steps—in matched cadence, creating a pulse resembling a heartbeat. The air in the passage, at first cold and dank, became warm and comforting.

Kurt felt feather light, as though he were drifting on air, and at length, he realized he could no longer feel the cold stone beneath his feet. He *was* drifting. He was floating. He thought Charlie must be floating, too, for gone now were the heavy panting and the sound of paw steps pounding a rocky floor. While still he could feel the dog's tail in his hand, now there was no pulling, no need to struggle to keep hold of it.

Savoring the weightlessness, basking in its delightful abandon, free from the constraints of earthly existence, Kurt felt a great peace come over him, as though those quintessential elements of his human nature—mind, body, and spirit—had been drawn into perfect alignment. He sensed he had crossed a threshold to some distant dimension—the one, perhaps, for which the soul of man, while earth-bound, so earnestly desires; the one which houses the wellspring from which flows the unseen rhythm—universal, mathematical, infinite—that guides the stars in their courses and lends to all living things balance and accord.

Kurt had lost all desire to be any place other than the blissful, fluid realm in which he found himself, when all at once he felt a tug, then a gentle nudge, as though a guiding hand had pulled him back across the threshold and steered him off in another direction. A rush of anger swelled inside him, and a moment later, anger turned to panic as he felt himself rolling, twirling, tumbling, unable to discern up from down, feeling only poleless motion. Unable to free himself—indeed, even to right himself—he allowed his body to grow limp and languid, and little by little, what remained of his sense of bodily substance melded with the darkness, until he felt he, like the cavernous womb in which he floated, consisted of nothing more than air and endless night.

He might have floated thus unceasingly had not his senses been awakened by a gentle stirring within the void—a stirring that caused the pitch of the heartbeat to rise and fall producing a strange, enchanting melody—a melody born of air, devoid of voice or musical instrumentation—a melody not unlike the whistle of wind, beautiful in its simplicity.

As he listened, enraptured, the voice of a deep-toned instru-ment—a double bassoon—slowly wended its way through the darkness, playing a second melody, low and strangely melancholy, that blended with the first. The sinuous strains, sadly sweet, entwined themselves around the boy, enfolding him, holding him close, comforting him like a mother's arms around her child.

Gradually the darkness faded and the passage filled with purple light. For the first time, Kurt saw the chiseled walls, the uneven floor, the low ceiling—rough-hewn surfaces that sparkled as though some-one had sprinkled them with particles of fine silver.

With the purple light came the scent of wisteria. Like a magic elixir sent to nourish an ailing soul, the rare perfume streamed into his nostrils, filling his head with mystical dreamscapes imbued with lavender pools, serene and deep, and shadows, long and purple, whose origins, steeped in darkness, bespoke a great mystery.

Soon, the purple light faded into blue. And with the blue came the scent of gardenia and images of flower petals falling like snow from an azure sky. Kurt felt as though he were but a breath of air floating among the petals, yet he could feel their coolness, their delicate touch upon his skin, as he drifted onward, still entwined in the strains of the melody—a melody now flowing from an instrument of a slightly higher tenor.

Gradually, the blue light faded into green, then yellow, then orange, and lastly, pink. With each color there came a most beautiful fragrance—mint with the green, rose with the yellow, honeysuckle with the orange, jasmine with the pink. And each fragrance brought with it a flood of images akin to itself—and the voice of an instrument more delicate and higher in tone than the one before.

With the coming of the pink light and the fragrance of jasmine, the soft tones of a flute caressed the boy, holding him securely, cradling him gently on the ebb and flow of the melody, as he drifted through an endless field of living stars.

All too soon, as when a pleasant dream abruptly ends with an unwelcome disturbance, movement in the air about him snapped Kurt out of his dreamlike state in time to see the pink color being replaced by scattered specks of silver light. From their flitting movement, the specks appeared alive. They grew in number until they consumed the pink altogether, filling the passage with a bright, silver glow. The glow became so concentrated in the distance it formed what seemed to be an opening—a doorway of light—a way out of the passage!

"Charlie, look!" Kurt cried, as he and his dog accelerated toward the light. It *was* an opening! Just as they reached it, the silver specs dispersed with a mighty *swish* toward the outside and disappeared into the glare of the sky. The next moment, Kurt found himself rolling uncontrollably in the tall grasses of a lush green meadow. When he came to rest, he looked about and saw Charlie sitting beside him wearing a stunned expression.

"You all right, boy?"

The words seemed to snap the animal out of his stupor. He blinked and the dazed look left his eyes.

Lightheaded and not at all certain of his ability to stand steadily, Kurt nevertheless rose to his feet and studied the landscape. Nothing appeared familiar. To one side of him stood a steep, gray wall of rock, but it was not the wall of rock near the lake. When he perused it, searching for the opening through which he had come, he found only solid, impenetrable rock. All that remained of the passage was the lingering smell of jasmine.

Neither was there a trace of the storm—unless one considered the lone, insipid little gray cloud hovering high in the sky above the wall. The sky was blue with a few fluffy white clouds, and the air was cool and clear and bright. The whole atmosphere sparkled and twinkled as though elfin beings had sprinkled the earth and all that grew from it with finely polished silver dust. Even the low-lying fog hugging the base of the cliff glowed with a silvery iridescence. Birds sang and a faint tinkling like wind chimes rose from a grove of copper-colored trees at the furthermost edge of the meadow—trees that had a metallic appearance and shimmered and sparkled in the sun.

Kurt turned to Charlie, who was standing close beside him, and nervously patted the dog's head. "I know one thing, Charlie. We're nowhere near the lake. Something is wrong. Something is very, very wrong."

CHAPTER 6

THE LAND OF WHISKERS

We're lost! thought Kurt. But it was worse than that. Being lost was simply a turning around—a glitch in one's internal compass. To find one's way again would mean deciding at which familiar tree to turn right, at which oft-seen rock to veer left, and so forth, until some recognizable pattern aligned the poles of one's internal compass and pointed the way home. Here, however, there was no familiar tree at which to turn right; no oft-seen rock at which to veer left. Nothing hinted of the slightest resemblance to the world on the other side of the passage. The air itself—even the time of year—seemed different in this place.

Earlier Kurt had breathed the hot, dry air of a late-summer morning and walked past flowerless fields of faded grasses that mourned the passing of summer. He had shivered at the moist, chill wind of an approaching storm and watched as a biting gust prematurely snatched the first heralds of autumn from graying branches. Now the air was cool, and fresh as morning dew, and it smelled of spring flowers and green grasses.

Kurt gazed toward the strange metallic trees at the meadow's edge—trees that rang softly in the gentle breeze that played among their copper leaves. As he stood listening, wondering how trees of metal could possibly exist, a gusty breath rushed the leaves, stirring them to ring clarion-voiced upon the air. When the flourish reached his ear, Kurt saw, moving toward him across the meadow's grasses, long ripples, like waves across a field of grain. The ripples merged as they traveled, becoming at length one wave that headed straight for him.

The moment the wave reached him, Kurt felt a pressure against his body, as though a tidal surge, immense and invisible, were passing over him, leaving in its wake exhilaration and heightened awareness. For the first time, he sensed a magical quality about the meadow, and a veiled presence.

"Who's there?" he called out. But no one answered—at least not in words. He felt a tug at his shirttail, and another, and another still, until the tugging became a steady pulling, and for a moment he allowed the thought that elfin beings, too small and too much of air to be seen, were coaxing him to stay a while and look closer. And indeed he did look closer as he recalled again his grandfather's words, only this time with new meaning and great expectation: "You must sometimes see what is not there and temper the tune of what you hear . . ."

This time, with sharpened senses, he saw clearly the vast meadow that lay around him like the crazy quilt on Grandma's down bed, soft and billowy, inviting the roll and tumble—a patchwork of colors amid green grasses held together by sparkling threads of silver. Wild sweet peas here, bluebells there, pink mariposa lilies to the left and right, golden buttercups and daffodils and daisies in profusion.

Fragile wildflowers, knee-high on Kurt, fluttered in the breeze and tickled Charlie's nose. Fragrant blossoms that brushed Kurt's legs massed in the distance becoming vast splashes of color and spilled perfume. Butterflies in every color of the rainbow played hide-and-seek among the flowers. The entire meadow danced before the boy like a child at play.

And not without music—splendid music! Songbirds poured their melodies onto the breeze, and the breeze, meandering through the tinkling leaves of the strange metallic trees, wove note into chord, and chord into measure, and measure after measure into joyous strain until the air rang with rapturous celebration.

Kurt was basking in the pleasure of it all when a note of discord struck his ear. Charlie was barking at something moving in the nearby grasses. Kurt craned his neck to see and up popped two cotton-tail rabbits.

Charlie barked even more now that he had flushed the small animals out of hiding. Kurt had heard the dog bark at rabbits before, but something in this situation was peculiar. He seemed to be barking in phrases, almost as if he were talking to the rabbits, hurriedly, with arm gestures and wrinkled brow and wagging tail; and they to him, with thumping feet and wiggling ears and twitching noses. Kurt realized the absurdity of what he was thinking. "Animals do not talk to each other," he told himself.

Nevertheless, the rabbits and Charlie soon began scurrying in circles around Kurt, the rabbits to the fore, hopping and thumping, the dog to the rear, prancing and yipping and nudging the boy. It appeared the three were trying to tell Kurt something—something extremely important—for every few seconds they stopped for a brief discussion among themselves, looked at the boy, shook their heads, and resumed their activity. Stop, look, go. Stop, look, go. Kurt could do no more than stare in bewilderment.

He was standing thus when all at once a hush fell upon the meadow. The birds stopped their singing. The breeze became still. The copper trees ceased their ringing. The commotion at Kurt's feet halted abruptly as the animals stood fast—as animals will at times of impending danger, their bodies rigid, alert, their gazes fixed, lending full concentration to the illusive signal within the animal's hearing that man has neither the physical apparatus to discern nor the instinctual capability of understanding. Occasionally their ears twitched as though they were homing in on the signal. Charlie, standing close to Kurt, barely seemed to breathe. The entire meadow stood still and silent, much like a forest when a deadly intruder encroaches upon it.

Only the butterflies moved, continuing their sprite-like dance above the flowers. Kurt thought there were more of them now than a moment ago, and indeed there were. Hundreds gathered from all parts of the meadow, appearing from hiding places in the trees and among the grasses and beneath the flowers. Kurt watched in amazement as the air around him became thick with butterflies.

Perhaps it was the whisper of their wings—or perhaps it was illusion born of the vast profusion of color about him—but Kurt was certain he heard words—faint words of a song whose melody came from deep within his own memory:

See the sprightly meadow morphs
Dancing o'er the flowers,
Scintillating, entertaining,
Hiding magic powers.

The melody, clearly discernable now, rose and fell in like fashion to the upward-downward flittering motion that marks the butterfly's flight. The words became clear and sharp and easily heard:

Iridescent meadow morphs
Drinking in the sun's glow,
Lepidopt'ra wings ablaze with
Colors of the rainbow.

Now there were thousands of butterflies. They circled the boy until he became the center of a great whirlwind of stirred colors—pastel, paint-pot colors—violets flowing into blues, greens pouring into yellows, pale oranges melting into pinks.

Myriads of meadow morphs,
Roots within the Mountain,
Pouring forth their silver song,
A never-ending fountain.

The great swirl of color encircling the boy left him faint, and like his weakened state, the words themselves grew faint, and Kurt had to strain to hear them:

Fragile, gentle meadow morphs,
Sent to whisk the mute,
Dancing o'er the flowers
Until summoned by the flute.

A butterfly grazed Kurt's face. Its delicate touch tickled and Kurt brushed it away. And as though that small gesture had signaled an end, the whirlwind slowed, the melody grew weaker, the delicate words faded to a mere whisper, and Kurt saw individual colors again, and individual butterflies.

Down and up and high and low,
Casting their bestowment;
Changing things, arranging things to
Better suit the moment.

Soon, even the whisper faded away and the butterflies dispersed, most of them disappearing within the foliage of the trees and beneath the flowers and among the grasses, leaving only a scattering visible as before. Those that remained resumed their dance above the flowers, and the meadow returned to its previous state with birds singing and a sound like soft wind chimes riding the breeze.

"What was that all about?" Kurt asked, not expecting an answer

"Those were the meadow morphs," replied one of the rabbits.

"Who said that?"

"I did," the rabbit answered with a giggle. "You couldn't understand us before because you didn't have your whiskers."

Kurt's mouth dropped open. He stood speechless. It was not difficult to believe he was talking to a rabbit, but the fact the rabbit was talking to him was beyond belief.

Gathering his wits about him, he gulped and ventured a weak reply. "Whiskers? I don't have whiskers."

"Yes, you do," said the second rabbit. "The meadow morphs gave them to you."

Kurt's surprise at discovering yet another talking rabbit was overshadowed by the prospect of having whiskers. He touched his face. "I do have whiskers!" And wiggling his nose and crossing his eyes, he tried to see the terrible appendages. And there they were—long and stiff, and wiggling right along with his nose.

"Don't you like them?" inquired the first rabbit. "They're really fine—the nicest I've ever seen. They ought to work very well."

"What do you mean, 'work very well?'" Kurt asked warily, twisting and bending the hair-like protuberances, trying to tell if in fact they were securely fastened to his face.

"Do what whiskers do," said the second rabbit.

"And what do they do?"

"They help you talk—to the other animals. Everyone knows that. What kind of animal are you, anyway?"

"I'm not an animal," Kurt said.

The rabbits glanced at each other, after which one of them hopped in a circle around the boy, regarding him curiously. "I've never seen a *not an animal* before," he said when he had finished hopping.

Rather than trying to explain, Kurt gazed across the meadow. "Where are we?" He addressed neither animal in particular.

"We're *here*," said the first rabbit, matter-of-factly.

"Of course we're *here*," said the second. "Anyone can see we're not *there*."

Charlie, who had been listening to the conversation, whispered, "Ask them the name of this place."

"Ah!" said Kurt. Charlie's talking so unnerved him he could not bring himself to utter an intelligible word. Instead, he stood wide-eyed, staring at the dog.

Charlie lowered his head until his chin nearly touched the ground and rolled his eyes up at Kurt and waited. When after a time Kurt still had not spoken, Charlie cleared his throat and whispered again, "Ask them the name of this place."

"What's the name of this place!" Kurt blurted, only half realizing he was asking a question.

"Whiskers," said the first rabbit.

"What?"

"Whiskers," repeated the second. "The Land of Whiskers."

Kurt could not for the life of him recall ever having heard of a Land of Whiskers. He tried to remember all the maps he had ever seen—the ones in his geography books in school, and those in the huge world atlas in his grandfather's library. On none of them had he ever seen such a place mentioned

"Where is this land?" he asked.

"It's *here*," answered the first rabbit.

"Of course it's *here*," retorted the second, thumping his foot impatiently. "It most assuredly is not *there*."

With much difficulty, Kurt explained to the peculiar little animals that some terrible mistake must have brought him to the Land of Whiskers. He explained that he needed to find the way home as soon as possible. "I don't know *what* happened exactly—or *why* it happened. I only know I'm here and I don't know *where* home is."

"He doesn't know *what*," said the first rabbit to the second.

"And, he doesn't know *why*," said the second to the first. "But most importantly—"

"—he doesn't know *where*!" blurted the first; and a self-serving smile spread across his furry face.

"I was going to say that," the second rabbit murmured. With his teeth clenched, he glared at the first before announcing proudly, "He needs the Cornerstone!"

"Of course, he needs the Cornerstone," said the first. "If you want to know the *where* and *why*, or even the *what* and *who*, there's only one place to go."

"The Cornerstone," the animals said in unison, nodding their heads affirmatively.

"What's the Cornerstone?" Kurt asked.

"We don't know," said one of the rabbits, shrugging his tiny shoulders.

"Well, where is it?"

"It must be *there*," said the other.

"Of course it's *there*," said the first, aiming a sour little twist of his lips at the second. "As you can see, it isn't *here*."

Kurt was growing impatient. "Exactly where is *there*?"

The second rabbit cleared his throat and announced in a very conclusive sort of way—and in a very *loud* sort of way—"*There* is where *there is*!"

"Of course *there* is where *there is*," the first rabbit said, peering down his nose. "If *there* were *not* where *there is*, *there* would be *here*. And if *there* were *here*, it would not be *there* at all."

"That's precisely what I said," replied the second rabbit, his eyes narrowing to tiny slits. "*There* is where *here* is *not*!"

By now Kurt's patience had worn thin. "I don't think you know much about the Cornerstone at all. How do you know it exists?"

"We heard about it from a tail," said the first rabbit.

"You mean you heard *a tale about it*, don't you?"

"No. We heard about it *from a tail*," the rabbit insisted, thumping his foot. He turned to the second rabbit. "What was it the tail said? Oh, I know, I know. 'Sticks and stones may break my bones . . .' No, that was not it."

"'A rolling stone gathers no moss,'" the second rabbit said with no small degree of sarcasm.

The first rabbit shook his head in disgust and rubbed his chin and pondered a moment before a look of recognition swept over his face. "Now I remember:

'Locked within the Cornerstone,
Words to lead from here to there.
Answers you must find alone,
The who, the what, the why, the where.'"

"That's it!" proclaimed the second rabbit.

Both animals grinned from pink ear to pink ear.

Not to be befuddled by the daft little animals, Kurt asked, "Where is the one who told you this tale?"

"He's *there*," said the first rabbit.

"Of course he's *there*," replied the second. "He's certainly not *here*."

Kurt drew a deep breath as he searched his mind for a new approach—one that would not include the word *where* as part of the question. "By *cornerstone*, you must mean a stone at the corner of something, right?"

"We assume so," said the first rabbit, "though it certainly is not at the corner of *this* place. Certainly not *here*."

"Certainly not," the second rabbit repeated, perusing the vast meadow about him. "For, as you can see, *here* has no corners. So it must be *there*, and *there* must have corners."

Kurt sighed and shrugged. He was about to thank the rabbits and take leave of them, when he noticed a dark shadow moving swiftly across the meadow heading straight toward him.

"Oh, oh," said the first rabbit.

Both animals stood motionless except for a nervous twitching of their noses.

The shadow passed over, and as its darkness touched him, Kurt felt a strange tingling in his whiskers. When he looked up, he saw a flash of light as something large and swift crossed the sun. Blinded by the glare, he could not determine what the object was.

The rabbits must have noticed the quizzical look on the boy's face, for they answered his next question before he could ask it.

"That was . . . Parhelion," stuttered the second rabbit, as though he preferred not to pronounce the name.

"Par what?"

"Parhelion—the Nimbus," said the first, fidgeting. "We don't know much about him."

"He's from very high up," added the second.

"Yes. From up *there*," said the first, pointing to the sky.

"Of course, from *up there*," said the second. "He could not be from *down* there, because *down* is *here*. Were he from *here*, he would *not* be *up*, because *up* is *there,* and *there* is *not down*." He nodded once, firmly, as if to punctuate his sentence, and glanced sideward at his furry little cohort.

Kurt decided not to pursue the subject of Parhelion further, for the rabbits obviously did not find the topic a pleasant one. Besides, further pursuit would only lead to more *there's* and *here's*. He thanked the animals for their help, and they bade him goodbye and made a zigzag dash across the meadow, their cotton tails flashing white against the green grasses and brightly colored flowers.

One thing was certain. The Cornerstone was not *here*, so Kurt would have to find out where *there* was.

Searching the landscape for a likely direction in which to head, the boy noticed a break in the trees at the eastern edge of the meadow and immediately set out toward it. After only a few steps, something struck him as strange. There was an unfamiliar quality to his gait. Unsure of his footing, he took a few more steps. His strides were evenly spaced and each foot touched the ground with equal force.

"Charlie!" he cried out. "Look at me! I'm not lame!"

The boy jumped with glee and took a few more steps and jumped again. Charlie jumped too, with his nose held high in the air and a delighted grin on his brown face and his floppy ear flapping up and down in the sweet-smelling air.

The two of them jumped and hopped and skipped among the meadow's grasses, laughing all the while, running and chasing and frolicking still more until finally they fell exhausted in the middle of a vast cluster of wild sweet peas. When at last he had caught his breath, Kurt sighed deeply and hugged his dog. "Oh, Charlie. If only Mother could see me. Wouldn't she be surprised!"

Soon Kurt directed his thoughts to the task at hand and once again set his sights on the opening in the trees. Still, from time to time, he did a little hop and skip, just to assure himself that he could. And from time to time, he crossed his eyes and wiggled his nose and stared at the strange appendages protruding from his face to see if by chance the whiskers had been only a temporary affliction. But each time, there they were, long and stiff and still firmly attached.

The break in the trees marked a dirt road, and because it appeared to be well-trodden, it offered hope that perhaps Kurt would meet others along the way who could tell him more about the Cornerstone and possibly direct him to it.

He and Charlie followed the road for several hours, stopping once to share a sandwich from the backpack and numerous times to talk to animals passing in the opposite direction. Of all the animals they met along the way, each one had whiskers, including those who would not have had them in Kurt's world. Though none could tell Kurt where to find the Cornerstone (some had heard of it, but did not know its whereabouts; others had not heard of it at all), everyone, to a whisker, advised the boy to travel through the Copper Valley and into the Nickel Hills toward the tall mountain peak looming on the eastern horizon. "It's the Silver Mountain," they said. "It's always advisable to travel toward silver. Everyone knows that." Kurt did not know that, but it made as much sense as anything he had heard in this strange land, and the road did seem to be winding in that direction, so he set the mountain as his goal.

The road passed through friendly forests in whose shade *ostrich* ferns and *rattlesnake* ferns grew in profusion. Kurt and Charlie were careful not to tread on *toad*stools growing along the road on the chance they might be the wayside benches of some local toads. They ducked under the branches of ancient oaks and stepped over sunlit rocks on whose shady sides gray *reindeer* moss grew, and walked past delicate *dog*wood trees and romped through wayside fields of *buck*wheat and *buffalo* grass and *goat* grass, careful to avoid the *fox*tails. Once, they stood at the edge of a shallow pond and touched the hairy *horse*tails and furry *cat*tails growing along its marshy bank. And yet another time, they paused in a flowery meadow to snap the snapdragons and look at the *lark*spur and feel the soft billows of dande*lion* down and *pussy* willows and to pick *goose*berries.

Kurt was getting used to the strange appendages darting forth from the sides of his nose. He rather liked talking to animals, and the whiskers allowed him to ask questions he had always wanted to ask, such as, "What color is a chameleon, really?"

One such tiny fellow scampered up from a rock on which Kurt was resting and climbed onto the boy's shoulder. Upon hearing the question, the chameleon answered, "Sometimes green, sometimes brown, but always yellow," and he scurried away toward a nearby hollow log. That particular answer puzzled Kurt—the "yellow" part, that is. He had never seen a chameleon turn yellow at all.

Apparently the conversation disturbed another who was sleeping under an adjacent rock, for Kurt saw movement out of the corner of his eye and a large snake crawled out onto the roadway. Startled by the sudden appearance of the reptile, Kurt jumped to his feet.

"Always mis-s-s-understood," said the snake, "always mis-s-s-understood."

"What do you mean?" Kurt asked.

"Just then . . . the way you acted. You thought I was out to harm you. But I wasn't. My kind are always mis-s-s-understood. It all started with that apple thing. His-s-s-tory is wrong. I've never even seen an apple." And he slipped away.

Kurt tried several times to talk with Charlie. He had so many questions he wanted to ask the dog. But each time, the conversation ended after only a few words. This verbal form of communication, so natural between human and human, proved to be awkward between human and dog. Perhaps if Kurt and Charlie had been strangers it would have been easier. But they were best friends, and throughout their time together Charlie had communicated in typical dog manner— with wiggles and wags and postures and facial expressions. Perhaps that was why now, when Kurt expected a lengthy conversation, Charlie could offer no more than a word or two. It must have been simply too new, too strange to the dog. Perhaps with time, the situation would remedy itself. For now, Kurt's questions would remain unanswered.

CHAPTER 7

ANNELIDA BOOKNOTCH

"Look, Charlie!"

Kurt pointed to a mother duck leading a line of six waddling ducklings to a roadside pond. Peering over his shoulder as he walked, watching the yellow ducklings splash one by one into the shallow water, he failed to see the low-hanging bough stretched across the road directly in his path, but he did feel the sudden blow to the head when he crashed into it.

As he stood in the roadway recovering, he felt something land on his shoulder and drop to his foot. Shaking his foot vigorously, he knocked whatever it was to the ground.

"Ah!" screamed a small, but masculine, voice.

Seeing no one ahead of him, Kurt spun around to see who behind him might have screamed. But there was no one behind him.

Just then, he noticed Charlie sniffing something on the ground and he knelt to see what it was. To his amazement, it was a worm—a small, green, segmented worm wearing a brown tweed vest and a matching tweed cap—and the worm had the tiniest whiskers.

The little fellow quickly busied himself brushing off his soiled vest and adjusting the hat on his head before looking himself over from top to bottom. "Thank goodness I'm still green! I was dreaming I was blue on the outside, too," the worm said, addressing no one in particular. And looking directly at Kurt, he added, "I couldn't tell inside the leaves. The light in there is so dim, you see."

"Uh . . . Who? . . . What? . . ." Kurt stammered, too much in awe of the tiny creature to formulate an intelligible question.

"Oh, I'm so very sorry," the worm replied. "I failed to introduce myself. I was rather shaken, having fallen from the tree. Under more favorable circumstances, I would have rendered a proper introduction."

"But . . . you're a worm," said Kurt. "Worms don't introduce themselves."

"I beg your pardon," the worm said indignantly. "Rules of etiquette require proper introductions on occasions such as this one. Besides, I'm not, by strictest definition, a true worm."

"You're not?" Kurt forced a crooked smile and sat down cross-legged in the roadway. Charlie sniffed the worm one more time and plopped down next to the boy.

Having been thus reminded of the propriety of proper introductions, Kurt took the initiative. "My name is Kurt. And this is my dog, Charlie."

The worm politely tipped his hat, first to Kurt, then to Charlie. "My name is Annelida—Annelida Booknotch."

"Annelida? That sounds like a—"

"I know, I know. It sounds remarkably like a girl's name. But I'm obviously not of the female gender."

"I can see that," Kurt said. "So how did you get a name like Annelida?"

"It all began at birth," the worm explained. "Of course, that *would* be the proper place for such an occurrence to begin, would it not? Everything in its proper place, I always say." He tugged at his vest and smoothed out a wrinkle before leaning back against a nearby twig.

"As I was saying, it began with my birth in the hospital, where a dreadful breakdown in communication occurred between my parents and the capable, though inattentive, hospital staff. My parents, bless their hearts, desired to name me after my dear Aunt Alida, which would have been no problem had I been a female child. But alas, I was a male, and that presented a problem of enormous magnitude."

"Enormous," said Kurt, glancing sideward at Charlie.

The worm inched his way over to the boy and crawled up onto his pant leg. "Do you mind?" he asked. "If I sit on your knee, I believe it will be much easier for us to converse."

"Go right ahead," said Kurt. So the worm climbed up to a lofty spot on Kurt's knee and settled himself comfortably before continuing his discourse.

"Anyway, the hospital staff apparently were not listening closely. They heard only the part about Aunt Alida and inscribed the name *Annelida* on my birth certificate. Alas! It was too late. The name is etched upon my soul for all eternity. But I've solved the problem to my satisfaction. I merely ask all I meet to call me Notch."

He sure is a wordy worm, thought Kurt. Why didn't he just say, "It was all a big mistake. Call me Notch."?

"Do you live in that tree?" Kurt nodded toward the low-hanging bow.

"I'm afraid so," the worm sighed. "It's the best I could do with no books around."

"No books?"

"Well, I *am* a booknotch, after all," said the worm. "You must know I would be living in a book if one were available." He paused and gazed into the distance. "Or perhaps you don't know now that I think about it. Booknotches are invisible in your world."

"My world?" Kurt pushed his face close to the worm and stared him in the eye. "How do you know about my world?"

"Well, since you're a boy, and there are no boys in Whiskers, you must be from that *other* world—which used to be my world until I lost my way and ended up here."

Kurt looked askance at the tiny creature. "If you're from my world, how come I've never heard of a booknotch?"

The worm smiled. "Because, as I said, booknotches are invisible in your world. And humans seldom believe in that which they cannot see, even when they hold the evidence in the palms of their hands." The worm stared at the ground pensively a moment, then looked up at Kurt. "According to a dictionary in which I once lived, I'm what you might call—an *intangible*."

"Oh," said Kurt, at a loss for words.

The booknotch was certainly *not* at a loss for words. "Every book has a booknotch. Haven't you ever noticed how books usually fall open precisely to the page you were last reading?"

"Yes," Kurt replied. "But what does that have to do with anything?"

"When a book opens thus, it's because a booknotch is marking the place. When it doesn't, it's because the booknotch is shirking his duty." The worm frowned. "There are always a few who do, you know."

Kurt recalled the library book he tossed on the ground when Charlie ran from the thunder. "That happened to me this morning—twice—when I was reading a library book by the lake. Both times it fell open right to the page I'd last been reading. Do you think there was a booknotch inside?"

"Without a doubt," said the worm. "And a fortunate one, too. Living in a library book is considered quite upper crust. One can travel and see the world when his domicile is a library book. Every time the volume is lent, he can journey to someone's home or school, perhaps ride a bus or a train. Ah! The drama! The spectacle!

"I once lived in such a book," the worm continued. "Often I'd climb onto the reader's head to enjoy the panorama or I'd peruse the book from a spot on his shoulder—I do delight in a good story. But such adventures can be dangerous."

"Dangerous? Why?"

"Why, indeed." The booknotch quivered as a shiver passed through his tiny green body. "If the reader should suddenly close the book, there may not be time enough for the booknotch to leap back inside."

Here the worm turned pale. He took a deep breath, and when after a moment the lovely green returned to his face, he went on. "That's how I came to be in Whiskers. Oh, that terrible accident! I shudder to think of it."

Kurt knew he would be in for another lengthy, perhaps incomprehensible, discourse should he ask the booknotch to explain, but curiosity forced him to inquire. Leaning even closer to the worm, he ventured, "Accident? What accident?"

"Well," said the booknotch, "I was living in the library book, and I very much wanted to read one of the stories—it was an anthology of short stories, you see—but since it was quite impossible to read from my vantage point inside the book—too close to the words, you know—it was imperative I leave the pages. Though the inherent dangers failed to justify such a course of action, I nevertheless dove wholeheartedly into uncharted waters, rushing forthright from the safety of my domicile. That proved to be folly of the highest magnitude."

"The highest magnitude," said Kurt. And he nodded, though he was not exactly sure what it was he was confirming.

"I had scurried out from the pages and was sitting on the child's shoulder, snuggled tightly against his collar, reading joyously," the booknotch continued, "when suddenly the boy was called to dinner. He must have been extremely hungry for he slammed the book shut before I could return to my friendly abode and ran bumpily toward the kitchen. For three days I clutched the spine of that ill-fated volume, praying the boy would open it again; and for three long days, he carried my beloved domicile around, unopened, unaware of the trouble I was in. Ah! I ended a sentence with a preposition." The worm blushed. "Well, it happens to the best and the least of us."

"That must have been a terrible experience," said Kurt. "Clutching the book, I mean; not the part about the preposition."

"An experience of great trepidation!" replied the booknotch. "Anyway, the boy had a puppy—a cute little fellow, but most voracious. The child went off to school one morning still having not opened the book, and the moment he was gone, the puppy, being very lonely I suppose, carried the book to a cozy spot on the living room rug and proceeded to devour it. I was devastated. I ran for my life—right out the door. That's when I became lost and stumbled upon the passage to Whiskers."

"That's awful."

"Awful, indeed," said the booknotch. And he looked up at the tree sadly. "Nevertheless, when the winds of circumstance ruffle the pages of our lives, we must be willing to turn a new leaf." He looked at the boy and smiled. But it was not a happy smile.

"I've resigned myself to living in that tree," the worm continued. "At first I tried to wend my way to Nickledown. I heard there was a book there. But, alas, the journey was too far for one as small as I."

"Nickledown?" said Kurt. "What's Nickledown?"

"It's a town at the foot of the Silver Mountain. A wonderful place it is, too, from what the animals say. But any place that has a book is sure to be wonderful."

"Does it have corners?"

"Does *what* have corners?"

"The town."

"I suppose it does," replied the booknotch. "Don't all towns have corners?"

"I'm looking for something called the Cornerstone. Have you heard of it?"

"Cornerstone," repeated the booknotch, rubbing his chin as he pondered. "As I mentioned before, I once lived in a dictionary—before my taste for fine phraseology necessitated my move to the short-story book. I seem to recall the word has various meanings. It can mean 'a stone at the corner of a building, often inscribed and laid at the ceremonial beginning of construction;' or it can simply mean 'the basic, essential, or most important part of something'—that is, 'the foundation.'"

"That's no help," said Kurt. "Oh, well. It was just something some rabbits told me about."

"Rabbits?" A quizzical look came over the booknotch's face. "Did these 'rabbits' by any chance have a misaligned sense of direction?"

"Everything they said had to do with '*here*' and '*there*' and '*not there*' and '*not here*,' if that's what you mean," said Kurt.

"There'n not-hares," said the booknotch. "Most difficult creatures."

"There'n not-hares?"

"That's what the animals call them. A most peculiar name, though strikingly definitive."

"But Notch, why are they called 'there'n not-*hares*' when they're obviously rabbits? Everyone knows a rabbit and a hare are two different things."

"It's all a matter of pronunciation"—said the booknotch—"where you place the emphasis. As I said, they're there'n *not*-hares, not there'n not-*hares*."

"Oh," said Kurt, thinking how very peculiar the name was indeed.

A faraway look came to the booknotch's eyes, and he began to reminisce. "I miss that old dictionary almost as much as I miss the short-story book. I so loved being inside those pages, the parchment leaves folding around me as I bundled myself in the words. There's nothing quite like it—feeling cozy and warm within the heart of words such as *hearth* and *hot soup* and *woolens* in wintertime; lingering within the coolness of *sea breeze* and *hammock* and *iced tea* in summer. Yes, lounging lazily among the letters . . .

In the curl of a Q

Or the crook of a T

In the bend of a U

Or the bow of a B

And the fun of it all! Ah, the fun...

To slide down an S

Or slip down a Z

To land in an X

Or the point of a V !

"But I do go on so, don't I?"

Kurt giggled. Then his expression became quite serious. "Notch, you're almost an inch long. How can you fit inside those letters?"

The booknotch smiled. "It's simple. When the book is closed, I become quite diminished in size."

"Just like that?"

"Just like that," the booknotch replied. He looked up at the leafy branch above his head and sighed. "Oh, to have real printed letters again. I carved some makeshift ones into the leaves of this tree as best I could, and they serve me well enough I suppose. I was sleeping in the bow of a *B* when I was awakened by the sound of your voice. When I saw you coming, I quickly jumped into the curl of a *Q*—a great place to hide—in that little squiggle. After all, you're the first human I've seen since I came to Whiskers, and you caused me some surprise. When you jostled the branch, I plummeted forthright from the squiggle."

"You mean you fell right out of it."

"Exactly," replied the booknotch. "I plummeted forthright." He smiled an embarrassed smile and blushed as he inspected his little green self. "At least I have no bruises. I'm blue on the inside, but I certainly do not want to be blue on the outside. I shouldn't mention that though. Blue is a very low color."

78

Kurt had no idea what the booknotch was talking about. How could anyone possibly know what color he is on the inside? Kurt let the remark pass. But the worm continued.

"Just the same, I prefer to think of my blue as indigo."

"As what?"

"Indigo—a dark, rich blue. Oh, the sound of it! In-di-go." He pronounced the syllables deliberately. "Magnificent word, intriguing word, with its two little *i*'s I sometimes feel are looking at me." The booknotch thought for a moment. "If ever I get to green, I think I'll refer to it as *chartreuse*. Ah! Chartreuse! Now there's a sonorous word. Perhaps someday my inside will match my outside. For now, however, I'm in di go."

By this time, Kurt was completely confused. The booknotch was green, not blue. Kurt thought perhaps the worm might be color-blind—or even a little mentally deficient. Or perhaps the fall from the tree had befuddled his thinking.

"I have an idea," said Kurt. "Charlie and I are traveling toward the Silver Mountain. Maybe you should come with us. You could ride in my shirt pocket. That tree is not a very safe place to be, and if there *is* a book in Nickledown—"

"Oh, could I!" said the booknotch. "The idea of having a book again—the thought is more than I can bear!"

"Then hop right up," said Kurt. And he placed his hand next to the worm and waited for him to climb aboard.

Kurt was about to put the tiny creature into his pocket when Charlie stopped him. "Wait," the dog said, and he plucked two leaves from the branch where the booknotch had been living and placed them in Kurt's hand next to the worm.

"How thoughtful," said Notch, squeezing between the leaves. "I would have missed my letters."

Kurt smiled at Charlie and slipped the leaves into his pocket, and the boy and his dog and the booknotch headed down the road toward the Silver Mountain.

They had not gone far when the fading daylight beckoned them to stop for the night. Kurt chose a campsite beneath one of the copper-colored trees at the side of the road and began gathering leaves from a neighboring oak to make a bed. Charlie busied himself sniffing the coarse brown fruit that lay in piles beneath the copper tree. The dog had just taken a piece into his mouth when Kurt happened to glance his way.

"Drop it, Charlie!" Kurt shouted, throwing down the armful of leaves he was carrying and rushing toward the dog.

Charlie lowered his head close to the ground and let the fruit roll from his mouth.

After catching his breath, Kurt patted the dog on the shoulder. "You don't know anything about that stuff, Charlie. It comes from a metal tree. For all you know, it's poison."

Charlie sighed and plopped down on the ground with his nose touching a large pile of the strange, biscuit-like fruit. "Can I smell it?"

"Of course, you can smell it," said Kurt.

When the boy finished preparing the bed of oak leaves, he and Charlie sat down upon it. Kurt took a sandwich from the backpack and handed half to Charlie, then peeked into his shirt pocket and invited the booknotch to join them.

The tiny worm inched his way out of Kurt's pocket and down to his knee, and when at last he had perched himself comfortably against a fold in the denim, he stared up at the warm, red-orange bows of the copper tree. "You've made a fine choice for a night's sojourn, Kurt. By definition, copper is a 'common reddish metal—ductile, malleable, and a good conductor of heat.'" The worm looked at Kurt and blushed. "Webster's Unabridged."

"Of course," said Kurt, trying not to chuckle.

"Yes, a very fine choice," said the booknotch, looking up at the tree again. "Heat flowing through those copper boughs should keep us warm through the night."

Kurt vaguely remembered studying metals in his science class, but he had not bothered to memorize their properties. The knowledge had seemed, at the time, to be of no practical use.

Changing the subject, Kurt offered Notch part of the sandwich, but the tiny worm refused, explaining, "Booknotches don't eat as people or animals do. Booknotches are sustained by a kind of ethereal nourishment born of the savoriness of an artfully embossed letter or the richness of a phrase well-penned."

"That stuff doesn't sound as tasty as good ol' peanut butter and jelly," Kurt said, biting into his sandwich.

"I'm afraid I shall never be able to make that comparison," said the booknotch. "*You* can, however. You can taste a sandwich—as you are doing this very moment; *and* you can taste phrases well-penned."

"Taste words?" Kurt mumbled, his mouth full of sandwich.

"As you read great literature," replied the booknotch.

Kurt pondered the booknotch's remarks for a moment before realizing what the little worm meant. "So—because I've read *Tom Sawyer*, you *could* say I've 'tasted' great literature. Right, Notch?"

The little worm smiled. "And—because you've read *Tom Sawyer*—I would say you 'have a taste for' great literature."

"Just like you do," said Kurt.

"Well—almost as I do," said the booknotch.

"I guess we have a lot in common, huh?"

"I guess we do," replied Notch.

Charlie had not said a word and by this time had finished his share of the sandwich.

"Then there's Charlie," said Kurt. "He can taste the sandwich but not the literature." Kurt leaned close to the booknotch and whispered, "He's a dog. He can't read."

"Don't be so certain," said the booknotch. "Besides—haven't you ever read out loud in front of him?"

"A few times."

"Well, there you have it! He's tasted good literature too." The worm thought for a moment before looking Kurt straight in the eye. "I do assume it was *good* literature you read out loud."

"I always read good literature," said Kurt. "And lots of it. Books are in my blood—that's what Father used to tell me. 'Books are the key to greater understanding,' he would say. Anyway, it was *Huck Finn*."

Charlie smiled at the mention of *Huck Finn*.

"You see?" said Notch. "Charlie, too, has a taste for great literature."

Kurt started to laugh, but his laughter was held in check by the note of seriousness in the booknotch's voice and the caring way in which the little worm looked at the dog.

While Charlie listened, Kurt and the booknotch talked until all three were quite sleepy. Finally, the booknotch said goodnight and Kurt tucked him safely away in his shirt pocket. The boy was about to lie down when he noticed Charlie staring longingly at the backpack. "A taste for great literature, huh?" Kurt said, and he removed two Chunkie Chewies from the pack and handed them to the dog. Charlie offered one to Kurt, who politely declined, and the two weary travelers curled up together in the bed of leaves.

Day's end brought a gentle breeze that played among the copper leaves and blew away the silver dust that all day long had glistened upon the landscape. Darkness brought a stillness that hushed the ringing of the copper trees and spread a blanket of sleep across the valley. Those who stirred in their beds heard a chorus of nocturnal tidings—the voice of the frog and the cricket.

"W-a-u-k, w-a-u-k," croaked the frogs. "Quickit! Time'a shaut. Quickit! Time'a shaut," retorted the crickets.

Kurt felt a sudden chill. It's only the night air, he told himself. Nevertheless, he wiggled down as far as he could into the bed of leaves. He was glad to have Charlie snuggled close beside him.

CHAPTER 8

TATTLE-TAIL

Always it starts slowly. First a faint glimmer, then a single gleam, as when a ray of sunlight strikes a diamond. A solitary sunbeam, dancing on tiptoe through the copper leaves, trips gently from leaf to leaf so as not to wake the sleeper. Soon another comes to frolic, then another, till myriad sunbeams dance and play among the leaves. They are joined by a gentle breeze that sets the leaves softly ringing, and fragile birdsong—a wren, a titmouse, a mourning dove softly cooing. A nearby brook, which had hushed its babbling for the night, springs to life with splash and tumble and endless chatter. Soon the forest animals, hearing the call to light, stir from their long night's sleep, allowing their presence to be known only by the rustling of leaves and the snapping of twigs trod upon by padded paws.

Anyone would have thought Kurt was one such forest animal, stirring as he did in his bed of oak leaves, coaxed to waken by the warm shower of sunlight cascading through the copper canopy above his head—silver sunlight turned golden by the orange-crimson foliage of the copper tree.

Kurt opened his eyes to a landscape awash with shimmering light, and with a flash of remembrance, recalled the passage, the meadow, the strange bestowment given him by the meadow morphs. He touched his face and there they were—the unfamiliar appendages—still long and stiff and fully intact—still protruding like little antennas near the sides of his nose.

Sitting up, he brushed away the oak leaves that clung tenaciously to his clothes, and finding Charlie asleep, nudged the dog awake.

"Good morning, all," came a wee voice from Kurt's shirt pocket. "Notch?"

Kurt peeked into his pocket, and the sight of the tiny booknotch, nestled comfortably between his leaves, spawned a flood of recollections of the day before. At once Kurt recalled his lameness—or lack thereof—and stood and began hopping, first on one foot, then the other. Drawn into the spirit of the moment, Charlie hopped too.

When at last Kurt paused to catch his breath, he held his pocket open and peeked again at the booknotch. "Sorry, Notch," he said, "I didn't mean to bounce you around, but it's all true, isn't it—the whiskers, the metal trees, the way I can walk?"

The booknotch scratched his head in contemplation. "It's a fact you do have whiskers; and it's a fact there are metal trees; and it's a fact you can walk with a bounce in your step, and since truth can be defined as 'that which is in accordance with fact,' it must, indeed, all be true." The little worm yawned. "I'm afraid deductive reasoning of this magnitude, this early in the morning, always makes me drowsy. If you don't mind, Kurt, I shall sleep a while longer." He crawled down deeper between his leaves, and soon Kurt heard the faintest snore coming from his shirt pocket.

Charlie had stopped hopping by then, and Kurt took one of the two remaining sandwiches from the backpack, tore off a piece, and handed it to the dog along with a Chunkie Chewie. Hoping a taste of his favorite snack would make the animal amenable to conversation, Kurt remarked, "You know, Charlie, if you're going to help me find the way home, you've got to talk. And I don't mean all that dog stuff. You've got to use words."

Charlie answered in the usual way, with wiggles and wags, and went about eating his breakfast.

"Maybe these whiskers aren't working," Kurt grumbled, wriggling his shoulders through the straps of the backpack.

"It's not the whiskers," Charlie said bashfully.

Though the sound of the dog's voice startled Kurt, he was delighted the dog was talking. "There," he said. "Was that so hard?"

Charlie lowered his head and a sheepish grin stole across his face. "It's embarrassing."

"You shouldn't be embarrassed to talk to me, Charlie. And you know what? You have a nice voice."

Charlie grinned again, only this time it was with an open display of satisfaction.

By this time, Kurt had positioned the pack comfortably on his back and was ready to travel. "Charlie," he said, stepping onto the road, "I was hoping you would tell me about your life before I knew you. Where did you live? What did you do?"

"You mean about me and Chrysalis?"

"Who?"

"Chrysalis, my sister."

"I didn't know you had a sister."

"I do, but I don't know where she is now. She lost herself."

"She what?"

"She lost herself," the dog repeated.

Noticing a crack in Charlie's voice, Kurt let the remark pass. "You must have other brothers and sisters."

"I did at first," said Charlie, "but . . ."

The dog's voice failed him and Kurt quickly interceded. "What about your mother? Where is she?"

"I don't know," said Charlie. "I think Mother was a stray. She gave birth to us on a cold cement floor. The place smelled damp and musty."

"Like a basement?"

Charlie nodded. "The house must have been deserted because I couldn't hear a sound. And I couldn't see because my eyes weren't open yet. But I remember the terrible cold. And I remember Mother pulling us close, trying to keep us warm. But by the time the caretaker found us, there were only two of us left—me and Chrysalis."

Charlie uttered a deep, quivering sigh. "The caretaker talked kindly to Mother. He said he would give her a home. I guess he figured we pups would be adopted, but an older dog like Mother . . . well . . . you know."

"I *do* know," said Kurt.

Charlie lowered his head and stared at the ground as he walked. "The man wrapped me and Chrysalis in a warm blanket and took us to the shelter. That was the last we knew of Mother."

Kurt swallowed the lump in his throat. "I'm sorry, Charlie."

The dog offered a sad smile. He seemed to be comfortable enough talking by now, and he went on. "Little Chrysalis depended on me for everything. It made me feel good—you know—needed. When she was adopted away, I thought I would die. It was so lonely in that pen without her. I guess she missed me too. She was in her new home only three days when she pushed her way under the backyard fence and lost herself."

"How do you know that?"

"I heard the keepers talking about it. I cried and cried. I ran away from the shelter and searched for her everywhere for the longest time. But the keepers found me and took me back. That's when you came and adopted me."

"So *that's* where you go on those days when I can't find you. You're looking for Chrysalis. I should have gone to the shelter sooner. I could have adopted both of you."

Kurt noticed tears in Charlie's eyes, and he felt angry at himself for coaxing the dog to talk. "I won't let myself think about Charlie's little sister," he told himself, and setting his sights on the Silver Mountain, he quickened his pace. But try as he might, he could not help thinking about the tiny girl puppy, lost and alone, desperately searching for her big brother.

Kurt and Charlie walked without speaking after that. In time, their steps slowed, and as they meandered down the winding road, Kurt's thoughts fell in tune with the gentle chiming of the copper trees.

Perhaps it was this relaxed state that left him ill-prepared for what happened next, for when a lightning bolt tore through the clear sky ahead of him, he found himself knocked to the ground by the thunderous *BOOM!* that followed—a *boom!* that sent Charlie howling and pouncing on top of him. The two lay sprawled on the roadway when a second *BOOM!* shook the countryside.

"Thunder," said Charlie, his body trembling.

"The first one was thunder," said Kurt, pushing the dog aside, "but the second was something else."

Walking around bend after bend in the road, scanning trees and thickets and small clearings to the right and left, they found not the slightest sign of disturbance to explain the second *boom!* They would have given up the search had it not been for a sudden tingling in Kurt's whiskers that caused him to stop and listen. Grabbing hold of Charlie's collar, he pulled the dog up short. "Charlie, did you hear that?"

Charlie stood still and alert.

"There it is again," Kurt whispered.

This time Charlie heard it, too, for his stand-up ear turned toward the sound—a faint, small voice coming from somewhere up ahead.

> *"Weave and tat,*
> *Weave and tat,*
> *Till the tale is told;*
>
> *Weave a tale,*
> *Tat a tale*
> *Till I'm very old."*

Kurt and Charlie glanced at each other and crept along ever so slowly, homing in on the sound, straining to hear. The voice, which grew louder the closer they drew, sounded old and timeworn—somewhat like an old man.

"Weave and tat,
Weave and tat
Till the tale is told;

Weave a tale,
Tat a tale
Till I'm very old."

Rounding a sharp bend in the road, they came upon a terrible sight. There, sprawled across the center of a wayside clearing, lay a mighty oak, its massive trunk split down the middle, its splintered wood charred and ashen. The voice was coming from the direction of the fallen tree. Now they could hear it clearly.

"How could this have happened? Oh, weave and tat," moaned the tired old voice. "What am I to do? Oh, weave a tale. Someone help me!"

"Charlie! That's what the second *boom* was! The tree!" And he ran toward the fallen oak.

Charlie wasted no time. Dashing past Kurt, he raced to the tree and began sniffing the dense foliage.

Kurt arrived a moment later, and pushing aside a bushy limb at the tree's outer edge, peered through the mass of tangled branches. Again he heard the voice. It was coming from deep within the foliage.

"There, Charlie!" Kurt pointed as he climbed over the limb. He paused when the voice fell silent.

For several seconds, neither one moved.

Kurt's face turned pale. "We're too late, Charlie."

The dog stared at Kurt and his brow crinkled down to a point between his eyes. His eyes filled with determination. He looked to where Kurt had pointed, and in one well-aimed lunge, plowed through the foliage and disappeared into the thick of it.

"No!" Kurt shouted. But he could do no more than fix his gaze on the foliage where Charlie disappeared and watch it shiver and shake as the dog rummaged through it.

All at once Charlie's head popped out from among the leaves. He was carrying something in his mouth—something long and wiggly.

He zigzagged through the tangled branches much too fast for Kurt to determine what it was, and it was not until the dog was well away from the tree that he dropped whatever it was on the ground.

Kurt hesitated a moment then ever so cautiously crept toward the long and wiggly thing. By the time he reached it, the creature was lying straight and stiff at Charlie's feet.

Never had Kurt seen such a peculiar being. It looked like a tail—a long, gray, furry tail with no animal attached—tapered and plain at one end, and having on the other end, which was more or less blunt, a tiny face with whiskers and big blue eyes and puffy round cheeks.

Kurt crouched on the ground and stared at the lengthy animal—if indeed it could be called an animal. "Was that you talking before?" he asked the creature, craning his neck to get a better look at its face.

"It was," the tail answered huffily, pulling itself straight up and balancing on its tapered end while pushing its whiskered end up tight against Kurt's nose, causing the boy's eyes to cross. "And is that *you* talking now?"

Kurt quickly pulled his face away. "I'm sorry. I guess I was rude, staring at you like that."

"Rude attitude, a pesky mood," replied the tail in a most disgruntled voice. The mouth on his round little face bent downward in a frown, and he stared at Kurt intently before rambling on: "You—staring at me without a tree. Staring, glaring—never caring."

Soon the frown turned to a look of curiosity as the tail studied Kurt from foot to head. After a time, he glanced at the fallen tree, sighed a mournful sigh, and relaxed to a flattened position on the ground.

"I'd offer you a seat on the root over there—somewhere—should you care to sit," he said, nodding toward a large root growing above the ground at the base of what was once a stately old tree. "Used to be the finest seat in the house. But it's buried in splintered wood now. What's an old tail to do without his oak tree, dear me? By the way, thank you for pulling me from the foliage. I was afraid no one would hear me under all the leaves, so bereaved. Few animals pass this way anymore."

"It was no trouble," said Kurt, as he sat down next to the tail. "Besides, Charlie did all the work."

The old tail seemed not to be listening. He was staring absent-mindedly at the tree. "Terrible rumble, rum-tum-grumble."

"What?"

"Rum-tum-grumble," the tail repeated. "That's what I felt just before the terrible light, terrible fright, terrible fall and all. I didn't *hear* the rum-rum-grumble. I felt it in the ground. We tails are on the ground day and night, as you must know. And lately I've felt something strange. A vibration, a rumbling, a rum-tum-grumbling. Yes, that's what I felt—just before the terrible sound—just before the tree fell down."

"It was thunder," said Kurt. "And lightning."

The tail looked at the boy quizzically.

"It was lightning that felled your tree," Kurt explained. "A bolt out of the blue."

"He was frightening," said the tail.

"He? Lightening is not a *he*. It's a thing. It's—"

The tail interrupted, his voice shaking. "He pointed to my tree—and me. He must not like tails, you see."

The old tail stopped talking, and raising his fore-end high in the air, studied Kurt again from foot to head until a look of recognition spread over his face. After drawing a breath so deep it inflated his body like a balloon, and releasing it with a windy sigh, he appeared much more at ease. In a moment or two, a rosy-pink glow spread across his puffy cheeks, and a soft twinkle danced in his sky-blue eyes. To Kurt, the twinkle looked more like a gleam—the gleam on a just-licked peppermint stick. When the tail spoke again, it was with a delight in his voice that reminded Kurt of popsicles, icicles, tricycles, bicycles; ribbons for girls and kites for boys; wishing wells and wind-up toys.

"You're the first Nickle-Dickle I've ever seen," the tail said, with a tickle in his smile.

"How did you know my last name was Nickle-Dickle?" Kurt asked, surprised the tail would know.

"I didn't know your name; I only know you're a Nickle-Dickle. I've never seen one, but from what I've heard of them, I'm sure you *are* one, *am* one, *is* one." He thought for a moment then quickly corrected himself. "Yes! That's it. You *are* one."

"No, I are not one . . . I mean, *am* not one," said Kurt. He was sure they were not talking about the same things. "I don't understand. What do you think a Nickle-Dickle is?"

The tail stared thoughtfully into space then looked at Kurt as though he had just made a great discovery.

> *"One Nickle-Dickle—ten to a rhyme;*
> *Ten Nickle-Dickles—twenty at a time;*
> *Twenty Nickle-Dickles—never will they find*
> *The one Nickle-Dickle they left behind."*

"That doesn't make sense," Kurt said indignantly.

"Of course it does—*if* you use logic," said the tail. And his voice rang happily with a jingle like Christmas bells.

> *"One nickel makes five cents.*
> *One dickle makes no sense.*
> *One Nickle-Dickle makes scents.*

"And that's what Nickle-Dickles do. They make scents!" He laughed till his voice rattled like a jar full of jellybeans.

"Well, Nickle-Dickles may make sense, but *you* don't," said Kurt.

"Of course I don't," replied the tail. "I'm a tail. Tails don't make scents. Nickle-Dickles do." And he laughed all the more.

"Ah," Kurt moaned, holding his hands over his ears. "Never mind."

The tail's sky-blue eyes opened wide, and he chuckled.

> *"Never mind? I've never mined*
> *For copper, silver, nickel;*
> *For if you please, they grow on trees,*
> *So mining them is fickle."*

Kurt shook his head in disbelief.

Charlie had wisely stayed out of the conversation, and when Kurt looked to him for help, Charlie pretended to be sleeping.

Though vexed by the strangeness of the conversation, Kurt took it upon himself to venture another question. "I don't mean to be nosy, but I've never seen anything . . . I mean, any*one* like you before. Exactly what are you?"

"I'm a tattle-tail," answered the tail. "You can call me Tattle."

"For short."

"That's right. For short. Though I'm really quite long as tails go."

"I can see that," said Kurt. "I've seen plenty of tails." He paused a moment to choose exactly the right words. "But they were always . . . uh . . . connected. I've never seen any like you before—not anywhere."

"Not here, not there, not anywhere?"

"Not anywhere," Kurt replied emphatically. "What are you doing without your . . . other end?"

The tail stared wide-eyed at the boy. All color drained from his face. "Other end? You know about my other end, dear friend, dear friend?"

All at once Kurt felt an uncomfortable tingling in his whiskers. For a moment, deep despair overtook him and he could not bring himself to make further mention of the tail's other end.

"Ah, no. I don't know a thing about it. I was mistaken."

"Mistaken. Forsaken. My soul shaken," the tail said sadly.

"So, how did you come to be in Whiskers?" Kurt asked, in a weakish attempt to change the subject.

"This is where I was dropped," said the tail. The pink slowly returned to his cheeks and a mischievous twinkle appeared in his eyes. "Here I lie telling tales, but telling tales, I do not lie. Though I *lie* here, I do not *lie* here, you see." He was obviously amused at his clever use of language.

"I see," replied Kurt, somewhat confused.

Tattle told Kurt he had been in the same spot under the oak tree all his life. He had no memory of a time when he was *not* under the oak tree. "But I once had roots in the animal kingdom," said the tail.

"How do I know? My whiskers say it's so. They speak to me of another end—a sort of friend—running free—unlike me." A look of longing befell the tattle-tail's face, and the sadness returned to his voice. "But now my roots lie beneath this tree—buried, as it were, in antiquity." He shook his head as though perplexed. "My history is a mystery."

"I guess you'll have to go someplace else now," said Kurt, glancing toward the fallen oak. "You know . . . find another tree."

"Go someplace else? Me? Unheard of! Not a word of! I'm a tattle-tail. We tails stay where we're dropped—where we've stopped."

The tail forced a smile. "I've been fortunate, though. This spot by the road has been a good place for a tail to be—a tail like me. I've gathered all sorts of material to weave into tales from animals passing this way. A prickle-pine, perhaps a toad, along the road near my abode.

"Lots of animals stop here, too, to hear me tat a tale or two—though none like you." The twinkle left his eye. The rosy rushed from his cheeks. "Or, at least, they used to. Few animals travel this part of the road now. I don't know why. I don't know how to bring them back to here and now. Many have moved to the Nickel Hills. And the ones who do pass this way have heard my tales for many a day. So most don't bother to stop anymore—to seek my door here on this floor of grass and ground. They're not around. They can't be found."

The tail looked toward the fallen oak tree and tears glistened in the blue of his eyes. "Now, without a shady tree to rest under, it's no wonder no one will stop."

"We stopped. Me and Charlie," Kurt said quietly.

The tail smiled. The rosy rushed back to his cheeks. "Yes! You did!" The peppermint gleam returned to his eye. "Enough about me. Tell me about you—the two—the you and you." He nodded at Kurt then Charlie, and looking back at Kurt, said, "You say you're not a Nickle-Dickle. What are you?"

"I'm a boy," Kurt replied.

"Joy, toy, ploy, coy." The tail appeared puzzled, as though searching his mind for the word. "No, there's no *boy*," he concluded at last.

"Yes, there is," Kurt insisted. He told the tattle-tail about home, and how he and Charlie had come to the Land of Whiskers, and about his adventures in the Meadow.

The tail listened with great interest, but when the subject of Parhelion the Nimbus came up, Tattle's long body stiffened. "I have felt Parhelion's shadow pass over on occasion—shudder, stutter, shadow, shade—it made me so affright, afraid. But never could I see him through the foliage of the tree. For that I am thankful, for he could not see me—see me ēither, nēither, neīther—neīther hear me blăther, blīther."

"That's blăther, blīther," said a small, sleepy voice from Kurt's shirt pocket.

"Who said that?" the tail asked, craning to see what the boy had in his pocket.

"It's a booknotch," said Kurt, and he peeked in at the worm just in time to see him yawn and fall asleep.

"Book, notch, cook, blotch, look, botch," rambled the tail.

"Tattle," said Kurt, "I notice you speak in rhyme from time to time." Realizing he was doing so himself, he quickly threw his hand over his mouth, but not in time to keep Tattle from laughing

"In Whiskers we all speak in rhyme from time to time, oh 'boy' of mine. Rhyme paints better pictures than prose, as everyone knows. And the better the pictures, the greater the understanding . . . or is it *over* standing?

"Our whiskers seem to like rhyme, too—a rhyme from me, a rhyme from you. Whiskers translate words from one animal's language to another. *To an other*," he repeated deliberately, "and they do much better with rhyming words. Something to do with rhythm and bounce—more rhythm, more meaning, more pounce to the ounce."

"I never thought about that," said Kurt.

"Even when we speak in prose—when we have something to say that nobody knows—our whiskers cause the other animal to hear the words in rhyme—in proper meter, in proper line—for better understanding. We speak in rhyme at other times, too. It's fun for me and fun for you. Why don't you try it, and if it fits, buy it!"

"Oh, no. I couldn't," said Kurt, embarrassed by the prospect of performing in any way before anybody, even if the audience did consist of only a dog, a booknotch, and a tattle-tail. "That was just an accident before."

"Come on, come off, come over, come under. Give it a try; it's full of wonder. Start with something happy and simple—a face with a smile, a cheek with a dimple."

"Well . . . okay," said Kurt. "Here goes.

> *Once upon a glitch in time,*
> *I stumbled on a world of rhyme."*

"Very good," said Tattle. "Go on."

> *"Where people spoke to crocodiles,*
> *Who greeted them with friendly smiles,"*

"Yes, yes. That's it. That fits."

> *"Where one could joke with polar bears*
> *And laugh with lions in their lairs."*

"Wonderful, wonderful!"

> *"Where is this place? Oh, where, oh where?*
> *Over here? Over there?"*

The tattle-tail's smile soured. "That part needs work."

> *"Where rainbows touch upon the ground,*
> *The Land of Whiskers can be found."*

Kurt stared at the tail with great expectation. "How did I do?"

"For a first attempt . . ."

"Yes, yes," Kurt urged.

"For a first attempt . . . I think . . ."

"Tell me," Kurt demanded.

"For a first attempt . . . it was wonderful, funny, and FUNderful!"

Kurt smiled and Charlie giggled. The tattle-tail laughed a laugh that was dandy, till his little cheeks puffed like pink cotton candy.

When the laughter subsided, Kurt stood up. He had lost all track of time. "I'm sorry to leave you, Tattle, but we really have to be going."

The sugar-pink faded from the tattle-tail's cheeks; his long, furry body turned limp on the ground. But Kurt took no notice. His thoughts were on the journey ahead. "Do you know anything about a Cornerstone?" he asked the tail.

"A cornerstone, a cornerstone," Tattle mumbled. "I know a tale about a cornerstone."

"Tell it to me, please," said Kurt.

Tattle cleared his throat and recited in a dull monotone:

> *"Locked within the Cornerstone,*
> *Words to lead from here to there.*
> *Answers you must find alone,*
> *The who, the what, the why, the where."*

Kurt stared at Charlie. "That's the same rhyme the there'n not-hares told us, Charlie. Now I know what they meant when they said they heard it from a tail."

"Goodbye, Tattle," Kurt said, and he began walking toward the road. When he was some distance from the tail, he called back, "It was FUNderful talking to you." But the tail did not answer.

After a few more steps, Kurt heard the familiar voice again and stopped to listen. The voice sounded weary and timeworn, much the way it had when he and Charlie first discovered the tail. The creature's words, slow and somnolent, were steeped in despair and lamentation: "Afraid, frayed, betrayed, dismayed. Me, without a tree, for all to see. Is it right to be left? Is being left right? Is it correct? Does it reflect a lower place, a tail disgraced?"

The tattle-tail rambled on mournfully:

> *"Riddle, rattle, prittle, prattle,*
> *Just who is this tail named Tattle—*

Dropped, discarded, quite immobile,
From his birth, most ignoble—
Once together, now apart;
Then a whole, now a la carte?

That other end, now just a squiggle,
Once was waved, but now must wiggle.
Does it cry to think me lost?
Does it mourn the terrible cost
Of someone's whim, of someone's pride
In disconnecting its other side?

Does it ever think of me
Lying here beneath this tree?
Does it know my spirit begs
To romp through woods on lanky legs—
Legs that should have carried me—
Legs that would have set me free?

Who would shear my roots, my will,
And leave me here alone and still?
Who would do this? Just what sort?
Is there no justice? No retort?
Riddle, rattle, prittle, prattle,
Just who is this tail named Tattle?"

Poor Tattle, thought Kurt. "C'mon, Charlie." He turned and ran back to where the tail was lying.

The tattle-tail, his body limp and flat on the ground, was so immured in melancholy he barely noticed Kurt had returned.

"Tattle," said Kurt, kneeling down next to the tail, "we can't leave you here with no tree to lie under."

"Though I *lie* here, I do not *lie* here," the tail mumbled.

"I know, Tattle. As I was saying, you said no one stops to hear your tales anymore. Why don't you come with us to Nickledown? In a town, there's sure to be lots of animals to hear your tales."

The tattle-tail's eyes popped wide open. "Me? Go to Nickledown?" He raised his head and stared at Kurt. The rosy rushed to his little round cheeks. His sky-blue eyes twinkled like wishing stars. But all too soon the twinkle faded. "How could I go to Nickledown?" he said. "I've never been anywhere but here under my oak tree, you see. I have no legs, you know. Such woe. Tattle-tails always stay put."

"Legs are no problem," said Kurt. "You can ride Charlie's tail. You can wrap yourself around his tail and ride all the way to Nickledown, just like a real connected tail."

"He can what!" said Charlie.

Kurt nudged the dog. "You've always wanted a spare tail, haven't you, Charlie?"

The dog forced a smile and tucked his tail between his legs.

Tattle stared at Charlie's tail. "I don't know . . . one tail or two? What should I do? I don't think tails are supposed to, do you?"

"Who says?" said Kurt. "Why don't you give it a trial run?"

"A trial run?" said the tail.

Kurt smiled. "It could be fun."

The old tail looked at Charlie. Then he looked at Kurt. Then he looked at Charlie's tail again.

"A little trial run—
What could it hurt?
A wiggle, a waggle,
A romp in the dirt . . ."

In the tattle-tail's eye
Was a hint of a gleam,
Like the shine on a scoop
Of blueberry ice cream.

At last the tail grinned
And nodded his head.
"I'll do it! Hop to it!"
The tattle-tail said.

Charlie moaned and sat down next to Tattle, stretching his tail full-length alongside the tattle-tail. The dog stared intently at Kurt and his brow crinkled down to a point between his eyes. His eyes filled with determination. Tattle wound himself around Charlie's tail and off they went!

Kurt suspected the dog planned to discourage the tattle-tail, and when he saw Charlie in action, he was certain of it.

Charlie wiggled and wagged. And he wagged and wiggled. He scampered and pranced and scampered again. He hopped and he jumped, he stumbled and bumped . . . But still the tail held fast.

"Yahoo!" shouted Tattle with a jingle in his voice. "Yahoo! Yahoo! Yahoo! Whoopee do!"

His heart must have raced
A bipidy bop,
For his cheeks became pink
As raspberry pop!

"Yahoo!" the tail said
As faster he flew—
"Yahoo! Yahoo!
Yahoo! Whoopee do!"

Charlie began to laugh as he romped—as he jumped and wiggled and stumbled and bumped. After a time, he seemed proud to be sporting two tails.

When at last the jumping
And bumping stopped,
The dog was so tired
His stand-up ear flopped.

The tattle-tail dropped
With a thud on the ground
Saying, "Nickle me! Tickle me!
Take me to town!"

So it was settled. The tattle-tail would be going to Nickledown.

Kurt woke the booknotch, took him out of his shirt pocket, and introduced him to the tattle-tail. Having in common the same basic shape and a certain propensity for words, the two liked each other straightaway.

After a time, Kurt put the booknotch back in his pocket and adjusted the pack on his back, Tattle wrapped himself around Charlie's tail, and the four were off to Nickledown!

CHAPTER 9

THE PINK STINKLE-DUNK

It was well into afternoon when Kurt, Charlie, Tattle and Notch reached the interior of the Copper Valley. The booknotch had earlier defined copper as a "common reddish metal." Now Kurt could see for himself the truth in the worm's definition. Copper was indeed common. Here in the valley's innermost part, the metal trees grew in such profusion they choked out all but an occasional oak. Thick stands lined both sides of the road, interrupted only now and then by a small breach through which Kurt could catch a glimpse of a meandering stream, or perhaps peer through to a grassy expanse of meadow. But always beyond the stream or meadow there rose another stand of copper trees, vast, gleaming like golden topaz in the afternoon sun. Everywhere the boy looked, sunlight reflecting in crimson highlight across the myriad metal leaves turned field and meadow and stream alike a fiery red, imbuing the air itself with a rich, warm glow that reached up to the sky, painting even the undersides of clouds the golden-red of burnished copper.

The number of copper trees in this central region were equaled in measure only by the abundance of fruit they bore. In fact, they were so heavily laden with the strange, brown, biscuit-like fruit that from time to time Kurt would hear the clamorous ringing of a single tree and would turn in time to see it shed its entire crop at once, strewing fruit in all directions upon the ground. In places, huge piles had accumulated beneath the trees.

Charlie had just stopped to sniff a particularly large pile, and Kurt was about to warn him for the second time not to eat the fruit, when the boy saw something dart across the road up ahead. Before he could determine what it was, the creature disappeared into a wayside thicket.

"Follow me, Charlie," Kurt said in a quiet voice and carefully began making his way toward the thicket.

With Tattle wrapped tightly around his tail and his nose pressed to the ground, Charlie followed closely on Kurt's heels, sniffing the earth like a bloodhound.

When Kurt reached the spot where the creature vanished, he heard a rustle. Picking up a fallen branch, he stripped away its side shoots to make a stick and cautiously stepped into the thicket, using the stick to push aside the heavy underbrush.

Again came the rustle, which now seemed to be coming from a bramble bush a few feet ahead. Leaning as far forward as he could, Kurt carefully pushed the end of the stick into the bush. He felt a bump when it struck something solid, and out from the bush sprang a blur of bristling black-and-white fur with two large, dark eyes.

The animal screamed and Kurt screamed and the animal screamed again. A moment later, Kurt smelled the most god-awful smell he had ever smelled. "Skunk!" he cried, dropping the stick and pinching his nose shut as he ran back through the thicket. Charlie zoomed past him with a blood-curdling howl that set the nearby copper trees clanging. Having escaped the worst of the smell, the two came to rest in the middle of the road.

"That was awful!" Kurt said in a muffled voice, his hand held firmly over his nose and mouth.

At the first opportunity, Charlie buried his nose in Kurt's pant leg, and following the dog's lead, Tattle pushed his end with the face deep into the fur on Charlie's hindquarters.

"You all right, Notch?" said Kurt, peeking into his shirt pocket. The booknotch replied with a weak, "Cough, cough, cough."

As the four huddled in the roadway, a small, rather inquisitive-looking animal cautiously poked its head out from behind a nearby deerberry bush and stared at Kurt curiously. Trying not to choke on his words, Kurt mumbled, "I'm sorry, but you *are* a skunk."

The animal's eyes opened wide. He seemed to be taken aback at being identified in such a brash and impertinent manner. With an air about him that exuded pride and pomposity, as well as some degree of indignation, he stepped out onto the roadway, where Kurt was better able to see him.

Despite his diminutive stature, the animal appeared stately—though a bit stodgy. He was impeccably dressed from head to foot in a finely tailored black three-piece suit, rather like a tuxedo, and a white, starched shirt with a high, stiff collar. Even his tasteful paisley ascot was stiffly starched, making him appear a bit stuffy as well. His silver watch fob dangled properly from its appointed pants pocket, and his black shoes were polished to a rain-slick shine.

Throwing his shoulders back and his chest forward, and raising his nose high in the air as though something (perhaps an affront to his societal station) had given him courage to face Kurt head-on, the imposing little animal proceeded to defend his rank in a manner hinting of ivy-covered halls and old encyclopedias well read. "A *skunk*? A *skunk*? *I* most assuredly am not a *skunk*, whatever that may be. *I* am a *stinkle-dunk*! A *pink* stinkle-dunk if you please. For the most part."

"Oh," Kurt replied in a nasal voice, his fingers pinching his nose shut. "I didn't know."

"And what may I ask are you?" inquired the stinkle-dunk, looking Kurt over from head to toe. "You *look* like a Nickle-Dickle, but you're oddly dressed."

"He's a boy," came the muffled voice of the tattle-tail, whose face was still pushed deep into the fur on Charlie's hindquarters.

Kurt glanced at the tattle-tail, and looked back at the stinkle-dunk. "My name is Kurt, and I'm not a Nickle-Dickle. That is, I don't make scents. My *last name* is Nickle-Dickle."

The stinkle-dunk appeared puzzled. "You most certainly don't make sense," he said huffily. "What's the waggle-lick's name?"

"The *what's* name?"

"The waggle-lick's name," the stinkle-dunk repeated, looking directly at Charlie but not addressing him as such because much of Charlie's face was still buried in Kurt's pant leg.

"His name is Charlie," said Kurt, "but he's a dog, not a . . . What did you call him?"

"A waggle-lick," the stinkle-dunk insisted. "I certainly know a waggle-lick when I see one. By the way, you can release your nose now. That's not likely to happen again. It's just that sometimes . . . when I'm startled, that is . . . I, ah . . ."

Realizing the stinkle-dunk's embarrassment, and blaming himself in part for the malodorous mishap, having frightened the animal as he did, Kurt released the hold on his nose. After taking a small sniff to test the air (which had greatly purified itself by then), he said, not too convincingly, "It really wasn't so bad." But he couldn't look the little skunk in the eye. Instead, he looked down at Charlie. "You've smelled skunks—I mean stinkle-dunks—at home, Charlie. It wasn't that bad, was it?"

Charlie, wearing a pained expression from holding his breath too long, peeked cautiously at the stinkle-dunk, withdrew his nose from Kurt's pant leg, and shook his head no.

"You'll have to excuse him," said Kurt. "He's a waggle-lick of few words."

The stinkle-dunk glanced at Charlie. "At home, you say. Where is home?"

"Over the mountain," said Kurt, pointing behind him. "Or through it. Or . . . Well, I'm not sure exactly. But I'm going to Nickledown to find the Cornerstone. The there'n not-hares said the Cornerstone might help me."

"Harumph," said the stinkle-dunk. "The there'n not-hares. I'm not certain I would wager a wag on what *they* have to say."

"Well, do *you* know anything about it—the Cornerstone, I mean?"

"I know it is rumored to exist. And it is said to be in Nickledown."

Kurt proceeded to tell the stinkle-dunk about his conversation with the there'n not-hares, and about the meadow morphs and the whiskers and the shadow. The stinkle-dunk listened attentively until the mention of the shadow, whereupon a horrified look befell his face.

"Parhelion," said the stinkle-dunk.

"Yes," Kurt replied. "Or at least, that's who the there'n not-hares said he was. Is something wrong?"

"Oh, no," replied the skunk, removing a white silk handkerchief from his vest pocket. "It's just that Parhelion . . . I mean . . . that is to say . . . Well, there are stories about the Nimbus. But no one really knows much about him. And some animals think . . . that is, I think . . ." The stinkle-dunk wiped a bead of sweat from his forehead and put the handkerchief back into his pocket. "In actuality, I don't know exactly what I think about Parhelion. I truly hope I never *have* to think about him."

Uncertain what to make of the animal's strange behavior, Kurt turned to Charlie, only to find the dog standing over the tattle-tail, his brow wrinkled with worry.

"He fell off," said Charlie, staring at the tail. "You said 'Parhelion,' and he fell right off." And indeed he must have fallen with a solid *cur-plop!* for now he lay rigid and trembling on the roadway, mumbling incoherently, sounding much like a broken record: "Oh, weave a rattle, tat a prattle . . . coy, toy, joy, boy . . . no boy, no boy, no boy . . ."

Charlie glanced up at Kurt, and with a look of desperation, gave the tattle-tail a long, motherly lick across his rosy-cheeked end, which now was looking rather pale.

The old tail responded with a shake of his head, and having thus become lucid, said nervously to the dog, "Would you please put me under a tree. Out in the open is no place to be."

Charlie wagged his tail and gently picked Tattle up with his teeth and placed him under a copper tree by the side of the road.

"Thank you," said the tail. "Under a tree is the best place to be."

In light of the tattle-tail's distress, the stinkle-dunk quickly turned the topic of conversation away from the Nimbus. "I'll tell you what, ah . . . What did you say your name was?"

"Kurt."

"That's a short, quick little name."

"It's really Kurtis Francis—Kurtis Francis Nickle-Dickle. But I use Kurt for short. Everyone used to call me Francis, but a boy at school said it sounded like a girl's name, so I told everyone to call me Kurt. It sounds more grown-up, don't you think?"

"Harumph," said the stinkle-dunk. "And what does your mother call you?"

"She calls me Kurt now, too—when she isn't calling me 'dear.'"

"I see," said the stinkle-dunk. "And your surname is Nickle-Dickle." The little animal rubbed his chin and mused deeply as he studied Kurt again from head to foot.

"Well," he said, withdrawing his silver watch from its appointed pocket. After quickly checking the time, he tucked the watch away. "You have a long trip ahead of you, Kurtis, and it's getting late. Perhaps you and your friends would like to stay the night at my cottage and get an early start in the morning. We could partake of supper and enjoy some good conversation. I do have a taste for conversation, and it appears I'll be having little of that in the future." A look of dismay came over the stinkle-dunk's face and Kurt was not sure what to make of it.

"But Nickledown—where you're going—there's the place for conversation." The stinkle-dunk stared into the distance and his face took on the look of one who has just seen a divine vision. "In Nickledown, I hear, the conversations are stupendous! Especially those with the Nickle-Dickles. Most eloquent conversationalists, the Nickle-Dickles. And animals from all over Whiskers come to Nickledown to trade and visit and celebrate; and they bring with them all sorts of stories about the Far Regions. Ah, yes. To journey to Nickledown and converse with the Nickle-Dickles. It's been a dream of mine for years."

"Why haven't you gone?" asked Kurt.

"Procrastination, I suppose," said the stinkle-dunk, "though justi-fied procrastination. I wanted to wait until I was fully prepared—fully pink, that is. One must be at his best to hold his own in a conversation with a Nickle-Dickle."

Kurt had no idea what the stinkle-dunk was talking about. And there was that word "*pink*" again. The stinkle-dunk certainly did not look pink to him. Kurt recalled thinking the booknotch was color-blind earlier. Perhaps the stinkle-dunk, too, was color-blind.

"About the invitation," said Kurt. "I think we'll take you up on it. Thank you Mister . . . ah . . . Mister . . ."

"Just call me Stinkle-Dunk. For short."

CHAPTER 10

STINKLE-DUNK'S HOUSE

Despite the unpleasant way he and the stinkle-dunk met, Kurt was glad to have the company of the peculiar little skunk. He welcomed, too, the animal's kind invitation to stay the night at his home, for nightfall was rapidly approaching. Already the deep crimson rays of the setting sun streamed across the valley floor, drawing forth strong shadows and bathing the landscape in hues of darkish red that washed away all remains of afternoon's warm copper glow. Like supple fingers, the shadows, long and purple-crimson, directed the travelers onward, eastward, pointing the way to the Silver Mountain

As the reds gave way to the cool purples of approaching nightfall, Kurt felt a slight tingling in his whiskers. Soon thereafter, he was sure he heard quiet voices whispering, "Evening draws nigh; sleep tight, sleep tight." But a short time later, the air became so full of night sounds—the chirping of crickets and croaking of bullfrogs—he could no longer hear the quiet voices.

Kurt listened intently to the night sounds as he walked along the road with the stinkle-dunk and the others. Something within the sounds disturbed him. He was certain he heard words amid the croaking and chirping—words that evoked a sense of urgency, yet made no sense at all. At last he concluded his whiskers must be at fault. They must not be interpreting correctly.

The boy stared cross-eyed at the strange appendages jutting forth near the sides of his nose. He wiggled his nose, carefully studying every inch of every whisker. Having inspected all of them thoroughly, and having assured himself the whiskers were properly aligned, and finding no defect in them whatsoever, he concluded the fault must be his own. He simply needed more practice using his whiskers.

The croaking and chirping grew unbearably loud the farther the little band journeyed up the road, and when it reached a pond by the wayside, the noise was so raucous it became impossible for Kurt and his friends to hear one another without shouting.

"W-a-u-k. W-a-u-k," croaked the frogs. "Quickit! Time'a shaut. Quickit! Time'a shaut," retorted the crickets.

Stinkle-Dunk put his hands over his ears and quickened the pace. "The night-chirps and leap-lops are especially loud this evening," he shouted above the din. "I've never known them to be so boisterous."

"It sounds like they're saying, 'Walk'—and 'Quick! Time is short,'" Kurt shouted back. "But what do they mean?"

"I'm not certain," said the stinkle-dunk, "but surely it has nothing to do with us. Hurry on, now."

Despite Stinkle-Dunk's lack of concern, Kurt felt uneasy, the way he did at the lake when he thought someone was behind him and no one was there. He was glad when they were well past the pond.

After a time, the night creatures' voices became faint in the distance, and soon thereafter Kurt heard a gentle ringing like wind chimes as a breeze rustled the metallic leaves of the copper-colored trees.

"Are the trees really made of copper?" Kurt asked the stinkle-dunk.

"They are," the animal replied. "That's where the Copper Valley gets its name. As you go through the Nickel Hills in a day or two, the copper trees will gradually disappear and be replaced by nickel ones. The nickel trees are not so numerous, but they're much more beautiful to behold, and their music puts these to shame."

"It's hard to believe trees can be made of metal," said Kurt.

"You find that unusual?"

"Where I come from, it would be impossible."

"Harumph," said the stinkle-dunk. "I assume you don't have silver ones either."

"Silver ones?" Kurt's eyes opened wide. "You have silver ones too?" He imagined how rich he would be if he had a tree made entirely of silver.

"Actually, I don't know for a fact that we have them," said the stinkle-dunk. "No one I know has ever seen one. But legend says there's a grove of them high on the Silver Mountain—higher even than where the abacus flowers grow. According to the legend, if you draw near enough to a silver tree to hear its music, you'll fall asleep and never come down the mountain."

Kurt was lost in thought about the silver trees when the stinkle-dunk came to an abrupt halt in the road.

"What is it?" Kurt asked.

The stinkle-dunk stood motionless. "Did you hear it?"

"Hear what?"

"A rumbling. Charlie heard it. Look at him."

Charlie was standing with his head held low, his eyebrows crinkled to a sharp point between his eyes. He looked up at Kurt and the little white crescents formed beneath the brown of his eyes.

"Charlie, please use words," Kurt begged. "What did you hear?"

Charlie whimpered, but said nothing.

"Perhaps we animals are more sensitive to these things," said the stinkle-dunk. "I'm sure I heard a rumble. And there was an article in this morning's newspaper—a short article—just a line or two. I thought nothing of it, but now I wonder." He took a deep breath and resumed his walk.

"What did it say?" said Kurt.

"Probably nothing important. Let us talk of more pleasant things."

Kurt turned his thoughts to Nickledown. "What are the Nickle-Dickles, exactly, Stinkle-Dunk?"

"Oh, they're fine beings. They look very much like you, except for their size. Yes, very fine beings. Were they a color, I'm certain it would be at least pink. You know, like me. Well, sort of like me. I'm pink for the most part, though I slip now and then."

Kurt could not imagine what the stinkle-dunk was talking about. There was that mention of *pink* again. The boy stared at the little skunk. From his fur to his finely tailored clothes, there was not a speck of pink on him. Kurt suspected "I slip now and then" had to do with the unpleasant way they met, and knowing the embarrassment that caused the stinkle-dunk, he thought it better not to discuss the slippage. His curiosity about the color was more than he could bear, however, so he ventured a question.

"What did you mean, 'if the Nickle-Dickles *were* a color?' They must be *some* color; everyone is *some* color. Otherwise, they'd look ghostly."

"Color has nothing to do with the way you look, Kurtis. Quite to the contrary. It has to do with—"

The stinkle-dunk interrupted himself. They were rounding a bend in the road and a small cottage was coming into view. Stinkle-Dunk's chest swelled with pride at the sight of it. "Ah," he sighed. "Home at last."

The house standing before them was an immaculate cottage made of antique brick, with two windows on the front graced with shutters made of hammered copper. The steeply pitched roof and the door, too, were hammered copper. Tiny tea roses and miniature gardenias growing in boxes beneath the windows filled the air with a delightfully sweet scent that blended with that of the star jasmine spilling over the side of a large copper urn at one side of the door. The walkway leading invitingly to the front steps was a long path of shiny pebbles that glistened in the moonlight and crunched as Kurt, Charlie, Tattle, Notch, and the stinkle-dunk made their way along its length.

"It's a beautiful house," said Kurt.

The stinkle-dunk smiled and hurried ahead.

When moments later Kurt and the others reached the steps, they found the stinkle-dunk standing at the door mumbling to himself, nervously reading a note.

"What is it?" Kurt asked.

"Nothing," said the stinkle-dunk, his voice trembling. "Just a notice left on the door by a friend. Nothing out of the ordinary." He crumpled the paper and quickly stuffed it into his pants pocket. But even in the moonlight, Kurt could see the little skunk's face was as pale as though the blood had been drained from it, and he dared not question him further.

Kurt had to duck to get through the doorway of the stinkle-dunk's cottage, since the opening was not made for someone of his height. Once inside, however, he could stand up quite comfortably, for the cottage had cathedral ceilings, a rare feature for a house in the Land of Whiskers, as the stinkle-dunk was quick to boast.

Kurt felt safe and secure inside the cozy cottage—it reminded him of his own home. The tattle-tail, on the other hand, was nervous. He'd never been inside a house—inside anything, for that matter. He promptly asked Charlie to place him under something. The dog dropped him on the living room floor in front of Stinkle-Dunk's big green overstuffed sofa, and with a gentle nudge of his nose, pushed him under. "Ah," said Tattle, "green like my tree, a good place to be," and after breathing a long, fervent sigh, he smiled at the dog, closed his eyes, and fell fast asleep.

Despite his efforts at cheerfully playing the proper host—rushing around turning on lights, fluffing pillows, and in general, making the place comfortable—the stinkle-dunk still appeared pale. Thinking it might serve to take the skunk's mind off whatever was in the note, Kurt took the booknotch and his leaves out of his pocket and introduced the worm to the stinkle-dunk.

"Thank you for your kind hospitality in graciously inviting us to stay the night in your exquisite abode," said the booknotch.

A look of surprise came over the stinkle-dunk's face upon hearing the booknotch's words. "You're quite welcome," he replied in a flowery tone of voice. Right away, much of the color returned to his face, and from the sparkle in his eye, it was apparent he took great pleasure in Notch's eloquent use of language. "I can see you're a fellow who knows how to use his whiskers with maximum efficiency," he said to the booknotch.

The booknotch smiled a shy smile. "I'm happy to have met you, sir. I believe, if you will forgive my lack of social grace, I shall retire early this evening. I'm unaccustomed to traveling so far in so short a time. Good night, all." And he slipped back between his leaves, which Kurt gently placed in a copper bowl on the coffee table.

"What a fine little fellow!" said the stinkle-dunk. "Did he come with you from that other world?"

"No, I found him when he fell out of a tree. He had no book, you see, and . . . well, it's a long story." Kurt explained Notch's predicament, adding, "I'm worried about him. There's nothing for him to eat in those leaves. Not the kind of stuff booknotches eat anyway; 'phrases well-penned,' or something like that."

The stinkle-dunk's look of delight turned to one of concern and he began pacing back and forth, his hands clasped behind his back, his eyes perusing the room intently. "If only I had a book for him. But there are no books in Whiskers of which I'm aware, except for one rumored to be in Nickledown, and who knows if there is truth to the rumor. Knowledge of lasting importance is passed by word of mouth here."

The little skunk stopped pacing and stared thoughtfully at the leaves in the copper bowl. "There *is* our little Copper Valley Gazette, of course, but it contains matters of fleeting interest only—nothing significant enough to be bound and kept."

Because it was early spring, the evening air brought a slight chill, so the stinkle-dunk built a crackling fire in the hearth before going into the kitchen to prepare a supper of homemade vegetable soup and home-baked biscuits with honey. Though he had fully regained his facial color by this time, he nevertheless stared into the distance now and then as though his thoughts were miles away.

"My mother makes biscuits like those," said Kurt, when he saw the stinkle-dunk remove a piping-hot batch from the oven. The skunk took off his apron and set it aside, and he and Charlie and Kurt sat down at the dining table with the starched, white linen tablecloth. They did not wake Tattle for supper because tails, like booknotches, do not eat as humans or animals do. Tails draw nourishment from the rhythm of a rhyme or a rightly metered line, as Tattle explained to Kurt on the road earlier that afternoon.

The table at which the three dined was low to accommodate the diminutive stinkle-dunk, and Kurt had to sit cross-legged on the floor to fit up to it properly. Charlie, however, appeared to be quite comfortable in one of the tiny chairs—so much so, in fact, that when he saw Stinkle-Dunk and Kurt place white linen napkins at their necks, he asked Kurt to help him tuck one into his old brown collar. The air of fine dining thus created seemed to strike a chord of gentility deep within the dog, for Charlie wore his napkin like a pedigree. Kurt could not help chuckling at the sight of Charlie, the vagabond dog, wearing a formal white napkin.

"Oh! I almost forgot," said the stinkle-dunk, jumping up from his chair. He took a large copper bowl down from a shelf and placed it in the center of the table, and put a small boat of bean gravy and a pitcher of cream to one side of the bowl.

Charlie's eyes opened wide at the sight of the substance in the bowl.

"What's that?" Kurt asked, recognizing it as the strange brown fruit he had warned Charlie not to eat.

"It's tribble, the fruit of copper and nickel trees," said the stinkle-dunk. "And I've heard it grows on silver trees, too, though I couldn't attest to it." The stinkle-dunk pushed the bowl toward Charlie. "Wonderful stuff! It comes in all sizes so animals large and small can have just the proper-sized morsels."

Kurt glanced at Charlie, who was peering back condescendingly from behind his formal white napkin. "I knew it was tribble," said the dog. "Tattle told me on the road."

Kurt felt a bit silly.

"Those who don't eat other fruits—or vegetables, or nuts, or grasses—eat tribble exclusively," explained the stinkle-dunk, handing

Charlie a large spoon, "but I prefer a small portion on the side, topped with bean gravy or cream. Yes, there's nothing like vegetable soup and home-baked biscuits, and if you have honey to go with the biscuits and a bowl of tribble on the side . . . well, it's all an animal could ask for."

Charlie placed two large mounds of tribble next to each other on his plate and put honey on one and bean gravy on the other. He then poured cream over the whole thing, giving his dinner the appearance of a huge, floating sundae. "Luscious!" he declared, picking up his spoon. Kurt and the stinkle-dunk glanced at each other and chuckled as Charlie grinned and dug joyously into the swirling mess upon his plate.

As the three dined, Kurt grew increasingly quiet. He seemed far away as he absent-mindedly picked at his meal. The stinkle-dunk watched the boy curiously for quite some time and said at last, "You know, Kurtis, I was born in Whiskers—in the Southern Region. Dreadfully hot down there. I moved farther north seeking a cooler climate, and here I live till this day. But I missed my home in the south terribly at first."

The stinkle-dunk waited patiently for Kurt to reply.

After a long pause in which no one spoke, Kurt swallowed hard and finally said, "I miss my home too," and having pronounced those difficult words, he allowed a flood of thoughts and feelings to pour out of him. He told Stinkle-Dunk about his house, his mother, his school, his secret place by the lake.

The stinkle-dunk listened attentively to all the boy had to say, but when Kurt described the thunderstorm at the lake, the skunk jumped up from the table and hurried over to a desk in the corner, where he picked up a folded piece of paper.

The Copper Valley Gazette was printed in columns like a newspaper, but consisted of only one small page. The stinkle-dunk did not unfold the paper; apparently, the article he was interested in was right on top. He stood by the desk reading to himself while Kurt resumed his discourse about home.

"Mother must really miss me. She needs me. I'm the man of the house now, you know."

"What did you say?" the stinkle-dunk said, absent-mindedly.

"I was telling you about my mother."

"Oh, yes. Forgive me. I *was* listening. It sounds very nice, except the part about school." The stinkle-dunk placed the newspaper back on the desk and returned to the table. "Imagine those children calling you names just because you were lame. That should have been even more reason to be nice to you—to make you feel at ease. Why, if they had color, I'm sure it would be no higher than purple." He reached for a biscuit, but his hand stopped in midair. "Lame? You're not lame."

"I was before I came to Whiskers," said Kurt. "It happened in the meadow. One minute I was lame. The next, I wasn't. My father was lame, too, and my grandfather, and his father before him, for who knows how many generations. I guess *my* son will be lame, if ever I have one. Father said being lame was a blessing. He seemed glad about it. Can you imagine that?"

The stinkle-dunk stared at Kurt in a deeply contemplative way. "I Iarumph," he said presently, letting the subject drop. "You mentioned you were the man of the house. Where is your father now?"

"I wish I knew. He just disappeared." Kurt pulled the chain holding the tarnished key out through the neck of his shirt and held the key up for the stinkle-dunk to see. "This is all I have left of him." After staring at the key himself for a moment, he carefully tucked it away again.

"Father was never without the key, but the morning he disappeared, when he heard the thunder, he ran out the door without it—ran out mumbling something about a bell and so little time. Annie, our dog, ran after him."

The stinkle-dunk looked at Kurt quizzically. "This thunder you talk about—"

"'Rumbling,' I guess *you* would call it," said Kurt. "Anyway, Mother saw the key on the dresser and knew how important it was to Father. She grabbed the key and chased after him—all the way across the field toward the woods. But a clap of thunder knocked her down."

"How dreadful!" said the stinkle-dunk.

"It was the loudest thunder I'd ever heard," said Kurt. "I saw her fall. I ran to her and found her crying and holding the key to her heart. I've never been so afraid in all my life. Mother looked at me and kissed me and put the key around my neck. I'll never forget the words she said or the look on her face. 'This is yours now,' she said. 'Your father is not coming back. I can feel it. He's not coming back.' He *didn't* come back."

The stinkle-dunk used his white linen napkin to wipe a tear from his eye. "And Annie the Waggle-Lick? Did she come back?"

"We never saw her again."

Kurt decided it would be better for everyone if he changed the subject. "You started to tell me about reaching pink. Now you say those kids would be no higher than purple. What do you mean?"

"Finish your supper and we'll go into the living room and sit by the fire and I'll explain," said the stinkle-dunk.

When they finished eating, Charlie asked Kurt for a Chunkie Chewie from the backpack. The dog offered one to Kurt and the stinkle-dunk, but they declined, and Charlie took his into the living room to eat it.

As Kurt sat on the woolen rug near the crackling fire with Charlie lying close beside him, the stinkle-dunk, from his position in his old down-filled wing chair, told Kurt about the colors of Whiskers.

"You see, in the Land of Whiskers," said Stinkle-Dunk, "colors are very important. They are what make us rich, in a manner of speaking. Here, everyone is a certain color—on the inside, I suppose you would say. No one is certain just how one moves up in color; it has something to do with the way an animal uses his whiskers, and whether he does good deeds or bad deeds. One day you've moved up, and you know it, and others know it too."

"But how can you be sure you've moved up if you can't *see* the colors?"

"You know through your whiskers and in your heart," replied Stinkle-Dunk.

Kurt was beginning to feel very relaxed with the kindly skunk, and he took the liberty of calling him Stinkle—for short.

"Is pink the highest color, Stinkle?"

Upon hearing the new form of address, the stinkle-dunk raised an eyebrow, but Kurt detected a slight smile on the skunk's face after a moment or two.

"No, there's silver," replied Stinkle. "That's the highest color. But few have ever achieved silver—only some webber-tats and a few weery-dawdles, as far as I know."

"Webber-tats and weery-dawdles?"

The stinkle-dunk described the tiny creatures, and Kurt determined they were spiders and snails.

"It's funny only webber-tats and weery-dawdles would have reached silver," said Kurt. "I mean, of all creatures to be silver! Snails—I mean, weery-dawdles—aren't good for much; Mother says they eat her vegetable garden. And webber-tats—they're only good for scaring girls."

"I must disagree," said Stinkle. "Webber-tats are wonderful, creative creatures, especially the silver ones. The sight of their webs shimmering in the sun ... Oh! What lacy magnificence!

"And as for the weery-dawdles, you have to be patient with them, of course. They're so very slow in all they do. But you couldn't ask for a finer friend. And their artwork! The silver ones leave a shining trail they use to paint masterpieces on trunks of trees, or wherever they decide to practice their craft. Their work is breathtaking!

"But getting back to the colors—below silver, it's pink, then orange, then yellow, green, blue, and finally purple at the bottom. However, I don't believe anyone in Whiskers is as low as purple."

"I wonder what color I am," said Kurt. "And Charlie."

Charlie opened his eyes slightly at the mention of his name and closed them again. Kurt was not sure if Charlie had been listening to the conversation or sleeping.

"There's one thing of which I'm certain," said Stinkle. "Waggle-licks are always at least yellow. Something to do with their loyalty makes them so."

Charlie *was* listening now. Kurt saw the dog's mouth turn up at the edges to form a hint of a smile when the stinkle-dunk said waggle-licks were "at least yellow."

Kurt and Stinkle talked into the wee hours of the night, and the stinkle-dunk remarked it was some of the best conversation he had had in many an evening.

"Stinkle," said Kurt, "why don't you come to Nickledown with us? You said yourself you've always dreamed of going there."

"Oh, no, no. I cannot. That is, I could not. I mean to say . . . we cannot always do what we would like to do. There are obligations, you see. And I *am* just an old homebody at heart. Besides, I—"

"What's to keep you here?" said Kurt.

Stinkle thought for a moment and a faraway look came to his eyes. "Well, perhaps I *could* reconsider—*if* I could control it."

"Control what?" asked Kurt.

"Nothing," said Stinkle, and he shook his head as if to bring himself to his senses. "No! It's out of the question. I cannot go and that's that! Let us talk of other things."

The fire eventually dimmed to a faint glow, and Stinkle offered to show Kurt and Charlie to the guest room.

As Kurt followed the stinkle-dunk down the long hallway, he noticed a door standing ajar, and peeking behind it, he saw a staircase leading to a cellar. At the bottom of the stairs stood a wall of ceiling-high shelves filled with row upon row of copper bottles and various-sized buckets.

When the stinkle-dunk saw Kurt looking down the stairs, he rushed to close the door. "There's nothing down there," he said nervously, pointing the way to the guest room, "just a drafty old cellar."

Kurt had come to Whiskers without shoes, and now his feet were dirty and aching from the long walk through the Copper Valley. For that reason, he was glad to accept Stinkle's offer of a warm, sudsy bath before bed. The boy soaked in the stinkle-dunk's big copper bathtub until the suds melted away and the water turned cold. After drying and dressing himself, he climbed into the guest bed with the hammered copper headboard—a bed considerably oversized by stinkle-dunk standards, but just big enough for Kurt. Charlie managed to find a small space at the foot of the bed to curl up in a ball next to Kurt's feet.

"Good night, Stinkle," Kurt called out when at last he was snuggled comfortably beneath the covers.

"Good night, Kurtis," the stinkle-dunk replied from his bedroom across the hall.

Kurt could see a light under Stinkle's door. Soon the light went out; but shortly thereafter it came on again and Kurt could hear the stinkle-dunk pacing back and forth, talking to himself.

"Oh dear, oh dear. Dare I go to Nickledown? First the one notice slipped under my entry door this morning and another fastened to it this evening. What am I to do? I really should stay and tend to the matter. But Nickledown . . . Ah, the thought of Nickledown."

The skunk breathed a long, mournful sigh and said emphatically, "I *must* do the responsible thing."

Stinkle's shadow crossed back and forth across the light under his door as the little skunk paced to and fro in silence. After a time, the animal began talking again, even more loudly.

"How could this have happened? I assumed the notice this morning was a mistake, a misunderstanding. But when I found the other this evening . . . Surely it's true—too painfully true. And me pink—for the most part. To think, after all these years, I could slip downward in color. Dear me, dear me."

The pacing grew faster then stopped, but the talking continued. "Just look at that face in the mirror. A stately face. Oh, perhaps a bit stiff and stodgy, but a stately face, nonetheless. A perfect face for a stinkle-dunk. A *pink* stinkle-dunk. A stinkle-dunk who accepts responsibility.

"Kurtis called me a 'skunk.' What a short, quick, carefree name it is, 'skunk.' I'm certain a 'skunk' would cast his cares aside and go to Nickledown. Ah. To be a 'skunk.'

Skunk, skunk, a funny word,
Strangest word I've ever heard.
Lacking grace, lacking care,
Lacking all the savoir-faire
Of stinkle-dunk, stinkle-dunk,
Stately, stodgy, stinkle-dunk.

Still . . . What a word!—short!—splendiferous!—
For one as I—sweet!—odoriferous!
Short it is, and sweet—like me;
Sweet—as when I set it free.
Should I consider, should I dare,
The name, 'Skunk,' to boldly wear?

Skunk, skunk, stupendous word!
Most wondrous word I've ever heard!
If 'Skunk' my name could truly be,
I'd grow me wings, I'd fly me free.
I'd soar above the highest clouds,
I'd sing out praises—sing out loud."

The animal paused a moment before continuing.

"What would others think of me—
This stinkle-dunk so fancy-free?
Would they cheer and think it grand
That I had spawned a marvelous plan
To lift my spirit weak and lame
By donning a simple, carefree name?

"But," said Stinkle, "nothing will change. The face in the mirror remains the same.

What good to dare? What good to care?
What good to harbor dreams so fair?
I must accept the who I am;
One can't have flim without the flam.

Alas, I fear, my dreams have sunk.
I'm stately, stodgy, Stinkle-Dunk."

"No," he sighed. "I could never be a 'skunk.' My collar is too stiff. My tie is too starched. My shoes are too polished. I am what I am, a stinkle-dunk—and pink—for the most part. Yet! In Nickledown, I hear, life *is* wonderful!"

Kurt watched the light go out again under Stinkle's door and wondered at the animal's strange soliloquy. He remembered the unpleasant way they met—the less-than-desirable slippage. Pink or no pink, he thought, a skunk is still a skunk.

The boy got up, opened the window slightly, and hopped back beneath the bed covers. As he lay nestled in the copper bed, he thought about the webber tats and weery-dawdles. He had seen lacy, shimmering webs before, and the silver trails snails leave behind. Could it be there were silver spiders and snails in his world and nobody realized what they were?

Through the open window he could hear the soft tinkling of a copper tree and the faint, faraway sounds of the night-chirps and leap-lops. "Quickit! Time'a shaut. W-a-u-k," called the night creatures. Kurt wondered at the strangeness of it all and thought about how far he was from home.

CHAPTER 11

THE NUT DRUGGLES

Sunlight streaming through the bedroom's east window woke Kurt early the next morning. Remembering his whereabouts and the formidable task that lay ahead, he pulled himself sleepily out of bed, and with Charlie trailing close behind, made his way down the long hall toward the kitchen. Halfway there, he heard the oven door opening on Stinkle's cast-iron stove. The high-pitched squeak fell with such a familiar ring upon his ear that, for a moment, he felt as if he were about to walk in on his mother preparing breakfast. In the kitchen, he found the stinkle-dunk busy removing a batch of freshly baked biscuits from the oven.

"Kurtis! Charlie! I'm glad you're awake," Stinkle said excitedly, as one by one he popped the hot biscuits onto a wire rack to cool. "We must hurry. The sooner we leave for Nickledown, the sooner we will get there."

The skunk tossed his kitchen mitt on the counter top and rushed about the room, busily gathering wares for the journey. "Let's see. Biscuits and honey to eat with tribble along the way. Knives, spoons, and plates to set a proper wayside table . . ."

"And napkins," Kurt said happily, grabbing a stack of the freshly laundered linens from a nearby shelf and handing them to the stinkle-dunk.

"Oh, yes," said the skunk. "One cannot dine properly without napkins." The animal's eyes sparkled with excitement as he stuffed the napkins into Kurt's backpack.

Remembering the booknotch and the tattle-tail, Kurt hurried to the living room, calling, "Notch! Tattle! Wake up! Stinkle is coming with us to Nickledown!" He reached into the copper bowl on the coffee table, lifted the corner of one of Notch's leaves, and peeked underneath.

The tiny worm yawned, and pushing the leaf aside, straightened his cap and smoothed his vest before smiling up at Kurt.

"Perhaps the little fellow would prefer to travel in this," said Stinkle, rushing into the room, waving the *Copper Valley Gazette*. He handed the newspaper to Kurt. "Though it's not bound, it's somewhat like a book, having actual printed letters."

Kurt held the *Gazette* close to the booknotch so he could inspect it, and having done so by a quick column-by-column perusal, the worm grinned from little green ear to little green ear. "Thank you ever so kindly, sir," he said to Stinkle, as he climbed onto the newspaper. After surrendering to a deep and intoxicating breath, he smiled again and added, "Ah. The delightful aroma of fine typography," and nestled himself comfortably on the paper, which Kurt promptly folded and stuffed into his shirt pocket.

"Oh! One more thing," said Stinkle, hurrying to the hall closet. He soon returned carrying a bright blue umbrella. "Just something I thought we might need for our journey."

Till then, Charlie had shown no interest in the frenzied preparations, but when Kurt returned to the kitchen and began closing the backpack, the dog peeked into the side pouch and quickly inventoried his Chunkie Chewies, smiling at the sight of at least a dozen stored safely in the bottom of the pouch.

When at last all was prepared and perused and pondered and packed, and Kurt, Charlie, and Stinkle had eaten a quick breakfast of biscuits with honey and tribble with fresh strawberries, which the stinkle-dunk hurriedly, though properly, placed upon the table, it was time to travel.

Charlie hastened to the living room and stretched out his tail alongside Tattle so the old tail could wrap himself around. After the dog had given both his tails a brisk wag, to which the tattle-tail cried, "Whoopee do!" Kurt and his friends set out toward Nickledown.

What a fine day it was for traveling! The sky was sunny and bright, the air sweet and full of birdsong. Along the way, Charlie stopped at copper tree after copper tree to smell the fruit Kurt now knew to be tribble. It seemed tribble not only grew in various-sized pieces, but also differed in flavor and aroma from tree to tree. Playing the connoisseur, Charlie sniffed and tasted with an air of pomposity as he compared the subtle nuances of each variety.

The little band traveled for several hours, and much of the time Stinkle seemed, in thought, far away. At one point, the little skunk looked toward the Silver Mountain and cleared his throat to speak. "If my calculations are correct, we should reach Nickledown before the next Silver Day."

"Silver Day?" said Kurt.

"Didn't I tell you about them?" Pausing a moment, Stinkle rubbed his chin thoughtfully. "No, I suppose I didn't. Remember the first day you arrived—how bright and silvery everything looked?"

"Yes. Everything sparkled. But the silver stuff was gone the next morning. I think the wind blew it away."

"You're right, Kurtis. The wind did blow it away—in a manner of speaking. You see, in the Land of Whiskers, every seventh day is a Silver Day. Early on those magical mornings, a silver dust settles over the land. The air remains still until the end of the day when the breeze comes to gather the dust."

"But the breeze started and stopped several times that day in the meadow."

"Things are different in the Meadow," replied Stinkle. "Strange things happen in the Meadow."

"I know. I got my whiskers there."

"So you did," said Stinkle. "Anyway, they say, on Silver Days, animals from all over Whiskers come to Nickledown, and throughout the day the Nickle-Dickles gather with their friends and the visiting animals to eat and sing and talk and play games. The festivities go on until evening when the breeze returns, and everyone leaves happy and content with life and living. It must be wonderful! We'll soon see for ourselves, Kurtis."

The stinkle-dunk's dreamy discourse was interrupted by a little "*Pop!*" as something struck him on the head.

"Ah! Those pesky nut druggles!" he cried, shaking his fist at a walnut branch hanging over the roadway. "You'd think they would be more careful druggling nuts above a road as well traveled as this one." Leaning over, he scooped up the offending nut and threw it into the bushes.

Kurt glanced up in time to see a little gray squirrel spill a load of nuts and scramble higher into the tree. "Harumph!" said the stinkle-dunk, doing a hop and skip to avoid the barrage of tumbling walnuts.

The group traveled free of mishap after that until the sun positioned itself directly overhead signaling time for lunch and a brief rest. In what seemed a well-timed stroke of luck, a gentle breeze appeared just as they arrived at a likely place to stop. They lauded their good fortune in having a breeze to play music in the copper trees while they dined in the shade. They lauded their fortune, that is, until all at once the breeze tousled some leaves by the wayside, scooped them up, and swirled them into a whirlwind that headed straight for Kurt. A moment before it reached him, the whirlwind swerved to one side and soared out of sight, but a few yards up the road, another took its place.

"I don't like this," Kurt said, his voice trembling. "Something is happening, Stinkle. I can feel it in my whiskers."

As he spoke, the second whirlwind billowed to twice its size and soared high into the air! And down it swooped—howling like a banshee—heading straight for Kurt. The venomous wind, ill-tempered as it was, struck the boy full in the face, pelting him with debris from the ground.

"Run!" Kurt shouted, covering his face.

The boy couldn't see the treetops begin to sway. He couldn't see Charlie, with Tattle on his tail, and Stinkle, fighting to keep their footing as they leaned into the wind. He couldn't breathe through the choking dust blowing in circles about him. But he did feel the terrible gust that hit him next—a gust that knocked him off balance and sent him staggering backward along the roadway.

As he fought to hold his footing, the air shook with a thunderous *THA-RUM!-BOOM!-BOOM!*

Tattle plummeted from Charlie's tail.

Stinkle screamed and ran into the nearby woods.

Charlie pounced on Kurt, knocking him to the ground.

Kurt managed to push the dog aside in time to see the wind rip the newspaper from his shirt pocket and carry it up in a whirlwind high over the trees.

"Notch!" Kurt screamed, struggling to his feet. "Stinkle! Help! Where are you! Notch is gone!"

With one relinquishing sigh, the wind died as quickly as it had come, and soon all was still again.

Charlie staggered to his feet amid a cloud of settling dust. With his tail tucked between his legs and his knees shaking, he licked the top of Tattle's head before laying his tail out full so the pale and trembling Tattle could twist himself around it.

"Oh, Charlie." Kurt scanned the road and nearby trees for some sign of the newspaper. "This is awful. Notch is gone. And we've got to find Stinkle."

Charlie wagged his tail—and Tattle—and he and Kurt and the tattle-tail began searching the woods. "Stinkle! Notch! Where are you?" Kurt shouted. But there was no answer.

Suddenly Charlie lifted his nose high in the air. He began to howl. In a moment, Kurt smelled it too. A familiar scent. An *unpleasantly* familiar scent. "Skunk!" he said, covering his nose. The boy peeked behind a nearby gooseberry bush, and there sat the stinkle-dunk, huddled close to the ground, babbling to himself.

"The *boom!* I managed well in the wind, but when I heard the *boom!* it so startled me that I . . . Oh, if only I could control it, but I cannot.

> *I slip, I slip,*
> *I most dis-STINK-ly slip.*
> *When I should stand with stately pride,*
> *I slip and show my baser side.*
> *I flee, but there's no place to hide.*
> *I slip, I slip, I slip!"*

"It's all right, Stinkle," said Kurt, his hand still covering his nose.

Upon hearing Kurt's voice, the skunk looked up. "It's *not* all right. Just look at you. You can't stand to breathe it."

With great effort, Kurt uncovered his nose, having first prepared himself to inhale only when necessary. "Stinkle," he said, his voice shaking, "that doesn't matter now. There's something more important. Notch is gone."

"Gone?" The stinkle-dunk rose to his feet. "What do you mean, 'gone'?"

"He flew away. The wind took the newspaper out of my pocket and carried it away with Notch in it."

"Oh, my!" said Stinkle. "We must find him!"

Kurt, Charlie, Tattle, and the stinkle-dunk searched everywhere, looking high in the treetops and low on the ground. They searched behind rocks and ahead of bumps, in ditches and niches and hollow stumps, calling all the while, "Notch! Can you hear us? Notch!" But their calls went unanswered. They searched and called, and they called and searched until their voices were hoarse, their energy spent. And still there was no sign of the newspaper or Notch.

"We can't just give up," Kurt said tearfully when he realized their efforts were futile.

"Perhaps if we rest a while we'll think of a way to find him," said Stinkle, and taking Kurt's arm, he led the boy back to the roadway. "I only hope the little fellow still has his paper about him—his dearly beloved comforting letters."

Filled with despair, the little group took refuge beneath a walnut tree a few yards up the road. Kurt slipped out of his backpack and placed it off to one side, and he and Stinkle and Tattle rested in the shade while Charlie went off to be by himself. Soon exhaustion got the better of them, and Kurt and Stinkle leaned back against the tree trunk and fell to troubled sleep. Tattle, too, fell asleep after mumbling a dull and doleful tale. None could know how short-lived their rest would be.

Indeed, not long thereafter, the three were startled awake by a terrible commotion. Charlie had returned and was running circles around the tree, barking furiously.

Kurt scrambled to his feet and chased after the dog, and grabbing his collar, pulled him to a halt. Charlie panted, breathless, his eyes wild with panic.

"It's okay, boy," said Kurt, stroking the dog's head. "Please use words, Charlie. If we're going to help you, you've got to use words."

Charlie whimpered piteously and glanced toward the backpack. And there, for all to see, lay the cause of the dog's despair. The backpack lay upside down, its contents strewn carelessly over the ground.

"Who could have done this?" said Kurt, releasing Charlie's collar, and he and Stinkle began gathering their scattered belongings and stuffing them into the pack. That's when Kurt noticed the side pouch was empty. "Charlie! Your Chunkie Chewies! They're gone!"

Charlie let out a blood-curdling howl. Stinkle made the churring sound stinkle-dunks make when they're sorely disturbed.

Kurt was about to close the flap on the pouch when he noticed one Chunkie Chewie lodged deep within the folds at the bottom. "At least there's one left, boy," he said, reaching into the pouch.

The sight of the one remaining Chunkie Chewie made Charlie howl all the louder, and Kurt quickly stuffed the precious morsel back into the pouch and secured the flap.

Just then, a lady nut druggle scurried down the side of the walnut tree.

"Hello, my friend," said Stinkle, recognizing the nut druggle. "It seems there's been a theft."

Stinkle introduced the squirrel to Kurt and told her about the theft.

"It was Tubbs. I'm sure of it," she said. "No one else would have done such a dreadful thing. It's this sort of mischief that keeps him stuck on green."

"The notorious Tubbs," said Stinkle, shaking his head.

"He's really a good little fellow," said the druggle. "He doesn't see too well, you know, and he has a voracious appetite. He hoards away anything remotely resembling a walnut. It gets him into all sorts of trouble."

"I'm beginning to think he'll never reach yellow," remarked the stinkle-dunk.

"Perhaps not," said the lady nut druggle. Gazing off into the distance, she flicked her tail nervously and turned to address Stinkle. "My dear friend, have you noticed anything unusual about the quality of light in the Copper Valley lately?"

"As a matter of fact, I have," Stinkle replied. "But I hoped it was just the fault of these old eyes. I suspected it was indeed the light itself when I read a newspaper article in yesterday's *Gazette* about—"

"You saw the article, too," she interrupted.

"Yes. And strangely enough, Kurtis and I, and Tattle and Charlie, were heading home last evening when we—or rather, Charlie and I—heard a rumble. Very faint it was. Kurtis failed to hear it at all."

"Oh, my," replied the nut druggle. "The article said rumblings started two days ago in the far northwest. Apparently they're making many of the animals there anxious. Nerves are on edge."

"That would have been the last Silver Day," replied Stinkle. "About the time *you* arrived in Whiskers," he said, turning to Kurt. "As I recall, something like this happened a few years back, but it never amounted to much—rumblings in the northwest, a fading of the light—and after a day or two, everything returned to normal."

"What do you make of it?" asked the nut druggle.

"Nothing, I suppose," said the stinkle-dunk. "We'll just have to wait for it to pass."

Kurt could tell the little skunk was uneasy despite his feigned lack of concern.

The nut druggle flicked her tail again. "Well, I hope it passes quickly. Tubbs's eyesight was already poor, and with the inferior light, his sight has worsened. He's been getting into all sorts of trouble, just as with this latest thing. I'm sure he mistook the Chunkie Chewies for nuts." She apologized on behalf of Tubbs and was about to scurry back up the tree when Stinkle reached out and stopped her.

"Kurtis, look!" he said, pointing to the nut druggle's apron pocket. Protruding from her pocket was a piece of folded newsprint.

"Pink Nut Druggle," Stinkle said anxiously, "is that your own newspaper in your apron pocket?"

"Why, no," she replied. "I found it in the tree just now. The breeze must have dropped it there. It was resting precariously on the end of an upper branch. I had only just read the front of it—the article about the rumblings—when I heard the commotion."

"Would you please unfold it," said Kurt, who by this time was bouncing nervously on his heels.

"Yes, quickly, please," added Stinkle, gesturing toward the newspaper.

"Of course," the nut druggle said with a puzzled look, and she withdrew the paper from her pocket.

As soon as she unfolded the *Copper Valley Gazette*, Kurt heard a familiar voice. "Oh," said Notch, looking pale and shaken. "I'm so glad to see you again. I've had a most unnerving experience."

"We know," Kurt said with a deep sigh of relief. "A whirlwind grabbed the paper from my pocket and took it away."

"Is that what happened?"

Kurt was so happy to see the wordy worm that he almost looked forward to the outpouring of syllables he knew would bombard them at any moment. The booknotch did not disappoint him:

"It was a most turbulent moment of tremulous, tumultuous, trepidation," said the booknotch. "I heard a terrible rush of wind, and suddenly, I felt a dizzying vertigo. Over and around I went, rolling in and out of my letters. Those staunch and sturdy letters—capital and lower case—came tumbling down around me. I had to dive into the bow of a *B* to avoid being hit on the tip of my head by the top of a *T*. I nearly was pierced by the point of a *V*. I would have turned green had I not already been so—on the outside, that is." The booknotch drew a long breath and sighed a lengthy sigh, and the bright, healthy green returned to his face. "I'm so thankful to be back with you."

"We're glad you're back, too," Kurt said.

Stinkle explained to the nut druggle about the whirlwind and thanked her for returning the newspaper and Notch.

"I'm happy to have helped," she said, and she scurried up the tree.

"A lovely lady," said Stinkle. "She's pink, you know."

"I guess there's nothing she can do about the Chunkie Chewies, is there, Stinkle?"

"I'm afraid not, Kurtis. Tubbs is probably far away from here by now."

Kurt put the newspaper holding Notch back into his shirt pocket, but this time he buttoned the flap, locking the paper in. "There," he said slipping his backpack over his shoulders. "Notch is safe in my pocket. And Charlie, your one Chunkie Chewie is safe in the pack."

When Charlie did not reply, Kurt looked around for the dog, but the animal was nowhere to be seen.

"I saw him sniffing around those shrubs a moment ago," said Stinkle, pointing to a thick stand of deerberry bushes a few yards from the walnut tree.

Kurt hurried over to the bushes and called after the dog. When he received no answer, he ran back to the walnut tree. "He's gone to find Tubbs. I know he has."

Pink Nut Druggle scurried back down the tree. "What's the trouble?" she asked.

"It appears Charlie has gone chasing after his Chunkie Chewies," said Stinkle.

Kurt wriggled out of the backpack and dropped it on the ground. "I have to go after him."

"Oh dear. That will never do," said Pink Nut Druggle. "You have no idea which way he went. It's better I send a band of my druggles. They know the territory and can fan out in all directions at once."

"But I can't just wait here. He's my dog and I—"

"She's right, of course," said Stinkle, giving Kurt a comforting pat on the arm. "The druggles are fleet and sharp of eye. They can find Charlie before he follows his nose to who-knows-where."

Reluctantly, Kurt nodded, and Pink Nut Druggle quickly summoned a dozen druggles. A moment later, Kurt, Stinkle, Tattle, and Pink Nut Druggle watched the fluffy-tailed fleet scurry away in all directions.

Five minutes passed—and six, and seven—and there was no sign of Charlie or the druggles.

"Something's wrong," said Kurt. "They should have found him by now."

Eight minutes passed—and nine and ten, as Kurt waited impatiently. "I'm going after him myself," he insisted.

"Wait." Stinkle grabbed hold of Kurt's shirtsleeve. "Here come the druggles now." And as he said, the first of the search party appeared from the south, then three from the north, and lastly, the others from east and west. But they all told the same hapless story. Nowhere could they find the lanky, vagabond dog with one ear up and one ear down.

Kurt's heart sank.

"I have an idea," said Pink Nut Druggle. "If Charlie's nose led him away from us, perhaps it will lure him back."

"What do you mean?" Kurt asked.

"Walnut confections," the druggle said with a smile.

She cinched her apron up tight around her waist and called out to a group of lady nut druggles who had gathered to watch the goings-on. "The Ladies' Auxiliary," Pink Nut Druggle announced proudly, and she motioned the druggles to hurry over. A moment later she was instructing them as a head chef might instruct her kitchen staff. "We'll need the most aromatic dishes: Cherry Walnut Jubilee, Hot Apple and Walnut Pie, walnut bread and walnut buns, toasted walnuts, roasted walnuts . . . And don't forget Aunt Fanny's Fabulous Walnut Flambé . . . And of course, Grandma Millie's Magnificent Minced Walnut Munchies. Now hurry along, scurry along, ladies."

The Ladies' Auxiliary chittered and chattered among themselves before scurrying off to various parts of the walnut grove. Soon the air was full of the sumptuous aroma of baking and roasting walnut confections, whose sugary whiffs and walnutty wafts wended and wound their way through the air high above the walnut grove.

The stinkle-dunk breathed deeply, savoring the mouth-watering aroma. "If this doesn't draw the waggle-lick back to us, I don't know what will."

Everyone stood motionless now as they waited and watched for some sign of the beloved brown dog.

"Look! It's Charlie!" Kurt called out. And he darted toward the north edge of the walnut grove.

Charlie made a dash toward the boy and pounced on him, covering his face with dog licks. "I lost myself," he panted. "I didn't mean to lose myself. Then I smelled the wonderful whatever-it-is, and I followed my nose, and—"

"It's okay," said Kurt, pulling himself from under the dog. "You're back and everything's right again."

By this time, Stinkle and all the nut druggles had gathered around Kurt and his dog. Charlie made a quick dash over to Pink Nut Druggle's walnut tree, scooped Tattle up onto his tail, and gave both his tails a jubilant wag before hurrying back to the group.

"Everything was fine at first," Charlie told the gathering. "I picked up the trail of my Chunkie Chewies—I never mistake the smell of a

Chunkie Chewie. There was no time to waste, no time to say goodbye. I had to leave while the scent was strong. I was deep in the woods, following the trail, when I detected the odor of something moldy. It brought back memories—terrible memories. I smelled just like the cold, damp cellar I was in as a pup—when Chrysalis and I almost died of the chill."

"Oh, Charlie. How awful!" said Kurt.

The dog's eyebrows came to a point between his eyes. He stared intently. "It was all around me. I sniffed to the left, and I sniffed to the right, and all I could smell was that awful odor. I heard a rumbling, and when I started to run, a gust of cold air knocked me down. I pulled myself up and dashed toward a hollow tree. I squeezed inside and closed my eyes and hid there until the smell went away and the rumbling stopped. When I crawled out of the tree trunk, I couldn't believe my nose. Roasting nuts and baking bread. I followed my nose and here I am. When do we eat?"

Everyone laughed except Kurt, Stinkle, and Pink Nut Druggle.

"He heard rumblings," said the druggle. "The article in the *Gazette* said—"

"I'm sure what Charlie heard had nothing to do with *those* rumblings," Stinkle said calmly. "Most likely it was just Charlie's imagination. He was lost and distraught over the loss of his Chunkie Chewies. The mind plays tricks under such circumstances."

"Perhaps so," said Pink Nut Druggle.

Kurt said nothing. Imagination? Like Grandfather's tales?

It was late afternoon by this time, and with supper still to be eaten, traveling farther was out of the question. As the lady nut druggles spread their walnutty feast on the ground beneath Pink Nut Druggle's tree, Kurt and Charlie and Tattle and the others chittered and chatted. Even the booknotch poked his head out of Kurt's pocket for a time to join in the moment of leisure and conversation and fine camaraderie.

Meanwhile, the stinkle-dunk busied himself preparing a generous portion of biscuits, which he withdrew from Kurt's backpack and placed properly on a plate along with a small pot of honey before offering it to Pink Nut Druggle as a contribution to the feast.

When at last the meal was served, everyone filled himself to the brim with biscuits and honey and all manner of fine walnut confections—the finest the Ladies' Auxiliary had ever prepared. Though still longing for his Chunkie Chewies, Charlie managed to find some degree of solace in a double helping of Grandma Millie's Magnificent Minced Walnut Munchies.

At last, with the quiet coming of day's end, the animals sought their places of rest. Full and content, everyone in the walnut grove fell fast asleep—some among and some beneath the sheltering bows of the walnut trees.

CHAPTER 12

FRAIDY SLINKLE-PURR

Considering the bountiful feasting the night before, one might have thought full stomachs and dreams of plenty would have caused the nut druggles to sleep soundly well into the morning hours. But such was not the case. The sun was up, and the busy druggles, having remained as quiet as they could for quite some time so Kurt and his friends could sleep, were anxious to go about the day's business. Kurt and the stinkle-dunk awoke to the faint chitter-chatter of the industrious little animals and the whispery "*Sh-h-h's*" of Pink Nut Druggle, whose repeated attempts at quieting her noisy band were growing more futile by the minute.

"A fine day to journey," said Stinkle, wresting himself from his grassy bed beneath the walnut tree. He smoothed his wrinkled suit to perfection, adjusted his tasteful paisley ascot till it aligned properly with his stiffly starched collar, and went about the daily task of winding his silver pocket watch.

Charlie stretched and shook himself from front to back and gently nudged the tattle-tail awake before sniffing the pouch on the backpack holding the one remaining Chunkie Chewie.

When they had thanked the nut druggles for their hospitality and voiced their highest praises for the scrumptious feast of the past evening, Kurt, Charlie, Stinkle and Tattle (and the booknotch, having peeked out of Kurt's pocket) bade the druggles goodbye and once again found themselves back in the role of travelers on the road to Nickledown.

Although the part of the Copper Valley through which they now journeyed lacked much of the warm, reddish glow that so saturated the atmosphere near Stinkle's house, enough persisted to cause the dirt road to lie like a crimson thread across the green velvet meadows that blanketed the valley floor. Copper trees, though sprinkled more sparsely now, continued to bejewel the countryside with scattered patches of sparkling citrine and golden topaz.

As they walked, Kurt and Stinkle watched large, graceful, soaring birds ride the wind currents overhead, their wings tinged reddish-gold by the valley's reflected light. They listened as tiny songbirds sang melodious greetings and peeped and chipped and chirped at each other.

"Gossiping," said Stinkle.

"What?"

"They're gossiping. The little ones—the twitter-flits. They see all, they hear all, they tell all. Nothing gets past them. And whether it's newsworthy or not, they pass it on. If you want to spread news, tell it to a twitter-flit.

"Not so, the wind-wafts," he continued, gazing up toward the several birds circling lazily overhead. "There is a noble fowl. They see as much as the twitter-flits but prefer to soar and drift on the breeze minding their own business. How graceful they are, riding the ebb and flow of the winds, spiraling, soaring to lofty heights and drifting ever so gently downward, only to soar again on the next current. Ah, to lead such a life."

Thus the band traveled, enjoying the marvels of the countryside, conversing, delighting in their friendship one with the other. After stopping some hours later for a brief respite and a midday meal, they traveled farther still until, just before suppertime, they came upon a small, dingy house by the wayside.

The house offered nothing in the way of visual amenities to welcome the visitors. Its once-white stucco was gray and cracked. Its window shades, tightly drawn, were tattered and frayed. The entry door leaned to one side, having partly fallen from its rusted hinges, and weeds grew in profusion along the shabby picket fence in front, having choked out any garden that might have once bloomed there. The only reasonably well-maintained plant was a small stand of catnip growing alongside the porch.

Considering its run-down condition, Kurt thought surely the house must be deserted, and for that reason, he was surprised when the stinkle-dunk halted at the front gate.

"This, I shudder to say, is the home of a friend of mine, a slinkle-purr." Stinkle kicked aside a small rock that abutted the gate. "I hope you won't mind if we make a brief stop. The poor fellow is so in need of a visit now and then, and I don't come this way as often as I should."

"I don't mind," Kurt said, although he hardly was thrilled with the prospect of entering the house. It looked as though it might tumble down should they step too heavily upon its floor.

"Perhaps Charlie should wait for a proper introduction," the stinkle-dunk suggested. "My friend *is* a slinkle-purr, and with Charlie being a waggle-lick . . . With properly functioning whiskers, I'm sure the two would get along well enough, but I'm afraid Fraidy is not known for his properly functioning whiskers. As a matter of fact, they function so poorly he's been stuck on blue ever since I've had the dubious fortune of knowing him."

Stinkle pointed to a large, sprawling evergreen at the side of the front steps and suggested to Charlie that he hide behind it until he could prepare the slinkle-purr to meet him. Charlie agreed, and Kurt and Stinkle carefully unlatched the rickety front gate and made their way stealthily up the walkway. Charlie followed, with Tattle on his tail, and when the dog was securely crouched behind the evergreen, Stinkle knocked on the drab front door and put his finger over the peephole. "A little game we play," he said with a grin. "A little signal. This way he knows it's me."

A moment later, a pair of yellow-green eyes peered around the edge of a tattered window shade and quickly disappeared. Shortly thereafter, the front door opened ever so slowly, squeaking on its rusty hinges.

"Fraidy Slinkle-Purr, my furry feline friend!" roared the stinkle-dunk, pulling a big blue yarn ball from the pack on Kurt's back.

The scraggly, ragtag slinkle-purr snatched the yarn ball, juggled it briefly, and tossed it behind him into the living room. Then, chasing it into a corner, he pounced on its top and tumbled over and over—he and the yarn ball—rolling and snagging, rollicking, dragging it to and fro and back and forth, hitting and batting and biting and fighting until finally he lay exhausted in a heap of mangled, tangled worsted upon the floor.

"That's his subtle way of saying, 'Come in,'" said Stinkle.

Stinkle and Kurt stepped into the room, whereupon the stinkle-dunk beckoned to Charlie, who had been peeking from behind the bush watching the ruckus.

"Fraidy, I want you to meet someone," Stinkle said to the cat. "This is my friend, Kurtis. And this is his waggle-lick—"

"Hiss-s-s-s!" spit the slinkle-purr, arching his back and baring his teeth. Razor-sharp thoughts rushed through the black crescent slits in his yellow-green eyes, and Charlie's whiskers read the thoughts well. He barked. He snapped. And with that, they were off!

> Over the sofa, under the chair,
> Charlie and Fraidy chased here and there,
> Hissing and snapping and slapping and scrapping,
> Running and falling, behavior appalling,
> Till finally Charlie heard Kurt loudly calling
> And came to his senses and stopped the rude brawling.

Charlie's "yellow" took over. Not the yellow of cowards, but of one empowered to give what is good when the other one should, but can't due to something embedded in kittenhood: bad dreams or bent whiskers—something like that—that keeps him from being a sociable cat.

With that, Charlie blushed and apologized
To the cat—so loathsome and uncivilized—
Who promptly ignored him and slinked away
To a place in the shadows, there to stay.

Poor little Tattle had managed to hold fast to Charlie's tail throughout the fray, but now he fell off onto the floor with a thud, looking rather green. After a moment, he managed a shy little smile and said weakly, "Yahoo. Whoopee do—" And he fainted flat out.

"Now, Fraidy," said the stinkle-dunk, shaking the tattle-tail to revive him, "the waggle-lick did not mean to frighten you. After all, you did startle him with your hissing and spitting."

Showing no sign of remorse, Fraidy emerged from the shadows, his feline head held high and aloof and his tail held straight up. Ever so slowly, he sashayed past Charlie, letting his tail slap the dog on the chin as he passed by him. With a look of delight, the sneaky slinkle-purr scooted across the floor and leaped onto a tattered chair in a dark corner and watched Charlie retreat in humiliation to the opposite corner.

Meanwhile, Kurt was trying his best to look about the room. "Why does he keep it so dark in here?" he whispered to Stinkle.

"He's afraid of his own shadow, and light casts shadows," the stinkle-dunk said in a hushed voice. "It's ironic, is it not? He lives within the very thing that frightens him most—shadow."

"Why is he afraid of his own shadow?"

"Because of something dreadful that happened when he was a young slinkle-purr. You see, Fraidy was not born in Whiskers. Fraidy is one of the lost animals. He remembers little about his kittenhood in that other world. He was so young when he became lost that his eyes were not yet fully opened. But he does recall the furry warmth of his mother, and her gentle purring, and how she held him down and washed him against his will—for his own good, of course. And he remembers having plenty of food to eat, and siblings pressing close against him. And he remembers four walls of a cardboard box. He felt secure within the dark confines of the box."

"How did he become lost?"

"He fell asleep one day and woke up cold and alone somewhere outside the box. It happened to be the very day his eyes were beginning to open, so he could see only dim shadows about him. He was so afraid he began to run, and one of the shadows followed him. The only way he could escape the dreadful menace was to find a dark spot somewhere, for the shadow would not follow him into a dark place."

"Poor Fraidy."

"Poor Fraidy, indeed," said Stinkle. "Every time he tried to come out of the darkness, there was the shadow, waiting for the tiny slinkle-purr. Little Fraidy ran with all his might toward a dark spot he could barely see, and suddenly he felt himself tumbling, tumbling. When he landed in the Meadow—in the Land of Whiskers—the shadow was still following him. He managed to find this old, abandoned house, and here he has lived ever since."

"It was his *own* shadow chasing him, wasn't it, Stinkle?"

"Yes, Kurtis, it was."

The stinkle-dunk glanced sympathetically toward the slinkle-purr and shook his head. "I've tried to convince him shadows can't harm him, but I'm afraid his fear is too deeply rooted. So I come to visit him from time to time and bring him a yarn ball and tell him stories—stories of unknown origin that have been handed down by word of mouth since the beginning of Whiskers time. He enjoys stories so—especially ones about knights in shining armor. Every time I get to the part about knights being brave and doing good deeds, Fraidy says, 'Tell me that part again.' I believe hidden somewhere within that cowardly slinkle-purr is the seed of a brave knight."

Stinkle had managed to revive Tattle by this time, and the old tail asked to be moved to a place under something where he would feel safe, so Stinkle gently lifted him up and placed him under a rickety chair. Soon the tail appeared quite himself again and began mumbling tales, swaying back and forth as he rambled on. When Fraidy caught sight of the swaying tail, his yellow-green eyes took on a sinister stare.

"Fraidy," said Stinkle, "whatever you're thinking, I suggest you put a stop to it."

Kurt's eyes by this time had adjusted to the dim half-light and he was able to look more closely at the room. It was a shambles. The furniture was pulled, the drapes were shredded, tangled yarn balls lay scattered in every direction. When Kurt's glance happened to fall upon the corner where Fraidy sat shrouded in shadow, he saw the cat still watching the tattle-tail intently, but now the feline was crouched, poised to spring.

"Fraidy," said Stinkle, stepping to position himself between the cat and the tattle-tail, "don't you think it's time you were civil to your visitors? This kind of behavior is most unacceptable."

The slinkle-purr turned his head away and closed his eyes, feigning disinterest in anything the skunk had to say.

"Fraidy Slinkle-Purr, get down from that chair and talk to us!" demanded the stinkle-dunk.

After an interval of what appeared to be deep feline thought, the cat replied in a pretentiously slinky tone of voice, "Per-r-r-haps I co-o-o-uld come down." And he rose from his crouched position, stretched his front legs, and peered around the stinkle-dunk to catch a glimpse of the tattle-tail. Hopping down, he slinked to the window and pulled the drapes shut over the already-drawn shade.

"Fraidy, you really are too much!" said Stinkle, "How do you expect us to visit in this darkness? We can't even see the whiskers on our own faces!"

Attempting to be helpful, Kurt turned on a lamp. When it came on high beam, Fraidy saw his own shadow—a giant slinkle-purr cast darkly against the drapes.

"E-e-e-k!" he screamed, leaping straight up into the air. He caught hold of the drapes on the way down and, rotten as they were, they began to tear.

Kurt and Stinkle rushed to catch the hapless slinkle-purr, but arrived too late. Fraidy landed in a pile of shredded drapery and shattered nerves, and at once his slinky drawl changed to quick, choppy chatter, its sole content focused on the whereabouts of the illusive, giant slinkle-purr. "What! Where! Who's it! Where'd it go!"

"It's all right, Fraidy," said Stinkle. "It was just your shadow. I've told you over and over, shadows won't hurt you."

Charlie stared at the pitiful hunk of frazzled fur that was Fraidy Slinkle-Purr and sighed a deep sigh. With a pained expression, he walked over to the backpack, removed his last Chunkie Chewie, smelled it, and after taking a long, hard, wistful look at it, held it out to the cat. "This is for you," he said.

"What's it?" snapped Fraidy.

"It's a Chunkie Chewie," said Charlie.

"Whatcha do with it?"

"You eat it," the dog replied, and he mumbled something under his breath.

Fraidy reached out ever so slowly, as though he intended to take the Chunkie Chewie. But at the last moment he slapped it out of Charlie's paw and batted it into the kitchen across the slippery floor, ricocheting it off the baseboards. Charlie watched in disbelief as the slinkle-purr played hockey with his last Chunkie Chewie.

When Fraidy finished his game, he smiled coyly at Charlie and sprawled out on top of the Chunkie Chewie so the dog could not retrieve it. In a slinky tone of voice, he asked, "Is it good for cu-u-u-te little slinkle-purrs to eat?"

"*Cute* little slinkle-purrs, yes," answered Charlie, "but in your case—"

"Charlie!" Kurt said sharply.

"What about preser-r-r-vatives?" continued the slinkle-purr. "Does it have any preser-r-r-vatives? What about sa-a-a-turated fats? Does it have any sa-a-a-turated fats? And what about a-a-artificial color?"

"Fraidy," said Stinkle, interceding, "perhaps you should keep it as a knickknack."

"Very well," said the cat. And carrying the Chunkie Chewie in his mouth, he leaped to a high shelf and placed the precious biscuit near the edge where Charlie could stare at it longingly.

"Speaking of food," said Stinkle, "we *have* been traveling all day. Would you think us too rude, Fraidy, if we invited ourselves to supper? I wouldn't want you to go to any trouble." ("Not that he would," Stinkle whispered to Kurt.) "We've brought our own biscuits and honey."

"Go ri-i-ght ahead," said Fraidy, and he jumped down from the shelf and proceeded to pour himself a big bowl of cream, letting the stinkle-dunk prepare the meal for the others.

The others dined frugally, and after supper, the time when Charlie usually had a Chunkie Chewie for dessert, Kurt noticed the dog staring wishfully at the "knickknack" resting high on the shelf. Fraidy must have noticed too, for a self-serving little smile crept across his feline face.

"Fraidy," said Stinkle, drawing the cat's attention, "remember how you used to talk about going to Nickledown someday—to sing with the other slinkle-purrs on the fences there?"

"Y-e-s-s," replied Fraidy.

"Well, Kurtis and I, and Charlie and Tattle and Notch—Oh! Remind me to introduce you to the booknotch. Anyway, we are all going to Nickledown. We would like it very much if you would come with us."

"We would?" said Charlie.

"Never!" Fraidy snapped. "I won't!" And with his voice quivering, he added ever so pitifully, "I can't."

Charlie smiled.

"Fraidy, if you're concerned about your shadow," said Stinkle, "I have solved that problem." And he picked up the blue umbrella he had brought from home and opened it. "Kurtis, would you please stand directly under the overhead light in the living room."

At the mention of the overhead light, Fraidy scooted under the chair in the corner.

Kurt stood beneath the light as the stinkle-dunk instructed, and Stinkle handed him the open umbrella.

"Hold it over your head, please, Kurtis."

Again, Kurt did as he was asked to do, and Stinkle flipped a light switch on the wall. The dim light cast upon the umbrella from the overhead bulb formed a large, gray circle on the floor—a shadow mimicking the shape of the umbrella.

"You see, Fraidy," said Stinkle, "if you were carrying the umbrella, your own shadow would not show. There would be no arms or legs—no frightening appendages to scare you. Just a circle like this one."

Fraidy stared at the umbrella while everyone waited. He paused and he pondered. He pondered and paused. Charlie, in the meantime, sat with his paws crossed, and Kurt was sure he heard the dog whispering, "No, no, no . . ."

"Yes! I'll do it!" Fraidy snapped. "This slinkle-purr will go!"

"Ah, no," Charlie moaned, uncrossing his paws.

It was settled. Everyone would be going to Nickledown.

For the sake of the tattle-tail's well-being, Stinkle suggested they travel some distance down the road and camp for the night. Tattle had been comfortable enough in Stinkle's house, but being inside with Fraidy had made him quite nervous. So, when the sun began to set and Fraidy felt it was safe to go outside, the group headed out the door with the slinkle-purr holding the open umbrella high above his head.

On the front steps they found a package addressed to Charlie, and a note was attached:

Dear Charlie the Waggle-Lick,
Returning the strange nuts on behalf of Tubbs. Says they're the funniest nuts he ever saw. Couldn't get the shells off. The twitter-flits told me where to find you. Tubbs sends his apologies.
—Pink Nut Druggle

Charlie was jubilant! He tore open the package and offered a Chunkie Chewie to everyone—even Fraidy! Everyone declined, and Charlie handed the Chunkie Chewies to Kurt, who stored them safely away in the side pouch of the backpack. When all was in order, the little band headed down the road with Charlie wagging his tail (and Tattle) as he pranced happily at Kurt's side.

Before long, Fraidy began to trail behind the others. The cat had a deeply contemplative, conniving look in his yellow-green eyes.

"I think that sneaky slinkle-purr has something up his feline sleeve," Stinkle whispered to Kurt. "We had better watch him carefully."

CHAPTER 13

ꟻRAIDY'S ꟻLIGHT

The stinkle-dunk glanced over his shoulder at Fraidy Slinkle-Purr. "He's definitely up to something," he said under his breath, leaning close to Kurt. "He smiled at me just then—an innocent little smile on his devilish little face. Fraidy never smiles at anyone—he smirks. And he's been picking flowers—wild sweet peas. Imagine Fraidy appreciating the beauty of flowers. Have you noticed how he keeps watching Charlie's tail where Tattle is riding?"

Kurt was about to turn and see for himself when the stinkle-dunk reached out and grabbed his arm. "No, no," he whispered. "Don't you look too. He'll know we're on to him."

"Fraidy," Stinkle called out, gazing back at the slinkle-purr. "You had better step lively. We don't want to lose you as we round the next bend. Why don't you come up here next to Kurtis and me."

Ignoring the skunk's remarks, Fraidy paused by the roadside, leaned down, and picked yet another flower, adding it to the small bouquet in his hand. Pressing his nose into the bouquet, he feigned delight in its sweetness, inhaling deeply before closing his eyes and breathing a rapturous sigh. After a moment or two, he opened his yellow-green eyes ever so slowly and glared at Stinkle.

The stinkle-dunk turned away, but as an afterthought, peered back over his shoulder in time to see Fraidy, still holding the umbrella, toss the flowers to the ground and spring toward Charlie's tail.

151

From out of nowhere came a ferocious gust of wind. With a *swish!* and a *swoosh!* it swooped down under the umbrella and, with one jarring jolt, snatched it high into the air. Up went the umbrella! Up, up, up! And up went Fraidy Slinkle-Purr, still holding fast to the handle.

"E-e-e-k!" screeched the feline, as he rose like a hot-air balloon. Higher and higher he rose! High over the heads of the others! High over the treetops! Screaming like a siren! Shrieking like a shrew! with the sweet peas from the bouquet, caught in the updraft, whirling around him like a rainbow tornado.

"Let go of the handle!" Stinkle shouted frantically. "Jump before it's too late! Jump, Fraidy!" he screamed. But the slinkle-purr held fast.

"Now you're too high! Hold on! Don't let go! You're too high to jump!"

Soon Fraidy disappeared into a gray cloud—the only one in the sky—and the wind stopped blowing.

Stinkle slumped to the ground. "Where is he? I can't see him. Where is he?" he lamented, his voice trembling.

Kurt heard a whistle, faint and shrill at first, but growing louder by the second. Out of the corner of his eye, he caught sight of something dark plummeting from the cloud, and in a moment he perceived it in all its undeniable felinity.

"There he is!" Kurt shouted, pointing skyward. And indeed, there was Fraidy—his umbrella turned inside out, his back arched, his tail pointing up, his scraggly fur standing on end, three legs held stiff as boards in front of him, one paw still holding fast to the umbrella handle. And the entire flying menagerie was whistling like a Piccolo Pete!

Down, down, down the cat plummeted until he and his strange kite disappeared with a clatter in the top of a faraway copper tree.

"Oh, no!" cried Stinkle. "We have to find that tree!" And hastening to his feet, he took off running. Kurt and Charlie ran after him, and when they arrived at what they thought to be the correct copper grove, they searched through the midst of it, shouting for the slinkle-purr. "Fraidy! Fraidy Slinkle-Purr! Where are you!" But there was no answer.

Just when they thought surely they were searching the wrong grove, they heard a meek "me-o-o-o-w," followed by another even more pitiful than the first. Upon hearing the weakish cries, Charlie halted in his tracks and listened, his stand-up ear stiff and alert. When Fraidy cried again, Charlie's head turned sharply to the left. At the dog's poised and ready stance, Tattle twisted himself tighter around Charlie's tail and braced himself for the run that surely would come. "Whoopee do!" the tail cried. And *zoom!* They were off—Charlie and Tattle—dashing toward the tallest, most dazzling tree in the grove.

Kurt and Stinkle chased after the dog, arriving at the tree seconds later. Their relief at finding the cat was at once overshadowed when they saw the inextricable predicament the animal had got himself into. There in the uppermost branches, near the end of a fragile limb, clinging with his claws to a frail clump of foliage, hung Fraidy Slinkle-Purr, his eyes staring blankly into space.

"One of us will have to climb up and get him," said Kurt. "But how do you climb a copper tree? They're so slippery."

Inspired by Kurt's question, Tattle began one of his tales:

"How do you climb a copper tree?"

"Not now, Tattle," Kurt said. "Can't you see we're trying to think?"

"No. Let him continue," said Stinkle. "His tale might be of help. Go on, Tattle, please."

Tattle cleared his throat and began his tale again:

"How do you climb a copper tree?
You don't!"

"Well, that's a great help," said Kurt.

Tattle smiled at the boy and continued:

"How do you climb a copper tree?
A copper tree will bend to thee."

Kurt and Stinkle looked at each other. "Of course! That's it!" said Stinkle, his eyes opening wide. "The branches of copper trees bend in the breeze causing the leaves to strike one another to play chords. The trees are very particular concerning which leaves strike which leaves as they strive to play the chords properly—to make them harmonious. With a slinkle-purr in the treetop, the leaves on the disturbed branches will not be able to strike properly. Those branches will naturally bend down so their leaves might still strike the proper chords—an octave or two lower, of course, but proper just the same. When the branches bend, Fraidy should slide right down. All we have to do is wait for a breeze and be ready to catch him."

Hurriedly they gathered oak leaves, spreading them under the tree to cushion Fraidy's fall should they miss him.

"It could take forever for a breeze to come up," said Kurt, spreading the last of the leaves.

"Not with this strange weather," said Stinkle. "Haven't you noticed how often the breeze comes and goes?"

No sooner had Stinkle spoken than Kurt felt a gust ruffle his hair. "Stinkle! It's the breeze!"

"Yes!" said Stinkle. "And look at the tree!"

The branches began to bend. The leaves began to play. Music filled the air! And Fraidy joined the chorus, singing louder than the copper tree.

Suddenly the upper branches bent way down, and the slinkle-purr began to slip. He slipped an inch—then two—then three and four—then—"Ye-e-e-o-o-ow!" he shrieked as he tumbled through a clamor of copper leaves and shattered chords.

Kurt and Stinkle reached out to grab the cat, but drew back when they saw his stiffened legs with their sharp, protruding claws plummeting toward them. *Thump!* went Fraidy, falling between them, landing with a jolt on the cushion of oak leaves. Dazed by the fall, the cat sat without making a sound.

"Fraidy," Stinkle said, kneeling down and shaking the slinkle-purr, "are you all right?"

Fraidy sat staring into the distance, his eyes two big, glassy, yellow-green marbles.

"Fraidy!" Stinkle repeated, shaking the cat again.

At last Fraidy blinked and his eyes fell into focus. "Who's it! What's it! Where's the wind!" he blurted, pressing his claws into Stinkle's arm.

It was some time before Fraidy regained his composure, but when at last he seemed himself again, Kurt suggested they go back to the road. Just before the wind took Fraidy, Kurt had noticed a sprawling oak beside a roadside clearing—a tree much like the one Tattle lived under before his was felled by lightening. After Fraidy's fantastic flight, no one felt like traveling farther, and the oak would provide shelter for the night.

As the little group made their way back through the groves, they watched the coppery pinks of the early evening sky slowly give way to purples and grays, as night descended over the land. They welcomed the rising moon with its flood of silver light—light much too diffused to cast sharp shadows and frighten Fraidy, yet strong enough to light the way back to the road. Before long, they arrived at the oak.

What a wonderful tree it was in Tattle's opinion, its thick and sturdy limbs spreading open-armed toward them. There was even a dent in one of the roots growing above the ground that made a fine seat for Kurt.

Right away, the tattle-tail settled himself comfortably beneath the bows and began extolling the virtues of living under an oak tree. Soon his discourse retrogressed to tales of times past, and as the old tail drifted deeper into thought, his lengthy body began swaying gently back and forth until it drew the attention of Fraidy, who watched with great interest. When the stinkle-dunk aimed a look of disapproval at the slinkle-purr, the cat stood up and stretched before walking ever so casually over to a thicket of brambles growing a short distance from the oak. After a quick glance about, he jumped into the thicket and disappeared.

"What's that sneaky slinkle-purr up to now?" said Stinkle, and shaking his head, he followed the cat into the brambles.

The stinkle-dunk and slinkle-purr were gone for quite some time, and Kurt was feeling some concern, when suddenly something sprang up over the top of the thicket and lunged at the tattle-tail.

"Get off me, you fiendish slinkle-purr! You ball of fuzz! You wad of fur!" cried Tattle, pulling himself free of the cat. "You're enough to tie an old tail into knots jumping out of the bushes like that, like that."

The incorrigible Fraidy, having speedily withdrawn some distance away, crinkled his brow into a frown and licked his lips and swished his tail in short, choppy movements, making no attempt to disguise the wily stare in his yellow-green eyes. He crouched, he froze, he lunged again, and in a rapid-fire game of slap-and-miss, attempted to trap the dodging tail between his paws.

"That's all I can take of you, you sassy slinkle-purr," said Tattle, and raising his tapered end high in the air, *whack!* he smacked Fraidy full in the face.

"Yeow!" cried the cat, leaping into the bushes.

The tattle-tail shook himself from end to end. "It's bad enough a tail has to lie in one spot all day—what dismay!—without some ill-mannered slinkle-purr pouncing on him—trouncing on him! I doubt his whiskers work at all. Such gall!"

Stinkle reappeared just in time to see the end of the tiff between Fraidy and Tattle. "I knew that slinkle-purr was up to no good," said the stinkle-dunk. "You all right, my friend?" he asked the tail. "Sorry I didn't find him in time to stop him. Imagine him attacking you that way! And you being orange besides. He simply has no respect for anyone."

"I'm all right, Stinkle—I thinkle," laughed Tattle, having recovered from the fray. "It's not the first time a slinkle-purr has done that to me, and I'm sure it won't be the last. It has passed."

"Just the same, I had better see where he's gone to this time." And the little skunk disappeared again into the brambles.

The tattle-tail looked up at Kurt. "Stinkle's a good friend to that pesky slinkle-purr. I wouldn't bother with him myself—that elf. I'd place our friendship on the shelf."

"I guess that's why Stinkle's pink," said Kurt.

Moments later, Stinkle returned, wearing a look of utter dismay. "Fraidy Slinkle-Purr will not be going to Nickledown," he announced quite formally.

"What do you mean?" Kurt asked.

"I caught up with him a little way down the road. He realized he would have no umbrella now to protect him from his shadow. He's headed home."

"And all for the good," said Tattle.

"All for the good," Charlie added, smiling, and he looked at the others and blushed.

The stinkle-dunk seemed to take no notice of Tattle's and Charlie's remarks. Instead, he sat and stared at the ground, contemplating. After a time, he spoke. "I'm afraid I have more bad news. I, too, have reconsidered. Neither shall I be going to Nickledown."

"But Stinkle, why?" Kurt asked, surprised the stinkle-dunk would so brashly change his mind.

The skunk took a deep breath and sighed. "I dare not, Kurtis—not after that terrible slippage.' You know—when the thunder struck and I ran and hid—out by Pink Nut Druggle's place."

"I remember," said Kurt.

"Well, I've been debating the question in my mind ever since. I wanted so very much to go. I even deluded myself into thinking I could control the slippage, but I cannot. I won't allow myself to be embarrassed in front of the Nickle-Dickles. Besides, I have urgent business to attend to at home. And now that Fraidy won't be going—that's all the more reason to stay. He needs someone to look after him, you see, and . . ."

Kurt noticed tears glistening in the stinkle-dunk's eyes. "We understand," he said. But he didn't understand fully.

The tattle-tail, who had been listening quietly to the conversation, stared up at the moonlit foliage above his head. "Do they have oak trees in Nickledown? Can they be found?" he asked.

"I don't know," Kurt replied, and he glanced at Stinkle in time to see the skunk discreetly wiping a tear from the corner of his eye.

The stinkle-dunk must have heard the question, for he quickly cleared his throat and rejoined the conversation. "There must be very few oak trees in the hills between here and Nickledown. I once over-heard a group of nut druggles discussing a shortage of acorns in the lower hills. One must conclude that in Nickledown, at that higher elevation, there may be none."

"I was afraid of that," said Tattle. "I don't dare leave this oak tree—not I, you see. You saw what the lightening did to my *old* tree; just think what he would do to me, should he see me lying without a tree. I don't think lightening likes tattle-tails, you see. *I* can't go to Nickledown ēither. Ēither, eīther, nēither, neīther. I shan't. I can't," he said sadly.

There fell a great sorrow among the travelers after that, and for a time, no one uttered a word. At last Stinkle's voice broke the silence. "Harumph!" he said, rubbing his chin. "I've been thinking about the lightening—also the thunder and wind. I had thought they were new to Whiskers, having never experienced them myself. But when Pink Nut Druggle said the light out by her place had diminished enough to be troublesome to Tubbs, and she mentioned reports of unrest in the northwest, it brought to mind a tale I heard a while back. I meant to ask you about it, Tattle," he said, turning to the tail, "but it slipped my mind and—"

The skunk stopped talking. He cocked his head to one side and sat very still.

"What is it, Stinkle?" said Kurt.

"Sh-h-h. Do you hear it?"

"I don't hear anything."

"A rumble, dim and far away, growing louder. Surely you must hear it now."

The others heard it, undoubtedly, for Charlie's stand-up ear aligned itself as though it had locked onto some secret signal, and he sat very straight and rigid. Tattle collapsed on the ground, and his long body stiffened until it resembled a stick.

"Now I hear it," said Kurt. "Thunder."

"My tree, my tree!" cried Tattle.

Stinkle jumped to his feet and churred loudly.

"Wait," said Kurt, listening more closely. The sound had taken on a rhythm, a cadence, like hoofbeats. "It's not thunder," he declared at last.

A look of horror came over the stinkle-dunk's face. "Whin'ny-ga-lop—whin'ny-ga-lop—whin'ny-ga-lops!" he screamed, his voice shrill and full of panic. "Coming this way! Take shelter! Take shelter!"

Charlie scooped Tattle up in his teeth and ducked behind the tree trunk. Stinkle dove into the brambles. Uncertain where to turn, Kurt stood his ground and waited. He was not sure what a whin'ny-ga-lop—whin'ny-ga-lop—whin'ny-ga-lop was.

From northwest of the clearing came a thunderous rumble. Before Kurt could fully focus his sight, they were all around him. Horses—wild ones—stangs—fleet animals galloping at full speed through the trees. To the left and right they darted past, a montage of hoofs and tails and heads and manes amid a cloud of blinding dust.

One of the animals, a stallion, running to the rear of the others, stopped short of trampling the boy and reared up on its hind legs. Circling the clearing as it worked to catch its breath, it snorted and whinnied, and steam poured from its nostrils. When the dust in the clearing settled, the sleek black stallion came to a halt in front of Kurt, and with a heartfelt "neigh," apologized to the boy for almost running him down.

"We've traveled a great distance—from the Far Regions of the northwest," said the whin'ny-ga-lop—whin'ny-ga-lop—whin'ny-ga-lop. "It's no longer safe there. I'm moving the herd south."

By this time, Stinkle, Charlie, and Tattle had emerged from their hiding places.

"Why is it unsafe, friend?" Stinkle asked.

The horse stamped his hoofs on the ground nervously. "It started with rumblings—faint at first. But the rumblings grew louder, day by day.

And as the rumblings grew, the light began to fade. Hour by hour now, it grows dimmer. With the failing light, many of the animals have slipped downward in color, some of them two steps or more. They fuss and quarrel and feud with each other. It's as though they no longer see things in the light of Whiskers, but in a grim and perilous light—a light full of shadows and ill intent. Something strange is happening in the northwest."

"Something strange, indeed," said the stinkle-dunk.

The whin'ny-ga-lop—whin'ny-ga-lop—whin'ny-ga-lop apologized again for the intrusion, and after bidding all a hasty goodbye, ran to catch up with the herd. Kurt and the others listened to his hoofbeats until they grew faint in the distance.

"Stinkle," Kurt said, when all was quiet again, "before the whin'ny-ga-lop—whin'ny-ga-lop—whin'ny-ga-lops came through, you mentioned a tale. What did it say?"

"All I remember is something about a confrontation between a rather large Nickle-Dickle and a creature never before seen in Whiskers. I think Tattle would be a better one to ask." He turned to the tail. "Think way back, Tattle. Do you remember a tale from a few years ago about a battle of some sort in the northwest, and strange happenings there, similar to what the whin'ny-ga-lop—whin'ny-ga-lop—whin'ny-ga-lop described?"

The tattle-tail, lying on the ground, scratched his fore-end with his aft end. "Humm. Now that you mention, I do recall a tale such as that—details and all. I heard it from a passer-by—a flutter-fly—who said he had seen the actual skirmish. I told the tale two times over—to a portly prickle-pine and an oinker named Rover. A few of the other tails told it too—ones out by the Meadow where you came through." He nodded toward Kurt. "I doubted its truth, so I told not again the disputable tale—that was the end. I tell *tales*, mind you, not *lies*."

"We know you do, dear friend," said Stinkle. "Please continue."

"I heard the tale from only one source—the flutter-fly, as I told you, of course. Since so few spoke of it, and some made a joke of it, I doubt it spread much past the northwest itself."

"The tale," Stinkle reminded Tattle. "What did it say?"

The tattle-tail hesitated. He seemed to be reaching deep within himself to gather his thoughts before speaking again.

"It seems there *was* a confrontation—a ruckus, a fracas, of great consternation. But the conclusion itself remains in dispute. As to the winner, I must remain mute. Both parties vanished in the heat of battle—amid the terrible uproarious prattle of watchity widgits and kratchits and kridgits—whatever they are, whatever they am, whatever they be—it's all beyond me." The old tail paused to catch his breath. "The battle was preceded, as I recall, by a terrible tempest—a tempest of gall! And dim light, and rumblings—dark rum-tum-grumblings."

"What more can you tell us about the battle?" asked Stinkle.

"Nothing more about the battle itself—and nothing about the large Nickle-Dickle. But I do recall, details and all, something about the creature."

"Tell us what you know, please," said Stinkle.

This time the tattle-tail cleared his throat before proceeding. Anticipating a lengthy tale, Kurt sat on the root beneath the oak tree and made himself comfortable. Stinkle and Charlie sat beside him, and all three listened with great interest as the tattle-tail spoke in metered rhyme:

> *"Hear thee now a tale of old,*
> *Of shadowed chambers, damp and cold,*
> *In earth's dark womb, in blackest Sheol,*
> *The hiding place of the Thunder Troll.*
>
> *Buried in the earth so crusty,*
> *Mired within his cavern musty,*
> *Lurks the seed of rumbling roll,*
> *The foul, the fetid, Thunder Troll.*
>
> *This gnarly, twisted, ashen ball*
> *Of furrowed flesh with blood of gall*
> *Sleeps in silence in his tomb*
> *Till tolled awake by treading Gloom.*
>
> *Summoned by the gathering veil*

Of clouded legions grim and pale,
He stirs and growls from deep within
And rumbles forth to spirits kin.

At first a dwarf, a nubbin small,
A mumbling, grumbling, rumbling ball,
This hideous, heinous, haggard hob,
This scraping, scratching thingamabob,

Passes dimly, dark to light,
And cursing all within his sight,
Drums the air with grumbling roll—
The voice of the terrible Thunder Troll.

As hills and valleys shun his rumbling—
Scowling, growling, rum-tum-grumbling—
Up he swirls and twirls and flees
And whirls the wind through swaying trees.

Rolling long, and ever longer,
Full he grows, and ever stronger,
Till in billowed, burgeoned size
He stretches forth in giant's guise.

Hunched upon the thickened clouds,
Veiled from sight by vaporous shrouds,
He gazes down through sunken eyes,
Immured within his dim disguise.

With icy breath in labored thrusts,
He whips the wind to thrashing gusts
That wrench from fertile soil with ease
Tender roots and fresh young trees.

Plodding on the welkin floor,
He pounds the earth with thunder's roar
That numbs the nerve, lays bare the bone,

And turns the trembling heart to stone.

His fury mounting stride for stride,
He roars and howls the heavens wide
Till all about him, lightning flashes!
In its wake, the thunder crashes!

From his flaming fingers fly
Blades, like rapiers, through the sky
That rent the veil, that rive the vein,
And spill to earth the drenching rain.

In fear of cleansing rain, his legions
Flee the sky for darker regions,
Hence, to sound again the toll
That hails the heinous Thunder Troll.

The Troll, with weak and waning din,
Shrinks within his furrowed skin
And plummets through the welkin floor,
A gnarled and twisted nub once more.

Mid fleeing clouds and chasing light,
He pales and shrinks from earthly sight
And twists and turns till head meets toe,
And rolls to dungeons deep below.

This nasty, nimble, gnomish nib
Tumbles to his earthen crib
Where cradled in earth's brackish womb,
He sleeps once more within his tomb.

Remember thee this tale of old
When rumbles roll from chambers cold—
From earth's dark womb, from blackest Sheol—
From the hiding place of the Thunder Troll."

When the tale ended, Kurt could do no more than sit frozen to his place on the root. A chill ran down his spine as he recalled the ashen face in the clouds above the lake—and the cold that swished by him at the entrance to the passage, with its terrible stench, like that of a body long decayed. He recalled Charlie's encounter with something cold and moldy in the woods near Pink Nut Druggle's place. And the bell—that dark and dreary bell.

It was the Troll who battled the large Nickle-Dickle, thought Kurt. Could the Troll be in Whiskers again? And who is there to stop him this time? The animals can't fight something as terrible as the Thunder Troll. Most have never even seen a storm.

Despite his concerns, Kurt said nothing. After all, what could he, a mere boy, do? It was beyond his capabilities to fight anything as powerful as the Troll.

He glanced at Stinkle. He hoped the little skunk would think Tattle's tale was just foolish prattle born of an old tail's imagination.

"Well, Tattle," said Stinkle, breaking the silence, "you were right in not repeating that tale. Certainly there's no truth to such a story." But even in the moonlight, Kurt could see that Stinkle's face had turned sickly pale.

Weariness brought on by the day's adventures soon caught up with the travelers. Charlie drifted off to sleep lulled by the sound of night-chirps and leap-lops. Stinkle made himself a bed of leaves and tossed and turned in it for some time before falling asleep.

Kurt was far too restless to sleep. He checked his pocket, and finding the booknotch awake, moved the little fellow to a place on his knee.

"You haven't peeked out of my pocket all day, Notch. Been catching up on your sleep?"

"Quite to the contrary," said the tiny worm. "I thought it wise to keep a low profile. I have no desire to be anywhere in close proximity to a cat—to Fraidy Slinkle-Purr in particular based on what I've heard through the fabric of your pocket. I fear, with my diminutive size and my brown tweed accouterments, I might resemble too closely a tasty piece of tribble."

Kurt assured the booknotch the cat was gone and, after a time, tucked him away again in his pocket. Leaning back against the trunk of the oak, he set about the business of getting some much-needed rest, a task that proved to be none too easy as he drifted in and out of sleep to the sound of Tattle's droning voice telling tales into the night:

"Deep in the river that flows from the Silver Mountain lives King Aegis, King of the Swishin-Figgles. The mighty King Aegis, guardian of the precious jewels that adorn the Opal Lake. Rainbow jewels. Priceless ones abounding in the Opal Lake . . ."

Jewels? Opal Lake? King Aegis? Kurt was wide awake again. He listened intently as Tattle told a tale of a lake filled with precious opals.

A pirate's treasure! That's what it sounds like, thought Kurt. But the lake probably doesn't exist. It's probably all just an old tail telling tales.

Tattle finished the tale of the Opal Lake and began another:

"I think I've never seen a sight
That brought my heart such fond delight
As the curious one I saw this night—
Fraidy's fabulous feline flying machine.

Its wings were wobbly, its throttle stiff,
But all and all, it gave a lift
To the slinkle-purr when set adrift—
Fraidy's fabulous feline flying machine.

Up it pulled the poor little fella—
Up to a cloud with his folding umbrella.
I knew that feline could sing a cappella—'
Fraidy's fabulous feline flying machine.

For a moment it hovered within the shroud,
Then down it plummeted out of the cloud,
Umbrella and feline, whistling loud.
Fraidy's fabulous feline flying machine.

With its wobbly wings turned inside out,
Its stiff little throttle thrashed about,
But all and all, it was steady and stout.
Fraidy's fabulous feline flying machine.

It clamored and clanked as it crashed to its mark—
The top of a copper tree, cold and stark.
What a strange and unusual place to park!
Fraidy's fabulous feline flying machine.

Now close your eyes and imagine the sight:
The flying feline's fantastic kite
That took to the sky this very night—
Fraidy's fabulous feline flying machine."

Kurt giggled and closed his eyes.
Tattle rambled on until his voice faded to a whisper:

"Weave and tat,
Weave and tat
Till the tale is told;

Weave a tale . . .
Tat a tale . . .
Till I'm . . .
very . . .
old."

Soon they were all asleep under the oak tree.

CHAPTER 14

SPINNERET THE WEBBER-TAT

Terrible things, goodbyes. Kurt held bad memories of them. He recalled the time he had to say goodbye to his only true friend, who was moving away. The two promised to write each other every day, and they did for a while. But as their interests grew apart, they wrote less often. Finally, the letters stopped altogether. Sad things, goodbyes.

Now it was morning and Kurt was having to bid farewell to Stinkle and Tattle—Stinkle, his newest friend, his nurturer, his teacher, his companion—and Tattle, one of the first friends he had met in the Land of Whiskers. Kurt disliked being among those who visited the tail briefly and moved on, leaving him alone under his tree. But he *had* to move on. He had to find the Cornerstone and the way home. With a heavy heart, but an equally grievous longing for home, Kurt waited for Charlie to bid the tail goodbye then headed down the road, occasionally glancing over his shoulder to see Stinkle and Tattle still watching and waving. Just as the waning letters from his childhood friend became fewer and less desired, so Stinkle and Tattle gradually became smaller and fainter in the distance. Finally, a bend in the road blocked them from sight altogether, and Kurt and Charlie and the booknotch found themselves alone on the road again.

As the flat land of the Copper Valley gradually gave way to rolling hills, the warm reddish glow so prevalent in the valley faded, and the soft silvery glow of the Nickel Hills grew in intensity, allowing the delicate pastels of spring to show forth in all their fragile glory. Now Kurt beheld a countryside awash with springtime color. The clear, crystalline light—as yet appearing undiminished to all except the most discerning eye—danced across fragile young leaves and delicate spring grasses, bringing to life the warm greens and soft, buttery yellows of the season in a way that the red-imbued light of the Copper Valley could not. It played unimpaired among the pink and purple petals of freshly opened flowers, and shimmered on dew-covered stems, and spread a virgin, rainbow iridescence over moist young buds. Even the shadows felt the benevolent touch of the pure crystalline light, for it lent them a sheer transparency, revealing within them delicate neutrals and warm, subtle grays forever lost in lesser light.

Shortly after noon Kurt saw his first nickel tree. Thereafter, the copper trees became fewer, the nickel trees more numerous, as Kurt, Charlie, and the booknotch traveled farther into the hills. Stinkle had correctly described the nickel trees. The music they played as the breeze gently touched them was more delicate, purer, and higher in tone than that of the copper trees, and their beauty was a delight to behold.

When the travelers reached the crest of a hill, the magnificence of what they saw overwhelmed them. There, in vast display, as far as their eyes could see, lay groves of nickel trees. The afternoon sun striking the highly polished leaves sent a shimmer among the branches that danced from leaf to leaf, bringing the trees to life with light. Like graceful ballerinas in white chiffon dresses, they danced their dance of light, choreographed by the breeze, all the while filling the air with siren's song, coaxing the weary travelers to dream waking dreams—dreams resplendent with lofty aspirations—dreams designed to lift the soul on wings of song to heights unfathomable.

Kurt was entranced by such a dream, when all at once a brilliant glow in the distance caught his eye and snapped him awake. The glow appeared to be coming from a grove of nickel trees up ahead. Rays of radiant light shooting high into the air above the grove reminded him of the nimbuses painted around the heads of saints in religious paintings he had seen in books. The light was far brighter than the nickel trees themselves. Surely this could not be Nickledown, he thought. It was too soon. Stinkle had said it would take two days to reach the town.

Kurt quickened his pace, walking briskly around bend after bend. After a particularly sharp turn in the road, he stood before it—the source of the light.

At the side of the road lay a circular clearing, its furthermost edge defined by a semicircle of nickel trees that appeared as though they had been draped in Chantilly lace. A vast network of glistening webs stretched from the ground, up through the trees, and from treetop to treetop; and woven into the webs were countless sparkling droplets of morning dew—tiny prisms that reflected the sun's light upward, creating the brilliant glow Kurt had seen from the distance

As beautiful as the webs were, their vastness was overwhelming, and Kurt wondered for a moment if the size of the spider that wove them might be proportionate.

Charlie, too, appeared to have misgivings, for he darted a few yards up the road and barked for Kurt to hurry along. But when Kurt crossed the clearing and drew close to one of the trees, Charlie slinked up behind him and crouched near his feet.

As Kurt peered up through the shining webs, he was surprised to hear a voice coming from above in the branches. "Whatever have I done with it?" said the small, feminine voice.

Craning his neck, Kurt scoured the branches, hoping to see whoever was speaking.

"I know it must be here somewhere," said the voice. "I was using it only moments ago."

"Who's up there?" Kurt asked cautiously.

"I am," answered the small voice. "Spinneret the Webber-Tat."

Kurt noticed movement amid the webs and a small spider dropped abruptly from a point high in the tree and came to rest at the end of a length of silken thread directly in front of Kurt's nose.

The boy jumped back, startled by the sudden appearance of the brown spider. When he had recovered from the fright, he looked closer at the webber-tat and noticed it had tiny whiskers he could barely see.

"I didn't mean to startle you, dear," said the fragile creature. "I'm not quite myself this morning, you see. Either my eyes are failing me, or there's something errant in the quality of light."

The spider scurried a few inches up the thread and looked around in every direction and slipped down again. "I've misplaced my silver needle and I must find it to weave dew into my webs. I've gathered fresh dew from the Silver Mountain and it must be used quickly or it will all go to waste."

Silver needle? thought Kurt. He had an idea. He removed his backpack and, reaching inside, pulled out the smallest fishhook he could find and handed it to the webber-tat. "It's not silver, but it might do."

"Oh, my dear, it's perfect," said the webber-tat. "It's bigger than I'm used to, but it's a fine, sharp needle."

Kurt smiled and introduced himself and Charlie. Remembering the booknotch, he took the little worm out of his pocket, and placing him on his shoulder, introduced him as well. The webber-tat seemed pleased to meet them all. She asked Kurt where he was traveling from and he told her the Copper Valley. "I shouldn't be here at all," he said. "I came to the Land of Whiskers by mistake, and I'm heading to Nickledown to find my way home."

"You're definitely headed in the right direction," said the webber-tat; and looking at the boy's feet, she added, "Kurt, dear, you've walked all this way without your shoes?"

"Yes. I was going fishing when I ended up in Whiskers. I always go barefooted when I go fishing."

"Well, dear one, perhaps you will find shoes to fit your needs when you reach Nickledown. In the meantime, why don't you rest here for a time."

Being painfully aware of the sad state of his feet, Kurt accepted her kind offer and made himself comfortable in the dappled shade of the web-covered tree. As Spinneret sat on a nickel leaf and began weaving a new web, Kurt told her his story. He described the lake and the passage and his adventures in the meadow; and he told her about Stinkle and Fraidy and Tattle, and how he had met the booknotch.

"I'm not sure how I got my whiskers. Suddenly, there they were. The there'n not-hares said the meadow morphs gave them to me."

"Did a meadow morph touch you?"

"Yes, one did," replied Kurt. "They were swirling all around my head and one touched my face. It tickled and I brushed it away."

"That's how you got your whiskers," said the webber-tat. "The meadow morphs give them to animals—and crawling creatures, such as webber-tats and weery-dawdles and night-chirps—that don't already have them when they enter the Land of Whiskers. The slightest touch does it."

"And booknotches, too?" asked Notch. "One did touch me the day I arrived."

"I'm sure booknotches are included," said Spinneret. She glanced at Kurt. "The meadow morphs are responsible for changing things, arranging things, to better suit the moment. And whiskers were what you needed most at that moment."

"What I needed most was to go home," said Kurt.

"The meadow morphs hadn't the power to send you home," replied the webber-tat. "Besides, it would have been quite out of the ordinary for someone to want to leave the Land of Whiskers. You are somewhat of a rarity."

"I am?"

The webber-tat nodded. "Usually, only animals come here. When an animal is lost or frightened, a passage opens to the Land of Whiskers. The animal uses his whiskers to find his way through the passage. You were fortunate that your love for Charlie caused you to hold fast to his tail. Without whiskers of your own, you could have lost your way and been locked within the passage forever."

"But *some* animals don't have whiskers. How do they find their way through?"

"Guidelithes are sent to guide them," said Spinneret.

"Guidelithes?"

"The silver specs of light you described."

"So why wouldn't they have helped me if I had let go of Charlie's tail?"

"They are sent to guide lost or frightened *animals* and *crawling creatures*, Kurt. You are neither an animal, nor a crawling creature. You, dear, as I said, are somewhat of a rarity. I'm sure the wind knew that. I'm sure that's why it fought so hard to keep you out. But when it realized your love for Charlie would not allow you to let go of his tail, it let you come through."

All this time, Spinneret was working feverishly, weaving a heavy web that started out long and rope-like and expanded into something resembling netting. She wove the rope-like end around the trunk of a nickel tree and worked her way across the ground, spinning and weaving toward another tree a few feet away. At one point, she stopped and recited a little verse as she checked her progress:

> *"Spin a thread from old to new;*
> *Weave a web of summer dew.*
> *Silver shuttle passing through;*
> *Silver needle stitching, too."*

Whatever she was weaving, its size in proportion to the tiny spider was overwhelming. Though curious to know what it was, Kurt was too busy reflecting upon his whiskers and the trip through the passage to ask.

"I guess for an animal, the Land of Whiskers is a pretty good place to live," said Kurt. "Doesn't seem to be anything bad here—except maybe Parhelion." (And the Troll, he thought. But he didn't want to mention that to Spinneret. After all, the Troll was not *his* problem.)

"Are you worried about Parhelion, dear?" asked Spinneret. "You said yourself you've seen nothing but a shadow. And you told me you thought it was foolish for Fraidy to be afraid of shadows. Doesn't the same apply to you?"

"That's different. Fraidy's afraid of his *own* shadow, and everyone knows your *own* shadow can't hurt you. But Parhelion is real, and the animals in the Copper Valley are afraid of him. Is he evil?"

"Some things we must learn for ourselves, Kurt."

The webber-tat's answer disturbed the boy, and he thought he would be wise to change the subject for the time being. "Have *you* ever been to Nickledown?"

"Oh, yes, dear. I've been to many Silver Days there. It's a wonderful place, but I prefer the country life in the Nickel Hills. I go through Nickledown, too, on my way to the Silver Mountain to gather dew. The finest dew is found on the mountain. I weave it into my best pieces of work."

"Have you ever seen Parhelion on the Silver Mountain?"

The webber-tat glanced up at Kurt before looking down at her work again. "The Nimbus is from high up, Kurt. *Very* high up. Much higher than I've ever been."

Her words were disquieting, and again Kurt changed the subject. "Spinneret, have you ever heard of the Cornerstone? My friend Stinkle said it's in Nickledown."

"I have heard of it," replied the webber-tat. "It's said to be large and very real. And it *is* said to be in Nickledown, though I've never seen it. According to legend, there are words locked within the stone. But that's all I can tell you."

"What about a book?" asked Notch, who had been listening to the conversation from a spot on Kurt's shoulder. "Is there a book in Nickledown?"

"There is a legend about a book. But no one has ever seen it to my knowledge."

"Oh." Notch hung his head. "I think I should like to go back into my paper now, Kurt, if you don't mind."

Kurt held the newspaper open so the booknotch could crawl inside, and after folding it, tucked it away in his shirt pocket.

By this time, the sun was low in the sky, and Kurt realized he and the webber-tat had been talking all afternoon. It was not until

Spinneret suggested they have supper that Kurt considered how hungry he was.

While Spinneret dined on dew from the web she was weaving, Kurt ate biscuits and honey from the backpack, and Charlie ate tribble with a Chunkie Chewie for dessert. As evening approached, Kurt heard the familiar sounds of night-chirps and leap-lops, and he asked the webber-tat about them. "I'm sure they're saying, 'Walk' and 'Quick! Time is short,' but what do they mean?"

Spinneret had resumed her weaving, but now she stopped and looked directly at Kurt. Her expression became serious.

> *"The meaning of 'Quickit'*
> *You'll soon discover.*
> *The meaning of 'W-a-u-k'*
> *You must uncover."*

"Uncover the meaning of 'W-a-u-k?' How do I do that?"

"Do you like riddles, Kurt?"

As if I had time for riddles, thought Kurt. I have more important things to think about. But he answered, "Yes, I do. I love riddles."

"Then listen well:

> *Here's a riddle short and sweet:*
> *Use your whiskers **and your feet**."*

"Use my whiskers and my feet? I don't know what you mean."

"I'll give you another clue," said Spinneret. Listen carefully:

> *The leap-lops speak with meaning hidden,*
> *Croaking their message in common sound.*
> *'W-a-u-k,' they say in cloaked confusion;*
> *'Tread upon the common ground.'*

> *Whiskers to words,*
> *Footsteps to light;*
> *Walk in the shoes,*
> *Lace them up tight.*

Truth in the step,
Light at the top;
Leap-lop to silver!
Leap-lop, leap-lop."

Kurt was even more confused. Why doesn't she just say what she means, he thought.

Spinneret was weaving again, but now she was acting strangely. Time after time she looked at the weaving then looked at Kurt. The boy had the feeling she was sizing him up.

Despite her diminutive size and friendly manner, Spinneret was still a spider. Kurt realized the web she was weaving was large enough to hold him, and it appeared to be sturdy and strong as well. And the webber-tat had avoided giving him straight answers to his questions about Parhelion—his questions about the night-chirps and leap-lops, too, for that matter.

A chill ran up the back of his neck. What if he had fallen into a trap? Certainly the little spider wasn't big enough to trap him herself, but what if she had friends? Huge, horrible, eight-legged webber-tat rogues! Kurt's mind painted pictures of gray, sticky webs, and spiders with mandibles larger than he.

"There," said Spinneret. "It's done. I was afraid it wouldn't be finished before nightfall. Now, if you will just lift this loose end up to that tree, I'll fasten it on."

"Lift what?" Kurt said nervously.

"The hammock, dear. If you'll just help me fasten this end to the tree, you'll have a soft, comfortable bed to sleep in tonight. There's even room for Charlie. It's the least I could do for one who was kind enough to provide me with a new needle."

"Oh," sighed Kurt, relieved by the fact it really was a hammock—a beautiful white silk one with silver dewdrops woven into the edging.

He held the loose end close to the tree while Spinneret crawled up and spun more web to secure it to the trunk. When the hammock was firmly fastened, Kurt thanked the webber-tat and climbed in. Charlie climbed in, too, and found a perfect spot to curl up near Kurt's feet.

The hammock felt cozy and comforting and reminded Kurt of his bed at home. Sitting up, he watched the webber-tat crawl into a tiny niche on a nearby tree trunk. "Spinneret," he said, "do you think the Nickle-Dickles will be able to help me get home?"

"I'm afraid not, dear," said the webber-tat. "Only from silver will you find what you're seeking, and the Nickle-Dickles are not silver. In fact, they're no color at all, though if they were a color, it would most certainly be silver. Color is a state among animals and crawling creatures, and Nickle-Dickles are neither."

"Well, what are they?"

"No one knows, exactly. They were led to the Land of Whiskers from a place called Hamelin. Since then, they've been caretakers of all that's beautiful here."

"Oh," said Kurt, and he thought for a moment. "Spinneret, what did you mean when you said, 'only from silver' will I find what I'm seeking?"

"Answers are always found within silver, Kurt dear. That's where the greatest knowledge lies."

"Are *you* silver?" Kurt asked. He was sure she was. It was a feeling he had. He couldn't explain it. It had something to do with a tingling sensation he felt in his whiskers when he thought about her being silver. Still, he wanted to hear her say it.

"I am silver, dear," replied Spinneret. "But I haven't the answer you seek. Perhaps another who is silver can help you. Sleep now, dear one. Good night." And she nestled lower into the niche on the tree trunk.

Spinneret's words offered no direct help, but at least now Kurt knew he would have to seek other silver ones. "What's so special about silver, anyway?" he asked himself. Oh, well. Notch would know. Booknotches know all that stuff. He would have to remember to ask Notch in the morning.

Kurt curled up with his dog in the silken hammock just as the moon appeared in the night sky and shed its silver light upon the sparkling dewdrops woven into Spinneret's webs. The moonlight transformed the silken masterpieces stretching from treetop to treetop above his head into a silver canopy that sheltered him while the hammock cradled him—while its silken threads held him safe and snug like a mother's arms around her child. Length of day and length of night seemed of no consequence now, as he lay in this gentle place—in this dew-bejeweled domain of one tiny webber-tat whose gift, it seemed, was not only to weave a world of light and fragile lace, but also to weave with tender threads the silken veil of time.

From out of the dark, a gentle breeze appeared and played soft music in the nickel trees. It held within itself a breath of warmth, as though somewhere in its travels it had come upon the sleeping Summer, stirring her to wake, coaxing her to rise and claim her rightful place in due season. Ever so slowly, the ambling breeze rocked the hammock back and forth, back and forth, like the pointer of the metronome on Grandma's piano.

> *Tick—tock—*
> *Tick—tock—*
> *Tick—tock—*
> *Tick—tock—*

The breeze bore upon its fragile wing a lullaby—a gentle song plucked from the grasp of a faraway wind—a Never-Ending Lullaby that sifted through the trees like fairy dust, settling lightly upon the boy, filling his mind with silver dreamscapes.

> *Tick—tock—*
> *Tick—tock—*
> *Silent—words—*
> *Silken—words—*
>
> *Tick—tock—*
> *Tick—tock—*
> *Whispered—words—*
> *Elfin—words—*

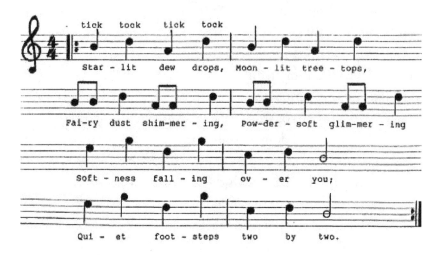

Starlit dew drops, moonlit treetops,
Fairy dust shimmering, powder-soft glimmering—
Dew-soft petals, sugar sweet,
Drifting down around your feet . . .

Starlit dew drops, moonlit treetops,
Fairy dust shimmering, powder-soft glimmering—
Floating gently on the air,
Gathered fragrance lingers there . . .

Starlit dew drops, moonlit treetops,
Fairy dust shimmering, powder-soft glimmering—
Loving arms around you tight,
Peaceful dreaming through the night . . .

Starlit dew drops, moonlit treetops,
Fairy dust shimmering, powder-soft glimmering—
Swaying breezes softly pull you;
To and fro they gently lull you . . .

Starlit dew drops, moonlit treetops,
Fairy dust shimmering, powder-soft glimmering—
Voices calling soft as dew,
Whispered promises all for you . . .

Starlit dew drops, moonlit treetops,
Fairy dust shimmering, powder-soft glimmering—
Quiet footsteps steal away,
Comes the dawning of the day . . .

Kurt was fast asleep.

CHAPTER 15

∾ℯ℥

MOSEY THE WEERY-DAWDLE

Morning! Glorious morning! Sunlit dew drops! Silver treetops! The phrases danced in the boy's head like fairytale sprites.

Peering up through Spinneret's dew-studded webs, watching the nickel leaves shimmer in the morning sun, Kurt wondered how the trees could have been any more beautiful had they been the progeny of purest silver and not that of lower-born, lesser-valued nickel.

"What is nickel, anyway?" Kurt mumbled to himself.

"Nickel," answered a small voice from his shirt pocket. "A silver-white metal capable of polish, resistant to corrosion, used in alloys and as a catalyst.'"

Kurt giggled. "Good morning, Notch. Webster's Unabridged?"

The booknotch peeked up over the edge of Kurt's shirt pocket. "Unknown origin, I'm afraid. I memorized the definition while visiting a sick relative in a rather drafty old dictionary whose cover was missing. The poor fellow insisted on nestling himself among the *n*'s, believing he would recover sooner near 'nurse' and 'nurture.' I strongly recommended he move to the *s*'s near 'strength' and 'stamina,' but he was too afraid to make the long journey past 'operation,' 'palpitation,' 'quarantine,' and 'respirator.'"

"Speaking of *s*'s," said Kurt, "what do you know about silver?"

The booknotch thought for a moment and smiled. "Silver, 'a white, metallic element that is sonorous, ductile, very malleable, and capable of a high degree of polish.'"

"Unknown origin?"

"Certainly not," said the booknotch. "Recognizably Webster's." And he slipped back down into Kurt's pocket.

The booknotch's definition of silver was no help to Kurt. But what about nickel? What did Notch call it? A catalyst? What was a catalyst, anyway? Kurt tried to remember the definition from his science class. Something that makes things happen or something like that. Well, Kurt thought, looking up at the nickel trees, I wish *this* nickel would make things happen. I wish it would send me home.

"Good morning, dear ones." Spinneret scurried down the tree trunk. "You were sleeping so soundly I let you sleep in. You should be up and on your way now. You have a great task ahead of you."

A great task for certain, thought Kurt. And another goodbye.

Despite his distaste for goodbyes, Kurt knew they were necessary at times—parting rituals that must be performed to close a chapter in one's life and open another. Saying goodbye to Spinneret would be a little like saying goodbye to his mother. He had not had the chance to do so the fateful day he was drawn through the passage. Perhaps this morning's parting sentiments would in some way make up for that terrible omission.

After a quick breakfast and the dispensing of the much-dreaded goodbyes, Kurt and Charlie and Notch once again found themselves traveling toward the Silver Mountain. The air was warm now, the season having taken a definite turn toward summer. The farther the three traveled, the bluer became the sky, the sweeter became the air, and soon Kurt felt excitement welling inside him at the prospect of reaching Nickledown. He was deep in thought, imagining what he would find there, when out of the corner of his eye he spotted a narrow, shining trail running along the edge of the road. The trail was moist and took on a silvery appearance as it glistened in the sun. Upon closer inspection, Kurt found it to be quite lovely in design. "A snail. It has to be," he said to Charlie.

Charlie sniffed the trail and began tracing its length with his nose. Kurt followed Charlie, who followed the trail, and soon they arrived at its leading edge. But nowhere was there a snail to be found. The trail simply ended abruptly near the base of a sprawling digger pine near the side of the road.

Just then, from high in the tree, came a weak voice calling frantically—frantically slow, that is, if such a thing can be. "Help me! I'm up here! Help me!"

Kurt looked up and could barely see a tiny snail clinging to the tip of an upper branch. He thought it strange the little snail could get there without leaving a trail on the tree trunk. Nevertheless, he carefully climbed the tree, stretched his arm out toward the end of the branch, and ever so gently lifted the trembling snail and placed him securely on his shoulder. "How did you get up here?" he asked the wee creature.

"It's a long story," said the snail, his voice quivering. He glanced down at the ground, and "Ah!" he screamed.

"Are you afraid of heights?" Kurt asked, knowing of nothing else that could have caused such a reaction.

"Yes!" the snail cried, closing his eyes.

"Well, hold on," said Kurt. "I'll have you down in no time." And with the snail still trembling, Kurt made his way to the ground and placed the little fellow safely on the roadway.

The snail breathed a sigh of relief. "Thank you ever so much," he said in his weak and weary voice. "Now I must hurry." And he rushed off in dawdling flight, if such a thing is possible. "Hurry, scurry. Oh, what worry," he mumbled, as he moseyed along, stopping to pant and catch his breath after every few inches. "Monumental, mountainous task!"

The snail's weary manner of speaking was contagious, and Kurt found himself talking as slowly as the snail. "Wait! Why are you hurrying?" he said, as slowly as the snail would have said it. "I mean, why are you hurrying?" he repeated in his normal manner of speaking, realizing his mimicry, and not wanting the tiny fellow to think he was mocking him.

"I'm trying to get to Nickledown," drawled the snail. "For Silver Day," he added. "Week after week I try to get there, but I always arrive a little too late. I turn around and head home just in time to turn around and try again. Back and forth and back and forth. Ah," the snail sighed wearily.

The mere thought of all that superfluous travel made Kurt tired. He offered to carry the snail, and that delighted the tiny creature.

"What's your name?" Kurt asked.

"Mosey the Weery-Dawdle," the snail replied.

A *silver* weery-dawdle from the look of his trail, thought Kurt, and with renewed hope of finding answers that would lead him home, he reached down and gently lifted the little fellow to his shoulder.

"Ah!" the snail screamed. "Too high, too high!"

"I'm sorry. I forgot," said Kurt. And he moved the wee creature to a place on his right foot.

Noticeably relieved at being closer to the ground, Mosey drew a deep breath and released it slowly. "Yes. That's much better."

Kurt began walking, and each time he took a step, he swung the snail forward, whereupon the weery-dawdle gave a little cry of delight. "Whee!" he said. "I've never moved this fast in all my life."

Kurt chuckled to himself. He's such a cute little guy—tiny whiskers and all. Even if he is silver, how could someone this innocent know something as important as the way home?

As they traveled, Kurt told Mosey his story, and Mosey told Kurt how he came to be in the tree.

"It was Tubbs. He's a nut druggle—a far-sighted one and—"

"I know," said Kurt. "He mistook Charlie's Chunkie Chewies for nuts and stole them."

"He mistook me for a nut, too," said Mosey, "and he carried me high in the tree. I was so frightened I couldn't utter a sound. It was not until he tried to remove my shell that he discovered his terrible error. He panicked and ran away, leaving me stranded."

"That's awful."

"It's not the worst of it," Mosey continued. "The twitter-flits saw it all. They're certain to spread the story, and that will surely cause trouble between the weery-dawdles and the nut druggles."

Oh, yes, thought Kurt. The twitter-flits. The little winged gossips.

"Perhaps in Nickledown I can find a way to make everyone see more clearly," said Mosey.

Kurt had no idea what the snail meant, but it seemed unimportant.

The terrain gradually steepened as Kurt, Charlie, and Mosey (and Notch in Kurt's pocket) walked the long road through the Nickel Hills. Pines and cedars, as well as dense groves of nickel trees, lined the roadway at this higher elevation, and here the nickel trees played even more melodiously than the ones in the lower foothills. The higher they climbed, the more sweetly fragrant became the air, as a flowery perfume spilled down the hillsides, suggesting a garden hidden somewhere in the distance.

Toward sundown, the four stopped for the night, and Kurt quickly prepared beds of leaves and pine needles for himself and Charlie.

It took a while for Mosey to regain his sense of balance—he was dizzy from riding on Kurt's foot—but as evidenced by his delighted expression when Kurt placed him on the ground, the wee snail had enjoyed the experience all the same.

"That was invigorating," he drawled. And he added timidly, "If you don't mind, Kurt, I'd like to make a request."

"Sure. Anything."

"I am a weery-dawdle who enjoys an adventure as much as the next crawling creature. Do you think it would be possible . . . That is, do you think it would be too much to ask . . ."

Just hurry and ask me, Kurt thought, though he wouldn't have said that to the weery-dawdle. Instead he said, "What kind of adventure did you have in mind?"

Mosey looked at the boy shyly. It was a long moment before he spoke. "Do you think tomorrow I could ride on your—*left* foot?"

Kurt almost burst out laughing. So that was to be Mosey's great adventure!

"Of course, you can ride on my *left* foot," said Kurt.

The weery-dawdle was delighted. His chest puffed to twice its normal size with pride. How daring he was to ask to pursue such a spirited adventure! How brave! How debonair! First a right foot, then a left—and within a day of each other.

Kurt still held little hope for such a demure and unassuming creature as Mosey knowing the way home. Nevertheless, he decided to approach the subject, just in case. He told the weery-dawdle about Spinneret, and about how she had said another who is silver might help him. "You *are* silver, aren't you," he asked the snail.

"Yes, Kurt. I am silver, and answers *are* always found within silver. But another who is silver must help you. I do not have the answer you seek."

Kurt tried to disguise his disappointment. "How much farther is it to Nickledown?"

"Not far," said Mosey. "You can probably see it from that knoll over there." He nodded toward a high, grassy knoll a few yards away.

Kurt hurried to the knoll and climbed to its crest just as the last rays of the setting sun were disappearing below the horizon. "You're right!" he shouted to Mosey. "I can see the tops of houses!"

When he turned to climb back down, he happened to glance toward the west. What he saw sent a chill down his spine. There, looming tall and dark against the reddening sky, stood a vast legion of thick thunderclouds.

Kurt ran back to where Mosey and Charlie were camped and described the clouds to the weery-dawdle.

Mosey's face turned pale. "I must see for myself. Put me on your shoulder and take me to the top of the knoll."

"But, Mosey, you're afraid of heights."

"I must see it, Kurt. This is too important to worry about my petty fears."

Kurt placed the trembling snail on his shoulder and climbed again to the top of the knoll. Somewhat unsteadily, Mosey raised his head as high as he could and stared into the distance. "This is not good," he said, his weary voice shaking. "I've seen this before. It's the Gathering Gloom."

❧

CHAPTER 16

ᏫHᏋ ᏟORNERSTONE

Kurt spent a restless night camped on the outskirts of Nickledown, tossing and turning in his leafy bed, his dreams of the splendorous town turned nightmarish by the ever-present shadow of the darkly looming specter Mosey called the "Gathering Gloom."

In the morning, as they journeyed, Mosey told Kurt he had seen the Gloom several years earlier while visiting the northwest.

"It loomed in the sky for days and made the animals so anxious that tempers ran high. Many slipped downward in color—some all the way back to purple. Animals stole and lied and fought with their neighbors. I believe all of Whiskers would have fallen to destruction had not the Gloom been checked. But it *was* checked."

"How?" asked Kurt.

"There was a battle. Those who saw it spread word that a large Nickle-Dickle and a terrible creature fought within the Gloom until both combatants disappeared and the Gloom rolled away."

"I heard about that battle—from the tattle-tail. I wondered why more animals didn't hear about it."

"The Far Regions of the northwest are cold and sparsely populated," said Mosey. "News travels slowly there, and word of the battle soon faded. To my way of thinking, the Gloom and the terrible creature were gone and finished. I, for one, saw no reason to spread ill tidings."

After some time, Kurt and Mosey set aside their fears of the Gloom, insofar as talking about it was concerned. They were rapidly approaching Nickledown, and the sweetly intoxicating scent of fresh flowers soon chased all unpleasant thoughts from their minds.

"That smell. What is it?" Kurt asked the snail.

"The Rainbow Garden," said Mosey, inhaling deeply. "The perfectly balanced perfume of the Rainbow Garden. Legend says the garden's roots lie in an *ancient* garden—one that flourished before Whiskers time."

"It smells like the flowers I smelled in the passage," said Kurt, "only stronger and all mixed together."

The morning breeze carried the sweet perfume like heaven's breath down through the hills. A slight turn of his head to the left, and Kurt breathed the ennobled bouquet of vintage wisteria; a turn to the right, the rich ambrosia of old-world gardenia. A shift of the breeze brought the coolness of mint, and the satiny warmth of antique rose. A shift yet again, and the dulcet elixirs of honeysuckle and jasmine flowed down like nectar poured from a flask.

The sweet flower scents swirled about Kurt's head, blending again into the perfectly balanced perfume, and like a magic potion, the perfume consumed him, casting its spell, causing him to dream of a garden of long ago—a lost garden beyond waking memory.

What must that garden have been like if this one, the Rainbow Garden, were but a shadow of its ancient predecessor? What abundance it must have yielded in fruit and flower!—fruit to feed the body, flower to feed the soul. What earthly joys! What unearthly pleasures! Sugary sweetness to tickle the palette; richness of color, delight to the eye; heavenly scents to set the mind dreaming; contented beasts dwelling in flowering fields, resting in shaded glens.

Just as seeds are lost that fail to heed the call of spring—that lie too long dormant in earth's dark womb—so the garden's first keepers were lost, and with them, the beasts of the flowering fields and the shaded glens, and the fields and the glens themselves.

What master gardener in his benevolent wisdom called the Nickle-Dickles with sweetly piped music, brought them to Whiskers to replant the seeds and care for the garden, and opened the door for lost beasts to return? Did he know, as lost seeds might with time and nurturing push their way again to the light, so the beasts, with time and nurturing, might rise through the colors to silver, there to blossom in fullness once more? Pray the lost and frightened beasts might find the open door—the passage that leads narrowly through the rock to the Land of Whiskers, to Nickledown, to the Rainbow Garden.

"Kurt! Kurt!" cried Mosey.

"Oh, I was daydreaming, I guess." Kurt shook his head to waken himself. "Something about a lost garden. I can't quite remember."

"The perfectly balanced perfume can have that effect the first time you smell it," said Mosey. "If the effect is that strong, we must be close to Nickledown."

And indeed they were. When they reached the top of the next rise, there it was! Nickledown—nestled cozily on a hillside at the foot of the Silver Mountain.

What a sight it was in the morning sun with its gleaming, white-stucco houses and well-manicured hedges and cheerfully winding cobblestone streets! Set like an emerald among it all, was the Town Square with its Rainbow Garden—a patch of grass of the greenest green, bordered on all sides by mound upon mound of colorful flowers—flowers splashed with all the hues of an artist's palette.

From the top of the rise, Kurt could see a shimmering river winding lazily along the edge of town, down through the valley, and out of sight. Sunlight reflecting from the river's crystalline surface lent a particular brilliance to the clear, sparkling air above the town.

"What's that music?" Kurt asked, upon hearing the opening strains of a melody more beautiful than any he had heard thus far in the Land of Whiskers.

"It's the voice of the Great Nickel Gate," said Mosey.

The sound was of nickel trees tuned to perfection. Every note, every chord, seemed the voice of a heavenly messenger. The music, floating in and out on the breeze, beckoned the travelers to draw nearer.

"Come on," Kurt said excitedly, signaling Charlie to hurry along. Mosey held fast to Kurt's left foot as the boy made his way with bounding strides down the rise and up the hill leading to Nickledown's gate.

When they arrived at the Great Nickel Gate, Kurt stopped to listen and stare in awe at the two gigantic nickel trees that stood side by side to form the gate. He stood entranced by the sheer beauty of the silver-white trees whose leaves sparkled in the sunlight as though cascading diamonds tumbled unendingly through their myriad branches. Now he heard clearly the enchanting call of the perfectly tuned, finely sculpted arbors, whose middle branches reached each toward the other tree to form an arch, whose upper branches intertwined to form a steep spire pointing heavenward, whose lower limbs spread like open arms to welcome the lost and weary to Nickledown.

When Kurt and his friends passed through the gate, nickel trees all over Nickledown rang out in greeting. They quieted to gentle chiming as the boy and his entourage made their way along the cobblestone streets past immaculate whitewashed houses adorned with brightly colored shutters, and flower-filled window boxes, and windows dressed to a tea in white lace curtains that ruffled gently in the breeze. Here and there, the fragrance of freshly cut lawns and sweet grasses drifted on the air. Everywhere the aroma of herbs and spices, freshly baked bread, and hot-from-the-oven cakes and pies cooling on sills beneath open sashes invited the travelers to linger.

The town was a hubbub of activity with animals scurrying here and there cheerfully tending to chores, talking, laughing. Kurt felt a surge of hope arise within him. Surely in a place such as this there would be someone silver—someone who would know the way home, or at the very least, someone who could guide him to the Cornerstone.

They were nearing the Town Square when Charlie suddenly raised his nose high in the air, took a deep breath, and darted off before Kurt could stop him. "Charlie!" Kurt shouted after the dog.

When the animal gave no heed, Kurt looked down at Mosey, who was still riding his left foot. "I'd better go after him before he gets lost," he told the snail, and he lifted Mosey and placed him on the ground.

"I can take it from here," drawled the weery-dawdle. "Ah, Nickledown at last. Thank you so much for the ride, my friend."

Kurt and Mosey bade each other goodbye, and Kurt hurried after Charlie. He could see the dog in the Rainbow Garden standing shoulder-deep in a mound of honeysuckle, smelling the blossoms.

"Charlie! Get out of there! You'll trample the flowers!" he called to the dog.

"He can't harm them. And he's enjoying them so," said a voice from behind him.

Kurt turned to find a small woman, only as tall as he, but looking the age of his mother. She was dressed in piebald clothes: a long dress made entirely of pink-and-yellow patches, a crisply starched apron of the selfsame stripe, and a kerchief of pink-and-yellow check tied loosely about her head. And her smile was as cheerful as the garden itself.

"Are you a Nickle-Dickle?" Kurt asked, feeling certain she must be.

"Yes," the woman replied, "but I'm certain you are not, though you look as one of us."

"My name is Kurt, and I'm a boy. And this is my dog—I mean, my waggle-lick," he said, pointing to Charlie. "We've been traveling for days, all the way from the Copper Valley."

After telling the tiny woman something of his situation, he decided to get straight to the point about her color—or lack thereof—just in case Spinneret had been wrong and the Nickle-Dickle might in fact be silver.

"Mother Nickle-Dickle," he said (he had not been told the Nickle-Dickle's name, but calling her Mother Nickle-Dickle seemed perfectly natural and quite appropriate), "is it true Nickle-Dickles don't have color?"

"It is true," said the Nickle-Dickle. "We move neither up nor down. Only animals and crawling creatures live within the colors."

"Then you're not silver."

"I am not. But if you're seeking silver ones, tomorrow Nickledown will be filled with visitors, and you will most certainly find some who are. Tomorrow is a Silver Day, you see."

Tomorrow. Another whole day to wait, thought Kurt.

Just then, he noticed a peculiar stand of nickel trees in the center of the lawn that formed the Town Square. It consisted of twelve perfectly matched trees, spaced evenly, one from the other, like the numbers on the face of a clock. What purpose such an arrangement was meant to serve was not at all apparent. If there had been some sort of spire at their center, the trees could have perhaps served as a sundial. But there was nothing at the center but lush, green lawn.

"What's that ring of trees?" Kurt asked Mother Nickle-Dickle.

"The Circle of Beginnings," the woman replied.

"What's it for?"

"It is believed all nickel trees have their roots in the Circle."

"Then it's a monument."

"It's thought of as a wellspring," replied the tiny woman.

"Mother Nickle-Dickle, I need to find something called the Cornerstone. Some animals say it's in Nickledown. Do you know anything about it?"

"I know all there is to know about it. The legend of a Cornerstone has been with us since the beginning of Whiskers time. As for the stone itself, I'm afraid it's only legend. No one has ever seen such a stone."

"It doesn't exist?"

"Only as myth," replied Mother Nickle-Dickle.

Kurt's heart sank along with his hope. No Cornerstone. How could it be? He had truly believed the stone existed. The there'n not-hares, though uncertain of its whereabouts, had not questioned its existence. What was it they said?

> "Locked within the Cornerstone,
> Words to lead from here to there.
> Answers you must find alone,
> The who, the what, the why, the where."

Kurt felt angry at himself for being so gullible. "I should have listened to Stinkle. He warned me not to wager a wag on anything the there'n not-hares had to say. Now I have to find someone silver to help me, just like Spinneret said. But who can say if Spinneret knew what she was talking about. After all, she believed the legend of the Cornerstone, too. Maybe no one in Whiskers knows the way home."

Kurt was jolted from his angry lament by the realization that Mother Nickle-Dickle had heard every word of it. The tiny woman looked troubled. "You're weary," she said. "Come home with me and have a hot bath. Soon Father Nickle-Dickle will be home, and we'll have supper and a warm bed for you and Charlie. You may stay with us as long as you like."

The words were welcome, and Kurt was about to accept the Nickle-Dickle's kind invitation when his attention was drawn elsewhere. From behind him there came a flurry of chimes. When he turned to look, he found the nickel trees in the Circle ringing wildly, as though they had been set upon by a strong wind. But there was no wind, only the ever-present soft and pleasant breeze. After a moment, the trees settled to gentle chiming again.

"What was that all about?" Kurt said, turning to Mother Nickle-Dickle.

"What was *what* all about?" the woman replied.

Kurt realized she had not noticed the flurry, and he was about to explain to her what he had heard, when all at once something more incredible happened. In the center of the Circle there appeared a gigantic rock.

Kurt wondered if perhaps his eyes were playing tricks on him. "Mother Nickle-Dickle, what's that?" he asked excitedly, pointing toward the rock.

"It's as I've told you. The Circle of Beginnings."

"No. The other. The . . ."

Kurt stared at the woman. Was it possible she couldn't see the rock? Perhaps he was only imagining it himself. When he looked again at the Circle, Grandfather's words flashed across his mind. "You must sometimes see what is not there and temper the tune of what you hear . . ."

Kurt glanced quickly at Mother Nickle-Dickle then turned and ran toward the rock. He stopped short outside the Circle of Beginnings and stared curiously between the trees at the huge stone, which he half expected to disappear upon closer observation. But there it stood, steadfastly waiting for him, as staunch and solid as it first appeared.

Kurt was certain the rock was real, but due to the unexplained way it had manifested itself, he was reluctant to move closer. Someone—some *force*—must certainly have placed it there. Someone powerful, no doubt. Perhaps someone terrible!

Despite his apprehension, he felt drawn to the rock. At length, he mustered his courage, took a deep breath, and stepped resolutely between the trees and into the Circle.

The rock was very large indeed. "Boulder" would better describe it, for it was several feet taller than Kurt and its width nearly equaled its height. But it did not appear to have been naturally formed, as boulders are. Instead it was roughly chiseled, as though it had been shaped by the hand of a sculptor to resemble the Silver Mountain.

On the rock's face was a smooth, polished area, one foot by one foot square, upon which was carved in relief yet another mountain—another representation of the Silver Mountain—at its foot, a pastoral scene of an animal kingdom, and atop its peak, the finely engraved bust of a bird—a vulture by all appearances—whose head was ornately adorned with scrollwork resembling a crown.

A chill ran the length of Kurt's spine. He had seen that engraving before—that face of a bird.

Quickly, he withdrew his father's key from his shirtfront and compared the avian face on the key to the one engraved on the rock. They were identical.

The person who forged the key must have also carved the rock, he reasoned. But for what purpose? Drawing nearer to the carving, he looked to see if perchance there was a keyhole of some sort thereabout, knowing of no other purpose for which the key should be so tied to the mysterious boulder. Finding none, and feeling foolish, he tucked the key away.

It must be some kind of monument, he concluded at last; and with that he despaired. It *was* a monument—one that seemed even more formidable as he stood within reach of it, but a monument just the same, nothing more. He would find no help here.

Downhearted and discouraged, he ran his fingers over the carving. The moment he touched the stony surface, a shock like an electric current ran up his arm, and he jerked his hand away. He could hardly believe what happened next.

The ground beneath his feet began to tremble. He heard a rumbling, as though a mighty stone were being rolled away, and on the face of the boulder, there appeared a doorway.

The tall arched opening offered no clue as to what lay beyond. Kurt felt as though he were peering into a long, dark tunnel with no end in sight. As he gazed into the darkness, a strange tingling traveled the length of his whiskers and he felt his heart begin to pound. In one soul-shaking moment, he realized what was happening. This was no mere monument. This was the seed of hope for which he had been so grievously searching. Spinneret and the there'n not-hares had been right after all. The stone was real, the legend true—and he had proved its truth. He had found the elusive Cornerstone!

After hesitating a moment to gather his courage, he stepped through the doorway into the darkness and at once heard a massive *boom!* as though a great stone door had slammed shut behind him.

The tomb-like chamber in which he found himself quickly filled with a dim, gray light that coldly revealed the room's chiseled walls. When he looked about, he saw the floor, the ceiling, even the place where the doorway had been, all were solid rock. Strangely enough, he was not afraid. Instead, he felt comforted, as in the passage when the heartbeat nurtured him.

Soon, colored light appeared, just as it had in the passage—purple, blue, green, yellow, orange, pink. The pink remained.

Flower scents accompanied each color, too, as in the passage. But here, there was no sound—no heartbeat, no music. Only silence. Total and complete silence.

In the center of the chamber stood a pedestal made of solid oak. Kurt had noticed no pedestal when first he entered the chamber, but now, there it stood. And a book lay upon it.

"Notch!" he cried, hurrying to the pedestal. "There's a book!"

Into the thickness of the volume's brown leather cover was carved in relief the same likeness of the Silver Mountain he had seen on the face of the rock. He reached for the book, and the moment his hand touched it, a flute began to play, softly, sweetly, purer and clearer than in the passage. The music seemed far away, yet he heard its notes with such clarity he could almost feel the warm breath of the one who played it. The flute continued to play as, slowly, Kurt opened the book.

The volume's pages were of old parchment that in the light of the chamber took on a pale pink hue. The first page was blank. The second contained a chart of colors in the shape of a ziggurat—purple at the bottom, blue at the next higher step, and green, yellow, orange, and finally pink at the uppermost step. Above the ziggurat was an aura of sparkling light. Though Kurt was certain the aura was merely an image engraved on the parchment, it nevertheless glowed as though an actual light were coming from a source inside the ziggurat. The glow intensified and suddenly a stream of pure, silver light shot toward Kurt's face. He squinted and quickly turned the page.

The next page was a fine lithograph—a map of the Land of Whiskers. Kurt saw the Twelve Gates of Whiskers and determined he must have entered from the west, at the Ninth Gate. He located the Copper Valley and the Nickel Hills and the Silver Mountain with Nickledown at the foot of its western slope.

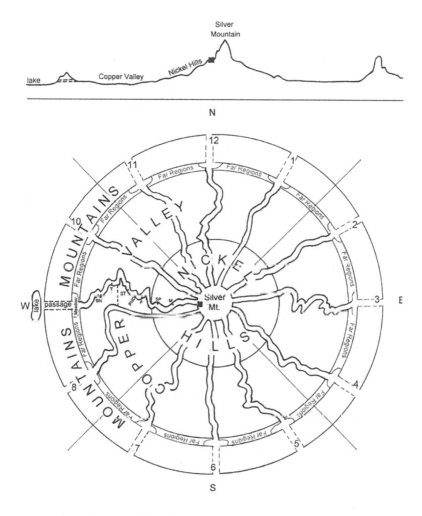

When he turned to the next page, he was bewildered by what appeared to be words of a puzzle. The words were written in bold script, and as he read them, a surge of excitement overwhelmed him. Here lay the key to his greatest desire. Here lay the longed-for ray of hope—steps on the path leading home. It seemed he had only to uncover three secrets:

> *For you who holds The Book in hand,*
> *Who seeks to leave this rainbow Land,*
> *A door awaits, so you are told,*
> *If first three secrets you unfold:*

199

Reveal the first, **set all aright**
So the door may appear *within your sight.*

Reveal the second and **bring to light**
The door itself *when the time is right.*

Reveal the third before the night
And **the door will open** *for homeward flight.*

Clues to the three secrets were there on the page, along with a firm directive: HONE YOUR WHISKERS AND KNOW THE TRUTH!

Kurt concentrated so intently his whiskers tingled as he read the clues to the three secrets:

The first is like unto the second:
REACH DEEP WITHIN THE HALLOWED GROUND;
FIND HARMONY THAT HAS NO SOUND.

The second is like unto the first:
CLIMB UP THE STEEP AND ROCKY GRADE;
FIND SWEETNESS THERE THAT DOES NOT FADE.

The third, unlike the other two,
A silver one must give to you.

Kurt could do no more than stare at the words. The clues made no sense. They would take a great deal of thought.

He turned the page again, and a poem appeared. It was written in silver script that glowed softly in the pink light of the chamber. He read the poem:

To him who reads The Book of Light,
Who heard the Piper's call to flight:
Gaze upon this parchment page;
Play upon this paper stage.
Read what others cannot see.
These silver words were penned for thee.

Lift The Book from off the shelf.
Hold its words within yourself.
Never let The Book be far.
Keep it close to where you are.
Turn its pages one by one.
Your rainbow journey has begun!

When again Kurt turned the page, he found the next one blank, and the one after that, and all the others after that. He was perplexed. The poem had instructed him to keep the book with him, but he was not sure why—he had read everything in it. Obediently, he lifted the volume from the pedestal and turned toward the place where the doorway had been. Instantly the tall opening reappeared.

Kurt stepped through to the outside, and when he turned and looked behind him, the doorway was gone. He glanced around briefly at the Circle of Beginnings, and when he looked over his shoulder again, the stone itself had disappeared.

"Notch, did you see that?" he said, remembering the worm. He dropped the book on the ground and snatched Notch's newspaper from his shirt pocket; but when he unfolded the paper, the booknotch was not on it.

"Notch!" he cried in panic as his thoughts flashed back to the Cornerstone. Could Notch have fallen out of his pocket inside the chamber? Had the stone disappeared with Notch inside?

All at once he heard a small voice coming from somewhere near his feet. When he looked down, he saw the book had fallen open when he dropped it, and there on one of the pages stood Notch, looking up at him, grinning from little green ear to little green ear.

"Here I am, Kurt."

"How did you get there?" Kurt asked, relieved to see the worm.

Notch smiled. "I crawled from the paper onto the book while you were reading. I guess you were too busy to notice me. Oh, Kurt! Isn't it wonderful! I'm in a book at last. And such a fine book! The script is exquisite! And the pages! Such delicate parchment! I never imagined there could be a book as splendid as this one. I should like to stay in it forever!"

"I don't see why you can't," said Kurt. "And I'm sorry I dropped you. I'll be more careful from now on."

"I'm sure you will, Kurt. No harm was done. Besides, I'm certain no ill could ever befall me in a book such as this one."

"I'm sure it couldn't," said Kurt.

He was happy for the booknotch—*and* for himself. The little worm's dream had been fulfilled, and now there was hope he and Charlie would find their way home.

Kurt looked around for Charlie and spotted him in the Rainbow Garden smelling the roses. When he called to the dog, Charlie came running. "Did you see that, boy?" said Kurt. "Notch has a book—this one. He's in it now. We were in a rock. It was the Cornerstone, Charlie. We found it!"

Charlie wagged his tail excitedly. He did not use words, but Kurt knew the dog was glad.

Just then, Mother Nickle-Dickle walked over to Kurt. "You ran away so quickly I was unable to hear your reply to my invitation," she said.

Kurt was surprised at Mother Nickle's lack of excitement. He had not imagined the Cornerstone. It was real and he had the book to prove it. Surely the tiny woman had seen him enter the stone, yet she acted as though nothing out of the ordinary had taken place. In fact, none of the animals in the Town Square seemed to notice the strange occurrence—an occurrence that should have caused quite a stir. Kurt recalled how, at first, he had not seen the huge boulder—only lush green grass within the Circle of Beginnings—and it occurred to him that perhaps Mother Nickle-Dickle and the others had seen nothing out of the ordinary after all.

"I'm sorry," Kurt said to Mother Nickle-Dickle. "Yes, I *will* come home with you. Thank you."

Kurt and Charlie followed the kindly woman to her little whitewashed house on the cobblestone street adjoining the Rainbow

Garden. Inside the house, Kurt opened the book and introduced the booknotch to Mother Nickle-Dickle before placing the volume, with Notch in it, safely away in his backpack. After a soothing bath, he sat at the kitchen table, with Charlie at his feet, and watched Mother Nickle-Dickle prepare a pot of vegetable porridge for supper. "Mother Nickle-Dickle," he said, "tell me about Silver Days in Nickledown."

"On Silver Days," said Mother Nickle-Dickle, "a flute plays at dawn and a silver rain falls. The flute is faint and far off in the distance, but you can hear it if you're awake. And a gentle breeze comes to play music in the nickel trees to waken all who sleep. The breeze dries the rain and leaves behind a silver dust that makes the day sparkle."

"It sounds beautiful."

"It is. And all throughout the day, we and the animals congregate with our friends to talk and sing and eat and play games. At the end of the day, the breeze returns to gather the dust. But there's more to Silver Day than just those things."

"What do you mean?"

Mother Nickle-Dickle put down the spoon she was using to stir the porridge and sat beside Kurt at the table. There was a tone of quiet reverence in her voice when next she spoke. "Silver Day is a time when lost animals from all over the land come together. Some have traveled for many days from the Far Regions. Precisely at noon, when the sun is highest in the sky, the lost animals gather with those of us who have always lived in Whiskers, and they say the names of the loved ones they left behind in that other world, so as never to forget them. It is believed, in some unexplained way, their thoughts touch the hearts of those they left behind, causing them to think of their beloved animals at precisely that same moment."

Charlie looked up at Mother Nickle-Dickle. "Do you think my sister, Chrysalis, will come for Silver Day? She could be in Whiskers. She lost herself a long time ago."

"If she's here, perhaps she will," replied Mother Nickle-Dickle, smiling kindly at Charlie.

The tiny woman got up from the table and resumed her cooking. The lull in the conversation gave Kurt time to reflect upon the lost animals. He thought about Parhelion the Nimbus and wondered if he were a lost animal, or if he had always lived in Whiskers. He wasn't sure just what a Nimbus was. "Have you ever seen Parhelion?" he asked Mother Nickle-Dickle.

The tiny woman seemed surprised at Kurt's question, so he told her about his brief encounter with the shadow in the Meadow.

"No one ever sees Parhelion," said Mother Nickle-Dickle. "They see only his shadow. No one knows where he lives, though some think it's high on the Silver Mountain—perhaps beyond. Some believe he is silver. Others believe him to be the color of darkness below purple."

"If he lives on the Mountain," said Kurt, "he would know about a door leading back to my world, wouldn't he? I mean, from up there, he could see anything—even a door if there is one."

"A door? Perhaps. But no one knows how to find the Nimbus. No one, to my knowledge, has ever tried to find him. And you dare not risk going up the Silver Mountain. According to legend, the silver trees that grow there can lull you to sleep—to a sleep from which you might never awaken. It's better you seek others for your answers and forget about the Nimbus."

Mother Nickle-Dickle had left the porridge to simmer on the stove and was putting icing on a large chocolate layer cake. "It's a birthday cake," she said when she noticed Kurt staring at it. "—a Silver Day tradition."

"Whose birthday is it?"

"Why yours, of course—and all the lost animals. They always arrive in the Land of Whiskers on a Silver Day, so every Silver Day is their birthday."

A great idea, thought Kurt. A birthday every week!

Kurt heard the front door open, and in walked a tiny man only a wee bit taller than Mother Nickle-Dickle, wearing piebald clothes much like hers. His shirt and pants were made entirely of pink-and-yellow patches, his vest was fashioned of the selfsame stripe, and round

204

his neck was loosely tied a scarf of pink-and-yellow check. The man removed a silver tuning fork from his vest pocket and carefully placed it in a crystal case on a nearby shelf. It was Father Nickle-Dickle, home from a day of tuning the nickel trees.

The diminutive man's cordial manner, when he was introduced to Kurt and told something of his story, immediately made the boy feel welcome. "Our home will be your home," he said.

Father Nickle-Dickle glanced at Kurt's feet. "You have no shoes. That will never do," and he left the room and soon returned with a pair of his own shoes, which he handed to Kurt. "A little gift to welcome you."

Kurt thanked the Nickle-Dickle and placed the shoes on his feet. They felt a bit strange, being not exactly the right size.

Father Nickle-Dickle watched Kurt walk awkwardly around the room. "It's hard at first to walk in the shoes of another," said Father Nickle-Dickle, "but it becomes easier the longer you try."

Mother Nickle-Dickle called Kurt and Charlie and Father Nickle-Dickle to supper. It was a delicious supper of porridge and biscuits with pudding for dessert. The birthday cake, after all, was for the morrow—the morrow, with its promise of wondrous delights: silver rain at dawn, and silver dust, and festivities with food and games and friends. And the search—the search for the first two secrets and a silver one who might know the clue to the third secret. Perhaps even—if no silver one was found—a search for Parhelion.

CHAPTER 17

SILVER DAY

Kurt awoke to the gentle *tap-tap-tap* of early morning rain. As he lay nestled amid the folds of soft bed linens, he could hear ever so faintly the distant, dulcet tones of a flute, whose melody called to him from beyond a dew-soaked mist. Gradually the rain stopped falling, and the melody faded as though the last of the raindrops had washed it away.

Soon a breeze began to play among the nickel trees—the breeze that comes to dry the drops and leave behind the silver dust. It tripped among the metal leaves and drew from them a silver song that rang throughout Nickledown, calling animal and Nickle-Dickle alike to waken. When the drops were dry, the work complete, the breeze gathered itself and went its way as gently as it had come. And in its wake, Nickledown lay glistening under a delicate veil of purest silver.

Recalling Mother Nickle-Dickle's words of the night before, Kurt sprang from his bed and peered through the window glass. It was just as Mother Nickle-Dickle had said. The warm summer morning sparkled with bright, crystalline light. The air itself seemed full of hope and jubilation. It was Silver Day! "Surely on a day such as this I'll find someone who knows the clue to the third secret," Kurt told himself. "Then I can uncover all three secrets and go home."

He quickly grabbed his backpack, withdrew the book, and peeked in at Notch. Finding the little worm fast asleep, and not wanting to wake him, he closed the book and placed it gently on the bedside table.

In the kitchen, he helped Mother and Father Nickle-Dickle pack wares for the day's festivities before he and Charlie headed outside to the Town Square. Already a large crowd had gathered in the square and set up tables whereupon they had spread every culinary confection imaginable.

Kurt watched in amazement as streams of animals filtered in from the side roads and from along the riverbank carrying packs laden with offerings for the celebration. All was abuzz with activity. Hither and thither they moved—in the air above, on the ground below, the young and the old, the large and the small, the long-eared and short-tailed, the short-eared and long-tailed, and others with no tails at all; the winged and the scaled, the fluffy, the fuzzy, the slinky and slick, the spotted and not, the portly, the skinny, the prickly and smooth; slipping and sliding ones, hopping and jumping ones, barkers and purrers and squeakers galore; and an oinker or two, and also a few who carried trunks way up front. And some had pouches with young ones inside who happily came along for the ride and giggled and squealed at the sight of it all, especially the cakes and the pies.

Charlie's hopes of finding his sister rose when he saw the vast number of animals parading into Nickledown. "Look at them all," he said to Kurt. "Someone must know if she's here."

The dog romped up and down the lines of visitors asking everyone he met if they knew his little sister. "Her name is Chrysalis. She's a waggle-lick just like me, only she's smaller and beautiful and kind of shy and she has a small white spot on her neck that's shaped like a freshwater pearl. Have you seen her?"

Finally a group of waggle-licks from a neighboring region recognized the description and gave Charlie directions to where they thought she might be found. Charlie was overcome with joy, and he quickly told Kurt his plan to find Chrysalis.

"Charlie, that's so far away," said Kurt. "And what if it's not even her?"

"I have to find out," Charlie said excitedly. And he jumped up and gave Kurt a quick lick on the chin and dashed away.

"Wait!" Kurt shouted after the dog. "If I find the third clue and learn the secrets"—Charlie was too far away to hear him—"we'll be going home," he added quietly.

Kurt's fear for the dog's safety was somewhat dispelled by the fact there were so many animals on the roads leading to Nickledown. Convinced Charlie would easily find help if needed, Kurt turned his thoughts to the task at hand and set about walking around the Town Square looking for animals he thought might be silver. At one point, he stopped to watch a group of tiny Nickle-Dickle children laughing and giggling as they skipped rope to the rhythm of a rhyme:

Tree kibble, tribble, tribble,
Tree kibble, take a bite.

Tree kibble, dribble, dribble,
Down the chin and out of sight.

Tree kibble, nibble, nibble,
Double helping late at night.

Double trouble, tree kibble,
Tribble trouble, what a fright!

When the children finished the rhyme, they dropped the rope and formed a circle, holding hands. "Let's sing the Piper's song," one of them said, and they began singing as they danced in a circle:

Hear the pipe and skip along.
Sing the Piper's happy song!
Leave your cares and come along to Nickledown.

See the twinkling nickel trees
Hear their music in the breeze,
Softly calling, "Hurry, please, to Nickledown."

209

Except for their diminutive size, the young Nickle-Dickles looked much like the children at Kurt's school playing at recess on a bright sunshiny day.

"What's that song they're singing?" Kurt asked a hedgehog, who had also stopped to listen.

"It's a song that's been passed down from generation to generation among the Nickle-Dickles," said the hedgehog. "No one knows where it came from."

Kurt watched the children a moment longer and smiled a melancholy smile and walked on.

The morning passed quickly, and precisely at noon, when the sun was at its highest, the merry-making ceased and all became quiet. The Nickle-Dickles and those animals born in the Land of Whiskers gathered in silence with the lost animals, the way kindred spirits will, and the lost animals remembered loved ones left in that other world and spoke their names so as never to forget those who shared their lives before. When the sun moved past the midday point, Silver Day festivities resumed, but now there existed a renewed and cherished bond among the celebrants.

Kurt talked to many animals in the Town Square after the noon ceremony and found a few who were silver, but none could give him the clue to the third secret. He decided his only hope lay in finding Parhelion, so in early afternoon he went to the riverbank to contemplate the first two secrets and devise a plan to find the Nimbus. After all, he reasoned, he had always done his best thinking by the water's edge. Why should it be any different here?

As he sat with his back resting against a large boulder, he realized fully the difficulty of the task. How does one find a Nimbus? How does one summon a shadow? Perhaps he would have to climb the Silver Mountain and seek the creature's dwelling place. But Mother Nickle-Dickle had warned against that.

He was beginning to doubt he would find the Nimbus at all when suddenly he felt a penetrating chill. He glanced up just as a dark shadow passed over him. The shadow was huge and of bird-like proportion, its depth of blackness so frightening that Kurt jumped up, darted behind the boulder, and crouched there waiting for the shadow to glide out of sight. It was not until the darkness was well past him that he realized his blunder and called after the Nimbus, "Parhelion!" But the creature was well on its way upriver.

Kurt was furious at himself. The Nimbus had been directly above him. "All I had to do was shout," he scolded. "I could have asked him about the secret. But what did I do? I acted like a coward." He grabbed a stick from the ground and took a well-aimed swing at the boulder before throwing the stick down. "First I was afraid of that bully, Duff Skruggs. Then I was afraid of a bird. How could I be so stupid? Next time I won't hide. Next time I'll face him square-on and ask him about the secret."

Kurt headed back to the Town Square more determined than ever to find Parhelion. He was thankful Charlie had not been present to witness his cowardice.

Back at the square, Silver Day festivities were in full swing. Despite invitations and coaxing from several animals, Kurt had no heart for joining the celebrants. Even the pies and cakes looked unappealing. All he could think about was finding the Nimbus.

He looked up at the mountain looming above the town and realized what a formidable task it would be to climb it. "The map!" he said to himself, remembering the one in the book. "If I study the map, maybe I'll come up with another place to find Parhelion—someplace other than the mountain."

Without hesitating, he ran to Mother and Father Nickle-Dickle's house, fetched the book, and hurriedly returned to the square, where he plopped down under a shade tree. When he opened the book's cover, the volume popped open precisely to the page he had last been reading—the page with the poem.

"Ah!" screamed a familiar voice from the ground.

"Notch! I'm sorry. I didn't mean to knock you out of the book."

"I'm all right," said the booknotch, brushing dust from his green body. "I'm a bit jostled, but uninjured. I was sliding down a z when you opened the book, and I *z-z-zipped!* right off the page." The little worm blushed.

"Come sit with me and pull yourself together," Kurt said, and he lifted the booknotch up to a place on his knee. "I was just about to look at the map."

"Oh," said the booknotch. "I thought perhaps you were going to read the other pages."

"Other pages? *What* other pages?" Kurt quickly flipped through to the back of the book. "The rest of the pages are blank."

"Oh, but there are many things written in that book," said Notch. "The pages may *appear* blank, but I can feel the letters. They're very close—just beneath the surface."

"Really!" Kurt speculated on what might be written there, and recalling his reason for opening the book, quickly turned to the page with the map and ran his fingers over it, searching for a likely spot to find the Nimbus. "I have to find Parhelion. I thought the map would help."

The booknotch turned pale. "Parhelion? Parhelion the Nimbus?"

"Yes," said Kurt. "I have to ask him if he knows the clue to the third secret."

The worm shuddered. "When I was living in the Copper Valley, I heard talk of Parhelion—talk of his shadow, that is. I'm not sure anyone has ever seen *him*. But where there is shadow, there must also be substance. And the shadow is shaped like a bird, they say. And if there's one thing a worm learns to distance himself from, it's a bird."

"But Notch, Stinkle said no one in Whiskers was lower than blue, so how could Parhelion possibly hurt you?" Kurt said the words, but he recalled the fear he felt when the shadow passed over him by the river's edge.

"I also heard Mother Nickle-Dickle say some believe him to be the color of darkness below purple," said Notch. "How can we be certain *what* color he is?" The little worm held the back of his palm to his forehead as though he were checking his temperature. "Could you put me back in the book now, Kurt. All this talk of the Nimbus has made me rather ill."

"Of course," said Kurt. "You do look a little pale."

"Thank you," the booknotch replied. "I believe I shall find a comforting c in which to cradle myself."

Kurt picked up the worm and placed him in the book—on the page with the map—and closed the book ever so gently.

CHAPTER 18

LEGENDS

Since his study of the map provided no likelier place to find the Nimbus, Kurt decided he would have to seek Parhelion on the Silver Mountain. But climbing the mountain could prove fatal. Stinkle and Mother Nickle-Dickle had warned him about the legendary silver trees rumored to grow there. As a precautionary measure, he decided to find out as much as he could about the trees before embarking on such a dangerous venture. With that in mind, he returned the book to the house and made his way back to the Town Square, where he spent the rest of the afternoon talking to as many animals as he could. All of them echoed the same warning: "Do not climb the Silver Mountain." But none could tell him any more than he already knew about the silver trees.

One animal, a friendly raccoon who was orange, said, "If you must go up the Mountain, try not to trample the abacus flowers." Kurt recalled Stinkle mentioning the abacus flowers and he asked the raccoon what they looked like.

"They're believed to be the sweetest flowers in the Land of Whiskers," said the raccoon. "Pure white they are. And according to legend, each blossom is just as it was since the day it first bloomed. Some have been with us since the beginning of Whiskers time—when the first Nickle-Dickles planted the seeds. There is thought to be one blossom for every animal and Nickle-Dickle and crawling creature living in Whiskers, so the number increases, but never decreases."

"Would they die if you picked them?" asked Kurt.

"Die?" said the raccoon, looking puzzled.

"You know—fade," explained Kurt. "I would like to take a bunch to my mother when I go home, but not if they're going to die." He corrected himself. "Fade, I mean."

"I can't be certain," said the raccoon. "No one has ever picked them to my knowledge."

Kurt thanked the raccoon for his help and returned to the shade tree to mull over what he knew about the silver trees and abacus flowers, and to ponder the first two clues. "If I find Parhelion and he gives me the third clue, I still won't know the first two secrets. What was it the book said? 'Reach deep within the hallowed ground. Find harmony that has no sound.' Maybe it's the nickel trees. Father Nickle-Dickle tunes them and makes them harmonious." He paused and considered. "But they can't be as harmonious as the silver trees. *Their* music is so beautiful it can put you to sleep forever. It's *got* to be the silver trees. And they grow on the Silver Mountain. If that's not hallowed ground, I don't know what is." He considered again. "But that's no good. The book said, 'harmony that has no sound' and silver trees have sound—a sound so beautiful you can't listen to it."

Suddenly he realized what he had said. "That's it'! You can't listen! If I cover my ears, I won't be able to hear the music. The trees will have no sound. The silver trees *are* the answer to the first secret!"

Feeling proud of himself, he turned his attention to the next clue. "'Climb up the steep and rocky grade. Find sweetness there that does not fade.' The flowers in the Rainbow Garden are sweet. They're the sweetest things I've ever smelled. Only . . . they're no secret. Everyone knows where they are. Besides, Charlie stepped on some yesterday and they faded."

Just then a mother raccoon passed by with three young ones following close behind. "Abacus flowers!" Kurt cried out, recalling his conversation with the raccoon who was orange. "The raccoon said they're the sweetest flowers in the Land of Whiskers, and no one has ever seen them fade. And they grow on the Silver Mountain, so I would have to climb a steep and rocky grade to get them. The abacus flowers are the answer to the second secret!"

Again Kurt felt proud of himself. He knew if he put his mind to it he would find the answers. Now he would have to find Parhelion and ask for the third clue. Then he could figure out the third secret, and he would have all three.

He quickly devised a plan: "I'll climb the Silver Mountain and find the abacus flowers and pick a huge bunch. And I'll find the silver trees and break off a large branch. Then I'll go to the top of the mountain and call Parhelion and ask for the third clue. I'll bring the flowers and the branch back to Nickledown for everyone to see. Then I'll figure out the third secret, and when Charlie comes back, we'll go home. And to think, I can do it all in one day!"

Despite the fact animals and Nickle-Dickles were busy all around him packing wares and folding tables and streaming in long lines out of town, Kurt took no notice of the activity until he felt the breeze that comes to gather the silver dust. His mind was on the task ahead. "I'll get a good night's sleep and start out in the morning," he told himself. And he hurried as quickly as he could to the little house on the cobblestone street.

CHAPTER 19

THE SILVER MOUNTAIN

Kurt awoke before dawn, having spent a restless night, his dreams besieged with images of Parhelion's shadow and voracious, man-eating raptors, and steep walls of blistering rock towering above dark, bottomless pits. He worked hard to convince himself he had only been dreaming and the climb up the mountain would hold no such terrors. This was the day that could bring the much-longed-for journey home if he followed his plan to the letter, and he was not about to have a few bad dreams interfere with his plan.

Anxious to be on his way, he called his dog, forgetting for a moment Charlie's quest to find Chrysalis. He understood Charlie's need to find his sister, but he would rather have had the dog safe at home with Mother and Father Nickle-Dickle as he embarked on his perilous climb.

Quickly, he dressed himself and packed a lunch, putting the book, with Notch inside, into the backpack. The poem had said to keep the book with him. He had forgotten to do so yesterday, having become preoccupied with Silver Day activities and finding the Nimbus.

Before the sun was fully up, he was on his way to the river's edge. He walked until he reached a spot that offered a clear view of the mountain, and there he stopped to study the steep, narrow path running upward and out of sight on the mountain's side. The mountain itself appeared much higher now that he planned to climb it. He had not noticed before how its uppermost peak reached almost to the clouds. "Perhaps I won't have to climb all the way up," he told himself. "Perhaps I'll find the silver trees and abacus flowers halfway up. No one said they grew all the way at the top. And I'm sure Parhelion would hear me from only halfway up." Realizing his resolve was weakening, and determined not to allow that to happen, he forced himself to walk on.

The sun was well up by the time he reached the foot of the mountain path and began his climb. At first he walked with ease, enjoying the fresh mountain air and warm sunlight on his face. He even stopped once to chat with two mountain goats traveling in the opposite direction. But the air grew uncomfortably thin as higher and higher he climbed, watching Nickledown grow smaller and smaller below him. When he reached a great height, there was still no sign of the abacus flowers or silver trees. Only sweet grasses and scraggly shrubs grew among the many outcroppings of barren rock lining the path.

Gradually the trail became less and less a path and more and more a narrow shelf, as the land to one side of it dropped away. At one point Kurt had to turn sideways and inch his way past an outgrowth of jagged granite projecting from the mountain's side to travel on. Not far past the protruding rock, the trail widened again and turned sharply inward. Soon thereafter Kurt found himself at the base of a rocky knoll. Though greatly in need of a rest, he pushed himself to climb upward past the many small boulders and scattered patches of brush that littered the knoll. When at last he found a soft stand of grass near the top, he slumped to the ground, lightheaded and out of breath.

Perhaps it was this brief, involuntary respite that gained him strength to stand and gaze at the land on the other side of the knoll; or perhaps it was the sweet elixir drifting toward him from the blanket of white covering the field beyond. Whatever his source of strength, he stood. And there before him, spread across a vast mountain meadow, as far as his eyes could see, lay a dazzling display of pure white blossoms.

"Abacus flowers!" he cried, running wildly down the knoll and through the meadow. "Wonderful, glorious abacus flowers!"

The blossoms were larger than he expected, looking very much like Easter lilies, so gathering a bunch as he had planned was out of the question. "I'll pick two—one for me and one for Charlie," he said when he had caught his breath. "And one for you, too, Notch!" he called out.

The boy snapped the long, thick stems carefully so as not to damage the plants themselves. That way, he reasoned, they would bloom again someday. As he separated each blossom from its mother plant, a strange sadness overtook him; but after he had pushed the stems securely into his backpack, the feeling subsided and he felt jubilant at having achieved his first goal. "We did it, Notch!" he shouted. "We got the abacus flowers! Onward to the silver trees!"

He found the place on the far side of the meadow where the path resumed and again started upward. An hour passed, but still there was no sign of the silver trees. He was feeling more lightheaded now due to the extreme thinness of the air at this higher elevation. As climbing became more and more difficult, the terrain became more and more creviced and barren. In places, deep ravines crossed his path, and he had to jump them to continue.

Nickledown was but a speck on the hillside below now, and Kurt began to worry that, should his search for the silver trees take him much past noon, he might not make it back to the town before nightfall. In the dark, he would risk falling into one of the ravines.

He was weighing the wisdom of climbing farther when he heard a faint tinkling. It was a light and delicate sound, like a crystal chandelier caught in a breeze. "The silver trees!" he cried, as a stand of the glistening arbors suddenly appeared on the path in front of him. He was sure they had not been there a moment earlier, but there they stood, fixed like sentinels, their leaves shimmering in the morning sun.

The trees began to play. Their music sifted over the boy like fairy dust strewn from the tip of a magic wand.

Kurt felt a weakness overtake him and he quickly threw his hands over his ears. But already the soft, sinuous strains had engraved a song of enchantment upon his memory. He felt his eyelids grow heavy, his muscles weak. He reeled aimlessly as he fought the overwhelming urge to sleep.

In one frantic effort to reach his goal, he released his hands from his ears and lunged headlong toward one of the trees, aiming to pluck a low-hanging branch. But the branch had no substance. His hand passed through it as though through air.

Suddenly there was no ground beneath his feet. He felt himself falling—headfirst and down—down into the black cleft of a deep ravine. A short tumble, a jarring jolt! and he found himself lying on his stomach on a slanted slab of rock, several yards below the top of the ravine.

Shaken but unharmed, he dug his fingers into the slick surface seeking a crack or crevice—any kind of handhold that might allow him to pull himself up and out, or at the very least, anything that might keep him from sliding farther into the cleft. But there was no handhold. He felt his fingers slip—and down he went!—down, down, down like a child on a sliding board—down until he stopped with a *thump*! on the cold, hard floor of the rocky ravine.

The pit in which he landed was black as pitch. With his heart pounding wildly, he peered into the darkness waiting for his eyes to adjust enough to show him if further danger lay about—more clefts perhaps that would use a careless move on his part to thrust him deeper into the pit. But the darkness was too dense, too black, to be penetrated by the eyes of a mere mortal; and for the sake of his sanity, it was good he did not surmise an *im*mortal might be lurking nearby.

When he had caught his breath and gathered his wits, he ran his hands over the ground on all sides of him. Finding it solid, he stood shakily and looked up at the small speck of light hanging like a shiny jewel at the top of the ravine, dangling well out of reach. Knowing he would never be able to climb to it, he realized fully the dire consequences of his predicament, and despair overtook him. He would surely die in this fathomless pit, alone and cold and hungry. No one would know what happened to him, for he had not told Mother or Father Nickle-Dickle his plan to climb the mountain. And what about

Charlie? The dog would think he had discovered the secrets and left for home without him. Charlie would feel betrayed by the one he loved most; his heart would be broken. And Notch—Kurt remembered the book was in the backpack and Notch was in the book. "Notch!" he called out, half crying. The thought that his foolish endeavors would forever entomb the tiny worm made his pain even more unbearable.

"Can anyone hear me!" he shouted, looking up at the tiny speck of light above his head. "Help me! I'm down here! Help me!" In reply, his words bounced off the cavern walls, echoing, "Help me . . . Help me . . . Help me . . ."

When the last of his words drifted into nothingness and all became still again, his ear detected a sound it had not noticed before. Ever so faint it was at first—and airy—like someone breathing. The breathing turned to sighing, and the sighs led to stirring, and the stirring led to deep and troubled breaths, as when a sleeper is rousted from a much-needed nap.

All at once a rumble filled the cavern—a dim and dreary rum-tum-grumble.

In the far recesses of the pit there appeared two small dots the size of marbles, red and glowing. They disappeared and reappeared—quickly—like eyes blinking.

Now the eyes remained open, fixed and staring, spitting out hot red embers that zigzagged upward, sizzling, and snapping like tinder in a well-stoked fire.

With a sudden chill, Kurt remembered Tattle's tail about the creature who battled the large Nickle-Dickle:

> *"Buried in the earth so crusty,*
> *Mired within his cavern musty,*
> *Lurks the seed of rumbling roll,*
> *The foul, the fetid, Thunder Troll!"*

Kurt's heart began to race. From deep in the darkness, the thirsty eyes began to move. Ever so slowly they inched toward the boy, growing redder and hotter the closer they drew.

Kurt took a deep breath and, despite his trembling, held himself fixed and fast, hoping he would seem to the one who owned the eyes but a smudge of shadow against the cavern wall.

A rumbling growl—a lumbering footstep! The chamber shook! And the eyes advanced.

All at once Kurt heard a long and hollow inward rush of air, as though a massive breath were being drawn into an empty chamber. A moment later, a frigid rush of musty air blew toward him, filling his nostrils with a stale, rancid, mummy-like stench. The sickening gust swirled about his shoulders, wrapping his body in a bone-chilling cold.

Another lumbering footstep—and the ground began to shake, the walls began to rattle. Small boulders, dislodged from cliffs above, tumbled down the steep ravine and bounced like spilled beads across the cavern floor.

With so great a fury did the eyes burn now, they cast a red and flickering light upon the chamber walls. Against the stony backdrop, Kurt could see dimly the misshapen form that owned the eyes—a nebulous figure blacker than the pit itself—a figure the color of darkness below purple—moving toward him.

The creature drew to a halt in front of Kurt and stooped, peering down into the boy's eyes. Kurt's knees began to buckle. All strength left his body. Surely he would collapse at any moment. With all his might he fought to shun the creature's gaze. But his will was no match for the thirsty stare. It locked his gaze. He could look neither left nor right, only stand transfixed by the mesmerizing flames that writhed within the molten eyes.

From the corner of his eye, Kurt saw the creature lift a moldy arm whose hanging folds of rotting flesh gave off a stench more putrid than the creature's breath. Kurt tried not to breathe as a shadowy hand, gnarled and claw-like, reached toward him, aimed at his shirtfront where hung his father's key.

Kurt felt the key grow warm against his skin. Hotter and hotter it grew until he thought it would surely sear his flesh. He longed to cry out, but the scream lodged itself like a lump in his throat. Just when he was certain his breath would fail him, he felt a rush of wind upon his face and heard a sound from high above—a sound like the mighty flapping of wings.

The molten eyes glanced upward. With his gaze set free, Kurt looked toward the small speck of sky at the top of the ravine. There, cast darkly against the light, was the unmistakable silhouette of a bird!

Kurt watched the silhouette circle, growing larger and larger until it eclipsed the opening, leaving only a dim corona where the light had been. As if to set its mark, the dark raptor raised itself high and away, gave a shrill cry of warning, and dove headlong from the top of the pit. Part way down, it spread its wings to right itself and continued its plunge, its legs stretched to the fore, its razor-sharp talons held open like two colossal claws aimed directly at Kurt.

The lump lodged in Kurt's throat burst forth as a primal scream and he collapsed on the cavern floor.

Reaching its mark, the mammoth bird scooped the boy up by the waist of his pants and soared skyward toward the light. Up and out of the ravine it carried him! Out into the bright sunlight! High over the silver trees! Down the mountainside past rocky outcroppings and steep slopes and mountain meadows filled with abacus flowers! Down to the foot of the Silver Mountain. Landing on the riverbank, it deposited him by the water's edge, and with a powerful flapping of wings and a mighty rush of wind, it ascended into the sky, disappearing into the glare of the noonday sun.

Kurt had been holding his breath so long he had to force himself to breathe. Realizing he was safe and Parhelion was getting away, he shouted after the Nimbus, "Parhelion! Come back! The secret!" But the Nimbus did not answer.

Exhausted, Kurt pulled himself up the riverbank, slipped out of the backpack, and let his trembling body slump to the ground. "At least I have the abacus flowers," he told himself, pulling the pack toward him. But the abacus flowers—the precious answer to the second secret—lay wilted against the blue cloth of the backpack.

"No, no, no!" he wailed. "It was all for nothing. No Parhelion, no branches; not even the abacus flowers. I'll never get home." And he snatched the dead flowers from the pack and threw them to the ground.

That's when he remembered the booknotch.

"Notch, are you all right?" He frantically tore the pack open and grabbed the book. The book opened to the place he had last tucked Notch away. And there on the page sat the booknotch, a little pale, but alive, nonetheless.

"It was terrible. I must have passed out—twice," said Notch. "First when I heard a tinkling sound, and again when I awoke to the unmistakably horrifying flap of approaching wings. What happened?"

"It was Parhelion. We fell into a ravine and he rescued us. You see, he wasn't the color of darkness below purple at all."

The booknotch grimaced. "He may have saved us this time, but who knows about next time. It could very well be he wasn't hungry. Next time we could be his midday snack. I shudder to think of it."

"Maybe," said Kurt. "But that's the chance I'll have to take if I'm ever to see him again. I have to learn the third secret—the first and second now, too, for that matter."

A dark shadow gliding along the riverbank drew Kurt's attention. "It's Parhelion!" he said, scrambling to his feet.

"Close the book!" screamed Notch.

Kurt snapped the book shut and stuffed it into the pack just as the shadow reached the place where he was standing. The shadow circled the boy several times and cast a cool darkness over him—a darkness that grew larger and larger as the substance of the shadow, Parhelion himself, slowly descended from the sky.

Billows of dust rose high into the air as the force of Parhelion's wings stirred the loose soil round about. For some time after the bird touched ground, Kurt could see nothing through the dust but a dim silhouette of gigantic proportion looming above him. When the dust settled, he found himself staring directly into the face of the Nimbus.

CHAPTER 20

PARHELION THE NIMBUS

The bird's head and neck were pink and fleshy, naked like a vulture's. Its strong, hooked beak and long, curved talons marked it as a bird of prey. But this Great Winged Creature was neither vulture nor common bird of prey. Its physical composition suggested a lineage lost in antiquity—behemoth and leviathan of ancient fame coming to mind.

Colossal size and formidable countenance alone, however, could not account for the aura of dominion and might permeating the very atmosphere in proximity to the Nimbus, for surpassing in magnitude the creature's size or countenance was a premier intelligence that revealed itself in the bird's deeply penetrating gaze—an intelligence perhaps omniscient that seemed capable of searching the hearts of lesser creatures and rendering judgment upon their quivering souls.

As Parhelion's cold, yellow eyes stared down at Kurt from the bird's fleshy head, the boy felt other eyes watching him. He looked closer at the dark feathers covering the Nimbus's body—feathers that appeared solidly black from a distance—and realized, to his overwhelming fright, that eye was meeting eye. The bird's feathers were studded with a multitude of lesser eyes, even to the undersides of the creature's wings, and these eyes, unlike those on the feathers of a peacock, were no mere colored markings. These eyes changed direction when the eyes on the bird's head changed direction. These eyes stared when the eyes on the bird's head stared.

The terrible raptor studied the boy from head to foot as method-
ically it folded its massive wings. Kurt could do no more than watch
in awe, mesmerized by the colossal creature's stolid, bone-chilling
stare. What was this Nimbus, he wondered—this all-seeing, vulturous
apparition that cast a dark shadow, yet had appeared in the Meadow
as a flash of light against the sun? This phantom-like avian that one
moment seemed as illusive as a specter veiled in a shroud, the next as
real as its shadow upon the ground?

At last, the Nimbus spoke. "You are the one," said the bird, in a
voice somber, deep, and resonant.

Kurt swallowed the lump in his throat and tried to speak, but
only a soundless breath rushed forth. He cleared his throat and tried
again. "The . . . one?" he stammered weakly.

"The one who seeks the door," replied the Nimbus.

"Yes." Kurt's voice trembled. "And you're P . . . Parhelion."

"You say that I am," said the raptor.

Gathering what little courage he had within him, Kurt begged
the Nimbus, "Please, I need your help. I called to you yesterday, on
Silver Day, when your shadow passed over, but you were too far away
to hear me. I needed to talk to you."

"I could not commune with you then," said the Nimbus. "You
had not *The Book* with you. Were you not instructed to keep *The Book*
with you?"

"Yes," Kurt answered, his voice still shaking. "The poem said to
keep it with me, but I forgot. Besides, there's nothing in that book
except the poem and a chart and a map—and some stuff about secrets."

"Still, you must keep *The Book* with you always. Dwell upon
its words. Take by faith that which you cannot see. Only then can
we commune."

"How can I 'dwell upon' blank pages?" Kurt asked.

"There are many pages in *The Book*," replied the Nimbus, "some
written, some as yet unwritten; others written, but not yet seen. Only
by keeping *The Book* with you will you be able to see what others
cannot see."

Still fearful, but driven by desperation, Kurt forced himself to question the bird further. "You *are* silver, aren't you?" he asked with great caution.

"You have said," replied the Nimbus.

Kurt breathed a sigh of relief, but his ease was short-lived as he felt the creature's icy stare lock upon him and saw the multitudinous eyes follow suit. He wondered if it were possible for an animal to be both silver and evil.

"If you're silver," he said to the Nimbus, "why don't you come to Nickledown on Silver Days? Why do you stay on the mountain all the time?"

"The mountain is my home. And I do not remain there always, as you can see. Am I not here with you now? And did you not see my shadow in the Copper Valley?"

Kurt could find no fault with the bird's logic, and feeling somewhat more relaxed, he stepped back, intending to sit down. But when the Nimbus's myriad eyes followed him, he remained standing.

The stories Kurt had heard about Parhelion had been veiled in mystery. They portrayed the bird as wraithlike and menacing. Determined to learn the truth of the matter, Kurt marshaled strength to question the creature again. "Don't you have any friends? Don't you want to talk to the Nickle-Dickles and the animals?"

"My position necessitates a certain degree of detachment," said the Nimbus. "There *are* those with whom I commune, however. Some forms of communication transcend even the marvelous capabilities of whiskers, young Kurt."

Parhelion's words were lost on the boy. Kurt was more concerned with the fact the Nimbus had called him by name. "You know my name," he blurted nervously.

"I know it well," replied Parhelion, staring at the child intently.

Kurt was certain the Nimbus was reading his thoughts. He could feel a tingling in his whiskers. He was suddenly aware the bird might learn the depths of his fear, and having heard you should never let an animal sense your fear, he threw back his shoulders and stood very straight, attempting to make himself appear larger and strong.

The Nimbus stared a moment longer and relaxed until the skin on his fleshy neck folded down upon itself. "Perhaps I should tell you something of my beginnings in this land," he said. "I was not always as you see me now."

"You weren't?" Kurt's curiosity piqued, and he listened with great interest.

"My kind were almost extinct in your world when first I came to the Land of Whiskers," said Parhelion. "We were sought after and destroyed as harbingers of darkness by those in your world who allowed superstition to rule over reason. So adept had I become at avoiding others in the world beyond the passage that when I came to Whiskers, I continued my reclusive habit. I made my home on the Silver Mountain, far from the other inhabitants of the land."

"But things might have been different for you here," said Kurt. "Couldn't you have talked to the animals—tried to make friends?"

"In my own way, I did," said the Nimbus. "Somehow, not by chance, but rather by some inherent characteristic of my species, I presume, I began interacting with the inhabitants from my position high above them. My whiskers seemed to have a peculiar capability other whiskers did not possess. I had no need to be near the others to hear their voices and respond in secret. I moved rapidly through the colors and became silver. The silver has become more and more intense over time, and with its growing brilliance, I have felt the need to move higher and higher up the mountain."

"Have you reached the top yet?"

"Where do you believe the top to be?"

"Up there," said Kurt, pointing to where the mountain's uppermost peak loomed tall and distinct against the blue of the sky.

Parhelion glanced at the mountain. "Look again, young Kurt."

Kurt looked again and a cold shudder rolled through his body. The mountaintop had vanished from sight, having stretched upward into a high layer of nimbus clouds.

Parhelion's story seemed to make sense, and Kurt almost believed it completely—until he looked again at the vulture whose steel-eyed stare pierced him to the marrow. The sight of the bird's naked head and curved beak stirred in the boy's imagination frightening pictures of vultures circling the dead, feeding voraciously on rotting carrion. Perhaps those people of long ago had been justified in destroying his kind, thought Kurt. Perhaps he would be wise to turn and flee—now—before it was too late. But he so desperately needed to find his way home that at last he pushed the dark imagery aside and forced himself to confide in the bird, be he good or evil.

"Parhelion," he ventured, "the book said to get home I'd have to uncover three secrets. The first would make everything right for the door to appear. The second would make the door appear at the right time, and the third would open the door. The book gave me clues to the first two secrets, but someone silver has to give me the third clue. I searched all over Nickledown on Silver Day, but no one could help me."

"I possess the clue you desire," said Parhelion. "But even if you do uncover the secrets, you will have only one chance to pass through the door. It will open only at sunset on the third Silver Day from the time you arrived in the Land of Whiskers."

"That's only six days from now," said Kurt.

The Nimbus nodded. "Should you not be beside the door at that precise moment, possessing knowledge of the three secrets, the door will not open. Be forewarned and use your time wisely. Quickit! Time is short."

Quickit? Time is short? So that's what the night-chirps meant. "Please, Parhelion, tell me what I need to do."

The Nimbus cocked his head to one side and turned it slightly so that one eye on his naked head peered down at Kurt from beneath folds of wrinkled skin. And the penetrating gaze of that single eye locked itself on the boy's eye sending a shiver to the deepest recesses of his soul.

"Hone your whiskers and know the truth," said the Nimbus.

Kurt's whiskers tingled as he anticipated what Parhelion was about to say. But much to his dismay, the awesome bird stared as if to read Kurt's thoughts, then unfolded his mighty wings and lifted off into the sky.

"No!" Kurt shouted, shielding his eyes to protect them from the dust raised by the creature's wings. He felt his heart pound as panic overtook him. "Parhelion! The door! How will I open it?"

The imperious bird called to him from high above in a voice that echoed through the hills.

"MID COLORS CLEAR AND FLORAL SCENT,
FIND RICHES VAST THAT CANNOT BE SPENT.

"Now, quickit! Time is short . . . Time is short . . ." The voice trailed off in the distance, and soon the Nimbus disappeared in the blinding rays of the midday sun.

When the dust settled, Kurt took a deep breath and released it slowly, repeating the words to himself so he would not forget them. "Colors clear. Floral scent. Riches . . Riches!" He recalled Tattle's tale about a lake filled with opals. "That's it! The Opal Lake. Opals have clear colors. And the air around the lake *must* have a floral scent. *All* the air around Nickledown smells like flowers. And having opals would certainly make a person rich. If I can find the Opal Lake and get the opals, I'll fill my pockets with them and save them until I think of a way to find the 'harmony that has no sound' and the 'sweetness that does not fade.' Then I'll . . . Oh, but the clue said, 'riches that *cannot be spent.*' Well, opals can't be spent. But you'd be rich if you sold them for money. It all fits!"

Kurt reached down and snatched the backpack from the ground. Once again his spirit soared! Once again he had a plan of action! The journey home would not elude him.

CHAPTER 21

THE POLYGLOPS

It was all so simple. He had only to find the Opal Lake and bring back the opals to prove he knew the third secret. And there was but one way to find the Opal Lake. He would first have to find King Aegis, King of the Swishin-Figgles, the "guardian of the precious jewels that adorn the Opal Lake," as mentioned in Tattle's tale.

But how does one find a swishin-figgle? He catches him, of course. And how does one catch a swishin-figgle? On a line, of course. And what does one use for bait? Polyglops, of course. And Kurt knew just the place to find big, fat, juicy ones.

On Silver Day, he had overheard a conversation between two pigs about an island full of polyglops—an island in the middle of the river, across from the scrub oak tree. Kurt recalled having passed the scrub oak while walking along the riverbank on his way to climb the Silver Mountain. He hadn't noticed an island at the time, but his thoughts had been focused on the climb. The tree should be easy enough to find again.

"Notch!" he shouted, swinging the backpack by his side as he ran along the riverbank. "We're going to look for Polyglop Island!"

The scrub oak, which looked much like a ragged, twisted umbrella, proved to be easy to find indeed. Kurt spotted it at the tip of a long, narrow peninsula that jutted well out into the river. The peninsula jutted so far out, in fact, it left only a narrow channel between itself and the small island the pigs described.

Kurt was relieved to find he would need to swim only a channel and not a larger portion of the river. He had heard, however, that channels can be treacherous as they twist and turn, making their way between land masses, so he knew he could be in for a challenge.

When he arrived at the scrub oak, he opened the book and explained to Notch his plan for gathering the polyglops.

"I don't think that's such a good idea," said Notch. "Frankly, I'm quite disturbed by it all, and quite disappointed you would consider kidnapping poor little polyglops for the purpose of baiting hooks with them. After all, I'm a worm of sorts myself, and the thought makes me shudder."

"It's okay in this case, Notch. Polyglops are different. They're plain old fishing worms. They're not special like you. Besides, it's the traditional thing to do."

"It's wrong, Kurt. Heed my words. It's a big mistake."

"Well, I'm going to do it anyway. I have to. I can't swim with the pack on my back, though, so I'll leave you under the scrub oak."

"I wouldn't want to go, anyway," said the booknotch. "I've no wish to be part of such a dreadful endeavor. Please reconsider."

"See you later, Notch. And don't worry. Soon our troubles will be over." He stuffed the book into the pack and removed his shoes and shirt before jumping into the river.

It seemed to Kurt the water was much colder than it should have been at midday in summer, and there was a strange turbulence coming from somewhere in the depths. "Just river currents," Kurt told himself. "Water running over rocks and crevices on the bottom. Too far down to bother me."

No sooner had he swum the first few strokes than a sense of foreboding overtook him. He felt the same uneasiness he felt at home, on the road to the lake, when he thought watchity widgits were watching him from the clouds; only now he sensed something watching from below. "Grandfather never said watchity widgits could swim," he told himself, only half joking. "If anyone's watching, I'm sure it's just a school of fish."

At first the boy's strength and energy were as high as his aspirations, and he swam with ease. But soon matters took a turn for the worse. Though the channel appeared placid, far below the surface the currents twisted and turned, spawning treacherous undertows, and from time to time Kurt had to summon all his strength to keep from being pulled to the bottom.

Halfway to the island, he began to tire; and the more he tired, the stronger grew the currents. With each stroke, he found it harder to maintain a straight line toward the island. For the first time, he thought perhaps he had undertaken more than he could handle, and this time Parhelion would not be there to help him. He knew that to be a fact because from well out in the channel he could see for miles in every direction, and the Nimbus was nowhere in sight.

Three-quarters of the way to the island, his arms began to stiffen; his legs began to cramp. "Just a little farther," he told himself. But he was not certain his limbs would keep moving long enough to carry him to shore. The harder he struggled, the more distant the island appeared. With his strength waning, his muscles weak, and the island still beyond reach, he was forced to draw upon the one last seed of hope remaining—the same secret storehouse of will-inspired might he had called upon when he struggled against the wind at the opening to the passage. Through sheer want and determination, he mustered strength to swim the last few yards, and with one desperate push, reached the shore and pulled himself onto the sandy beach. There he lay, exhausted and frightened, feeling fortunate to be alive. He dared not think about the return swim. Perhaps Notch had been right. Perhaps he should not have come to the island. And what purpose had it served? There was not a single polyglop in sight. The island was deserted.

Just then, Kurt heard a funny little sound. *Glop! Glop! Glop!—Pop! Glop!—Glop! Pop!—Glop!*

From all over the island, little polyglops began popping up from tiny holes in the sand. Hundreds of them. Fat, juicy ones. *Glop! Glop! Glop!—Pop! Glop!—Glop! Pop!—Glop!*

As far as his eyes could see, friendly little polyglops popped. *Glop! Glop! Glop!—Pop! Glop!—Glop! Pop!—Glop!*

Kurt could not believe his eyes. He was surrounded. Everywhere he looked, smiling polyglop faces grinned at him.

Several of the tiny creatures wiggled out of their holes, and before long, a line of polyglops was inching its way toward him.

"Can we be of help?" asked a plump and pulpy one who appeared to be the leader.

"You wouldn't *want* to help if you knew what I came here to do," Kurt answered.

The polyglop seemed to have no idea what Kurt meant, for he went right on smiling at the boy.

"It doesn't matter now anyway," said Kurt, realizing he could not possibly harm one of the innocent little creatures.

He looked out across the channel, which appeared much wider now, and moaned despairingly. "How will I ever get back? I should have listened to Notch."

With hope all but gone, he caught sight of a glimmer of light in the scrub oak tree on the opposite shore, and as he watched, something strange and beautiful happened. A long white streamer, rather like a ribbon, slowly unfurled from the tree in the vicinity of the light. One end seemed tethered to the oak, while the other floated freely, fluttering gently in the breeze. Kurt stood mesmerized by the gracefully flowing strand that floated in the air as softly as dandelion down. Determined to catch it should it come near the island—to learn what magic kept it so blithely aloft—he waded into the shallows and waited.

Behind him on shore, hundreds of polyglops lined up watching curiously.

The strand, growing longer, drifted slowly toward the island, and when the breeze drew it close above Kurt's head, the boy jumped up and seized it.

A cheer went up from the polyglops—a weak cheer by human standards, but a cheer, nonetheless.

The boy examined the strange white ribbon and found it to be so light in weight he could barely feel it in his hand. Surely a feather would weigh more, he thought. But when he tried to snap it, he could not break it no matter how hard he tried.

He looked closer at the strange material—the strangely *familiar* material. He had seen this before—the silky texture, the satiny sheen—a material as strong as the rope ends on a hammock he once slept in.

Suddenly he realized what he was holding. A rope! And one that had to have been woven by none other than Spinneret the Webber-Tat! She must have happened along, and understanding his predicament, woven him a lifeline!

Kurt said goodbye to the polyglops, grasped the rope firmly, and waded farther out into the water. Confident the other end would be securely anchored, he plunged into the cold water, entrusting his life to one tiny webber-tat's invaluable offering.

It was no easy task hauling himself hand-over-hand back across the channel, but ever so slowly the length of rope before him grew shorter and shorter as the ribbon-like tail floating on the water behind him grew longer and longer. At last he arrived at the shore, where he stood on his feet in waist-deep water beneath an overhanging bow of the scrub oak tree. Spinneret was standing on the bow, waiting to greet him.

Relieved at making it across, he tossed the rope aside and had just begun pulling himself up out of the water onto the large limb, when something latched onto his foot—something that tugged furiously!

"Spinneret!" Something's got me!" he cried, struggling to free his foot.

The water beneath him began to churn. He felt the same unnerving stare he had felt earlier, and whatever was tugging at his foot grabbed hold of his leg and pulled him from the limb. "No!" he cried, plunging backward into the river. Spinneret screamed as she watched him disappear beneath the surface.

Kurt felt himself being swept down river—drawn again into the treacherous currents. He rolled and twisted and choked on the water, going under and up and over and under again until he thought he surely would drown. After a particularly deep plunge, he felt himself rising through the water—surging upward from the murky depths toward the light. A moment later he found himself gliding along the surface, coughing out the river water that nearly drowned him. Drawing a desperate breath, he filled his lungs with clean fresh air, and with his senses restored, he was able to feel the cool breeze blowing across his wet face. Realizing he was lying on his stomach on top of something—something huge and cold and slippery—he rubbed his hands along its scaly surface. It was a fish!—the biggest he had ever seen!—And he was on its back, sailing smoothly and swiftly over the water.

The fish swam upriver, and slipping toward shore, deposited the boy in the shallows near the scrub oak tree. Before Kurt could get a good look at it, the mammoth creature slid beneath the surface and was gone.

"What was that?" Kurt asked, seeing Spinneret walking toward him as he climbed onto the riverbank.

"That was King Aegis," said Spinneret, her voice trembling.

Kurt was stunned. It was the fish he had planned to catch—the fish that could tell him where to find the Opal Lake.

For fear of further frightening the webber-tat, Kurt did not tell her something had pulled him beneath the water. Instead, he allowed her to believe he had entangled his foot on an underwater branch and slipped backward into the river. After catching his breath, he did, however, tell her his ill-conceived plan to catch King Aegis.

"You needn't have gone to all that trouble, dear," said Spinneret. "You could have stood on the riverbank and *called* the King of the Swishin-Figgles."

If Spinneret noticed the look of embarrassment on Kurt's face, she did not choose to humiliate him by mentioning it. Instead she asked, "By the way, Kurt dear, have you solved the riddle? Remember?

Here's a riddle short and sweet:
*Use your whiskers **and your feet**."*

I haven't had time to think about it," said Kurt.

The webber-tat nodded understandingly. "Well, dear, I must be going. I was on my way up the Silver Mountain to gather dew when I came upon your predicament. I'm glad I happened by. Give some thought to the riddle when you have time." And she hurried on her way.

Kurt's disappointment at his foiled attempt to catch King Aegis was surpassed only by his anger at himself. He had wasted the better part of a day climbing the mountain and swimming to Polyglop Island and had gained nothing for his efforts. Now he would have to begin his search for the opals again, this time by *calling* King Aegis.

He put on his shoes and shirt and removed the book from the backpack. Remembering Notch's admonishment, he reconsidered and tucked the book away again. There was no way he was going to give Notch an opportunity to say, "I told you so."

CHAPTER 22

KING AEGIS

It was two hours past noon and the summer sun was its hottest. Kurt knew fish feed near the surface early in the morning before the heat of the day sends them to the depths to cooler water. He worried that King Aegis might be in the deepest part of the river now and might not hear him calling no matter how loudly he shouted for the swishin-figgle.

"King Aegis! King Aegis!" he yelled over and over, cupping his hands around his mouth, aiming his calls in every direction out across the water. "King of the Swishin-Figgles! Do you hear me!" But he received no response from the mammoth fish.

Frustrated, he sat down, opened the pack, and removed the book. He had not given Notch a chance earlier to reprove him for his folly concerning Polyglop Island, and he was glad the booknotch chose not to do so now. After a time, however, his conscience prompted him to approach the subject himself.

"Okay, I know, I shouldn't have tried to get the polyglops. But that's all over. I have a better plan, and it won't hurt anyone. I'm *calling* King Aegis to ask him where the Opal Lake is. When he tells me, I'll go get the opals."

By this time, Notch was perched comfortably on the spine of the book. "Hmm," he said, pondering deeply. "Finding the opals is one thing, but bringing them back with you sounds rather like stealing to me."

"It is not," said Kurt. "When people find buried treasure, it's theirs. It's the same thing."

"I'm certain the matter is open to interpretation," said Notch. "Anyone who might have had a legitimate claim to buried treasure would have been dead for centuries; therefore, a treasure would, in all probability, belong to no one. But the opals are a different matter. You don't know whether they belong to King Aegis or to anyone else."

"Well, finders are keepers," Kurt replied. "That's the rule. Always has been, always will be. It's every man for himself at times like this." He said the words, but he could not look Notch in the eye.

"I greatly desire to return to the book now, Kurt," said the booknotch. "I believe there is a beneficent *b* or a consoling *c* waiting for me." He crawled down to the middle of the page, and Kurt closed the book and returned it to the pack.

By now, Kurt was quite distraught. "King Aegis! King Aegis!" he yelled louder than before. Could Spinneret have been wrong? Could it be the King of the Swishin-Figgles would not answer his call?

Out of the corner of his eye, he caught sight of something large and silvery breaching the water. It shot up like a bullet before plunging again into the river. When Kurt turned to see what it was, a great splash showered him with river water. Not until he wiped his eyes was he able to see the mammoth fish swimming just below the surface a few yards away. Surely this must be the fish he had summoned. Surely this must be the renowned King Aegis—the mighty leviathan himself!

The fish disappeared for several seconds before bursting through the surface again. This time Kurt could see it clearly, for it loomed momentarily in the air above the water, its shiny body glistening in the sun. When it plunged again, the resulting splash knocked Kurt off his feet.

Over and over the fish flew upward and splashed downward, sending wave after wave crashing to shore.

What a kingly entrance for the great Ruler of the Swishin-Figgles! thought Kurt. He was about to call to the fish when once more the creature burst through the surface and loomed for several seconds before plunging again into the depths. Now it stayed under, and with its disappearance, the waves subsided and the river returned to its placid state.

Kurt searched for the fish, but saw no sign of it through the water. A moment after he decided King Aegis was truly gone, he saw the fish's silvery head slip ever so quietly above the surface.

"Why have you summoned us?" asked King Aegis, in a voice august and regal.

Us? thought Kurt. He looked around expecting to see another fish, but saw only King Aegis. "I called you because I need your help. By the way, thank you for rescuing me."

"It was our royal duty," replied the aqueous monarch, with a slight bow of the head that in no way compromised his sovereignty.

Deciding to waste no time, Kurt told the fish his plan to find the Opal Lake and bring the opals back to Nickledown.

"There is an Opal Lake," said King Aegis, but we are not certain it will meet your needs."

"I know what my needs are," Kurt snapped.

"Indeed," said the swishin-figgle, with no small degree of condescension. He said nothing more for several moments while he studied the boy intently. Kurt was beginning to feel uncomfortable as he stood before the swishin-figgle, subjected to his cold, fishy stare.

"Very well," King Aegis said at last. "We will tell you how to find the lake. It lies toward the northwest. You must travel westward, downriver, until you reach the Crescent Rock. The Crescent Rock forms a bridge which will allow you to cross the river. Once on the other side, you must travel due north until you see the Rainbow Mist. The mist indwells the air above the Opal Lake. We wish you safe travel." With that, King Aegis drew his head beneath the surface and was gone.

Kurt was excited beyond belief. It would be just like searching for buried treasure. He grabbed the backpack and emptied out the sandwiches he had packed for the day. After all, he could do without eating, but he must have room in the pack to bring back the opals.

The boy ran along the riverbank until he was too exhausted to run farther. Then he walked for what seemed a mile before the Crescent Rock came into view. "Notch! It's the Crescent Rock!" he shouted when he saw it.

And what a sight it was! It bridged the water at a spot where the river narrowed to only a few yards from shore to shore, and at either end of it lay a well-manicured patch of lawn bordered by wildflowers and graceful willow trees. The bridge itself was a high arch that, due to its unevenness, appeared to have been naturally formed from some sort of rock resembling white, unpolished marble. Inset every few feet in the rock were clusters of colorful, uncut gemstones—amethyst, sapphire, emerald, citrine, golden topaz, pink tourmaline—that looked as though they had been carefully placed by the gifted hand of a master jeweler.

The sight of the bridge renewed Kurt's strength, and he ran toward it, passing a small herd of sheep grazing at the edge of the lawn. Without pausing to greet the animals, he quickly climbed to the top of the arch. From there, he could see for miles in every direction. There was no mist to be seen, but trusting King Aegis's instructions, he scurried down the other side and headed due north. Not long thereafter, he passed through a dense forest, and when he stepped out of the trees into a vast sunlit meadow, he caught sight of what appeared to be a cloud—a cloud that glowed with every color of the rainbow—hovering close to the ground in the distance. It was a thin, airy cloud—more like a mist—that allowed the sun's rays to penetrate through to the glistening body of water lying beneath it.

"I've found it!" Kurt cried, running headlong toward the mist. "Notch, can you hear me? I've found the Opal Lake!"

Kurt felt the air around him grow cool and moist as he stepped into the outlying edges of the mist. When he arrived at the lake itself, he found it just as he had pictured it, crystalline-blue and serene. Much to his delight, it was shallow enough to reveal its sandy bottom; and there, strewn across the sand were hundreds of brilliant opals—enough of the precious stones to make a person rich beyond avarice. This one triumph made every struggle he had endured in the Land of Whiskers worthwhile. He could hardly wait to reach for the first handful of jewels. He knew he would have to come back again and again to fill the pack many times over.

With great anticipation, he wriggled out of the backpack and dropped it on the ground. Reaching into the water, he scooped a handful of the cold, hard stones. He could feel the opals rolling around in the palm of his hand and over his cupped fingers. He watched them shimmer with opalescent brilliance as the glow from the Rainbow Mist struck their polished surfaces.

Kurt knew freshwater lakes such as this were fed by underground streams, so he was not surprised when he felt a gentle current pass over his hand. The current must have disturbed the opals he was holding, for the stones seemed to move from his hand of their own accord.

The boy trapped another handful and pulled them from the water. As his fingers broke the surface, the opals took on the feel of something slippery and alive. They *were* alive! They jumped out of his hand and back into the water.

"Fish!" he screamed. "I came all this way for fish!"

And indeed he had. What he thought were opals were, in fact, tiny opalescent fish. When he looked at them through the water, they appeared to be opals; when he withdrew them from the water, they proved to be fish. Again and again he reached for another handful, and again and again the precious jewels jumped from his hand.

Kurt felt his temper rising. He snatched the backpack from the ground and threw it over one shoulder. He ran to the edge of the mist. He ran across the sunlit meadow and through the forest and across the Crescent Rock to the other side. He ran past the grazing sheep and along the riverbank. He ran and ran until he could run no more. He was tired and he was hungry and he was angry, and with every stride, he felt his anger building to an uncontrollable tempest. This was more than he could bear. Surely no one could stand such disappointment over and over again.

When at last he reached the spot where he had talked to King Aegis, he was overwrought with anger. "King Aegis!" he screamed in a tantrum. "Where are you! Come here now, King Aegis!"

The King of the Swishin-Figgles seemed in no hurry to respond, but finally arrived in the same grandiose manner as before, splashing and drenching the boy, giving rise to a turbulence that hammered the shore.

"I don't need this!" Kurt shouted above the pounding waves. "I don't care how royal you are—or how many fish you think you are with your '*we*' this and '*we*' that! I want an explanation! You lied to me! You had no right to lie to me!"

King Aegis waited for the waves to subside before slipping his head above the surface. "We do not lie," he said calmly to the boy. "It was never our intention to deceive you. You would not hear the truth, though it was given you. Did we not say we doubted the lake would meet your needs? And were not our instructions accurate? Did you not find the Opal Lake?"

"Yes, I found the lake," Kurt said, his face red with anger. "I found the opals too. But they weren't opals. They were fish. Stupid fish!"

"It is true they are not opals," said King Aegis. "But they *are* jewels—though not the kind you sought. They are our children, the jewels of the water world—more precious to us than the silver rain that gives life to our world."

By now Kurt was accustomed to the fish's use of the royal "we," but he still could not help looking around for another fish. When he glanced away for a moment, King Aegis dove into the depths and was gone.

So that was how his ambitious plan was to end.

Kurt pulled the backpack from his shoulder and was about to drop it on the ground, but in a sudden fit of temper, threw it instead. "Notch, are you all right?" he called frantically, remembering the booknotch. He hurried to open the pack and found the booknotch jostled, but unhurt. The worm had been securely braced in the point of a *v* and had taken the jolt quite well. Kurt apologized and Notch understood.

"Oh, Notch," said Kurt. And he slumped to the ground. "What will I do now? How will I ever get home?"

CHAPTER 23

THE BOOKNOTCH LOST

"When you have a problem, and you can't find a solution, free your mind of the matter. Think of something else. Before you know it, the answer to your problem will pop into your head." That's what Kurt's grandfather told him. At the time, the boy dismissed the idea as nonsense, but now it sounded like good advice, so Kurt decided to pretend he was home and the riverbank was his secret place. He would lose himself in daydreaming and talking to Notch, waiting for the elusive answers to the three secrets to pop into his head.

The booknotch agreed Grandfather's advice was well founded, so as Kurt sat under a tree at the river's edge with the book lying open on his lap, Notch sat on the boy's shoulder, and for almost an hour they discussed a vast array of subjects. But through it all, no answers came.

Kurt began to lose faith, but still he remained determined not to think about his predicament. Finally the talking stopped, and Kurt fell to daydreaming while Notch dozed in a crease on the boy's collar. From time to time, the worm popped up to check the progress of their wishful venture and to offer moral support before drifting off to sleep again.

It was well into afternoon by then, and the approach of day's end brought a noticeable coolness, as often occurs late in the Season of Light when Summer, on her downward side, struggles to fend off the untimely intrusion of autumn. Kurt watched a leaf drift slowly to the ground. Autumn, he thought—the first falling leaf of the season. But that was not possible. Summer had lasted only days. Could it be that seasonal changes, which took place over months in Kurt's world, spanned the length of days in the Land of Whiskers? The rapidly changing weather reminded him of how quickly time was passing and how pressed he was to complete his tasks. Time truly *was* short, and the boy had not the vaguest idea of how to uncover the secrets.

A second falling leaf caught his attention as it fluttered down from the branches above and landed near his feet. A rush of panic overtook him as the urgency of it all struck him squarely in the face. "I'll never see home again!" he said, and he sprang to his feet, knocking the book to the ground. "I don't know the secrets, and I'll never find the door!"

A breeze ruffled the pages of the book. "Notch!" Kurt cried, remembering the tiny worm had been asleep on his collar. The boy searched his collar and the front of his shirt and the length of his sleeves and all down his pant legs. "Notch! Where are you!" he screamed frantically. Dropping to his knees, he crawled on the ground under the tree and rubbed his hands over the soil. "Notch! Answer me! Please!" But nowhere did he find the booknotch.

How he wished to hear the wordy worm's voice. How he wished to see his tiny green face peeking from behind a pebble, or his little segmented body perched upon a blade of grass. But only the sound of the breeze rustling the leaves of the tree answered his calls.

A surge of tears began to build within him. The tears turned to sobs, and the sobs overtook him. "How could I be so careless?" he moaned. "How could I do this to poor little Notch?"

When all hope was lost, he slumped to the ground under the tree, weak with sorrow, and allowed his tears to flow freely. He vowed not to move from the spot until some miracle brought Notch back to him. But in his heart he doubted there would be such a miracle.

Several more leaves drifted down from the tree and landed near the water's edge. The breeze rolled them over and over until they tumbled into the river. Kurt watched sorrowfully as the current carried them away.

Now there was nothing. No branches, no abacus flowers, no riches, no hope. "Who knows when Charlie will come back if he has family in another region," Kurt said to himself. "And now I've lost Notch—dear little Notch, who trusted me so." The boy tried to imagine how the booknotch must feel with no pages to enfold him, and the mere thought of the little worm, lost and unsheltered, so disheartened him that he cried all the more.

At first, Kurt could not see what happened next, for when his tears sent everything out of focus, he buried his face in his hands. But a rare and wondrous thing was taking place—something that happens in the Land of Whiskers only under the most extreme circumstances— in this case, at a time of deepest pain and despair. A color rose from deep within the boy—not a color such as the animals possess inside, but the color he was feeling. A cold blue light glowed first around his head, then around his shoulders, then around the whole of his body until the entire space around him became saturated with the peculiar blue light. When he opened his tear-filled eyes, he was frightened by the sentient glow that undulated as though it were a living thing. But despite his fear, he did not move. Nothing would force him from the river's edge. He had made a vow to Notch, and he would keep his vow.

CHAPTER 24

THE LEGACY

It was approaching sundown and the longed-for miracle had not occurred. Kurt picked up the book and slowly turned the pages one by one, fervently searching, hoping Notch would appear from beneath the dot of an *i* or the curl of a *Q*. But he did not.

The weather had taken a definite turn toward autumn, and the emergent night air carried a chill that cut through the boy causing him to shiver. That chill was but a forerunner to the one he felt seconds later.

From the corner of his eye, Kurt detected a black vestige off in the distance—a huge bird-like shadow gliding smoothly over the surface of the water, moving upriver against the flow. The shadow reached a point near the place where Kurt was sitting and slipped up the river-bank and passed directly over him.

Despite their earlier meeting, Kurt was still unnerved by the thought of confronting the Nimbus. He shuddered at the sight of the colossal bird, who seemed very much within his element silhouetted darkly against the purple sky. Kurt watched with dread as Parhelion circled several times and began a slow, steady descent toward him.

When the Nimbus was still yards away, Kurt caught sight of something protruding from the bird's beak—something barely perceptible—no more than a tiny speck—perhaps a twig, or part of a leaf. But as Parhelion drew nearer, Kurt saw to his horror it was neither twig nor leaf. "Notch!" he screamed, recognizing the limp, lifeless form.

Parhelion touched ground, and as he walked toward Kurt, carrying the hapless worm, tears again welled inside the boy, giving rise to an onslaught of deep sobs that stole his breath and left him weak and trembling. Helpless to do otherwise, he watched the Nimbus lay the booknotch on the ground then turn and soar into the air.

"Why did you do it?" Kurt screamed after the bird, certain he had killed the booknotch.

Without answering, Parhelion flew to the top of the Silver Mountain and disappeared into the clouds.

Kurt stared at the ground where Parhelion left the booknotch. He could barely bring himself to look directly at the little worm. "I'm sorry," he whispered, dropping to his knees and reaching out to gently stroke the tiny body. The booknotch was surely dead, for he did not respond when Kurt touched him, and his face, once bright green, had turned a pale, sickly gray.

Kurt had seen dead things before—bugs and dead animals on the road—but the full meaning of death struck him now for the first time. Death, in all its finality—irrevocable, unalterable. Nothing he could do or say could undo it. Here lay little Notch on the ground in front of him, close enough to touch, yet not in essence there at all. Gone was the intangible spark that allows heart to speak to heart, mind to speak to mind. This gray, lifeless shell had not the means to comprehend Kurt's words of anguish—his heartfelt expressions of apology. Never would it hear his words and offer forgiveness. Even whiskers, with all their intuitive capabilities, could not penetrate the grim barrier standing between the boy and his tiny, lifeless friend.

Kurt picked up the book, and lifting the body of the booknotch, he placed it lovingly on one of the pages. "I wish I could leave you cradled in a *c* or nestled in a *u*," he said between sobs, "but this is the best I can do."

He was about to close the book when he thought he detected a slight movement of the worm's shoulder. He was certain he must have jostled the book, causing it to appear the worm had moved. Nevertheless, he raised the book close to his face, held his breath, and watched intently. He *had* seen movement! He knew he was holding the book very still, yet there it was again! A slight stirring—a blinking of eyes—a shake of the head—and the booknotch sat up. He was *not* dead! He was very much alive! "Notch!" Kurt cried, his heart pounding wildly.

"Don't eat me! Don't eat me!" screamed the booknotch, holding one weakish arm over his eyes.

"Notch, you're all right. It's me—Kurt."

Notch let his arm slide down slowly from his face, and when he looked up at the boy, the magnificent green rushed back into his tiny body.

"Oh, Kurt," sighed the booknotch. "I'm so thankful it's you. I had the most terrifying experience. I was reposing comfortably on your collar, drifting in and out of sleep when, without warning, you sprang to your feet. You forgot I was there, I suppose. How dreadful it was! The next thing I knew, I was tumbling off your shoulder. I grabbed for your sleeve on the way down, but your arm swung out toward the river and knocked me into the diluvial deluge."

The worm removed his waterlogged cap, leaned over the edge of the book, and wrung the cap out. After repositioning the stylish bit of haberdashery on his head, he continued his saga.

"The current grabbed me and pulled me downriver. Never was I a good swimmer. I called to you frantically, but my diminutive voice was muted by the sound of the rushing water. I spotted a leaf bobbing by and managed to grab its leeward edge and climb aboard. I floated downriver—I don't know how long—spinning round and round as the leaf swirled in the tumultuous torrent. I became so dizzy I thought the motion would surely kill me should the water choose to spare me. Then I saw *him*—Parhelion—plummeting toward me, his voracious countenance heralding my impending doom! There I was, perched on that precarious little raft, helpless in his menacing presence, certain I was to be his dinner—or at the very least, the first course."

"That's terrible," said Kurt.

"Terrible indeed," said the booknotch. "My entire life passed before me. All the words and letters I had ever encountered flew past my eyes in a swirl of meaningless confusion, gathering to write the final chapter in this booknotch's life. *THE END* was coming! The last thing I remember was Parhelion's patulous beak speeding toward me wide open. I could see all the way down his cavernous throat. Soon I would be scooped up and hurled into the dark abyss of his belly. Lost! Entombed forever! I must have fainted. Then I woke up here."

"Oh, Notch, I'm so sorry," said Kurt. "It was all my fault. I was careless. I knew you were afraid of coming out of the book, but I was too concerned about my own problems to think of yours. You trusted me and I let you down. But it won't happen again. I have an idea." And he took a length of fine fishing line from the backpack and tied one end of it through the buttonhole on Notch's vest. After punching a hole in the spine of the book with a fishhook, he tied the other end through the hole. "There," he said. "You can come out of the book any time you want to, and you'll never have to be afraid of getting lost again."

The little worm smiled warmly. "How pleasantly reassuring! Thank you so much, Kurt. I believe I shall find a restful *r* in which to recuperate now, if you'll kindly close the book."

"Of course," said Kurt, and he tucked the booknotch inside his favorite part of the book—the part with the poem, where he would have an abundance of *r*'s in which to recuperate—and told him goodnight.

The booknotch was safe. The miracle had happened after all. Kurt watched the cold blue light around him slowly fade away.

It was twilight now, and small, twinkling stars appeared in the night sky. Kurt took no notice of them as he sat under the tree brooding over Notch's ordeal, visualizing the tragedy that could have spelled *THE END* for the booknotch. He might have drowned, thought Kurt, or been swallowed whole by a hungry fish. It was such a simple thing to solve Notch's problem. Why had he not thought of the fishing line earlier?

Reflecting on his friendship with Notch and the pain he felt when he thought he had lost him, he recalled his other friends in the Copper Valley, and he realized for the first time how important they were to him. Just as Notch had been cast into a torrent that could have led to a shadowy grave, Kurt's other friends had let life's circumstances cast them into the shadows. Stinkle was living in the shadow of a lost dream. Fraidy was living within real shadows, fearing the good life has to offer. Tattle was living among shadowy memories of times past, when his stories were new and welcomed by friends and passers-by.

Kurt thought about Charlie too. He remembered how he felt when he was holding Charlie's tail in the passage. What if he had let go? What if he had deserted Charlie in the darkness? How would he have lived with himself?

What if he deserted his friends now? Could he ever experience joy in a future grounded in the abandonment of those he cared for? Time was running out. If he took time to return to the Copper Valley, he might never get home. "I can't go back! I can't!" he shouted to the air.

All at once he heard a sound like the thrashing of wings. It seemed to be all around him, yet he felt no movement of air. He was certain it must be the Nimbus, so he stood up and called out, "Parhelion!" but no one answered. A strange tingling sensation traveled the length of his whiskers, and the breeze that earlier had died away began to blow again. Soon thereafter, he heard a voice—a voice that was *not* a voice. The sound—if it could be called a sound at all—seemed to flow through his whiskers directly into his thoughts. The voice that was not a voice was deep and resonant. "I fear you do yourself great ill in not acknowledging the aspirations of the heart," said the voice that was not a voice. "The heart seeks more than a place of being within the body. It seeks a place of peace within the soul."

"Who's there?" Kurt shouted.

Again, there was no answer.

Kurt looked up as a shooting star streaked across the sky. A dying star, he thought—dying just like Stinkle's dream of going to Nickledown, and Fraidy's dream of singing on the fences there, and Tattle's dream of telling tales to animals who have never heard his stories.

The boy's mind filled with visions of darkness. Dying stars and dying dreams—faded wisps of once-bright hope—shining for only a moment before slipping away to nothingness—in the end, no more than objects wished upon.

I can't let it happen, thought Kurt. I can't let their dreams die. I've got to bring them out of the shadows. I've got to bring them to Nickledown!

The deadline for uncovering the secrets loomed above his head like the hammer of a clock poised to deliver the final stroke of midnight. Kurt knew hours spent traveling to the Copper Valley would be hours he could spend searching for the secrets. But he would not allow himself to think about that now. He had a job to do. And maybe—just maybe—with a little luck—he could still uncover the secrets in time.

"Notch! Can you hear me?" he shouted. "I have a plan. I'm going back to the Copper Valley to bring Stinkle and Fraidy and Tattle to Nickledown for Silver Day. Stinkle won't be afraid to be around the Nickle-Dickles anymore and he'll have lots of good conversations. And Fraidy won't have to be afraid of shadows—he'll be able to sing on the fences. There will be lots of animals who haven't heard Tattle's tales. I can do it, Notch! I know I can!" But he didn't know exactly *how* he would do it.

All at once a brilliant flash of light illuminated the sky above the Silver Mountain, and a moment later Kurt watched a dim, gray shadow glide swiftly down the moonlit mountainside. With the shadow's approach came a gust of wind and a thrashing of wings—and Parhelion the Nimbus landed directly in front of Kurt.

"I am pleased," said the Nimbus. "A new page has been written in *The Book of Light*. Open *The Book* and read, young Kurt. It was not by chance you came to the Land of Whiskers."

Kurt was dumbfounded. He opened the book carefully, so as not to disturb the booknotch, and to his amazement, it opened to a page on which was written a story—a story he knew had not been there earlier. By the light of the moon, he read:

THE LEGACY

A lame child, a boy, was left behind when the Pied Piper took the children from Hamelin. The boy missed out on all the promises the Piper made to the children. To make amends, the Piper vowed the child's descendants would have access to the Land of Whiskers for generations to come. They would be a blessing to Whiskers, and Whiskers would be a blessing to them. The boy's surname was Nickle-Dickle. All first-born sons descended from the boy would be partakers of the Legacy.

The Piper lured the children of Hamelin away from the greed and deceit that filled their land to a place where all was truth and light. He forged a key of silver on a chain of nickel with a clasp of copper and sent it by way of a sprite to the lame boy with the promise of the Legacy. The boy gave the key to his first-born son on his ninth birthday, as the sprite instructed him, and told his son of the Piper's promise that when the time was right, he would hear the music of the flute through the early morning rain, and a passage would open to Whiskers. To seal the bond, the Piper promised the boy: "Though lame when earthbound, your son and his descendants will be whole as they walk in the light of Whiskers."

And so it was.

The children from Hamelin became a family unto themselves and called themselves Nickle-Dickles in memory of the boy left behind. The name, too, became a bond between the boy's world and the Land of Whiskers. In his own world, the first descendant of the lame boy carried the name, Harry Nickle-Dickle. While in Whiskers, he bore his true name: Harry Nickle-Dickle of Whiskers.

The children vowed never to allow greed and deceit to abide in their land. They vowed to become the guardians of Whiskers; to welcome lost or frightened animals through their gates (for they, too, had once been lost and frightened); to tend the Rainbow Garden so its fragrance would forever spread throughout the land; to tune the nickel trees so their melody would forever be in tune with the music of the Piper; to live in light and help the animals grow in the colors.

And so it is.

When he had finished reading, Kurt stood speechless, staring at the page. He looked up at the Nimbus. "I'm part of that legacy, aren't I, Parhelion?"

"Yes," replied the Nimbus, "you are."

"And my father . . . What about my father?"

"Your father was here many times, young Kurt. But on his last visit, another was here also—the Troll—and his legions, the Gathering Gloom.

"No!" said Kurt, as full realization struck him. "My father was the large Nickle-Dickle who fought the creature, wasn't he?"

"Yes, young Kurt, he was. Your father defended Whiskers against the Troll, but in so doing, he forfeited his life. For the first time ever, death occurred in Whiskers. Those born here did not understand it. They thought somehow the Nickle-Dickle had simply disappeared, though their whiskers told them something terrible had happened. The lost animals, who once lived in your world, knew death for what it was, and none wanted to speak of it."

"And Annie, my father's dog? Mother saw her chase Father across the field that morning and we never saw her after that. She must have come to Whiskers too."

"She did," said the Nimbus. "She was deeply saddened by the loss of your father. She loved him very much and was very proud of him."

"Where is she now?" asked Kurt.

"She lives in the Southern Region among many friends."

Kurt smiled a melancholy smile. "Sweet little Annie. I missed her so much after she and Father disappeared. She's the reason I adopted Charlie. I couldn't stand not having a dog around."

"Now, young Kurt," said the Nimbus. "Turn to the front of *The Book*—to the first page."

"But there's nothing on that page."

The Nimbus's many eyes stared at the boy. "Read what others cannot see. These silver words were penned for thee."

The poem, thought Kurt—that's what the poem said. He turned to the first page—one that was blank when he first found the book. Now the page glowed with silver script. A quill pen lay in the fold of the book. The sight of the page made Kurt's chest swell with pride. There, in gleaming silver, were the signatures of his predecessors.

"They're all here," Kurt said excitedly. "My grandfather, William Nickle-Dickle of Whiskers. And my great-grandfather, Prescott Nickle-Dickle of Whiskers. And all the others before them. And look," he added, his voice quivering, "my father, Thomas Nickle-Dickle of Whiskers."

Tears welled in his eyes as he ran his fingers over his father's signature as though he could touch him through the letters on the page. He wished he could tell his father how proud he was of him. When he thought of the Troll, his face flushed with anger. "My father loved Whiskers enough to die for it," he said defiantly. And with that, he picked up the quill pen and signed *The Book of Light*. In bold letters, under his father's name, he wrote, KURT NICKLE-DICKLE OF WHISKERS.

The silver ink glistened on the parchment page. For the first time, Kurt felt at home in the Land of Whiskers. "First, I'll bring my friends to Nickledown where they'll be safe from the Troll and his Gloom," he said with conviction. "Then I'll find a way to destroy the Troll."

"Beware the Troll, young Kurt," said Parhelion. "He takes many forms. At times he appears as a giant, at other times a gnome. He may show himself as but a breath of cold or a trace of rancidness."

"Who is he, exactly?" Kurt asked.

"He is known by many names," replied the Nimbus: "Father of Confusion, Father of Catastrophe, The Dark Deceiver, Tiller of Tumultuous Soil, Warden of the Wicked Weir. His Gloom is The Trodden Seed That Sprouts Within the Blighted Soil, his forward guard, the Vanguard of the Vapors."

Kurt reflected a moment on the Troll, and on his father and all his ancestors, and he asked the Nimbus, "If my father and grandfather and all the generations before them have been to Whiskers, why wouldn't the Nickle-Dickles and animals remember them? Nobody's mentioned them."

"Understandably," said the Nimbus. "Each time a Nickle-Dickle child leaves Whiskers for the last time, the Piper puts to sleep the memories of the Nickle-Dickles and animals, in so far as the Nickle-Dickle child is concerned, so all will be new for the next generation."

"Oh," said Kurt. "So when my son turns nine—if I have a son—and he comes to Whiskers, no one he meets will remember me?"

"So it has been, and thus it remains—for the sake of your son."

"But *you* remember everything."

The Nimbus nodded. "Mine is a different responsibility. As Guardian of the Legacy, I *must* remember."

Kurt was not satisfied with Parhelion's explanation. "Well, some animals still remember my father's battle with the Troll. It sounds like *they* remember him."

"They recall having seen a 'large Nickle-Dickle'—an anomaly of sorts. They have no memory of your father as the Nickle-Dickle child. You must hurry now. As I speak, the Gathering Gloom reaches well into the Copper Valley. Quickit! Time is short."

The Nimbus spread his wings, and with a mighty thrashing, ascended into the sky.

Kurt had assumed a "monumental, mountainous task," as Mosey would have described it. He had no idea how he would go about defeating the Troll. He would simply have to take it one step at a time. "First, I'll think of a way to get Stinkle and Fraidy and Tattle to Nickledown," he told himself. "Then I'll worry about the Troll."

Kurt knew he would be late getting home to Mother and Father Nickle-Dickle's house and he did not want the tiny couple to worry. He had already caused enough trouble for one day. So he tucked the book under his arm, grabbed the backpack, and ran all the way home.

When he arrived at the little house on the cobblestone street, someone was waiting for him.

"Charlie!" he cried. "You're home!"

The dog wagged from the tip of his nose to the end of his tail. "I found her!" he said. "I found Chrysalis! She's here!"

Charlie pranced over to the corner of the room, where his sister was sitting shyly, and gave her a quick lick on the cheek before introducing her to Kurt.

Chrysalis was smaller than Charlie and quite timid. Her eyes looked down when Kurt spoke to her, and her eyelids fluttered, revealing long, lovely lashes. She was every bit as beautiful as Charlie had described her; and just as he had said, on her neck was a white spot shaped like a freshwater pearl. Appropriate, Kurt thought, for one as feminine and fragile as the pearl itself.

After a long session of barking and laughing and hugging and dog licks, Charlie told Kurt about his journey and about Chrysalis's home. "She has a family in Whiskers. I'm an uncle many times over. What do you think of that?"

Kurt was glad to hear it, for it would make life a little easier should he and Charlie have to remain in Whiskers. "I think it's wonderful," he said. And he meant it.

When Mother and Father Nickle-Dickle and Chrysalis were busy talking, Kurt took his dog aside. "I'm glad you're back, Charlie. I've missed you so much, and something's come up. We have to take a trip!"

CHAPTER 25

THE SWEET PERFUME

Kurt had lain awake half the night trying to think of ways to persuade Stinkle, Fraidy, and Tattle to leave the Copper Valley. He knew they would not be safe for long with the Gloom gathering there. If he could bring them to Nickledown, he would then be able to devote his attention to finding a way to drive the Troll from Whiskers.

The boy had not mentioned the Troll and the Gathering Gloom to Mother and Father Nickle-Dickle the night before. Charlie had just come home, and he did not want to spoil the happy occasion. But now he was anxious to tell Mother Nickle-Dickle the whole story.

Every morning, Father Nickle-Dickle left the house early to tune the nickel trees. And every morning, Mother Nickle-Dickle went to the Rainbow Garden to tend the flowers, but she always left a hot breakfast on the table for Kurt. This morning was no exception.

Kurt bypassed the breakfast and ran straight to the garden, where he told Mother Nickle-Dickle all about *The Book* and the Legacy and his father and the Troll.

"Oh dear," said Mother Nickle-Dickle. "The rumors must be true."

"What rumors?" Kurt asked.

"There has been talk of diminished light in the Copper Valley and color loss among the animals—apparently a great deal of color loss. It's rumored some of the larger animals have lost their appetite for tribble and are very restless and unfriendly. Many have developed phobias, too, becoming afraid of the most harmless things. One poor slinkle-purr, who was already afraid of his own shadow, is now said to be afraid of everything."

"Fraidy," said Kurt.

"I even heard a curious story about a stinkle-dunk who's got himself into a terrible fix."

"A stinkle-dunk?" said Kurt. "What stinkle-dunk?"

"I don't know his name, but it seems some time ago he devised a plan to bottle his 'fragrance of rare odoriferousness,' as a stinkle-dunk friend of his called it. To him, and to other stinkle-dunks, such scents were pleasing. And since he was pink—for the most part—he thought his was the most pleasing of all. According to the twitter-flit who told me the story, the stinkle-dunk sold his entire collection of antique honey pots to raise funds to manufacture elaborate, crystal-lined copper containers, grand enough to hold his exquisite fragrance. He filled the containers with the fine perfume and advertised the finished product for sale to the other inhabitants of the Copper Valley as 'Stinkle-Dunk's Sweet Surrender.'"

"Oh no!" said Kurt.

"Needless to say, it was a terrible failure. Many of the animals who sniffed the Sweet Surrender swooned and fell flat on the ground."

"It must have been awfully embarrassing for the stinkle-dunk," said Kurt.

"According to the twitter-flit, that was not the worst of it. Under normal conditions, the animals would have simply returned the perfume and explained the problem to the stinkle-dunk in a gracious manner. But as I said, conditions are rumored to be far from normal in the Copper Valley. The poor stinkle-dunk has undergone terrible hardship—threats, lawsuits—even a loss of color. And it seems he was left with tens of gallons of the product yet to be bottled, hundreds of empty elaborate copper containers, and a huge bill for advertising, not to mention the cost of veterinarian services incurred some time ago when he had to be treated for overwork and exhaustion brought on by the personal manufacture of the product."

"It was Stinkle," said Kurt. "That's what all those buckets and copper bottles were in the cellar. That's why he didn't want me to see them."

"Oh my," said Mother Nickle-Dickle. "It's going to be harder than you thought to bring him here."

"I know," said Kurt. "If he happened to 'slip' while he was here, everyone would know he was the stinkle-dunk who sold the Sweet Surrender."

The thought of the stinkle-dunk's unfortunate "slippages" and his vain attempt to market his less-than-desirable "perfume" gave Kurt an idea, and he quickly told Mother Nickle-Dickle his plan.

"I have just the recipe," she said. "Wait here." And she dropped her trowel on the ground, hurried to the house, and soon returned with a large basket, which she and Kurt filled to overflowing with flowers from the Rainbow Garden—some of every kind. "These should do nicely," Mother Nickle-Dickle said, as she and Kurt carried the basket to the house.

In the kitchen, they found Charlie asleep in the corner and Chrysalis napping under a bench. Charlie woke up just long enough to watch Kurt and Mother Nickle-Dickle place the basket on the table, and he dozed off again.

Kurt began removing petals from the flowers according to Mother Nickle-Dickle's instructions, while the tiny woman climbed up on a chair and took a strange-looking device down from a high shelf. The device appeared to be some kind of press made of glass and sterling silver. It had a handle and a bulbous chamber near the top, both made of silver, and glass tubing in the middle that twisted and turned in several directions, and a little silver spigot at the bottom that opened over a small silver bowl. The metal parts gleamed with the fine patina only age and loving care can bestow upon a metal.

Mother Nickle-Dickle placed the press on the table, carefully filled the chamber with flower petals, and pushed the handle down firmly. Droplets of pure, clear oil dripped from the chamber and rolled through the tubing and emptied into the bowl at the bottom. Mother

Nickle-Dickle glanced at Kurt, whose eyes were following the drops as they tumbled through the tubing. "The raw oil must go through many twists and turns before it can reach a high level of purification," she said. "That's how the finest oils are made."

The tiny woman pressed petals from each kind of flower—wisteria, gardenia, rose, honeysuckle, and jasmine—and leaves from the mint. As each oil was pressed and gathered, Mother Nickle-Dickle carefully measured a portion into a second silver bowl. When the last oil had been pressed and gathered and measured, Mother Nickle-Dickle stirred the mixture gently with a silver spoon, counting as she stirred: ". . . nineteen, twenty, twenty-one. It must be stirred twenty-one times—seven for copper, seven for nickel, and seven for silver—if it's to be properly blended.

"There! Now you have it!" she declared, and she set the silver spoon on the table and held the bowl up for Kurt to smell the blended oils.

The boy leaned over and sniffed the clear liquid. "It's the perfectly balanced perfume of the Rainbow Garden—in liquid form!"

Mother Nickle-Dickle smiled. "It's an old family recipe."

The woman poured the perfume into a small crystal flask, sealed it with a ground-glass stopper, and handed it to Kurt. "This should work, if anything will."

"If anything will," Kurt repeated.

"Now. I want to tell you a shortcut to the Copper Valley," said Mother Nickle-Dickle. "It will enable you to reach the stinkle-dunk's house in a day-and-a-half rather than three days by way of the main road. The shortcut parallels the main road, but it does not wind and bend. You must be careful, however. Do *not* leave the roadway. The shortcut is not well traveled and if you stray from its straight and narrow path, there may be no fellow travelers to help you find your way."

Mother Nickle-Dickle filled Kurt's backpack with more than enough food for the journey—bread and jam and vegetable tarts and cake and pie—and of course, all manner of tribble delights for Charlie. And as Kurt and Charlie (and Notch in the book in the backpack) readied themselves to leave, the tiny woman searched through a corner desk in the living room.

"Here it is," she said at last, and she opened a silver box and took out a small compass and handed it to Kurt. "You'll need this," she told the boy. "You must follow the shortcut until you reach the hollow oak tree. Then head due north, using the compass, and you will come out on the main road west of Stinkle's house. Do not cut across before reaching the hollow oak tree. The woods this side of the tree are thick and impassable."

Kurt and Charlie said goodbye to Mother Nickle-Dickle and to Chrysalis, who had accepted Mother Nickle-Dickle's kind invitation to stay with her until Charlie returned. Kurt was glad to be taking a shortcut to the Copper Valley. After all, time *was* short. Saving a day-and-a-half would certainly work to his advantage. He was not the least bit concerned that the road was not well traveled. After all, he had only to stay on it, and what could be so difficult about that?

CHAPTER 26

RETURN TO THE COPPER VALLEY

Traveling by way of the shortcut was *not* difficult, unless one considered monotony a difficulty, for never did the road twist or turn in the slightest degree. It ran straight as far as the eye could see, sloping downward toward the valley like a giant slough.

Around noon, the boy and his dog stopped for lunch, resting under the spreading boughs of a stately oak. As Kurt leaned back against the tree trunk, he felt a bit of debris from the tree strike the top of his head, and when he looked up, he saw a redheaded woodpecker darting among the branches. A moment later, he heard a rap-tap-tap like a little hammer as the bird pecked a hole in an upper limb. The sound reminded Kurt of Stinkle's house with its hammered copper roof and hammered copper shutters and hammered copper door. "Hammered copper!" said Kurt. "That's it! That's how I'll get Fraidy Slinkle-Purr to come to Nickledown!"

After sharing a vegetable tart and a piece of cake, Kurt and Charlie (and Notch in the pack) once again headed down the long, straight road. When the sun was two hours toward the west, they stepped from sunlight into cloud shadow.

"It's the Gloom," Kurt said to Charlie. "We must have crossed the boundary between the Nickel Hills and the Copper Valley."

And indeed they had. Moments later they passed a large grove of copper trees.

How different the Copper Valley appeared in early autumn, its deciduous oaks and maples having turned the golden yellows, rich browns, and warm reds of the season. How startlingly vivid—almost garish—the autumn colors appeared against the cold gray sky—against the grim backdrop of the Gloom.

Despite the colorful leaves, the villainous Gloom had robbed the valley of much of its seasonal splendor. The copper trees should have mirrored the autumn hues of the deciduous trees; the autumn hues should have complemented the rich, warm patina of the copper leaves. There should have been within the atmosphere the ever-present reddish glow that so distinguishes the Copper Valley from other regions of Whiskers. But there was no reddish glow; there was no warm patina to be found on the copper leaves. The leaves, dull and pallid under the Gloom, were incapable of rendering the strong reflections necessary to produce the familiar glow. They mirrored only the drear, dispirited visage of the grim, gray-purple Gloom.

For hours after crossing the boundary, Kurt and his dog plodded along with no unusual happenstance to draw their interest. It was no wonder when, just before sundown, a rustling in the bushes at the side of the road threw Charlie into such a frenzy he ran blindly into the woods.

"Charlie, come back!" Kurt shouted, remembering Mother Nickle-Dickle's warning. "We can't leave the road!"

The boy stood by the wayside calling frantically to his dog. When Charlie did not respond after what seemed a very long time, Kurt drew a deep breath and stepped through the bushes and into the trees.

As Mother Nickle-Dickle had said, the woods were thick and impassable. Kurt forced his way through dense thickets and climbed over fallen tree trunks and stepped carefully over low-hanging branches that lay like traps set to trip him. At one point, he stumbled and fell flat on his face on the prickly carpet of leaves, twigs, and pine needles covering the forest floor.

He was careful to take notice of the directions in which he turned to assure himself he would be able to retrace his steps back to the road. Left and right he turned, and right and left. Or was it right and left then left and right? He reached for the compass. It was not in his pocket. "I've lost it!" he said frantically. "It must have slipped from my pocket when I fell. Charlie, where are you!"

The woods were so dense, the canopy overhead so thick with foliage, that had there been a cloudless sky above, Kurt still could not have seen the sun. Had he been able to see the sun, he might have determined which direction was west, wherein lay the heart of the Copper Valley. Knowing which way was west, he could have headed due south and come across the road at some point. But not only was the sun not visible, daylight was quickly succumbing to darkness.

Kurt was about to call again for his dog but stopped short when he smelled a pungent odor—a putrid, stale, rancid, musty, stomach-turning stench! The Troll! he thought, his heart pounding. That must be what Charlie heard in the bushes.

Panicked, he began to run. It made no difference in which direction he ran, as long as it was away from the stench.

All at once he saw a shadowy figure dash between two trees ahead of him and he stopped cold in his tracks. With his knees shaking, he recalled the terrifying encounter with the Troll in the ravine.

The shadow dashed again, moving in the opposite direction. Before he could turn and run, the dark thing leaped from behind a bush and stood motionless before him.

Kurt held his breath as he stared at the formless shadow.

Suddenly the dark thing pounced on him!

"Ah!" he screamed, as he fell to the ground with the creature on top of him. "Ah!" he screamed again as the creature licked his face from his chin to his forehead.

Licked? "Charlie, is that you? Charlie!" he cried, as the dog pressed his nose to Kurt's nose. "Get off me, you nutsy mutt! You almost scared me to death!"

"I'm so glad I found you!" said Charlie, still trying to lick Kurt's face. "I didn't find what was in the bushes, and when I got back to the road, you had lost yourself."

"I had *lost myself*?" said Kurt, pulling himself up from the ground. "I had *lost myself*? *I* didn't lose myself, *you* lost myself. I mean, *you* lost *us*. I mean, *we're lost*! Yes, that's it! We're *lost*, Charlie!"

"We are, aren't we?" replied the dog, looking around. "And it's all my fault. Mother Nickle-Dickle said not to leave the road, and I did. I lost us."

"Don't worry about it, Charlie." Kurt realized there was no use fretting over what was already done. Now was the time to use one's head and find the way back to the road. Soon the sun would be down, and without a moon to light up the night, the woods would be as black as the inside of a cauldron.

"Now relax, Charlie," Kurt said. "We have to think this one out. You're a dog. Dogs are supposed to have all kinds of instinct. Concentrate, Charlie. Do you have any feeling at all for which way is west?"

Charlie looked at Kurt as though he thought the boy might be a few ounces short of a pound of tribble.

"Oh, never mind," said Kurt. "I'm the one who lost the compass. We'll just have to spend the night here. We can't search for the road in the dark. We might go deeper into the woods."

It was a frightening thought, spending the night in the black forest, especially after having encountered the terrible stench. Perhaps the Troll was lurking nearby. Perhaps any moment Kurt would turn to see those two sizzling red eyes staring at him through the trees. The boy dared not look around. He dared not think about the Troll lest he show fear and frighten Charlie.

He did glance up at the canopy overhead, however, and to appear calm and unafraid, he commented casually, "I'll bet the sky is full of beautiful stars somewhere up there."

"I see stars," said Charlie.

"What do you mean? You don't see stars."

"Yes, I do," said the dog. "Right there behind you."

CHAPTER 27

THE GUIDELITHES

Kurt turned to see what Charlie was talking about, and there, high in the trees, were hundreds of tiny, twinkling lights. The boy watched in amazement as more and more appeared. They seemed to come from nowhere in particular. Where one moment there was darkness, the next, there appeared a spot of light. Hundreds grew to thousands, and still more gathered in the treetops until the woods were aglow with their brilliant light. It seemed to Kurt all the stars of the heavens had gathered beneath one dark and lowly forest canopy.

The lights triggered a spark of remembrance in the boy and he recalled having seen them before. "These are the same lights we saw in the passage, Charlie—the silver specs. Remember?"

Before the dog could answer, one of the tiny lights, which was much larger and brighter than the rest, swooped down and landed squarely on Charlie's head. The dog stood very still, gazing upward with his eyes crossed, trying to see the uninvited guest.

Kurt could tell the tiny being was a firefly of some sort, though it was much brighter than any firefly he had ever seen. He remembered Spinneret saying lights such as this were sent to guide lost or frightened animals, and he and Charlie were certainly lost and frightened. Perhaps that explained their sudden appearance.

"Who are you?" Kurt asked the glowing light on Charlie's head.

"I am Polestar of the Highest Order of Guidelithes," replied the firefly. "I and my legions have been sent to lead you out of darkness."

"Who sent you?" asked Kurt.

"The one who guides those who guide," replied the guidelithe.

Kurt could only speculate as to the identity of "the one who guides those who guide."

"Follow the light," said Polestar, and he flew from Charlie's head and soared high into the treetops above the cloud of guidelithes. In a moment, he moved, and the entire lighted legion moved.

Kurt and Charlie followed, walking confidently now through the thick forest that had seemed so foreboding only moments before—walking within the brilliant glow that painted a silver path for them to tread.

Back they traveled over the prickly carpet of leaves and twigs and pine needles that lay like a silver tapestry beneath their feet; back through the dense thickets, over fallen tree trunks, past low-hanging branches that now seemed less like traps and more like the gracefully bowing limbs they truly were. After a time, they stepped out of the dense forest and onto the long, straight roadway.

The sky, unobscured by trees now, appeared black as pitch except in those places where light from the great multitude of guidelithes illuminated the undersides of low-lying clouds.

Having halted briefly upon reaching the road, Polestar's legions turned westward. On silent wing they flew through the soundless night, leading the boy along the straight and narrow way that would take him deep into the Copper Valley. Kurt could not bring himself to utter a word as he walked within the light. Instead, he listened intently to the irrefutable silence, amazed at how such a great gathering of winged creatures could fly above him with neither stir, nor flutter. He thought it peculiar that nowhere could there be heard a cricket or frog or other night creature. It was as though, out of divine reverence, all living things within proximity to the guidelithes had fallen silent with the passing of their light.

After a walk in which time seemed immeasurable, the boy caught sight of the hollow oak tree Mother Nickle-Dickle had described. Without direction from Kurt, the guidelithes turned northward at the tree, and the boy and his dog followed them into the forest.

There was no road now, only a path, and parts of it were so overgrown with weeds and thickets that it disappeared altogether in places. Before long, the path converged with the main road about a half-day's journey from Stinkle's house.

As Kurt stepped out from under the forest's canopy onto the familiar winding road, he was astonished at what he saw. The light from the guidelithes revealed a sky whose clouds churned the way they did over the lake the day Charlie ran from the thunder. Occasional breaks in their formidable ranks allowed streaks of cold, pallid moonlight to pass between wayside oaks causing the ill-fated arbors, draped in darkness as they were, to stand in silhouette against the shafts of moonlight—to stand like sprawling, twisted sentinels—grim apparitions in an equally grim landscape. Even the once-graceful copper trees scattered among the oaks appeared foreboding in this place, their branches misshapen and malnourished, their limbs elongated, as though by day they had stretched beyond their means to draw to themselves what little light was left in the valley in the presence of the ravenous Gloom.

Charlie stayed close to Kurt as the boy prepared a place to rest for the night. As Kurt gathered leaves to make a bed, he heard ever so faintly a familiar sound. "W-a-u-k," croaked a leap-lop. "W-a-u-k," repeated another. Their calls were joined by the crickety voice of a night chirp. "Quickit! Time'a shaut," warned the solitary voice, ever so urgently.

Kurt's whiskers translated the sounds into an intense uneasiness. The boy had discovered the meaning of the night-chirps' message in Parhelion's warning, but the leap-lops' message still eluded him. What had Spinneret said about the leap-lops? "The leap-lops speak in meaning hidden" and something about "whiskers to words" and "truth in the step" and "footsteps to light." And what was that riddle?

"Here's a riddle short and sweet:
*Use your whiskers **and your feet**."*

Kurt quickly dismissed the riddle. He had no time to think about it now. Besides, thinking of it only made him more uneasy.

The boy finished preparing the bed of leaves and was about to thank the guidelithes for their help when Polestar swooped down and landed on Charlie's head again. Accustomed to the uninvited guest by now, Charlie sat patiently, waiting for the guidelithe to speak.

"There is something I would like you to see," Polestar said to Kurt, and as if their leader had transmitted some invisible signal, several of the guidelithes flew down and hovered in front of the boy. They were carrying a small basket made entirely of light. Leaning over, Kurt looked inside the basket. And there, lying still and quiet on the bottom, was a tiny being whose body was completely transparent. She, like the basket, was made of light; but her light was dim and pale, and it flickered from time to time as if any moment it might go out altogether.

"What is it?" Kurt asked quietly, intending not to disturb the frail creature.

"A sunbeam," replied Polestar. "A rather faded sunbeam. She's very weak, the dear child, and I fear she may fade away entirely. We have been keeping her with us trying to feed her with our light, but I'm afraid she's not responding."

"What happened to her?" Kurt asked.

"She was in your world, playing in the air after an early morning rain—on the day you came to Whiskers. She wandered into shadows where sunbeams dare not go, and there she came upon the Thunder Troll. He devoured much of her light, leaving her dim and pale—too weak to climb back to the sun—to ride its rays back to Whiskers."

Kurt peeked again into the basket and waited for Polestar to continue.

"Sunbeams ride the rays freely back and forth between the two worlds. The Land of Whiskers is where sunbeams dwell when the sun is not shining in your world, you see. Her only hope was to find you and beg you to take her with you to Whiskers."

"How did she know I would be going?" Kurt asked.

"She heard the Piper's call at dawn, and she knew you were the Nickle-Dickle child, so she made her way to your house and whispered to you and tugged at your sleeve, but you neither heard nor saw her. When you left for the lake, she gathered all the strength she had within her and followed you. There she played upon the page of a book you were reading, but still you did not see her."

"I saw her"—Kurt corrected himself—"her little light, I mean. But I didn't know what it was."

"She had all but given up hope of your answering the Piper's call," Polestar continued, "when she realized the thunder might frighten Charlie enough to send him through the passage. And since she knew how much Nickle-Dickle boys love their dogs, she knew you would follow. With the last of her strength, she climbed into your shirt pocket. When you came through the passage, she came with you. When you tumbled into the meadow, she fell from your pocket. That's where we found her."

"If only I had known she was there," said Kurt, "I could have—"

"You could have done nothing," said Polestar. "When we found her, she had only enough strength to tell us her story; then she fell asleep. She hasn't wakened since."

"Oh," said Kurt, and all at once he felt as though his heart would break as he stared at the fragile being lying weak and helpless on the bottom of the basket. At last he forced himself to look away.

"Polestar, why didn't I hear the Piper's call that morning? I'm sure I would have answered if I'd heard it."

"Did you hear a flute play at dawn?

"Yes. Well, no. I mean, I heard one for a few seconds in my dream, but some awful bell drowned it out. It woke me up."

"The leaden bell," said Polestar. "The Gloom must have struck the bell for that very purpose—to quell the Piper's call. Had you heard clearly and answered, a passage would have opened where you were, and that would have been at cross purposes with the Troll's intentions."

"He wanted to be there when the passage opened so he could come through with me, didn't he?"

"I would say."

"And he used Charlie's fear of thunder to open the passage at exactly the right moment."

"It suited his purpose."

"Why couldn't he have come through the air like the sunbeams? He's in the clouds some of the time, isn't he?"

"The Troll is linked to sky and earth," explained Polestar. "This bound him to the earth to some extent and prevented him from coming skyward to Whiskers. The passage was his only means. The Gloom, however, is linked to sky and air. It is in no way earthbound. It could come skyward to Whiskers, but only if preceded by its master, the Troll."

Polestar flew to the basket that held the dying sprite. After hovering over it like a brooding parent, he returned to Charlie's head.

"Her light should have been restored upon reaching Whiskers, but with the Troll and his minions present in the land, the quality of light was quite diminished. For that reason, she failed to respond. Others would not have noticed the slight dullness, but to one whose essence is light itself, it was as though the sun had fallen from the sky."

"What can we do?" Kurt asked.

"Perhaps nothing," replied the guidelithe. "There's little hope of saving her unless the Troll and his Gloom are driven from Whiskers— unless the light is fully restored."

Kurt looked into the basket again. "What will you do with her now?"

"We will take her to the Nickel Hills. The Gloom has not yet gathered there and the light is only slightly diminished. Perhaps she will derive some degree of nourishment from it. We dared not move her that far before, but now we have no choice. We will be saying goodbye to you, Kurt. A safe journey to you and to Charlie. I pray you find the door that leads home." And with that, Polestar flew high into the air over his legions, and in a moment, he and the host of shining guidelithes ascended with a mighty *swish* into the night sky and were gone.

Kurt tried to fall asleep in the deep dark of the Copper Valley, hoping the long night would drive all thoughts of the dying sprite from his mind. But even with his eyes closed, he could see the sprite's pale light beckoning to him through the darkness. "I must save the sprite," he told himself. "Now more than ever, I must drive the Troll from Whiskers!"

CHAPTER 28

STINKLE-DUNK'S SWEET SURRENDER

Morning found the sky little changed from the night before. The clouds, still dark and churning, gave Kurt the feeling time had stopped, and night, seeking to cling eternally, had frozen all the land in one somber, endless moment.

Heading east toward Stinkle's house, Kurt and Charlie made their way uneasily along the old familiar road past stands of shadowy oaks that seemed to watch their every move. Kurt felt as though each leaf projecting from the tainted branches concealed a pair of peering eyes.

The morning air, stale and dank, hung about the travelers like some thick, oppressive substance poised to choke the very breath from out their nostrils. Even the copper trees, which tended to ring at the slightest breeze, stood motionless, their leaves hanging like lead in the burdensome air.

Kurt thought it strange that, with the clouds churning more furiously than the night before, there should be no thunder. Surely in a gathering storm there would be rumblings at the very least. Where was the Troll if not here to rumble above him?

Kurt and Charlie (and Notch in the backpack) traveled for hours and met no animals along the road. The boy found this odd, for they had met many the last time they passed this way. Are they hiding, or have they fled? thought Kurt.

In early afternoon, they came within sight of the little house with the hammered copper roof—Stinkle-Dunk's cottage. How glad Kurt was to see it! He quickened his pace, anxious to feel again the warm welcome extended by the cheery front door and the gleaming roof and shutters. But the house offered no warm welcome. Instead, it looked deserted and unkempt. Perhaps the drawn curtains made it appear so, or the tall weeds in the window boxes where roses and gardenias once bloomed. Or perhaps it was the hammered copper turned dull and lifeless under the Gloom.

A terrible thought occurred to the boy. What if Stinkle were not at home? What if he were out foraging? Or worse yet, what if he had fled the valley, as the other animals appeared to have done?

Kurt hurried ahead until he felt the familiar crunch of the pebbled walkway beneath his feet. When he reached the house, he found the door covered with pieces of white paper, notices of some kind haphazardly tacked there. Grabbing a handful of the papers, he quickly perused them. They were subpoenas—all of them—the result of lawsuits against poor Stinkle.

"Stinkle!" Kurt shouted, pounding on the door. He soon heard footsteps within the house. The footsteps came as far as the door and stopped. The boy pounded again and called, "Stinkle! Are you in there? It's me—Kurt!"

The curtain to the side of the door moved slightly and Kurt saw a little black eye peering at him. In a moment, the door opened ever so slowly, and Stinkle stuck his head out, quickly looked to the right and left and pulled Kurt in by his shirt collar. It was all Charlie could do to make it through the door before it closed again.

"Kurtis!" blurted Stinkle. "I never thought I'd see you again. I hoped I wouldn't, for your sake. That is, I hoped you would have found your way home by now, but obviously you haven't, and under the circumstances, I'm so glad to see you!"

He hugged Kurt with a grip so tight it took the boy's breath away.

"And Charlie! Charlie, too!" And he patted the dog firmly on the shoulder. "When you knocked at my door, I was afraid it was one of *them*. I almost didn't answer. But I'm so glad I did!"

"Oh, these are for you," said Kurt, handing Stinkle the notices. "I found them on the door."

Stinkle snatched the papers from Kurt's hand, and without looking at them, quickly stuffed them into a desk drawer. "Now Kurtis, tell me all about you. What have you done? Where have you been? You must have found the way home by now. Why have you come back here?"

Kurt dropped his backpack on the coffee table and made himself comfortable on the green overstuffed sofa. As Stinkle listened with great interest from his place in the old wing chair, Kurt told him all that happened since last they were together.

"A most amazing series of adventures, Kurtis. You are lucky to have come through unscathed."

"I know. Anyway, when I read the Legacy, I knew I had to find a way to rid Whiskers of the Troll. But I had to bring you and Fraidy and Tattle to Nickledown first."

"Now, hold it right there," said Stinkle. "I'll help you in any way I can to get the others to Nickledown, but as for me—"

"You *have* to come, Stinkle. It's not safe here."

"Harumph," said the stinkle-dunk. "As I told you before, I am an old homebody at heart. I have no desire to go traipsing off to Nickledown. I'll stay right here in the Copper Valley if you don't mind."

"But I do mind," said Kurt. "I mind because I care about you."

He paused a moment to weigh his words. "Stinkle, I know about the Sweet Surrender."

The stinkle-dunk looked as though he had been struck dead. His face turned ghostly white. A hush fell between the two of them for several seconds before Stinkle spoke again. "I should have known you would hear about that—with all your travels and adventures." He slumped in his chair and a look of forlorn came over his face.

"Oh, Kurtis, what am I to do? This is all so terrible. How much do you know?"

"Enough to get the general idea. I heard a rumor in Nickledown—"

"Nickledown? Oh my, oh my. The news has traveled that far, has it? Now I'll never be able to go there. Even if this terrible situation with the Troll is resolved, I'll never be able to show my face in Nickledown."

"Stinkle, you've got to come with me. You know what's happening outside. The Gathering Gloom is growing darker by the hour. The other animals have already left this part of the valley. We didn't pass a single one on the road. I don't know where the Troll is, but I know you're in danger. I can feel it in my whiskers."

The stinkle-dunk's head fell forward; his chin dropped almost to his chest. "It doesn't matter, Kurtis," he lamented. "Nothing matters now."

Kurt was at a loss for words. He had never seen the skunk so distraught.

"My color is fading, you see," said Stinkle. "I'm slipping downward toward orange."

The stinkle-dunk sat in silence a moment before raising his head to speak again. "You see, it was all so innocent. My intentions were good. I just wanted to share my Sweet Surrender with others, and if I could make a little profit in so doing, all to the good. The extra money was to allow me to stockpile a supply of yarn balls for Fraidy. It was even going to pay for repairs to his house. I thought if I could improve his condition a little, he might . . ." He stopped talking and swallowed hard. "But then the notices started coming. Not at first, mind you. At first, no one complained."

"Why not?"

"As I think back on it, I realize the animals were trying to be kind in the beginning, not telling me the truth about my Sweet Surrender—trying to spare my feelings. They respected my color and were attempting to move up in color themselves. But on that Silver Day—the day you came through the passage—it all began to change. From that day on, something was not quite right in Whiskers."

"It was the Troll," said Kurt. "I'm sure he came through the passage ahead of me."

"That *could* explain it," said Stinkle. "On that afternoon, when I went out to forage, I noticed the animals were avoiding me. The ones I managed to speak to acted rudely and ran away. I'm sure they ran off to chortle and choke and talk about me behind my back. No one seemed concerned about color at all. I never thought I'd see such a thing in Whiskers. I would not be surprised if some of them were fallen all the way back to purple." He paused a moment to reflect. "Yes. Perhaps it *was* the Troll. You say he feeds on light. That would explain why the light diminished as it did. It's most alarming, for the very existence of Whiskers depends upon the light. Light is what nourishes the Land of Whiskers—what feeds it—what allows the animals to grow in the colors. Colors are not merely measuring devices, as it might appear, Kurtis. Colors are a form of light within us. And the light within us is a form of life. Should the light be destroyed, it would mean . . ."

"The end of Whiskers," said Kurt.

The stinkle-dunk stared at the boy with a blank expression, seeming to have no desire to embrace the words he, himself, had dared not say. But at last he nodded. "We—the animals, the Nickle-Dickles—all that is Whiskers—would fade away."

"You would die, you mean," said Kurt.

The little skunk said nothing, but he seemed to comprehend the word with fullness of meaning, for he drew a long, labored breath and gave a slight nod.

"Anyway," he continued, "the next morning—the day I met you—I found a paper attached to my front door—a legal notice. I thought at first it must be a mistake, a misunderstanding. It said my Sweet Surrender was causing some of the animals to swoon, and some had fallen and injured themselves." Stinkle's eyes filled with tears. "I would never intentionally harm anyone, Kurtis."

"I know you wouldn't, Stinkle."

"As I was saying, when I first met you, and you startled me and I slipped . . . Your reaction told me it was all true. For the first time,

I realized how the rest of Whiskers viewed my crème de la crème. When we arrived at the house, you may recall, there was another paper on the door. I stuffed it into my pocket. I preferred not to have you know of my shameful dilemma. But that was just the start of it all. Since then, I've had to pay fines and court fees and the cost of fumigating half the countryside. And the embarrassment! Oh, the embarrassment. Unbearable! And to make matters worse, I'm stuck with all those bottles; those useless, empty bottles."

The stinkle-dunk slumped deeper into his wing chair. "I could never go to Nickledown now. Can you imagine how humiliated I would feel in front of the Nickle-Dickles should I slip? Oh," he moaned, pressing his hand to his heart. "That terrible Sweet Surrender.

> *I stunk, I stunk,*
> *I most dis-STINK-ly stunk.*
> *What I had thought was silver scent*
> *Was nothing more than flatulent.*
> *They sniffed one sniff, and down they went!*
> *I stunk, I stunk, I stunk.*
>
> *I erred, I erred,*
> *I most dis-STINK-ly erred.*
> *I never would with ill intent*
> *My 'sweet perfume' misrepresent.*
> *What a vain entanglement!*
> *I erred, I erred, I erred.*
>
> *I ail, I ail,*
> *I most dis-STINK-ly ail.*
> *I, without premonishment,*
> *Much to my astonishment,*
> *Invited this admonishment.*
> *I ail, I ail, I ail."*

The stinkle-dunk breathed a deep, mournful sigh.
"But Stinkle, what about Fraidy and Tattle?"

The little skunk sat up straight. "Oh yes. You must get them to Nickledown, to safety. But how?" He stood and clasped his hands behind his back and began to pace.

"Stinkle, I have a plan," said Kurt. "But I'll need your help."

"Anything," said Stinkle, and he stopped pacing and settled back into the chair.

Kurt briefly explained his plan for taking Fraidy Slinkle-Purr to Nickledown. "I haven't thought of what to do about Tattle yet, but there's still enough time for that."

Hoping talk of Fraidy and Tattle going to Nickledown had made the stinkle-dunk amenable to going himself, Kurt took the flask of sweet perfume out of the backpack and showed it to Stinkle. "Mother Nickle-Dickle and I picked the flowers from the Rainbow Garden ourselves. She made the perfume from an old family recipe, especially for you."

"What!" said the stinkle-dunk.

"You can wear it when you go to Nickledown," said Kurt. "No one will know you're the stinkle-dunk who made the Sweet Surrender. And if you slip now and then, no one will notice. All they will smell will be the sweet perfume."

The stinkle-dunk leaped to his feet. He made the churring noise stinkle-dunks make when they're sorely disturbed. "Me? Wear perfume? Out of the question!" And he turned and headed toward the kitchen.

"But Stinkle, just smell it," Kurt said, pulling the ground-glass stopper from the flask. He followed Stinkle into the kitchen, and when the stinkle-dunk stopped near the table, Kurt held the flask toward the little skunk's nose. The animal threw up his hands and turned his head away.

"Never!" Stinkle said angrily. "Never in Whiskers has a stinkle-dunk worn perfume, and I will certainly *not* be the first. That is the end of the matter." After a short silence, he added, "I will, however, help you get the others to Nickledown. Now, what was that plan you mentioned? Copper armor for Fraidy?"

The two sat down at the kitchen table, and Kurt began explaining his plan in detail. With talk of copper armor for Fraidy, Charlie left his cozy spot beside the living room sofa, plopped down on the floor next to Kurt, and held his stand-up ear stiff and alert.

"We'll make him a suit of hammered copper—copper armor!" said Kurt. "No one would be afraid to go anywhere if he were protected by a suit of armor."

Charlie moaned and lowered his ear.

"What a wonderful idea!" said Stinkle. "Ever since that terrible 'flight' he took with the umbrella, he's been afraid of more than his *own* shadow; he's afraid of *all* shadows—and just about everything else, too. I couldn't convince him the wind caused the flight. He thinks a shadow grabbed him and pulled him up to the cloud and dropped him in the tree. It will take a great deal of convincing to get him to wear the armor. But I've had my share of experience handling Fraidy, and I'm sure, between the two of us, we can accomplish the task."

"We have to," said Kurt.

"However," Stinkle continued, "in addition to the armor, why don't we provide him with another umbrella to protect him, should the sun peek out along the way. He *is* still afraid of his *own* shadow, you know. A splendid addition, don't you think?"

"A splendid addition," said Kurt.

Stinkle disappeared into the hallway and soon returned with a large, green umbrella, which he placed on the kitchen table before sitting down again.

"Now," said Stinkle. "How do you propose to build the armor?"

"From the leaves of the copper trees," said Kurt.

Stinkle's expression soured. "Do you know how long it takes to harvest copper leaves?"

"Not really."

"Harumph," said the skunk. "Copper leaves grip the branches tightly. Each leaf must be twisted and turned until it snaps. It's a time-consuming process, even under ideal conditions; and with that dreadful darkness outside . . . I'm afraid it's out of the question."

"But there must be a way."

Stinkle shook his head. "It's useless to try."

"It can't be," Kurt insisted, and he thought for a moment. "Stinkle, didn't you say you still have those copper bottles you were going to use for the Sweet Surrender?"

Stinkle's eyes popped wide open. "The copper bottles! Yes, I still have them! I have a whole basement full of copper bottles! I stocked hundreds before I stopped producing the Sweet Surrender. I have enough for two suits of armor. And I have the tools to shape the suit. We can start right away."

He stood up from the table and hurried toward the hall, beckoning Kurt and Charlie to follow.

When Stinkle opened the basement door, Kurt could see at the foot of the stairs a set of shelves holding row upon row of shiny copper bottles, neatly stacked. When the boy descended the stairs and stepped onto the basement floor, he could not believe his eyes. Every wall was filled from floor to ceiling with wooden shelves upon which were piled, six high and four deep, bottles and bottles and more bottles—highly polished, finely crafted copper bottles fitted with fragile, crystal liners and topped with ground-glass stoppers—bottles whose only purpose could be to hold the finest and rarest of perfumes. And engraved on the face of each bottle were the words, "Stinkle-Dunk's Sweet Surrender."

Kurt was anxious to get started on the suit of armor, but he was not sure exactly how to go about it. "Where do we start?" he asked the stinkle-dunk.

"Harumph," said the skunk, looking puzzled. "I suppose . . . That is . . . If only we had instructions . . ."

"Instructions!" said Kurt, realizing he knew someone who could tell them *exactly* how to build a suit of armor. "Just a minute." And he ran upstairs and grabbed the book from the backpack, brought it to the basement, and placed it on the end of the long wooden workbench that filled the center of the room. When he opened the book, the booknotch appeared.

The little worm had apparently overheard the conversation in the kitchen, for he immediately offered to supervise. He was familiar with cut and style in suits of armor, having lived for a time close to a picture of such a suit next to the word *armor* in his old dictionary.

Charlie, on the other hand, chose to sit in the corner and watch the others work. He seemed unable to cope with talk of a cat wearing a suit of armor. After a time, he did help Kurt remove the crystal liners from the copper bottles. He took great delight in seeing how high he could stack the glass without it toppling over.

Kurt and Stinkle worked all afternoon and into the early evening. They worked straight through the dinner hour, snacking on biscuits and honey as they cut and snipped and soldered and hammered and molded the many small pieces of copper. Kurt had half expected the stinkle-dunk to glow blue earlier, during their conversation about the Sweet Surrender, but now the skunk seemed his old exuberant self again.

"Stinkle," Kurt said as they worked, "does anyone's color ever show? On the outside, I mean."

"Not the color he *is*," said Stinkle. "If an animal were yellow, for instance, his yellow would never show on the outside. Animals do some- times glow pink or blue, but it has nothing to do with the color they *are inside*; it reflects the color they're *feeling*. If they're exceedingly happy, they might glow pink. If they're deeply saddened, they might glow blue. But it seldom happens—only in extreme cases. Why do you ask?"

"Because I glowed blue when Notch was lost."

"I see. You've had a rare experience, Kurtis. I assume this doesn't happen in your world?"

"Oh no," Kurt answered. "But we do have the expressions, 'in the pink' and 'feeling blue.'"

"I'm surprised you have those expressions if no one in your world ever glows," said Stinkle.

It was well into evening when Kurt and the stinkle-dunk soldered the last pieces of copper onto the armor. After buffing the suit to a high shine, they propped it up on the workbench to admire it.

What a fine suit it was! Any slinkle-purr should have been proud to wear it. The booknotch said it was far more exquisite than the one pictured in his dictionary. Even Charlie smiled proudly when he saw his face reflected in the highly polished surface.

After carrying the suit upstairs and setting it on the sofa, Kurt and Stinkle built a fire in the hearth. They and the booknotch (who was perched on the open book on the coffee table) talked into the wee hours of the night, while Charlie snoozed before the fire. When at last the flames flickered and faded away and the few remaining embers dimmed to a faint glow, Kurt tucked the book, with Notch in it, safely away in the backpack, and he and Charlie made their way to the guest room where they had slept on their previous visit to the cottage.

Kurt lay awake for a time after Stinkle turned off the lights. He was thinking about the expressions "feeling blue" and "in the pink" and finally concluded his father or grandfather or great-grandfather—one of them—must have taken those expressions back to his world. He felt very proud of his family, and he wondered what the school bully, Duff Skruggs, would have to say if he were told Kurt's family had done something as noteworthy as that.

Thinking perhaps he would fall asleep easier with a bit of fresh air, Kurt hopped out of bed and walked to the window and raised the sash. The night was black, and quiet except for the distant croaking of leap-lops and the familiar reply of the night-chirps. "W-a-u-k," called the leap-lops. "Quickit! Time'a shaut!" warned the night-chirps. Kurt quickly slammed the window shut and jumped back into bed.

CHAPTER 29

SHELLS, SHELLS, AND MORE SHELLS

Kurt awoke to the sound of a low rumble. "Stinkle, are you awake?" he called, hurrying toward Stinkle's room.

"I'm in here," came a voice from the kitchen.

When Kurt arrived at the kitchen door, he found the stinkle-dunk hard at work with pans and spatulas and spoons and mixing bowls, busily baking biscuits for the journey to Fraidy's house. Charlie, if he was helping at all, was doing so in a strictly supervisory capacity; for the dog, having by all appearances succumbed again to the air of gentility so pervasive in the stinkle-dunk's fine, well-appointed house, was sitting properly at the kitchen table with a white linen napkin tucked neatly into his collar, eating his morning Chunkie Chewie.

"I dare say, Kurtis, did you hear the rumbling?" said Stinkle, pulling a pan of hot biscuits from the oven.

"It woke me up," Kurt replied.

"Harumph," said the skunk, and still holding the pan of biscuits, he closed the oven door with his foot. "I slept very little last night. I thought I heard rumbling the whole night long—faint, you know. I was certain I heard it early this morning, and having little inclination to go back to sleep, I got up and began baking. It's a long journey to Fraidy's, as you may recall, and with the weather as menacing as it is, we may not be able to forage along the way. We had better prepare ourselves well with food and supplies."

"Have you looked outside?" said Kurt, making his way to the living room.

"I've not taken time," the skunk called after him.

Kurt drew the curtain aside and peered out. "Stinkle! Come look at this!"

The stinkle-dunk wiped his floury hands on his apron and hurried to the window.

"The clouds," said Kurt, "they've started to move." And he held the curtain back so Stinkle could see.

"Toward the east," said Stinkle. "The direction we'll be traveling. We had better be on our way if we want to outrun them."

They did not wait for the last batch of biscuits to bake. Instead, they quickly packed what they could into Kurt's backpack, grabbed the suit of armor and green umbrella, and headed out the front door.

"One moment," said Stinkle. He ran back inside and soon reappeared carrying a small pick, hammer, and chisel. "We'll need these if Fraidy's armor doesn't fit—if we have to pry it apart and make adjustments."

Stinkle stuffed the tools into Kurt's backpack, and off they went.

In the gray light of morning, the Gloom appeared even more ominous. For the first time, Kurt could see the depth of churning within the clouds. As far as his eyes could see, the clouds hung as a heavy net set to drop like a trap upon the unsuspecting. In places, they had thickened to a deep, purplish black.

"The color of darkness below purple," Kurt murmured.

"Did you say something?"

"It was nothing," said Kurt, quickening his pace. "I was just remembering something my grandfather used to say."

Charlie stepped up next to the boy and walked close beside him. The dog seemed especially jumpy, and Kurt suspected it had only a little to do with the Gloom and more to do with the fact they were now nearing the place where, on the previous trip, Charlie's Chunkie

Chewies were stolen. Only a few of the biscuits remained now, and Charlie had rationed those to one per day. Kurt suspected the dog's intent was to guard the pack while keeping a sharp lookout for Tubbs, for his stand-up ear was alert, his strides deliberate, his muscles tense. When by chance Kurt stepped on an empty walnut shell, the crunch sent Charlie leaping a foot into the air.

"He's worried about Tubbs," Kurt whispered to Stinkle.

"I doubt if we'll see Tubbs," said the stinkle-dunk. It looks as though all the animals have left this area too."

The talk of Tubbs reminded Kurt of Mosey. "Stinkle, I just thought of something. What will happen to the weery-dawdles if they have to flee the Gloom? They can't run. They can't even walk fast."

"I don't know," replied Stinkle. "If we come across them, we can carry a few, but certainly not all. They're much too numerous. I doubt we'll find any around here, however. This is nut-druggle country, and with the feud going on—"

"The feud?"

"The feud between the weery-dawdles and the nut druggles."

Kurt stared at the stinkle-dunk blankly.

"Haven't you heard? It started with that tiff between Tubbs and your friend Mosey—when Tubbs left Mosey in the tree. I overheard two twitter-flits discussing it on my windowsill. It seems a friend of theirs—a gossipy little chirper—saw the whole thing and spread the news. Now the weery-dawdles and nut druggles will have nothing to do with one another. Each accuses the other of having defective whiskers."

"Oh no," said Kurt. "Mosey was afraid something like that would happen."

"Indeed," said Stinkle. "Your friend must be well acquainted with twitter-flits. The little feathered babblers have always been gossips, but at least they used to carry worthwhile messages from time to time. Since the Gloom arrived, they do nothing but spread idle twitter. The more trouble they cause, the better they seem to like it. With them stirring the pot, I fear the nut druggles and weery-dawdles will be feuding as long as there's a Land of Whiskers."

The travelers were nearing the walnut grove where Pink Nut Druggle and her band lived, but there was no sign of the druggles, unless one considered the vast number of empty nut shells scattered about. Walnut shells were carelessly strewn everywhere, as though the druggles had left in a great hurry. One shell, whose top half was missing, still had the entire nut left in the bottom half. It caught Kurt's eye because, from a distance, it looked remarkably like a weery-dawdle sitting in a nutshell.

"Stinkle, look at that shell," Kurt said, pointing. "If we could just find a way to hook them together . . ."

"Hook what together?"

"The nutshells. If we get lots of empty walnut shells and hook them together, say in groups of six or seven, we'll have little caravans of nutshell cars. And if we find the weery-dawdles and put one in each car and get the nut druggles to pull the caravans to Nickledown—"

"You're dreaming, Kurtis. The nut druggles would never agree to pull the caravans. And even if they did, the weery-dawdles would not entrust themselves to the nut druggles. They would never get into the cars."

"Sure they would," Kurt insisted, "*if* we ended the feud."

"And how do you propose to do that?"

"I don't know yet." Kurt pointed toward a large walnut tree on the left side of the road. "Stinkle, isn't that the tree where we stopped for lunch the day Notch blew away in his newspaper? The tree where Pink Nut Druggle lives?"

"I believe it is, Kurtis."

"Well, maybe Pink Nut Druggle can help us. She knows all the nut druggles. And she's pink. They would listen to her."

"Perhaps," Stinkle conceded. "But I doubt if we can find her. I'm sure the druggles have fled."

"It's worth a try," said Kurt.

They stopped under the walnut tree and called loudly for Pink Nut Druggle. They were surprised when she scurried down the trunk and greeted them. "Stinkle! Kurt! Charlie! I thought I was the only one left in this part of the valley."

"It appears you are," said Stinkle. "You're the first animal we've seen since leaving home."

"They've all fled this terrible darkness," said Pink Nut Druggle. "You caught me just in time. I and the other druggles were about to leave for the Nickel Hills. We hoped this awful gloom would pass, but when it didn't, and when we heard what happened out at the Meadow—"

"Something happened out at the Meadow?" said Kurt.

Pink Nut Druggle shook her head sorrowfully. "What a pity. That beautiful Meadow."

"What happened to it, dear friend?" Stinkle asked.

"The Meadow is no more," said Pink Nut Druggle. "The light has been swallowed up—completely. A passing stand'n-stare told us about it earlier today—a white-tailed one—a gentle animal. It was his favorite place to graze. Now it's as though the Meadow never existed."

Kurt and Stinkle looked at each other, but neither said a word.

"I must hurry along now," said Pink Nut Druggle. "The other druggles are waiting for me in the next grove. I had to run back to get my nut cracker, you see." She blushed. "These old teeth aren't as strong as they used to be."

Before she could dash away, Kurt stopped her and explained his concern for the weery-dawdles, a concern more intense in view of what happened to the Meadow.

"I've felt the same concern," said Pink Nut Druggle. "I hoped if we met the weery-dawdles on the road, my druggles would feel compassion and help them. But with this gloom affecting our colors, there's no predicting how they might act."

Kurt quickly explained his plan for the nutshell caravans. "I thought maybe you could talk to the druggles and—"

"What a splendid idea!" said Pink Nut Druggle. "But perhaps *you* should talk to them. I've tried to convince them feuding is wrong, but to no avail."

"What could *I* say to them?" said Kurt.

"Perhaps it's not so much *what* you say as *how* you say it," said the nut druggle. "I truly believe you possess the necessary persuasive powers. Something about your demeanor makes it so."

Whether or not this was true is uncertain, but Pink Nut Druggle's belief in the boy gave him the measure of faith he needed, and he agreed to speak to the druggles.

They hurried to the next walnut grove, and Pink Nut Druggle put out the call. Nut druggles, too many to count, scurried from all parts of the grove and gathered in front of Kurt and Stinkle and Charlie and Pink Nut Druggle, chittering and chattering away.

Kurt glanced nervously at the lady nut druggle, and she returned a reassuring nod. The boy took a deep breath and swallowed hard and cleared his voice. Recalling the nut druggle's words, he stood tall and at once felt hope and confidence swell within him. When he started to speak, a hush fell upon the crowd. Much to his own amazement, he became the Great Orator. His speech was magnificent! "Put yourselves in the place of the weery-dawdles," he said. "Walk in their shoes— as slow as they may be. Count your blessings that you are swift and sure of foot."

When Kurt finished speaking, there was not a dry eye among the nut druggles. Even Tubbs, who was never the most sensitive of druggles, sobbed uncontrollably.

"Now quickly," Pink Nut Druggle said to the throng, "go and gather the shells." And off they went in every direction gathering the sturdiest shells they could find, six to a druggle.

Despite the darkness overhead, the spirit of light prevailed. Everywhere druggles were helping other druggles stack the shells six shells high, as they practiced walking with them like jugglers in a Big Top circus. The more they gathered and stacked and spilled and laughed and stacked again, the more they became caught up in the occasion. Their excitement turned to joyous murmuring among themselves, such as, "I know we can convince the weery-dawdles," and "Why didn't we think of it ourselves?" and "The feud's gone on long enough," and "How wonderful it feels to be doing this!"

When they had finished their gathering and stacking and practicing, Pink Nut Druggle asked, "How will we string the shells together?"

"That's easy," Kurt answered. "I know someone who makes the finest thread around."

CHAPTER 30

THE COPPER ARMOR

The band of travelers which had numbered only four that morning now numbered in the hundreds with the druggles. Three abreast they walked, with Kurt, Charlie, and Stinkle (and Notch in the backpack) leading the long line that twisted and turned with every turn and twist in the road to Nickledown.

One might have thought Kurt would feel less troubled now, considering the clouds in this more easterly part of the valley were somewhat thinner than those near Stinkle's house and therefore seemed less menacing. Here, they had not yet thickened to the dark purple-gray so ominous that morning, and neither did they churn. But still they moved, and that was enough to remind the boy of the urgency of his task. He kept a vigilant watch as, ever so slowly, the glowering Gloom crept, moving right along with the travelers, while faint rumblings resounded in the distance.

In late afternoon, the group caught sight of Fraidy's shabby house a few yards up the road. Stinkle had told the nut druggles about Fraidy and the suit of armor, and had warned them that the sound of a multitude of voices and tramping feet would surely drive the slinkle-purr into hiding. For this reason, a hush fell over the assembly as they walked on tiptoe toward the rickety gate.

The nut druggles camped quietly outside on the road, while Kurt, Stinkle, and Charlie (and Notch in the backpack) made their way stealthily through the gate and along the walkway leading to the front steps. Stinkle carefully stashed the suit of armor behind the sprawling evergreen near the steps and tiptoed to the door, where he knocked and put his finger over the peephole. Soon the familiar pair of yellow-green eyes peered around the edge of the tattered window shade. A moment later, the door opened squeakily, revealing the scraggly, ragtag slinkle-purr.

Stinkle, always thoughtful, had remembered to pack a new ball of yarn for Fraidy, and he whipped out a bright green one from the rear pouch on Kurt's backpack and tossed it inside the house. Fraidy pounced on the yarn ball and went through the usual feline frolicking, and when at last he lay tangled on the floor, part of a mass of mangled worsted, the visitors felt obliged to enter the house.

Upon seeing Charlie, Fraidy quickly disengaged himself from the tangled yarn and sashayed past the dog, slapping him in the face with his tail.

"Now, Fraidy," Stinkle scolded, "don't start that again. Such behavior is *not* acceptable."

The cat slinked over to a spot in the corner, where he sat with his nose held high in the air. "G-r-r-r," growled Charlie, plopping down in the opposite corner.

"Fraidy," Stinkle said slyly, diverting the cat's attention, "we have a little proposal to present for your wise consideration."

"What's it!" snapped Fraidy. He was being asked to do something important, and that apparently made him nervous.

"It's nothing to worry about, my friend," said Stinkle. "In fact, it's really quite wonderful. We have brought a gift for you, and we want to show it to you and have you consider our proposal for its use, that's all."

"Is it something g-o-o-o-d to e-e-a-t?" asked Fraidy, switching to his slinky tone of voice. "Is it a kn-i-i-ckknack like 'what's his name' gave me befo-o-o-re?"

"The name's Charlie," came a voice from the opposite corner. "And Chunkie Chewies are *not* knickknacks."

Fraidy glanced at the dog coyly. "O-o-o-oh," he whined disappointedly. "Then what have you brought for this cu-u-u-te little slinkle-purr, hu-u-u-h?"

"I'll go get it," said Kurt, and he went outside and returned with the suit of armor.

"Ah! What's it!" exclaimed Fraidy when he caught sight of the shiny metal suit. "E-e-e-e-k!" he shrieked, diving under a chair. "Take it away! Take it away!"

"Fraidy," said Stinkle, "It's just some copper shaped like a suit. It won't hurt you. In fact, I'll show you." He hurried to the broom closet and returned carrying a tattered mop. Turning to Kurt, he whispered, "Hold the suit rightly, please, Kurtis," and—*whack!*—he gave the suit a swift blow with the mop.

"See?" he said, glancing at Fraidy. "You can do anything to it, and it won't fight back."

Stinkle hit the suit again. *Whack!* And still it did not move.

"You see? It didn't mind at all. It's indestructible. There's hardly a dent in it. If you were to wear this suit, *you* would be indestructible. Nothing could harm you. Why, I'll wager a wag you could walk all the way to Nickledown with us, and nothing would harm you along the way."

"Yo-o-o-u're going to Nickledown, and you want me-e-e to come with you?"

Kurt detected a slight gleam in the slinkle-purr's yellow-green eyes—a gleam with a touch of the sinister—and when the black crescent slits in those yellow-green eyes narrowed to mere lines, Kurt was certain Fraidy had mischief up his feline sleeve.

"Le'me whack it," the cat said, and he slinked over to Stinkle, snatched the mop from his hand, and *whack.* He gave the suit of armor a swift blow to the midsection. *Whack* went the mop again. *Whack* it went a third time, as Fraidy delivered yet another blow.

"Willit fit?" he snapped, tossing the mop aside. And stroking his left arm with his right paw, he added, "Will it fit a tr-i-i-m physique like thi-i-i-s slinkle-purr ha-a-s? Willit?"

"It was made to order," replied Stinkle.

The cat smiled coyly. "Then per-r-r-haps I'll go."

"Wonderful!" replied the stinkle-dunk.

"Wait!" snapped Fraidy. "What about shadows? There will be shadows."

Stinkle picked up the suit of armor and placed it in an overstuffed chair on one side of the living room and turned on a lamp on the opposite side.

At the sight of the lamplight, Fraidy scooted under the sofa and peeked out cautiously.

"Look," said Stinkle, and he walked between the lamp and the armor so that his body cast a shadow across the copper suit. The suit did not move. "You see," he said, turning off the lamp, it's not afraid of shadows. If you were inside the suit, you would not have to worry about shadows ever again."

"But what about *my* shadow?" said Fraidy. "What about my *own* shadow when I'm inside the suit? Hu-u-u-h?"

"Not a problem," said Kurt, whipping out the green umbrella.

"Ye-e-o-ow!" howled the cat.

"Now, Fraidy," Stinkle said in a soothing voice, "it's unlikely you'll take flight with *this* umbrella. That was just an unfortunate fluke before."

"We-l-l-l," drawled Fraidy, thoughtfully. "Yes! I'll do it!"

Charlie moaned and covered his eyes with his paws.

After they all had a quick bite to eat, Fraidy donned the suit of armor. It fit him perfectly. Hoisting the big green umbrella high over his head, he stepped cautiously out the front door and peeked around as though he expected something dreadful to happen. Seeing he was unharmed, he quickened his stride, and with a clang and a clank, made his way down the walk and through the gate to where the druggles waited on the road.

The nut druggles cheered at the sight of the scraggly, ragtag slinkle-purr wearing the suit of armor. When they'd bestowed congratulations all around, Kurt, Charlie, Stinkle, Fraidy and Notch, and the whole procession of nut druggles juggling little stacks of nutshell cars, headed down the road toward Tattle's oak tree.

CHAPTER 31

UP WITH TATTLE-TAIL

Kurt and Stinkle led the line of travelers, followed by Charlie and the procession of nut druggles, and Fraidy to the rear. It was nearing nightfall when the group came to the sharp bend in the road that signaled they would soon be arriving at Tattle's oak tree. Fraidy had been trailing farther and farther behind claiming the suit of armor was slowing him down, and when the column rounded the bend and the road straightened out again, Fraidy was nowhere to be seen.

"He's out to cause trouble," said Stinkle. "Quickly! We must hurry ahead and warn Tattle." And he and Kurt rushed ahead, leaving Charlie to lead the nut druggles.

Soon Kurt and Stinkle were within sight of the tree, and shortly thereafter, they heard a familiar drone.

> *"Tattle-Tail, untethered tail,*
> *Left to lie, but not to 'lie;'*
> *Tattered tail, unfettered tail,*
> *Seeing all that passes by;*
>
> *Weaving tales and tatting stories,*
> *Hiding longings deep inside;*
> *Holding fast to faded glories,*
> *Yearning for a place to hide ..."*

A moment later, they caught sight of the old tail himself, lying flat and listless on the ground.

"Tattle, my friend!" Stinkle bellowed, hurrying to where the tail was lying. "It's so good to see you again!"

Tattle lifted his head wearily, and as he peered up at the stinkle-dunk, his eyes began to twinkle. He smiled a delighted smile, and when he spoke, his voice rang as joyously as the music of a carousel. "Stinkle-Twinkle-Dinkle-Dunk! Kurt! Is it really you?—the two—the you and you?"

"It is," Kurt replied.

"Oh, that reminds me of a tale I've often told about a wind-waft— makes me joyous, makes me laugh—who returned home after riding the winds for many years; and when his family and friends saw him descending from the sky—Oh my! Oh my!—"

"Tattle," said Stinkle, "we would love to hear your tale, but there is a pressing problem we must attend to immediately. It involves Fraidy."

"Fraidy? That slinkle-purr, that ball of fur, is not with you, is he?"

"I'm afraid he is," said Stinkle, "and he's up to his old tricks."

Kurt told the tattle-tail about Fraidy's suit of armor and about his sudden disappearance on the road. He told him, too, a little of his adventures since last he and the tail were together. But before he could so much as mention the perfectly balanced perfume, Stinkle interrupted.

"It's Fraidy. He's going to attack. I can feel it in my whiskers." And he scurried away into the bushes.

"Tattle," said Kurt, "something terrible happened to Stinkle."

"I know. Such woe! The Sweet Surrender. I heard. My word!"

"I have to take him to Nickledown, away from the Gloom, but he won't even consider going. It's not safe in this part of the valley. You should see how dark it is back at his house. Pink Nut Druggle said the Gloom has swallowed the Meadow completely and—"

"Swallowed the Meadow?"

"Completely," said Kurt.

The tattle-tail's body went limp on the ground. The rosy rushed from his round cheeks.

"I brought this perfume for Stinkle to wear," Kurt continued, pulling the flask from the backpack. "You know—to cover up if he should 'slip.' But he won't even smell it."

"He's probably afraid it might not be strong—won't last for long," said Tattle.

Kurt removed the stopper from the flask, sniffed the perfume, and replaced the stopper. "I'm sure it's strong enough. If we could just get some on him, he would see it too."

"Shhh. Did you hear that?" Tattle whispered.

"Yes," said Kurt. "It must be Fraidy. Or Stinkle."

"Or both," added Tattle.

"I've got an idea," Kurt said, opening the bottle. "I'll pretend I'm letting you smell the perfume. If Fraidy attacks and Stinkle is nearby, I'll spill some of it on him in the confusion."

"Let's do it, go to it, do it," Tattle whispered. He swayed his fore-end to make himself enticing, should the cat appear.

Kurt heard the clank of metal, and all at once Fraidy Slinkle-Purr leaped over the bushes and landed squarely on top of Tattle. "Ah!" screamed the tail from somewhere beneath the pile of cat-filled copper.

Stinkle, in hot pursuit, dove through the air and landed squarely on top of Fraidy.

"Ah!" the tattle-tail screamed again, as over and over they rolled—the three of them—in a cloud of dust and metal and flying fur.

At the first opportunity, Kurt splashed some of the perfume on Stinkle, who was too busy battling to notice where it came from. When the tusslers smelled the perfume, the fighting drew to a halt. And when the dust settled, there the three sat, ruffled and rumpled and staring blankly at one another.

"I'm sorry, Stinkle," said Kurt. "I was letting Tattle smell the perfume when Fraidy attacked and—"

"That's quite all right," said Stinkle, with a peculiar expression on his face—a strangely delighted peculiar expression. "May I see that flask, please, Kurtis."

Kurt handed the flask to Stinkle, and the skunk sniffed the perfume directly from the crystal container. "Ah! What a fine fragrance! Why didn't you tell me it smelled this wonderful, Kurtis? Nothing could smell distasteful in the presence of *this* fine perfume."

Still wearing the peculiar expression, Stinkle held the flask to his nose and sniffed again. "Wearing this, a stinkle-dunk could go to Nickledown and not have to worry in the least about a slip now and then."

"That's what I've been trying to tell you, Stinkle. You *will* go to Nickledown with us, won't you?"

"Nickledown. Wondrous Nickledown! Town of my dreams. Perhaps—just maybe—with this perfume—I most certainly—quite possibly—could be persuaded . . ."

Kurt held his breath in anticipation.

The stinkle-dunk glanced around at the others and a look of delight filled his face. "I *am* persuaded. I *will* go to Nickledown!"

"Wonderful!" said Kurt.

"Funderful!" added Tattle. And they all laughed, except Fraidy.

Just then, Charlie and the whole band of nut druggles arrived at the oak tree. By this time, Fraidy Slinkle-Purr was sitting alone near the bushes looking extremely forlorn. In the excitement about the perfume, he had been ignored completely.

While Stinkle and Tattle were busy telling Charlie and the nut druggles about Stinkle's happy decision, Kurt walked over and sat down next to Fraidy, who appeared very much like a defeated knight in his dusty suit of armor. Kurt spoke quietly to the slinkle-purr. "Fraidy, I want to tell you how much I appreciate your help in getting the perfume on Stinkle. If it hadn't been for your clever plan to attack, we never would have convinced him to wear the perfume. I'm glad I caught on to your plan in time to help you carry it out."

Fraidy stared at Kurt with a look of bewilderment on his feline face.

"Yes," Kurt continued. "It was a brilliant strategy. I'm sure the wisest knight in any king's court could not have thought of a more clever plan or carried it out with more skill and daring. You really do deserve to wear that suit of armor. If I were a king, I would dub thee 'Sir Fraidy Slinkle-Purr, Noblest Knight of the Realm!'"

"Oh-o-o-h," Fraidy said, proudly. "You wo-o-o-uld?" And after reflecting a moment, he added, "Ye-e-e-s—you're absolutely right. I wa-a-a-s brilliant, wasn't I. I'm just glad you caught on to my scheme in time. We make a go-o-o-d team, don't we, Kurt? Ye-e-e-s. This slinkle-purr was tru-u-u-ly brave and daring."

The cat stood up and threw his shoulders back and held his furry chin high in the air, standing proudly, as a Knight of the Realm would stand.

Kurt was awed by the animal's sudden transformation. Gone was the stealthy, skulking posture. Gone was the sneaky slyness of eye. For the first time in his life perhaps, the cat had done something good for someone, even though he had no idea he was doing it at the time. Could this one, unintentional, yet ultimately benevolent act have spawned a "new Fraidy?" Had this slinkle-purr, through no effort of his own, finally realized how wonderful it felt to do something good for someone else?

Fraidy took a moment to groom his whiskers, which until then had been dirty and drooping, and they perked up and took on a healthy sheen. What a fine pair of whiskers they were in actuality!

"Fraidy," Kurt whispered. "A Knight of the Realm is honorable above all else. A Knight of the Realm would apologize to Tattle."

"Of co-o-o-urse he would," said Fraidy. "And this knight will do the honorable thing."

He clanked over to Tattle and stood at attention before him.

The tail quickly rolled behind the trunk of the oak tree.

"I have com-m-m-e to apologize," said Fraidy, leaning over to peek at Tattle behind the tree.

"You've come to what?" said Tattle, peeking back.

"I have com-m-m-e to do the honorable thing. I have com-m-m-e to apologize."

Tattle lifted his head high and away from the slinkle-purr. "A trick!" he said. "A slick trick!" But the surprised expression on the tail's face when he saw the cat's refurbished whiskers soon revealed he knew it was no trick. The tattle-tail's whiskers were working properly, and with Fraidy's shined up as they were, his must be working properly too. There could be no miscommunication—the cat truly did intend to apologize.

Kurt pretended to be as surprised as the rest at Fraidy's unexpected transformation. He *was* surprised at the degree of the cat's remorse. Never did he expect his intimate talk to work this well. At most, he had hoped to squeeze a long-overdue apology out of the cat.

Tattle smiled as he stared at the "new Fraidy." What a tale he could tell about this someday if anyone should care to hear it. The tattle-tail said how happy he was that Stinkle would be going to Nickledown, and how happy he was for Fraidy too. But after a time, the smile left his face, and a faraway look came to his eye.

Noticing the tail's melancholy, Kurt said, "Tattle, you do know you have to come to Nickledown with us, don't you? It's not safe here."

"I know. The darkness, the starkness," said Tattle.

"The Gloom," said Kurt, nodding.

Tattle glanced up at the sky. "That's why all the animals have been passing by. I wondered why."

"They're headed for the hills," said Kurt. "You remember how to ride Charlie's tail, don't you, Tattle?"

"You-u-u can ride my-y-y tail," Fraidy offered.

"I think he'd better stick with Charlie's," Kurt told the cat. "You'll have all you can handle with that suit of armor. But thank you just the same. Besides, how would it look for a knight to have two tails?"

"A knight?" said Tattle, looking at Stinkle. Stinkle looked back at the tattle-tail and shrugged his shoulders.

"Tattle," said Kurt, "it's true there are not many oak trees in the Nickel Hills, but there are some. And there are plenty of overhanging rocks, so you wouldn't have to sleep out in the open along the way.

And the oak trees in Nickledown . . . Wait. Notch can tell you. He's seen them."

Kurt grabbed the book from the backpack and opened it and waited for Notch to perch himself on the edge of the page.

"Tell Tattle about the oak trees in Nickledown, Notch."

The booknotch smiled, obviously glad to see his friend the tattle-tail again. "In Nickledown," said Notch, "there are wonderful oak trees—ancient ones, big and spreading and deeply rooted, with thick, rich-green foliage, and plump, shiny acorns. They are, by any comparison, the finest oaks I have ever seen, either in reality or depicted in books."

"Please come with us, Tattle," said Kurt. "Out by Srinkle's house, the clouds are black and churning, and they're moving this way. There might even be lightning by now. You remember what lightning did to your *old* tree."

"I know, I know. I'll go, I'll go," the tail said as a shiver ran the length of his body.

Charlie offered his tail so Tattle could take a practice run, and it was apparent during the excitement of the ride that hopes and dreams of Nickledown once again filled the tattle-tail's heart. For a moment at least, all fear of lightning seemed far from his mind.

To Kurt's great relief, the matter was settled. Everyone under the oak tree would be going to Nickledown. After much conversation and speculation about what Nickledown held in store, the band of travelers nestled beneath the spreading arms of the oak tree and listened attentively to Tattle telling tales into the night—happy tales Tattle borrowed from his early years under his *old* oak tree.

Sometime later, the breeze that had moved the clouds along throughout the day increased in strength, ushering in a harsh cold. Accustomed to life in the outdoors, the animals curled themselves into tight, furry balls, tucked their noses in, and fell asleep. Soon thereafter, the tattle-tail, having snuggled close beside Charlie, finished the last of his tales, closed his eyes, and joined the others in sleep.

Kurt tucked Notch away in the book and lay awake mulling over the feud between the weery-dawdles and nut druggles. He had persuaded the nut druggles to stop feuding, but persuading the weery-dawdles would present a greater challenge. After all, they were the offended party.

The boy tried not to listen to the voice of the chill wind playing eerily through the treetops, but when the wind grew colder still, he pulled some nearby oak leaves over himself to serve as a blanket. Following the animals' example, he curled up into a ball and waited for sleep to overtake him.

CHAPTER 32

WEERY-DAWDLE CARAVANS

The cold breeze that blew throughout the night gathered much of the Gloom to where Kurt and the others were camped. Now the thickened clouds, dark and onerous, stood perfectly still, poised and waiting, like a wild animal intent on trapping its prey.

Fear filled the animals' eyes when they awoke to see the nebulous beast looming above them—a beast that wickedly watched their every move. When the animals stirred from their beds, the clouds stirred. When the animals grouped themselves for the journey, the clouds began to churn. When Kurt and the others moved from the oak tree, the clouds moved with them.

"The Gloom is following us," Stinkle said to Kurt, as they walked along the road.

"It's following *me*," said Kurt. "First it was the Troll. Now it's the Gloom."

"What do you mean?"

"There have been too many coincidences. First the Troll came with me through the passage. And he was in the woods near Pink Nut Druggle's place when Charlie chased after his Chunkie Chewies. Then he was in the ravine when I fell, and later, in the woods when I lost the compass. I haven't seen *him* in a while, but now the Gloom seems to be watching everything I do."

"I see," said Stinkle. "It's as though the Troll has commanded the Gloom to take over the watch."

"Exactly. And Stinkle, I can feel those eyes staring at me again."

Stinkle glanced up at the Gloom. "It does seem to have a mind of its own."

"Or many minds," said Kurt.

"But why would the Troll have an interest in you, Kurtis? Surely you pose him no threat. Perhaps you have something he wants."

"I can't imagine what. All I have are the clothes on my back and the stuff in the backpack—and Father's key." Recalling how, in the ravine, the Troll had reached for the key, he withdrew it from his shirtfront, studied it a moment, and tucked it away again.

"Curious," said Stinkle, and he glanced at the clouds and hastened his pace.

With the faster pace, the Gloom moved faster. Whenever the pace slowed, the Gloom slowed.

After a time, the road took an upward slant, and shortly thereafter, Kurt heard a delicate tinkling like tiny bells ringing. "The nickel trees!" he said, and as if they had crossed some invisible boundary between darkness and light, the travelers stepped from cloud shadow into sunlight. They *had* crossed a boundary—the boundary between the Copper Valley and the Nickel Hills—and the Gloom, seemingly held in check by some invisible barrier, had drawn to a halt at the same boundary.

A cheer went up from the little band—a cheer of relief, a cheer of hope—as the joyous ringing of the nickel trees beckoned the travelers onward to Nickledown.

Only moments ago they had been traveling under a grim, gray sky. Now they found themselves in the delightful throes of a particularly *fallish* autumn day—the kind when the sun is sparkling, shadows are sharp, and the air is crisp and clear and clean—the kind of day that puts a skip in one's step and lends a certain vitality to life.

Around noon they arrived at Spinneret's clearing. What a sight it was in the autumn sun! Those who had never seen Spinneret's webs marveled at their magnificence. Even Kurt was overwhelmed anew by their beauty.

Spinneret was high in one of the trees busily weaving dew into her webs when the travelers entered the clearing. Upon seeing them, she scurried down the tree trunk.

"Kurt! Whatever are you doing back here?"

"It's a long story," Kurt said, staring at an incredibly beautiful piece of Spinneret's artwork, a freshly woven fringe studded with glistening dewdrops, hanging from the outermost edges of a leafy branch like the trim on a Victorian lampshade. "That looks like dew from the Silver Mountain," he said, pointing to the fringe.

"It is, dear one. I wove it this morning using some of the dew I gathered the day of your trip to Polyglop Island. By the way, did you ever find King Aegis?"

"Yes, but I'd rather not talk about that now, if you don't mind."

"As you wish, dear. What brings you back this way?"

Kurt told the webber-tat about the Troll and the Gathering Gloom and his efforts to bring his friends to Nickledown.

"I should have known something was amiss with so many animals passing this way and with the light diminished as it is," said Spinneret. "I've been dropping stitches and losing my needle repeatedly."

"Spinneret," Kurt said, "I think you should come with us to Nickledown. The Gloom has stopped at the boundary between the Copper Valley and the Nickel Hills, but if it starts to move again, it could be here in no time."

"Oh my! Perhaps I should." And she began unthreading her needle.

"Wait," Kurt said. "I need a favor." He told her his plan for ending the feud between the nut druggles and weery-dawdles.

Spinneret praised the boy's efforts and agreed to weave the thread that would link the shells together. "It will be a special thread," she said, "sturdy and finely woven. And such a noble cause deserves the finest silk." She put down her needle and began spinning a pure white silk. A short time later, she began weaving it into thread.

As the webber-tat worked, the stinkle-dunk sat nearby and talked to her, having first splashed on some of the sweet perfume—just to be safe should he slip.

Kurt, in the meantime, busied himself explaining to the nut druggles how they should connect Spinneret's thread to the empty nutshells.

After a time, Stinkle wandered off to a spot under a shade tree and fell asleep, leaving the webber-tat alone with her weaving. Kurt saw her drop her needle and hurried over to retrieve it.

"Thank you, dear," said Spinneret. "Now where was I?" She resumed weaving and glanced at Kurt. "Tell me, dear. Have you solved the riddle about the leap-lops?"

"No," Kurt answered.

"I see. By the way, I noticed you're wearing shoes."

"Yes. Father Nickle-Dickle gave them to me. They used to be his. They were uncomfortable at first, but Father Nickle-Dickle said it's easy to walk in someone else's shoes if you do it often enough. He was right. They feel just like my own now."

"Too bad you couldn't have walked in Notch's shoes," said Spinneret. "He may not have become lost."

"How did you know . . ."

"Word gets around, dear."

Kurt was puzzled. Walk in Notch's shoes? "If I'd walked in Notch's shoes," he told himself, "I would have realized how afraid he was of getting lost. I would have been more careful."

Suddenly Spinneret's words struck him fully.

"Walk in Notch's shoes! That's it! The answer to the riddle! 'Footsteps to light,' 'truth in the step,' 'use your whiskers *and* your feet.' The leap-lops were telling me to 'wauk'—walk in the other person's shoes. That's got to be the answer. Is it, Spinneret?"

"Yes, dear. That's the answer to the riddle. Here, in the Land of Whiskers, if you walk in the shoes of another often enough, you'll walk from color to color until one day, when you least expect it, you'll leap to silver, and a whole new world will open before you."

"Wow!" said Kurt. "I'd like to leap to silver."

"Stinkle says you told the nut druggles to walk in the shoes of the weery-dawdles,"

"I guess I did."

"Then it would seem you knew the answer to the riddle all along."

"I guess so," Kurt said, and he felt proud of himself.

"You said you would like to leap to silver, dear," said Spinneret. "But of course, since you're a *not an animal*, as you told the there'n not-hares, you would not experience color change as the animals do. I have heard from higher sources, however, that within the light of your world there dwells an entity akin to color—a celestial muse—a prompter—a changer—who speaks quietly to the hearts of *not an animals* just as color speaks to the hearts of animals here."

"I don't understand," said Kurt.

"You will in time, dear."

It took Spinneret most of the day to weave the thread for the nutshell cars. Just before sundown she completed the task, and Kurt and Stinkle cut the thread into measured lengths. They called the nut druggles into the center of the clearing and gave each druggle enough thread to tie six shells together to form his own little nutshell caravan, complete with harness. By the time all the tying was done, the moon was rising over the web-covered nickel trees.

What a sight the clearing was in the moonlight! Hundreds of nutshell cars joined together in sixes to form nutshell caravans; and the caravans lined up, row upon row, each headed by a nut druggle camped for the night, anxiously awaiting his chance to help end the feud. Moonlight shining on the dewdrops woven into the strands of silken thread lent a sparkle and shimmer to the clearing, giving the whole of it the look of a quiet lake on whose water silver moonlight played.

The group headed out early the next morning. Nickledown was now little more than a day's journey away, and according to Kurt's calculations, if all went well, they should reach the town's outskirts by sunset. After camping overnight, they would arrive in Nickledown the following morning—the morning of Silver Day!

Hours passed as the lengthy band trudged along, dutifully towing the nutshell caravans, keeping a sharp eye out for the weery-dawdles. But nowhere did they see the slightest sign of the little snails.

"What could have become of them?" said one of the druggles.

"They must be hiding from the Gloom," said another.

"We're too late to save them," said a third. "We should have done this days ago."

Suddenly the near-sighted Tubbs yelled, "Nuts ahead! Nuts ahead!"

"Those aren't nuts!" Kurt cried. "Those are the weery-dawdles!"

Tubbs slipped quietly to the back of the line as a hearty cheer—more like a battle cry—went up from the nut druggles. Eager to make amends and show the weery-dawdles their offering, the druggles began running toward the tiny snails, dragging the nutshell caravans like war wagons behind them, shouting, and flailing their tails in the air.

When the weery-dawdles, who were slowly inching their way along the road, saw the thunderous menagerie bearing down upon them, they screamed in horror. "Run!" they shouted. "Run for the hills!" In the chaos that followed, no one's whiskers worked properly. Weery-dawdles scattered in every direction—as well as weery-dawdles can scatter in any direction.

Mosey, traveling with the band of weery-dawdles, spotted Tubbs and held his ground in the dusty fray until the chubby little nut druggle came within calling distance. When he had drawn Tubbs's attention, he dropped a large package he was carrying on his back, and out spilled, of all things, a pair of glasses. Kurt, who had been scurrying around trying to quiet the scuffle, saw Mosey drop the package and stopped to watch.

Mosey said something to Tubbs, who picked up the glasses and put them on and giggled. "Look, everybody! I can see! I can see!" he called out. "No one has ever done anything like this for me." And he giggled again.

Mosey began to giggle, and so did Kurt. Charlie and Stinkle and Tattle and Fraidy and Spinneret and the other weery-dawdles and nut druggles noticed what was happening, and they began to giggle. Kurt even heard a tiny giggle coming from inside his backpack. Soon the air was full of laughter and good will. "After all," agreed the weery-dawdles, "if Tubbs and Mosey can become friends, so can we." And that was the end of the feud.

Kurt told the weery-dawdles about the darkness that had gathered in the Copper Valley, and about the dreadful disappearance of the Meadow, and about his fear the Gloom would spread to the Nickel Hills. He followed up by explaining his plan to carry them to safety in the nutshell caravans.

The weery-dawdles were grateful. They, too, had felt the troublesome effects of the fading light and had begun to fear they had waited too long to seek the safety of Nickledown.

The nut druggles helped the weery-dawdles into the nutshell cars, and when Kurt gave the order to "Move 'em out!" the caravans went rumbling (as well as nutshell caravans are able to rumble) along the winding road to Nickledown.

The troop managed to travel as far as the outskirts of town, as planned, before settling in for the night. There they found shelter beneath a cluster of overhanging rocks. The campsite was not far from the knoll where Kurt had shown Mosey the Gloom on their previous trip. Thinking it wise to check the Gloom's progress, Kurt, with Mosey on his foot, climbed the knoll; and when Kurt had lifted the weery-dawdle onto his shoulder, and Mosey had taken a deep breath to steady himself, the two looked toward the west. And there it was—the gray and ominous Gloom—standing tall like the grim stone wall of an evil fortress, still poised at the boundary of the Nickel Hills. Huge thunderheads now loomed high and dark at the Gloom's leading edge, towering over the other clouds like gargantuan generals waiting to lead their legions into battle.

"I don't like the look of this," drawled Mosey in his weak and weary voice. "When the Troll was in Whiskers before, the Gathering

Gloom stood still for a time. Some said the Troll was off in the far north, trying to harness the North Wind. If he should do that now, he and his Gloom could be upon us in an instant."

A chill ran down the back of Kurt's neck. "Let's not tell the others. There's no use scaring them."

"Yes," said Mosey, "I agree."

They returned to the overhanging rocks, and after the others had fallen asleep, Kurt opened the book to see if the booknotch was still awake. Finding him so, he took the little worm out of the book and discussed the day's events with him, being careful not to mention the thunderheads. Notch was so excited about returning to Nickledown that Kurt offered to let the worm ride into town on his shoulder. Notch thought that was a splendid idea.

Soon, weariness overtook the two of them, and when Kurt had told the booknotch goodnight and had tucked him back in the book, he curled up with the animals under the overhanging rocks and drifted off to sleep.

CHAPTER 33

ꙨNICKLEDOWNꙨ

Kurt awoke to the sound of gentle rain. It reminded him of the rain that fell the fateful morning he went to the lake.

As he looked around at his friends, still nestled in their leafy beds beneath the sheltering rocks, he felt as though he were the only living being awake in the entire universe. The night-chirps were right, he thought. Time *was* short. It had seemed plentiful enough at first—eight days from the time he discovered the book, six days from the time Parhelion gave him the third clue. But he had wasted much time in futile pursuits, failing to uncover even one of the secrets, and now there remained only this final day—this Silver Day.

Kurt did not notice the rain had stopped falling until he heard the faint *drip, drip, drip* of lingering drops rolling from the rocks above his head and splashing on the wet ground below. As he listened, a gentle breeze began to blow, coaxing the nickel trees to ring softly.

The boy noticed a stirring among the sleepers, and with much rustling of leaves and yawning and stretching, the small band of travelers slowly awakened, the way animals do after a long hibernation.

The breeze went about its magical task and dried the idle raindrops—every drip and drop and dribble and trickle—leaving behind a veil of silver dust that settled softly over the land. Every tree and flower, every rock and blade of grass, every living and nonliving thing welcomed the magic dust and waited patiently for the promised light.

Ever so slowly, the forward rays of the rising sun transformed the gray firmament of dawn into a canopy of rainbow colors. Soon thereafter the sun itself burst forth from behind the Mountain, pouring its bounty across the waiting land. Its enchanted rays kissed the silver dust, and the air exploded with silver light. It was Silver Day!

Time and distance separated the little band from the Gloom at that moment, and Stinkle, Fraidy, and Tattle allowed their fears of the impending darkness to be overridden by their lifelong yearnings to visit Nickledown. Their excitement quickly spread to the nut druggles and weery-dawdles, and to Kurt and Charlie and Notch and Spinneret.

Joyful exuberance filled the camp as everyone prepared to enter the town. The nut druggles busied themselves helping the weery-dawdles into the nutshell cars. Stinkle splashed on his sweet perfume. Fraidy polished his copper armor. Tattle wrapped himself around Charlie's tail and laughed as Charlie pranced and wagged both of his tails. At Kurt's suggestion, Spinneret climbed into one of the nutshell cars. Kurt took Notch from the book and hoisted him to a spot next to his collar and secured him with the piece of fishing line to the top buttonhole of his shirt. Finally, everyone was ready, and the strange menagerie headed toward Nickledown.

The travelers journeyed some distance, and with every step the nickel trees rang purer; with each breath, the air became sweeter. Soon they caught the delicate scent of florals that could only be coming from the Rainbow Garden.

"Nickledown is just over the next rise," Kurt happily told Stinkle. Filled with excitement, the two quickened the pace.

It was then that something peculiar happened. As they neared the next grove of nickel trees, they heard a sound that, though seeming like music, was flat and discordant. Kurt looked at Stinkle, who stared back wearing a sour expression.

"I don't understand," said Kurt. "I'm sure these are the trees Father Nickle-Dickle tunes."

"Perhaps he didn't tune them today," said Stinkle.

"That can't be. You don't know Father Nickle-Dickle. Nothing would stop him from tuning the trees."

Just then, a deer and a zebra came running toward them, away from Nickledown.

"Why are you running?" Kurt shouted, as the two animals drew near.

"They're gone!" cried the deer, zooming by.

"All of them!" shouted the zebra, as he too ran past.

Stinkle looked at Kurt with a deeply troubled expression. "What do you make of that?"

"I don't know," said Kurt, "but I'm afraid something is awfully wrong."

The little band climbed the last hill, and when they reached the top, there it was—Nickledown!

What a sight they were coming over the rise! The few animals who saw them later said they had never seen anything like it: a boy from another world with a booknotch on his shoulder, a waggle-like with two tails, a slinkle-purr wearing a suit of armor and carrying a big green umbrella, a whole procession of nut druggles pulling rows and rows of weery-dawdles in little nutshell caravans, one silver webber-tat riding in a nutshell car, and to top it off, a stinkle-dunk whose flowery scent arrived in town long before he did. Those same animals told Kurt there was a bright pink glow surrounding the whole troop as it marched through the Great Nickel Gate and headed toward the Town Square.

When they reached the Square, Kurt drew the little entourage to a halt. "Something's wrong," he said, scanning the Square. "Where are all the animals?"

"I've seen only a half dozen or so," said Stinkle, "and those were hiding—peeking from behind bushes."

"And the Nickle-Dickles," said Kurt. "And the food. There should be tables full of food. I don't understand. Mother Nickle-Dickle! Father Nickle-Dickle!"

He heard Charlie whine, and when he looked at the dog, he found him cowering, his head held low, his brow wrinkled, the familiar white crescents showing beneath the warm brown of his eyes.

"It's okay, Charlie. I'll find her. I'll find Chrysalis. You stay here with Tattle." And he patted the dog on the shoulder and ran toward the white house on the cobblestone street.

When he reached the house, he found the front door standing open and rushed in. "Mother Nickle-Dickle! Where are you?" When he received no answer, he ran to the kitchen, but no one was there. Pies, long-since cooled, rested on the windowsill; and a birthday cake, only partly decorated, sat on the kitchen table.

Calling again, he hurried to the bedroom. "Mother Nickle-Dickle! Father Nickle-Dickle!" Again, no one answered.

The boy heard a weak whimper coming from under the bed. Cautiously, he lifted the quilt that hung over the side of the bed and peeked under. Two soft brown eyes peered back at him.

"Chrysalis!" he said, recognizing the dog. "Where are Mother and Father Nickle-Dickle? Where are all the animals?"

"Oh, Kurt," replied Chrysalis, wiggling her way out from under the bed. "I'm so glad it's you! I didn't know what to do. I was so frightened."

"What happened?" Kurt asked.

"It was just before dawn," said Chrysalis, her body trembling, "during the silver rain. A flute played. The Piper. Only it wasn't the Piper. Something about the music was not quite right. It was played in a strange scale, and the melody was one I've never heard before. It was eerie—disturbing. And Mother and Father Nickle-Dickle—"

"Where are they?"

"I don't know," said Chrysalis. "They were in the kitchen, and when they heard the flute, they stopped what they were doing and headed toward the door. I tried to stop them. My whiskers told me something was wrong. But they didn't seem to see or hear me. They walked out the door in a daze."

"I'm sure we'll find them," said Kurt, attempting to comfort the dog. "Come on. I'll take you to Charlie. He's right outside."

"Thank you, Kurt," said Chrysalis, and she followed the boy to where Charlie and the others were anxiously waiting.

"Mother and Father Nickle-Dickle are gone," Kurt told Stinkle.

"I know," replied the skunk. "All the Nickle-Dickles are gone. I've talked to several animals who live in Nickledown. They saw it happen."

By now, most of the animals still in town had left their hiding places and were gathering around Kurt and his friends.

"The flute played," squeaked a guinea pig, "and all the Nickle-Dickles came out of their houses and headed toward the Silver Mountain."

"Mothers and fathers and children alike," brayed a donkey.

"The animals who came for Silver Day got frightened and left town," honked a goose.

"Their whiskers must have told them something was wrong," added a gander. "They've run away to hide in the hills."

"I saw where the Nickle-Dickles went," said a shy little sheep. "I saw the exact place where they disappeared."

"Where?" said Kurt.

"There," the sheep said, pointing to the side of the mountain. "All the Nickle-Dickles went up the Silver Mountain to the place where the rock is smooth—right there." And she pointed again. "Then the side of the mountain opened up. There was a big, black hole, and they walked into it. Then the mountain closed up and the Nickle-Dickles were gone."

"And the flute stopped playing," added a goat.

"Music soft and bitter sweet," said the tattle-tail, "full of lies and dark deceit."

Dark deceit? Kurt had heard those words before. But where?

Suddenly he remembered. "The Dark Deceiver! Parhelion called the Troll the Dark Deceiver! Stinkle, it wasn't the Piper who was playing the flute. It was the Troll. He's fooled the Nickle-Dickles into thinking the Piper was calling. He's kidnapped the Nickle-Dickles and locked them in the mountain!"

CHAPTER 34

THE RESCUE

"We have to rescue them," Kurt said, addressing his friends and the group of animals that, by this time, had grown rather large. "We have to find a way."

"Per-r-r-haps you need a knight in shining armor," Fraidy offered, bravely stepping forward in his copper suit.

"Thank you, Fraidy," said Stinkle, "but not just now. Perhaps we'll need a knight later."

"A night later, a day later. What does it matter? We're all the sadder," lamented the tattle-tail.

> *"Not one Nickle-Dickle, nor ten to a rhyme;*
> *Not ten Nickle-Dickles, nor twenty at a time;*
> *Not twenty Nickle-Dickles; none did they find;*
> *Not a single Nickle-Dickle was left behind."*

"I'm sorry, Tattle," said Kurt, "but that rhyme doesn't make sense."
"Of course it does, *if* you use logic," replied the tail.

> *"One nickel makes five cents.*
> *One dickle makes no sense.*
> *No Nickle-Dickles make no scents.*
> *So, open the door and let them make scents."*

"Open the door? What door?" said Kurt. The boy thought for a moment. "That's it! We'll *make* a door! We have tools—the ones we brought to adjust Fraidy's armor. They're small, but—"

"Yes," said Stinkle. "All we need is a *small* door. Just big enough for one Nickle-Dickle to squeeze through at a time."

The stinkle-dunk pulled the pick and hammer and chisel out of Kurt's backpack. "Follow me!" And up the trail to the mountain they went—Stinkle, followed by Kurt (with Notch on his shoulder); and Charlie (with Tattle on his tail); and Fraidy and Chrysalis and the nut druggles; and Spinneret and the weery-dawdles (who were still in the nutshell cars); and a whole procession of animals of all shapes, sizes, and species.

After a lengthy climb, they arrived at the smooth spot on the mountainside.

"I'll make the hole," said Kurt, grabbing the tiny tools. And he hammered and chiseled and picked and hammered and chiseled and picked and hammered again, but made only a small gouge in the rock. "This is very hard rock," he said, exhausted, and he dropped the hammer on the ground.

"Let me try it," said Stinkle. And he hammered and chiseled and picked and hammered and chiseled and picked and hammered again. "*Very* hard rock." And he let the hammer slide from his hand.

"Why don't we use the lug-a-trunk," said Tattle. "We lugged him along at the end of the line. That big lug-a-trunk could do just fine."

"The what?" said Kurt.

"The lug-a-trunk," said Stinkle, beckoning enthusiastically to a large gray circus elephant standing to the rear of the others.

Slowly lumbering, the lug-a-trunk made his way to the front of the group and stood before the smooth spot on the rock. The crowd stepped back a step and waited.

The lug-a-trunk took one step backward, hesitated a moment, and *boom!* he plowed into the mountain, but made not a dent. The crowd sighed with disappointment.

The lug-a-trunk lowered his heavy brow. He stared at the spot with a focused glare. He took careful aim and stepped back *two* steps. *Boom!* He plowed into the mountain again. This time a small crack opened in the rock, and a rousing cheer went up from the crowd.

Spurred on by the cheer, the lug-a-trunk stepped back *three* steps. His eyes filled with determination. He set his feet firmly. The crowd held its breath. But before the animal could lunge again, something unexpected happened.

From out of the blue came a bolt of lightning. It streaked across the sky like a jagged blade and slashed the mountain near its top.

Down the slopes came the roar of thunder!

"He's going up!" gobbled a turkey, flapping his wings and running for cover.

And indeed he was. The frightened lug-a-trunk reared up on his hind feet, raised his trunk high in the air, and sounded his mighty trumpet, sending animals scattering in all directions.

"He's coming down!" the turkey gobbled again, peeking out from his hiding place behind a rock.

And the lug-a-trunk's huge front feet came pounding down, shaking the earth, dislodging boulders from an overhead ledge.

"Run!" Kurt shouted. "Run!" He grabbed the tools, and he and the animals fled for their lives down the mountain path, leaping over rocks, dodging bouncing boulders, zigzagging past tumbling chunks of crusty earth.

When they reached the foot of the mountain and the dust and rocks settled, they made their way to the Town Square, where Kurt fell exhausted onto the grass under a spreading maple tree. When he had caught his breath, he checked on the booknotch and found the worm clutching his shirt collar, looking much greener than usual, but still securely fastened by the length of fishing line.

"Now what do we do?" Kurt remarked to the animals gathered about him, and he leaned back against the tree trunk.

Stinkle sat down on the opposite side of the tree, and he, too, leaned back against the trunk.

"Per-r-r-haps you need a knight in shining armor now," said Fraidy, walking up to his friends with a clamor and clank.

"Thank you, Fraidy. Perhaps later," Stinkle said, dismissing the cat with a wave of his hand.

The tattle-tail, in the meantime, had been staring absent-mindedly at Kurt and Stinkle as the two sat back-to-back under the maple tree. All at once the old tail's eyes began to twinkle and he cleared his throat to speak.

> *"Two hop-a-roos were talking,*
> *Standing back-to-back.*
> *'My baby roo is missing,*
> *And it's time for his snack.'*
>
> *'I'll help you,' said the other roo,*
> *Opening her sack.*
> *'If he can't find the front of you,*
> *Perhaps he'll find the back.'"*

"If he can't find the front of you, perhaps he'll find the back," Kurt mimicked. Front? Back? "Stinkle! We tried the front door; now we have to try the back! Maybe there's another way into the mountain—a cave entrance or something. You know, a back door."

"Harumph," said the stinkle-dunk, pondering deeply. "Perhaps. The fact the Nickle-Dickles went in where they did doesn't mean they have to come out the same way."

"Exactly," said Kurt. "Tattle, do you know any tales about another entrance to the mountain?"

The tattle-tail concentrated intently. "Humm," he said, after a lengthy pause. "Another door, something more . . .

> *A swishin-figgle*
> *Once did wiggle*
> *Through a door*
> *On the river's floor.*

He came upon an open sea,
A wet and wavy place to be,
And swam into a darkish room—
A shadowy, shallow, shivery tomb."

"That sounds to me like an underwater entrance to the mountain," said Kurt. "It could be a back door. And the room may be where the Troll is holding the Nickle-Dickles."

"A door under water?" said Stinkle. "We aren't swishin-figgles. We can't swim under water."

"I can," Kurt said, "with a little help from a friend." And he jumped up and ran toward the riverbank. The animals around the maple tree followed, and soon a crowd was gathered by the water's edge.

"King Aegis!" Kurt shouted. "King of the Swishin-Figgles! I need you!"

Not long thereafter, the whole mass of King Aegis's fishy counte-nance breached the surface, loomed in the air a moment, and plunged to the murky depths, drenching the onlookers with a huge wall of water. The fish stayed under for several seconds before his head quietly appeared amid a sea of undulating waves. "Why have you summoned us?" he asked.

"I need your help," said Kurt, and he told King Aegis about the missing Nickle-Dickles and about Tattle's tale. "Is there a door on the river bottom?" he asked.

"There is a passage," said the swishin-figgle, "but we do not allow our children to swim through it. It leads to a place of foreboding."

"I have to go there," said Kurt.

"It is dangerous."

"I don't care. I have to go."

"Very well, we will take you," replied King Aegis, moving close to shore. "Climb on our back. But you must hold tightly. The passage is dark, the currents treacherous."

Kurt untied Notch's fishing line from the buttonhole of his shirt and was about to tuck the worm into the book when Notch protested.

"I dare not go into the book just now, Kurt. Not with you risking your life in that treacherous torrent. I'd spend the time pacing circles around an *O* or thumping my fingers nervously on the top of a *T*. No, I will enjoy no solitude until you are safe on land once more."

"Perhaps a place near *my* collar would suit your purpose," offered the stinkle-dunk.

The booknotch agreed, and Kurt secured the tiny worm on Stinkle's ascot. He handed the backpack with the book in it to the stinkle-dunk for safekeeping, removed his shirt and shoes, and with the shirt in hand, jumped into the water. After tying the shirt around King Aegis's neck to form a harness, he climbed onto the fish's back and gripped the harness as tightly as he could. A moment later, he found himself gliding along the surface of the water, moving upriver toward the Silver Mountain.

"Prepare yourself," shouted King Aegis. "We're going under. Take a deep breath . . . right . . . now!"

Kurt drew in all the air his lungs could hold, and down they went—he and the swishin-figgle—straight to the bottom, where the water was cold and dark.

Kurt held onto the shirt with all his might, entrusting his life to the will of the mighty King Aegis. Though he could see nothing through the black water, at one point he did feel his ankles touch something on either side of him, and he guessed they were going through the passage—a passage that was much longer than he had expected it to be. Greatly in need of air, he began to panic. He was sure he could not hold his breath a moment longer. Just when he was convinced he would surely drown, his head breached the surface and he found himself gasping for air. A moment later he felt his body drifting, rising, falling, as he and King Aegis rode the gentle swells of an underground sea.

Looking around, he discovered the sea was inside some kind of chamber—a cave from the looks of it. A cold gray light filled the chamber, but nowhere was the light's source visible.

Though the chamber was vast, Kurt could distinguish a rocky wall on the far side of it where a tall archway loomed dark and menacing like the entrance to a sinister castle.

"That is the room," said King Aegis. "We will take you to it. We cannot go in, however, for the water in the room is too shallow. You may step off and go in if you wish."

King Aegis swam up to the archway and Kurt slid off the fish's back and onto the rocky ledge that formed the floor of the room. When he stood up, he found the water to be only a foot deep.

The room itself felt eerie, its space dimly aglow with the same cold gray light as the outer chamber. As with the outer chamber, there was no sign of the light's source. Worst of all, there were no Nickle-Dickles. The room held nothing more than a vast volume of frigid, musty air.

Kurt felt a weakness overtake him. He was exhausted from the swim, and now he was overwhelmed with disappointment. Just like his searches for the silver trees and abacus flowers and opals, his effort here had been for nothing.

He was about to turn and leave when he noticed what appeared to be another smaller archway in the shadows at the farthermost end of the room. Summoning all his strength, he waded through the murky water toward the shaded arch. When he reached it, he found a thin, dark veil covering the space within the archway, much like a sheer curtain. He was sure he could push the veil aside and step through the arch, or at least peek through to whatever was on the other side. But when his hand touched the veil, it was as though it had touched cold, hard stone, and he shivered and snatched his hand away.

Suddenly he heard a faint whisper—then another—then a murmuring as of many voices. There seemed to be a disturbance in the air around him, and he had the terrible feeling he was the cause of it.

All at once he felt the presence of many eyes. "King Aegis!" he shouted, turning and wading frantically toward the first archway.

The murmuring grew louder as Kurt plowed with all his might through the putrid water that, having thickened, now tugged at his ankles, growing more and more viscous with his every step.

"King Aegis!" he shouted again when he reached the archway. He could see the fish swimming just beneath the surface a few yards away in the underground sea. "Hurry, King Aegis!" he yelled.

He glanced over his shoulder in time to see the water in the room begin to churn. Desperate to escape, he jumped from the ledge and plunged into the dark waters of the sea. A second later he felt King Aegis's slick body draw alongside him, and he quickly pulled himself aboard the fish's back. "Get us out of here!" he cried, grabbing hold of the shirt.

When King Aegis turned from the archway, the voices grew louder; and within the voices Kurt heard another sound—a bleating, like the sound of goats. The surface of the underground sea behind him began to ripple. "Something's here, King Aegis! It's coming after us! Dive!" he screamed. "Dive!"

The fish sped out over the water, and after warning the boy to hold his breath, dove to the depths.

Soon thereafter, Kurt felt his ankles scraping against rock walls on either side, and he knew they were again squeezing through the narrow passage leading from the sea back to the river. Just before they emerged from the passage, he felt something graze the back of his neck. "An underwater branch," he told himself.

After what seemed an eternity, the boy saw sunlight through the water. Seconds later, he and the swishin-figgle breached the surface, and shortly thereafter, they arrived back at the riverbank, where the animals were anxiously awaiting their return.

Stinkle and Notch and the others must have known from the look on Kurt's face that something had frightened him terribly, for all signs of hope and expectation at once vanished from their faces, and they stood without saying a word.

"Thank you, King Aegis," Kurt said, his voice trembling; and after untying his shirt from the fish's neck, he climbed to shore.

"We are sorry you did not find the Nickle-Dickles," said the swishin-figgle. "The underground sea is truly a place of foreboding.

We are sorry we took you there." And he dove beneath the surface and was gone.

"Oh, Stinkle," said Kurt. "There's something awful down there. I'm glad the river blocks the entrance. And I'm glad King Aegis won't let his children go there."

Kurt wrung the river water out of his shirt and hung the garment over a branch to dry. "Now what do we do?" he said, slipping back into his shoes. "We have to rescue the Nickle-Dickles; and I have to rid Whiskers of the Troll. Until those things are done, I can't even think about going home. And time is short. This is the last day I have to uncover the secrets. If I don't, I'll never get home again."

"Per-r-r-haps *now* you need a knight in shining armor," said Fraidy, for the third time bravely stepping forward in his copper suit.

"Thank you, Fraidy," said Stinkle, "but I don't think—"

"I know," Fraidy interrupted. "You don't need a knight this time, either." And he turned and clanked away.

"Stinkle," Kurt said, "maybe we do need a knight in shining armor."

"What?"

"His suit—the copper. That could be the key to it all. Remember Tattle's tale—the one about 'dark deceit?' If the Troll could deceive the Nickle-Dickles with music, why can't we? I was just thinking that Fraidy's idea was full of holes—his idea for using a knight in shining armor to rescue the Nickle-Dickles—when I thought of something: copper that's full of holes. What would you have if you had little tubes of copper that were full of holes?"

The stinkle-dunk appeared puzzled for a moment. "Flutes!" he said, as a look of wonderment filled his face. "You would have little copper flutes! Lots of them if you used all the copper in Fraidy's suit."

"Exactly," said Kurt. "And we still have the tools. We can take the suit apart and make flutes."

"Then we can get the musically inclined animals to play them," said Stinkle. "Animals such as slinkle-purrs. They sing all the time on fences. They're very musically inclined."

"And we could get others to help with the music," Kurt added. "Twitter-flits who sing. And singing swishin-figgles. King Aegis can gather all the singing swishin-figgles together for us."

"And don't forget the yotees," said Stinkle. "Their fervent cries carry for miles. And the waggle-licks. Their howls are less refined, but no less fervent."

"And the whin´ny-ga-lop—whin´ny-ga-lop—whin´ny-ga-lops," said Kurt. "—wild stangs and saddle-ups and trot-alots. Their whinnies can be very musical."

"And the lug-a-trunks with their marvelous trumpeting," added Stinkle. "And the tails—we cannot forget the tails. We could put as many as we can find into the nickel trees to shake the branches. What a sound that will make! We have a whole wonderful chorus right here at our fingertips. It won't be practiced and well-rehearsed, but it will have one thing the Troll doesn't have."

"What's that, Stinkle?"

"Heart! It will have heart!" The stinkle-dunk said the words very deliberately. "All the animals want the safe return of the Nickle-Dickles. They will sing and play with all their hearts—in tune with the true spirit of silver. It will work, Kurtis. I know it will. Now all we have to do is convince the knight in shining armor to shed his copper."

"That could be a problem," said Kurt, reaching to grab his shirt from the branch. The shirt was still damp, but he donned it anyway then picked up his backpack and slipped it over his shoulders. "Come on, Notch," he said, intending to retrieve the worm from Stinkle's ascot.

"I believe I shall remain where I am," said the booknotch. ". . . *assuming* both of you are amenable to such an arrangement." He glanced up at the stinkle-dunk. "I've found a comfortable fold in which to sit, and with all the talk of a chorus, I hesitate to surrender such a choice seat from which to view the festivities."

"Of course you may remain on my ascot," Stinkle said graciously.

The little skunk had been patient until then, but now he seemed a bit anxious. "We must get about the task," he urged. "I shall handle Fraidy." And he turned to look for the slinkle-purr. "Oh, Fraidy," he called, spotting the copper-clad feline sitting forlornly beneath a nickel tree. "Would you come here, please."

"You need me no-o-o-w?" said the slinkle-purr, clinking and clanking toward them.

"We most certainly do," replied the stinkle-dunk. "You are most important to our mission."

"I am?" said Fraidy. "I-I-I-I am important?"

"Yes. *Very* important," said Kurt. "After all, you *are* the knight in shining armor."

"Yes," Fraidy replied. "I am Sir Fraidy Slinkle-Purr, Noblest Knight of the Realm!" And he stood straight and tall.

"Fraidy," said Stinkle. "I'm afraid we must ask you to do something that reaches beyond the call of duty. We must ask you to give up your armor."

"E-e-e-k!" Fraidy shrieked, slumping and holding his stomach as though he had been struck with a swift blow to the midsection. "What's it! Who? Me? Give up my armor?"

The stinkle-dunk placed his hand on the slinkle-purr's shoulder. "Fraidy, you have proved you are truly a brave knight. Three times you stepped forward to rescue the Nickle-Dickles. Such bravery does not go unnoticed."

"Yes. Three times," Kurt added. "And a brave knight doesn't hide behind his armor. It's not the armor that makes the knight. It's the slinkle-purr inside."

"Even without the armor, you are still a brave knight," said Stinkle. "And right now, we need that armor to make flutes. And we need *you* to direct a chorus. After all, you *are* very musically inclined. You proved that when you sang a cappella in your flying machine."

Stinkle and Kurt explained the plan for the flutes and the chorus, to which the slinkle-purr responded with a moment of quiet pondering. Then, with a sudden burst of valor, he said, "I will do it! This-s-s noble knight will give up his armor for the cause! I can keep the umbrella, though, can't I?"

"Of course," said Stinkle. And with that, Fraidy began taking off the suit.

With lots of help from the animals, Kurt and Stinkle pried the suit apart. They cut and hammered and bent and shaped and trimmed and smoothed and polished, as they formed and perfected the copper tubes. Finally, they bored the holes that turned the tiny tubes into flutes. Never were finer instruments shaped by the hands of man or animal. When they were finished, they had thirty-three flutes in all.

"Now, Fraidy," said Kurt. "Go and find all the slinkle-purrs you can. Bring them back here and choose thirty-three to play the flutes. The rest can sing. Charlie and Tattle and Chrysalis, you go and gather the tails—all you can find—and put them in the nickel trees. Pink Nut Druggle, will you and the other druggles kindly show the tails how to shake the branches. Stinkle, you and Notch find the lug-a-trunk that helped us on the mountainside. Tell him to gather all the other lug-a-trunks. We need their trumpets. Then go and find any yotees and whin ′ny-ga-lop—whin ′ny-ga-lop—whin ′ny-ga-lops that you can, and bring them here. Spinneret and Mosey, would you and all the weery-dawdles please stand in the Town Square and call all the singing twitter-flits together. Tell them the plan. I'll go find King Aegis and ask him to call the singing swishin-figgles. Now, quickit, everyone! Time is short!"

The group scattered in all directions to gather musicians for the chorus, and in no time at all, animals were assembling in the Town Square. All was abuzz and atwitter with singing and flute playing and organizing. At last the chorus was together, and Kurt called everyone to silence.

"It's up to you now, Fraidy. You are the conductor. I thought maybe you could lead that song the Nickle-Dickle children sing all the time, *Follow Me To Nickledown*. I think everyone knows it."

Holding the big green umbrella high over his head with his left paw, Fraidy raised his right paw in the air and began to conduct. The air became filled with music! Beautiful music! Beautiful because it was played with heart! And the flutes could be heard above it all.

Fol-low me to Nic-kle down, sweet-ly frag-rant ti - ny town.

The animals sang, and they joyously played;
The nickel trees rang as they clamored and swayed.

"Listen! A rumble, a roar, and a grumble!"
"Look at the mountain! The side of it crumbles!"

A hole opened up on the mountain's face
Where the lost ones had gone—precisely the place.

And then they appeared through the hole in the wall—
The Nickle ie Dickle ies! All of them! All!

Oh, what a cheer went up from the chorus!
A cheer that rang out over meadow and forest!

The animals ran and they hugged one and all!
The skinny, the tubby, the short and the tall!

Happiness filled the tiny-ish town.
Joy had returned to Nickledown.

A cheer went up from all the Nickle-Dickles and all the animals—a cheer that resounded through the Nickel Hills and stirred the nickel trees and set them ringing like a mighty carillon.

But when at last the ringing faded away, another voice took its place.

Bong!—it rang dimly.

Bong!—it tolled darkly.

A hush fell upon Nickledown as the animals stood frozen, entranced by the knell—entranced by the cry of the Trodden Seed—entranced by the call of the leaden bell.

Bong! Bong! Bong!

CHAPTER 35

❦

THE TEMPEST OF GALL

"Look!" cried a cow, pointing to a dark shadow gliding smoothly down the side of a dense stand of trees at one edge of the Town Square.

The shadow slid silently over the Rainbow Garden and steered a straight course toward Kurt.

"The Troll!" honked a goose, flapping her wings and running for cover.

"No, it's the Nimbus!" squealed a portly pig.

It may as well have been the Troll. Screams and squeals and squawks filled the square as animals scattered in all directions.

The shadow reached the place where Kurt and his friends stood, and as the dark vestige circled the ground round about them, a great bird-like form appeared overhead. A silver corona, bright and glowing, framed the creature's dark silhouette as he flew in circles high above sending forth a brilliant flash each time he crossed the sun.

All at once the creature dove, and as he descended, the Nickle-Dickles and all the animals gasped at the sight of Parhelion the Nimbus. When the awesome bird landed, the wind from his thrashing wings raised billows of silver dust that shrouded his dark and fearsome form. When the sparkling dust settled, the Nickle-Dickles, Kurt, and the few animals who remained with him, beheld unimpeded the fleshy face and many eyes of the great Nimbus.

The bird locked his gaze upon the Nickle-Dickle boy, who, standing transfixed, stared at the creature with fearful reverence. The steeliness of that avian gaze aroused old suspicions within Kurt—suspicions that the bird might in fact be the color of darkness below purple. When at last the Nimbus spoke, however, his words revealed a benevolent nature, and upon hearing them, those animals who had fled slowly withdrew from their hiding places and moved closer to the formidable black bird they called Parhelion.

As Kurt watched the animals draw near to the Nimbus, he saw them as children drawing near a loving father, and he knew for the first time with certainty the bird was indeed a creature of silver.

"I heard a cry of joy, and then the bell," said the Nimbus. "And I felt a great distress fall upon Nickledown—and a heavy foreboding."

Before Kurt could reply, he noticed the bird had turned his head sharply to the right and seemed to be listening intently. And when he looked around, he saw that *all* the animals had turned their heads toward that same direction—the west. They stood with bodies still, alert, rigid, their gazes fixed straight forward as though their whiskers had homed in on some clandestine signal known only to the more instinctual of living creatures—a signal that warned of impending danger.

Kurt heard a faint rumbling—muffled at first, and off at a great distance. The sound was marked and well cadenced, much like the rhythmic footsteps of a well-trained regiment. The tramping grew louder, and soon Kurt heard it clearly. An army! Its thunderous legions advancing toward Nickledown!

The light began to fade. The silver dust grew dull and lifeless. The air itself took on a grayish hue, as though a drear and dreadful shadow had fallen upon the land.

"There!" screamed a tiny turtle. "By the gate!"

Kurt turned quickly. And there, halted above the Great Nickel Gate, stood the forward battalions of the Gathering Gloom, grim and ghastly and ghostly gray. At their fore stood the Troll's Vanguard—his generals—the huge thunderheads Kurt and Mosey had seen from the knoll—lined up like sentinels.

Suddenly, as with an approaching train, the earth began to rattle, the sky above rumbled, a darkness rolled in with a rum-tum-grumble! The silver dust quivered and lifted and swirled as the wind in its fury lashed one and all. "Look!" screamed a donkey, "a tempest of gall!"

There in the north and the west as he told
Was the horrible face of the THUNDER TROLL!
Adrift in the clouds, aloft in a shroud,
Thickening, blackening, thundering loud!

"Run!" cried an elephant, packing his trunk.

"Hide!" screamed a kangaroo, closing her pouch, tucking her little one safely inside.

Animals scattered mid oinks and squeals—
Ducks and geese and cockatiels.
The large, the small, the short, the tall;
The scaly, the fuzzy, the smooth ones—all!

"He's harnessed the North Wind!" cried Mosey, hurriedly slow.

"It's worse than that!" Stinkle shouted over the howling tempest. "He's harnessed the North *and* West Winds. He's combined the cold treachery of the North Wind with the fleetness of the West Wind."

"Help us!" the animals cried, huddling close to Kurt.

"I can't help you!" Kurt shouted. "I don't know what to do!"

"You are the only one who *can* help them, young Kurt," the Nimbus said in a firm and steady voice. "You are the Nickle-Dickle child. You possess the key."

A raven landed on Kurt's shoulder. From his haggard appearance, he looked as though he had flown a long distance, and he was most distraught. "The Copper Valley is destroyed," he cawed frantically. "It is no more, no more, no more."

"My house!" cried Stinkle, slumping to the ground. "My dear little well-appointed house."

"Gone," said the raven, fighting to steady himself against the wind. "Swallowed by darkness. No more, no more." And with that, he dropped to the ground and hopped away.

Kurt looked at the animals, who were looking back at him helplessly, pleading, their fur and feathers blowing wildly in the wind. Believing there was still a chance he could find the door if he did not spend time fighting the Troll, Kurt turned to Parhelion. "Isn't there anyone else who can help them? What about you, Parhelion? Can't you fight the Troll?"

"I cannot," said the Nimbus. "Only the Nickle-Dickle child has the power to defeat darkness. The Legacy, young Kurt. Think of the Legacy."

Kurt thought about *The Book of Light*—the signatures—the purposeful lives of those who had come before him. When he looked again at the animals and Nickle-Dickles, his heart went out to them and his resolve returned. "Yes!" he said. "I'll do it. I'll fight the Troll!"

"Hooray!" the animals shouted.

As if to answer a challenge, a bolt of lightning struck the ground nearby.

"But how do I fight him?" Kurt asked the Nimbus.

"Your father was unarmed," Parhelion said over the roar of the wind. "He did not know the secret to defeating the Troll. You *can* know it. *The Book*, young Kurt. Read *The Book*."

"There's nothing in the book about fighting the Troll."

"Look again," the Nimbus said, and he spread his wings and cupped them around the boy to protect him from the tempest. "Believe, and read with your heart."

In the shelter of Parhelion's wings, Kurt withdrew the book from the pack, opened it, and read a new page:

> *Bell of shadow, forged of shade,*
> *Come to call the Troll to wake,*
> *Count the times your legions dark*
> *May wield their hammers, devil's wands,*

And strike the cold gray leaden bell,
The Piper's call to quit and quell;
For numbered are the dreary days
Governed by the leaden bell.

Tremble now, you watchity widgits.
Bow you low, you kratchits and kridgits.
Crumble down, you ghoulish cronies;
Rattle loud your broken bonies.
Another comes with music sweet
To wake a sleeper from his sleep.
The Piper calls above the knell,
Above the darkly calling bell.

His flute he plays with merry note;
His music sweet does gently float
Upon the wind to fetch the boy,
To turn the key and Gloom destroy.
Hear you well, you watchity widgits.
Hear me tell, you kratchits and kridgits,
The never-ending tale of light
That bids you flee in harried flight.

To him who holds The Book in hand:
Face you now the hellish band.
Take the key into the tomb;
Unlock the box, and seal the doom.
Don the robe! Begin the fight!
Upward soar in lofty flight
Above the mountain's open womb.
Cast the Troll into his tomb.

Kurt looked up from the book and stared at the Nimbus, whose many eyes were locked upon him. When the Nimbus spoke, his voice was filled with compassion.

"Your father did not have the key with him, young Kurt, yet he managed to drive the Troll from Whiskers. He lost his life in so doing. You *have* the key. Use it, young Kurt. Run to the rock. Turn the key and discover its true 'mettle.'"

Kurt reached for the chain that held the key, and to his horror, it was not there. "It's gone, Parhelion! The key is gone! I must have lost it in the underground sea." He remembered the "branch" that grazed his neck in the narrow passage. "They took it, Parhelion!—the Troll or his Gloom. They took it from me in the river passage!"

For the first time, the Nimbus appeared shaken.

Just then a mule came galloping up. "Look at that twitter-flit!" the mule shouted, pointing to a tiny goldfinch who was struggling to fly against the wind. The yellow bird was attempting to fly downward, toward Kurt. But the wind kept blowing him up and away. The twitter-flit was carrying something in his beak.

"The key!" shouted Kurt. "That twitter-flit has the key!" And there it was—the tarnished key, with the chain of nickel and the clasp of copper still attached, dangling from the twitter-flit's beak.

"Someone help him!" Kurt cried.

Several other twitter-flits bravely answered the call. Leaving the shelter of a nearby bush, they struggled to make themselves airborne, pressing hard against the wind that fought to pin them to the ground. The determined little sparrows managed at last to fly up behind the yellow twitter-flit and, despite some badly ruffled feathers, pushed him downward toward the boy.

Mother Nickle-Dickle had joined Kurt and his friends by then, and Kurt quickly handed the book to her. "Please keep this for me," he said. "And put Notch inside. I need to know he's safe."

Stinkle, standing next to Mother Nickle-Dickle, reached into the fold of his ascot where the booknotch was huddled, unfastened the fishing line, and placed the trembling worm in the book, which Mother Nickle-Dickle promptly tucked away in her apron.

By this time, the tiny twitter-flit was close enough for Kurt to catch the key and he dropped it into the boy's hand. "A swishin-figgle found it on the river bottom," the little bird chirped as loudly as he could. "He gave it to King Aegis, and King Aegis told me to bring it to you."

"Thank you!" Kurt shouted.

"Now run, young Kurt," said Parhelion. "Run to the rock! Discover *your* true mettle."

Chapter 36

The Battle

Kurt ran toward the Circle of Beginnings. When he reached the wildly clanging nickel trees and stumbled into the Circle, he was not at all sure the Cornerstone would appear, but he held out his hand in faith. A great gasp went up from the Nickle-Dickles and animals as the stone became visible for all to see. Kurt touched the carving on the boulder's face and the door appeared. When he stepped through it, the great stone sealed itself.

Inside the rocky tomb, all was quiet except for the muffled rumble of thunder that penetrated even the thick walls of the Cornerstone. Kurt watched the light change from purple through the spectrum to pink, and he smelled the fragrances of the colors. But no melodies accompanied the colors, and with the arrival of the pink light and the scent of jasmine, no flute played. Only the deep rumble breached the silence.

Kurt searched for a keyhole and found one on the front of the pedestal. Dropping to his knees, he read the inscription that appeared above the keyhole:

> *As silver fits the one who holds the key,*
> *The key now fits the lock that holds the power.*

Kurt pushed the key into the keyhole and turned it. With a blinding burst of light, the front of the pedestal dropped open revealing a garment of light lying on a shelf within. Kurt reached out to take the garment, but the moment his fingers touched it, the garment disappeared, and he found himself dressed in a robe—a robe of shining light.

As he placed the silver key around his neck—the key which, no longer tarnished, now glowed with the same fine patina found on Mother Nickle-Dickle's perfume press—he saw the chain of nickel and clasp of copper had both turned to silver. The boy felt a tingling in his whiskers, and all at once he knew what he must do. He stood up, and the door reappeared.

When he stepped from the tomb back into the roaring tempest, all the animals and Nickle-Dickles stared in awe at the boy who stood before them dressed in the Robe of Light, his fiery red hair blowing wildly in the wind. Even the Nimbus, who was waiting near the door, appeared humble before the Nickle-Dickle child.

"Parhelion," Kurt said, his voice strong and full, "you must carry me high above the Silver Mountain, into the darkest part of the clouds. I must meet the Troll on his own ground."

Parhelion nodded and knelt so Kurt could climb aboard his back. Kurt buried his knees deep in the thick feathers on the Nimbus's back to secure his position and took the chain from around his neck and raised the key high above his head in his right hand. "You must soar above the mountain's top and hold your position," he told the Nimbus. "The Troll will be attracted by the brightness of the robe. He will want to devour its light and will lunge for it. An instant before he touches it, I must touch him with the key. It must be perfectly timed."

"You realize you must look directly at the Troll to accomplish this," said Parhelion, unfolding his massive wings. "You will find yourself looking full into his face—looking without shield into the face of darkness itself. Beware his gaze, young Kurt—his eyes of molten coal. Should he fix your gaze for even a moment, you could lose your balance, your timing. You and all of Whiskers would become as a dying star—light reduced to darkness."

Kurt nodded. "Let's go!"

The Nimbus spread his wings and began the ascent. Kurt felt the force of the angry North and West Winds whirling about him, ripping at him, trying to dislodge him from the bird's enormous back. But with all his might he held on with his left hand to the sturdy feathers near Parhelion's neck, while with his right, he defiantly held the key aloft. As they ascended, the winds gave way, and after a time, Kurt and the Nimbus found themselves circling unimpeded in the air above Nickledown.

All at once, the many eyes on the Nimbus's back turned their gaze toward the Silver Mountain. Kurt braced himself for what he knew would be a sudden surge, and with a mighty burst of speed, up the side of the mountain they flew—soaring toward the highest peak! Nickledown, having grown smaller below them, disappeared altogether as they pierced the thick ceiling of dark storm clouds.

Kurt expected to break through to light on the clouds' upper sides, but the nebulous thunderheads stretched so high into the firmament there seemed no end to them. The boy and the Nimbus found themselves entombed within the heavy mists—entombed within the musty, murky mass that was the Gloom.

From within the terrible darkness, Kurt felt the bone-chilling stare of sad and sunken pupiless eyes as watchity widgits, kratchits and kridgits stared at him, glared at him, sneaked at him, peeked at him from behind every black and brackish billow. The boy's head filled with the rickety rattle of brittle bones as ghoulish cronies and terrible bonies danced grotesquely round about him, waving wildly their wizened limbs. Figures wispy, dark, and howling circled round him, soared above him, called like ghostly, ghastly banshees loosed from out a terrible pit! Horrible claws reached to grasp him, pulled and grabbed him, hooked and snagged him, but sizzled and hissed upon touching the robe.

"The Troll—where is he?" Kurt shouted to Parhelion, dodging the sweep of a grisly claw. He searched for the face of the Troll in every lightning flash—listened for his rumbling voice in every thunder crash. But the Troll hid himself well in his dark disguise.

As they circled within the Gloom—as the Nimbus fought to hold his course against the harrowing hoards—Kurt could see below him a darker black—the crater on the mountain's top—appearing, disappearing in the swirling mist.

Kurt smelled a sickening stench and felt a bone-chilling cold! *THA-RUM-RUM-RUM!* roared a voice that shook the welkin floor. And there, towering above him, grim and gray—towering in billowed, burgeoned size, staring down through bloodless eyes—was the giant himself! The Dark Deceiver! The Tiller of Tumultuous Soil! The Warden of the Wicked Weir!

The giant's eyes began to burn. Hot red embers hissed and spit, growing redder and redder the longer they burned.

The Troll stretched out a wizened hand and blades of lightning flew from the nails on his crooked fingers.

"Missed!" said Kurt, as the Nimbus swerved to dodge the bolts.

The giant whirled around and hurled his angry blades again. And again they missed and fell to earth.

Parhelion turned and dove toward the mountaintop. The Troll roared and tramped his feet upon the welkin floor. Reaching down to scoop the Nimbus up, he missed! The giant raised his head and roared again, pounding the mountain with a mighty *BOOM* that shook the highest peak and rattled the ground below. Spinning around and thundering loud, he fired his blades throughout the sky.

With his frenzied legions gathered round him—screaming, howling, scowling, growling—the Troll pointed a jagged nail at Kurt, and a bodiless vanguard rushed the boy, smothering him in a thick veil of putrid vapor. The vanguard's bleating cries so filled Kurt's head that he held his hands over his ears and lost his balance. The Nimbus swerved to one side setting the boy upright then fell back on course above the crater.

Well into the battle, Parhelion took a position that placed the mountain's crater between him and the Troll. He held his mark until the Troll crossed to a point directly over the chasm.

"Now!" Kurt shouted, and the Nimbus swooped down into the crater and out of sight then soared upward again behind the giant.

The Troll spun around. He lost his balance. He teetered. He stumbled. But just before toppling, he regained his footing.

Time and again the Nimbus swooped downward and soared upward, circling in great spirals around the Troll, while the multitudinous eyes on the bird's feathers remained fixed upon the nebulous giant. And time and again the Troll lunged at the bird and the boy as he twirled dizzily above the dark abyss, his fiery eyes tracing the circular path of the beleaguering Nimbus.

All at once Kurt felt the heat of the Troll's molten eyes lock upon him. "Look away, young Kurt," Parhelion shouted. "Do not meet his gaze. We have him now. He tires. See how he staggers."

Indeed, the Troll *was* staggering. Aimlessly he staggered, swaying to and fro, lunging wildly at the Nimbus and the Nickle-Dickle child with every pass they made in front of him.

Losing his footing, the Troll stumbled forward. Surely he would plunge through the clouds at any moment. Kurt and the Nimbus let down their guard. Victory was theirs!

But one must never count as done that which the hand of evil can undo. True to his name, Dark Deceiver, the Troll whirled around, sure of foot! Bending way down—turning his eyes upward in a ghastly stare—he peered directly into the eyes of the Nickle-Dickle child.

Mesmerized, Kurt felt helpless. The burning eyes of molten coal locked Kurt's gaze. He was losing his balance, listing to one side. He felt his grip loosening from Parhelion's feathers. He was slipping from the Nimbus's back! Ignoring the key, he used both hands to strengthen his hold.

Parhelion banked to one side, attempting to set the boy upright, but Kurt was tottering dangerously. "The key!" screamed Parhelion. "Use the key, young Kurt!"

Kurt fought to raise the key above his head as he struggled to regain his balance. The Troll glanced at the shining key and, in so doing, withdrew his gaze long enough for Kurt to pull free of the trance and right himself. The Troll roared with fury! With one terrible lunge, his eyes burning fire, he thrust a giant arm at Kurt, the fingers on his gnarly hand spread apart like an evil claw aimed to crush the boy.

He missed!

Kurt saw his chance. As the giant's arm swooped past him, he touched the key to the Troll's elbow.

The robe burst forth with a mighty blast of light never before seen in the Land of Whiskers! A light greater than the light of the sun! A light that sent all the colors of the rainbow showering down upon Whiskers.

A stream of brilliant light shot toward the Troll! He screamed! Becoming light itself, he lit the sky with a blinding FLASH!

When the light faded from his wizened body, he began to shrink. Turning a sickly gray, he shriveled to a wrinkled nib. Twisting and turning till his head met his toe, he plunged through the clouds to the crater below. With a strained roar and rumble—with a vain rum-tum-grumble—the gnarly, twisted, ashen ball of furrowed flesh with blood of gall disappeared into the black and bottomless hole in the mountain's top.

Kurt and Parhelion and the Nickle-Dickles and all the animals heard him rolling, rumbling, tumbling, grumbling, down, down, down inside the mountain to the depths of the pit, his rumbling growing dimmer the deeper he rolled.

The rim of the crater began to move. The Gloom began to wail! The watchity widgits, the kratchits and kridgits, the ghoulish cronies, the terrible bonies, the dark things—all! howled and moaned like dying souls as the mountain sealed itself—*THA-RUM!* The Gloom rolled away with one terrible scream! Then silence rested upon the air.

Sunlight poured down upon Nickledown, filling the air with silver light, and a gentle breeze began to play in the nickel trees. The whole of Whiskers seemed to sing to the Nickle-Dickle boy as he and Parhelion drifted down upon the breeze. While still high above the land, Kurt could see the Meadow where he entered the Land of Whiskers, and the Copper Valley—both flooded with light—both restored to their original splendor. He even thought he saw Stinkle's little cottage, its copper roof glistening in the sun.

A joyful cheer greeted Kurt and the Nimbus as they landed in the Town Square—a joyful cheer that never again would be silenced by the leaden bell.

It was finished. Light had defeated the power of darkness. The Nickle-Dickle boy had sealed the Troll in his tomb and driven the Gloom from Whiskers. Kurt's friends were safe, and the light was restored.

Kurt placed the chain holding the key back around his neck, and the moment he did, the robe disappeared and Kurt found himself dressed again in his lucky plaid fishing shirt and old blue jeans.

"Parhelion," he said, "if the Troll fed on light, why did he shrink when the robe *filled* him with light?"

"You see, young Kurt," the Nimbus replied, "darkness can *devour* light, but darkness cannot *become* light and survive."

CHAPTER 37

COLORS

The number of animals in Nickledown that day was greater than ever since so many had fled to the town ahead of the Gloom. Now they were filtering in from the hills, where they had hidden when the Troll kidnapped the Nickle-Dickles, and they were bringing with them packs overflowing with offerings for the celebration.

Some of the Nickle-Dickles ran to their houses and hastily prepared for the day's festivities, while others set up tables in the Town Square. Soon the Silver Day celebration was under way.

There were games of all sorts to play, and lengthy conversations— just the kind Stinkle so loved. And food. Ah, yes, food. Biscuits and honey and fruits and vegetables; and bowls and bowls of nuts and acorns. There was tribble of every size and consistency, topped with unfathomable delights—tribble with beans, tribble with cream, tribble with syrup, tribble with honey and butter; and baked goods—tribble loaf, tribble cookies, and tribble pie. And of course there was birthday cake because, after all, it *was* a birthday celebration. Everyone played and laughed and ate, then they laughed and played some more.

Charlie finished a huge bowl of tribble with cream and went off to find Chrysalis. Kurt was helping himself to a big piece of birthday cake when Tubbs scurried up to him.

"Hello, Kurt," said Tubbs. "Pink Nut Druggle says I have a good chance of becoming yellow now that my eyes are open. What do you think of that?"

Before Kurt could answer, Tubbs spotted a bowl of nuts on a nearby table and hurried over to it. "I've never had a good, close-up look at a nut," he said, examining one in detail. "Oh my! They're beautiful! They're almost too beautiful to eat! But not quite." He cracked the nut open and popped the sweet morsel into his mouth and grabbed two more. "See you later, Kurt." And he scampered away.

Kurt spotted Stinkle sitting under a tree across the way, deep in conversation with a group of Nickle-Dickles. He waved, and the stinkle-dunk excused himself and came over to the boy.

"Sorry to bother you," said Kurt.

"Oh, that's all right. I have to put on more perfume anyway. I've put on none since early morning, and I wouldn't want the effect to wear off. That could prove disastrous."

"But Stinkle, it has worn off."

A horrified look came over the little skunk's face. "It *has* worn off? Quickly, quickly! Oh, where is that bottle?" And he frantically searched his pockets for the flask.

"It's okay, Stinkle," Kurt said. "Don't you see what's happened? The scent wore off and you didn't even notice. The air is already so full of perfume you couldn't tell you weren't wearing any. Even if you slipped, no one would know. Nothing ever smells bad in Nickledown."

"Harumph," said Stinkle. Then the truth of the matter struck him fully. "Kurtis! I'm a skunk! Who cares if my collar is too stiff or my tie is too starched or my shoes are too polished. In Nickledown, I can be who I am—a skunk—without care, and fancy-free. Nothing ever smells bad in Nickledown!"

Kurt laughed. "Nothing ever does."

Just then they heard a familiar sound—a slightly off-key a cappella rendition of *Follow Me to Nickledown*—coming from the direction of a tall picket fence.

"Isn't that Fraidy singing on that fence?" Kurt remarked.

"It looks like Fraidy," said Stinkle.

Though they recognized the voice when the cat called to them from some distance, the animal that leaped off the fence and ran toward them was carrying an umbrella folded under his arm.

"Look!" the slinkle-purr said proudly. "I'm not afraid. Mother Nickle-Dickle said n-o-o-thing can hurt you in Nickledown, so I folded my umbrella and n-o-o-thing terrible happened. She also said copper can't exist for long in Nickledown, so my copper armor would have turned to cloth anyway. It wouldn't have protected me for long. Isn't it won-n-n-derful? Here I am—this cu-u-u-te little slinkle-purr—all in one piece. No cuts, no bruises, no nicks, no scrapes—as whole as e-e-ever I was! I guess I won't be needing this." And he tossed the umbrella aside and grinned a silly grin. "Nothing can harm you in Ni-i-i-ckledown. Everyone knows that."

"Fraidy, my dear Fraidy," Stinkle said with a chuckle, shaking his head.

"Fraidy," said Kurt. "Have you seen Tattle?"

"I-I-I've seen him," Fraidy replied. "He's been telling stories and riding the tail of e-e-very long-tailed waggle-lick and slinkle-purr in Nickledown. I offered him my-y-y tail, but he already had a waiting list. The Nickle-Dickle children have been following him around the way their ancestors followed the Pi-i-i-ed Piper."

"Here he comes now," said Kurt.

"And there he goes," added Stinkle, as Tattle frolicked past them riding the tail of a short-legged waggle-lick. The old tail was laughing and speaking in rhyme to a string of tiny Nickle-Dickle children, who followed close behind him, skipping and giggling as they listened to his tale.

"I guess I'll go see if my-y-y name has come up yet," said Fraidy. "I'm sure I-I-I was next on Tattle's list—right after that short-legged wa-a-a-ggle lick." And he followed the band of revelers down the street.

Stinkle turned to Kurt. "How full of jasmine the air is!"

"Stinkle," said Kurt, "you sure have a great nose. I can't believe you can smell jasmine when all the scents from the Rainbow Garden are in the air."

"Just the same, I do smell jasmine."

"Well, I smell just one big, beautiful scent," said Kurt, inhaling deeply and closing his eyes. "I can't even give it a name. 'The perfectly balanced perfume'—that's what Mosey called it."

The stinkle-dunk sniffed the air. "Only jasmine," he repeated. And he looked at Kurt strangely. "Only jasmine?"

Suddenly his eyes popped wide open. "*Only* jasmine!" And he did a little dance—a very unstately, unstodgy, carefree dance—the kind of dance a "skunk" would do. "Jasmine, Kurtis!" he said when he had caught his breath. "Do you know what that means? It means I'm pink! Not 'pink for the most part,' but *fully* pink! Truly and completely in every way wholly and wonderfully pink! I must tell Fraidy and Tattle the good news."

"There they are." Kurt pointed to the opposite side of the Square where Tattle was riding Fraidy's tail shouting, "Whoopee do!" and holding on for dear life. The slinkle-purr was low to the ground, dashing headlong toward Kurt and Stinkle as though he intended to zoom past them; but he stopped short when he saw the boy and the stinkle-dunk jumping up and down, waving their arms like children watching a circus parade.

"Good news! Good news!" said Stinkle. "I was just telling Kurtis how the air smelled strongly of jasmine, and he was surprised my sense of smell was so acute as to be able to pick out one particular scent, when I realized I'm pink! Not 'pink for the most part,' but fully and completely pink."

"That's won-n-n-derful," said Fraidy.

"It's more than wonderful," added Tattle. "It's funderful! And stupendous! And splendiferous!"

Fraidy sniffed the air. "*My-y-y* sense of smell most certainly *i-i-i-s* extraordinary, however. I *c-a-a-a-n* detect one scent above all the others. Mint. Coo-o-o-l, refreshing mint."

"No, no, no," argued Tattle. "We tails may not be known for our noses—I'm not exactly sure where our noses are, though they can't be far—but Stinkle is right. There's jasmine in the air for certain. Not *strong* jasmine; just a *hint* of jasmine—a *glint* of jasmine."

Kurt looked at Stinkle, and Stinkle looked at Kurt, and the two of them looked at the tattle-tail, whose mouth was hanging open.

"I'm pink!" said Tattle, twisting himself loose from Fraidy's tail. "I smelled jasmine, too—like you." And he smiled at Stinkle then plopped onto the ground and rolled over and over on the grass. "Not a deep pink, mind you, but pink! For the most part!"

Fraidy could not have noticed Tattle falling from his tail, for he was too busy gazing starry-eyed into space.

Stinkle grabbed the slinkle-purr by the shoulders and gave him a little shake, attempting to snap him out of his stupor. "Fraidy," he said, "didn't you see what happened to Tattle?"

Fraidy, still starry-eyed, mumbled, "Mint—mint—mint."

Stinkle gave the slinkle-purr another shake, and his yellow-green eyes fell into focus. "Mint!" he blurted.

"What?"

"Mint!" he said again. "I smelled mint! I'm not blu-u-u-e. I'm something ne-e-e-w. I'm green, green, green, green, green. Isn't gre-e-e-n the most beautiful color you've ever se-e-e-n?"

Everyone laughed with uncontrolled delight at Fraidy's sudden poetic eloquence; and they laughed with joy in the triumphant realization of what each of them had accomplished: a step up in color, a step toward the fulfillment of their highest goals.

The animals appeared content. Kurt had achieved what he had set out to do. He had brought his friends out of the shadows—to Nickledown and light. He began thinking about home, and soon his friends and some of the other animals noticed he was feeling blue, and they gathered close around him.

"In our happiness, we failed to think of you," said Stinkle.

Spinneret and Mother and Father Nickle-Dickle noticed the crowd gathering around Kurt, and they, too, drew near, followed by Charlie and Chrysalis and Tubbs and Pink Nut Druggle and Mosey. And Parhelion towered above them all.

"We heard the rejoicing," said Pink Nut Druggle.

"Yes," said Spinneret. "It's wonderful about the color changes. But Kurt, dear, why are you so sad?"

"The sun is almost down," said Kurt, "and I haven't uncovered the secrets. I'll have to stay in Whiskers forever. I'll never see my mother again."

CHAPTER 38

SECRETS

"One moment, dear," said Spinneret. "Are you certain you have not uncovered the secrets?"

"I didn't find the *harmony that has no sound*," said Kurt. "I thought it was the silver trees, but it wasn't. And I thought the *sweetness that does not fade* was the abacus flowers, but they faded. And I thought the opals were the *riches that cannot be spent*, but the opals turned out to be fish."

"Don't you see, dear," said Spinneret. You *have* uncovered the first secret. You've discovered the most beautiful harmony of all—the harmony that fills your life when you take time to understand the needs of others. In doing so, you've revealed to all the first secret:

> *UNDERSTANDING begins in the silence of*
> *the heart. A single note played upon a*
> *heart string and heard by another soon*
> *becomes a symphony.*

Rejoice in the music, dear. Conditions are right for the door to appear."

"Even so," said Kurt, "I didn't find the *sweetness that does not fade*. The doorway will never actually appear."

Mosey spoke up in his weak and weary voice. "Quite to the contrary, Kurt. You *have* uncovered the second secret. You've discovered the sweetness born of caring. In doing so, you've revealed to all the second secret:

CARING, like a fine fragrance,
penetrates and permeates all it
touches. The most delicate perfume, if
its oils are pure and finely balanced,
will drift upon the winds forever.

Breathe the fine perfume, Kurt. The doorway awaits you."

"But it won't open," Kurt replied. "I know I didn't find any riches. What good are the first two secrets without the third?"

"The door *will* open," said a voice deep and resonant, and the many eyes of Parhelion the Nimbus fixed their gaze upon the boy. "You *have* uncovered the third secret, young Kurt. *MID COLORS CLEAR*—the colors of the animals—*AND FLORAL SCENT*—the fragrance of their colors—you *have* found *RICHES VAST THAT CANNOT BE SPENT*. The third secret springs forth from the first and second. By example, you have taught your friends to understand and care about one another. Because of that, they have reached higher colors. And the light that shines within the colors is the essence of wealth in the Land of Whiskers. In revealing to them the first two secrets, you have given them the greatest treasure of all—*LOVE*.

Like the abacus flowers that bloom on
the Silver Mountain, love, when allowed
to grow, ever increases and never fades.

Like the music of the silver trees,
love, once felt, resides within our
hearts forever.

Cherish this sacred jewel, Kurt. You have heard and heeded the call to Nickledown and light. The door will open, indeed."

As Kurt looked at the faces of his friends, he realized fully what Parhelion meant. He *had* found the way home. And in so doing, he had formed a bond with the Land of Whiskers that would forever remain in his heart.

How at peace the animals were now that the Troll and the Gloom were banished from Whiskers. Kurt stared for a moment at the glistening nickel trees and breathed in the fragrance of the perfectly balanced perfume of the Rainbow Garden.

"Parhelion, what if I had not uncovered the secrets? Would I have remained in Whiskers forever?"

"You would not have been kept in Whiskers against your will, young Kurt. You had to be given the opportunity to uncover the secrets—the Legacy required it. Had you not uncovered the secrets, the Legacy would have ended. Never again would a human child have been allowed to enter the Land of Whiskers. Only in learning the secrets could you pass the Legacy on, for knowledge of the secrets allows you to carry to your world a portion of the light of Whiskers; and that light binds the two worlds together."

Kurt looked again at the friends gathered about him. From the sad looks on their faces, he knew they realized the sun would soon be going down. It was time to say goodbye.

Stinkle spoke for all of them. "Safe passage to you, my friend," he said quietly.

"Now, quickit," said Parhelion. "Time is short. You must climb the Silver Mountain and reach the door before the sun sets."

"Climb the mountain? Won't the silver trees put me to sleep?"

"Not if you hurry," said the Nimbus. "There will be no breeze to stir them until just before sunset, when the breeze returns to gather the silver dust."

Kurt felt tears welling in his eyes as he looked at his friends for the last time. The moment he had longed for had finally come, and with it came a sadness deeper than his heart could bear.

He bade his friends goodbye, one by one, and hugged Mother and Father Nickle-Dickle. After removing the shoes Father Nickle-Dickle had given him, he handed them back to the tiny man. "I guess

I won't be needing these anymore," he said. "You were right. It's not hard to walk in the shoes of another once you get used to it."

Charlie asked Chrysalis if she would come through the passage with them, but she reminded her brother that she had a family in Whiskers, and Charlie understood. After kissing his sister goodbye, he removed his old brown collar and placed it around her neck. She had never had a collar of her own, and tears filled her eyes.

Charlie asked Kurt to hand him the last Chunkie Chewie from the backpack, and he gave it to Fraidy with a half-smile. "It might not keep well on the trip home," he told the cat. "It has no preservatives, you know." Fraidy purred and rubbed up against Charlie affectionately, as slinkle-purrs will.

"You must hurry now," said Parhelion. "Time is short."

"Mother Nickle-Dickle," said Kurt. "Would you hand me the book. I'd like to say goodbye to Notch. And if you'll put the book back in the Cornerstone for me . . ."

"Of course I will," said Mother Nickle-Dickle (for the Cornerstone now remained visible for all to see), and she withdrew the book from her apron and handed it to Kurt.

"I'm glad you didn't forget to tell me goodbye," Notch said when Kurt opened the book.

"I could never do that," Kurt replied.

The boy no longer viewed goodbyes as parting rituals that must be performed. He saw them now as opportunities to wish those he loved all the good things his heart desired for them.

The booknotch looked up at Kurt shyly. "I've made green, Kurt."

"Notch, you mean 'chartreuse,' don't you?"

The little worm blushed.

"That's a full step up, Notch. Now your inside matches your outside."

Everyone laughed. Notch just nodded with a funny smile and spoke in that tiny voice of his that was cracking from the lump in his throat. "Goodbye, Kurt. Remember, I'll be in the book. If ever you come to Whiskers again, I would like it very much if you would come to see me."

"Of course I will. Goodbye, little Notch."

The booknotch had inched his way to the spine of the book by then, so Kurt gently lifted him and placed him on the page last read. He was sure Notch, being a proper booknotch, would want it that way. "Sleep tight," he told the worm.

He was closing the book when he noticed a new page had been written. Turning to it, he found instructions penned at the top: To be read to all the inhabitants of Whiskers. He read the page out loud:

> "One will come to defeat the darkness.
> He will take The Book through the passage,
> out from the Land of Whiskers and extend
> the Legacy to all who will hear. Though
> The Book be taken from Whiskers, those
> of you who remain in the Land will not
> be separated from it. Its words will be
> written in your hearts and will remain
> with you always.
>
> "The Book will be taken not that you
> should grieve, but rather that you may
> rejoice. A new page is to be written for
> those who live beyond the Twelve Gates
> of Whiskers—to give to them a portion
> of the light once meant for you alone.
> And the words of that page, too, will be
> written in the hearts of those of you who
> desire it.
>
> "And those of you who desire it will no
> longer see one another as purple or
> blue—as green or yellow or orange or
> pink—striving by your works to reach a

higher color. You will see one another
in a new light—a light from which all
colors are derived—a pure, transparent
light of brightest white shining as
silver in your midst."

"I guess I'll be going with you," said Notch, climbing to the page just read.

"Yes, Kurt," said Mother Nickle-Dickle. "Surely you are the one who will take *The Book*."

Kurt nodded and closed the book gently around the booknotch and glanced at Parhelion.

"Quickit! Time is short," the Nimbus reminded him.

Kurt grabbed his backpack from the ground where he had left it before entering the Cornerstone. He did not take time to put the book into the pack. Instead, he slung the pack over his right shoulder and tucked the ancient volume under his left arm.

"You must hurry now, young Kurt," said Parhelion. "Follow my shadow up the mountain path until you see the guidelithes. Follow them to the open door. When you go through the passage, hold tightly to Charlie's tail."

The Nimbus flew high into the air, circled several times, and headed toward the mountain. Kurt and Charlie arrived at the path in time to see Parhelion begin a slow ascent toward the mountaintop. Following his shadow up the path, they paused once to look back at Nickledown.

The boy and his dog passed safely by a grove of silver trees, and soon thereafter, Parhelion soared upward and turned and headed toward the setting sun. In a moment, he was gone.

"Goodbye, Parhelion!" Kurt shouted half-heartedly, knowing the Nimbus would not hear him—at least, not in the usual way.

CHAPTER 39

THE DOORWAY

Kurt saw the cloud of glowing guidelithes just ahead of him, poised above the path. When the cloud began to move, Kurt and Charlie followed.

The boy glanced over his shoulder just as the trailing rays of the setting sun began to color the sky a warm crimson. The sight of the huge ball of light disappearing on the western horizon filled Kurt with a sense of urgency, and he pushed onward at a quickened pace.

Suddenly, there it was—the door—an opening on the side of the mountain—a cold black hole at the base of a steep, gray wall of rock. The guidelithes quickly encircled the dark opening, their light revealing the fore-chambers of a deep, narrow cavern. Polestar, having positioned himself atop the circle of light, stood ready to lead the exodus at Kurt's signal.

"This is it, boy," Kurt said to Charlie, looking back at Nickledown one last time. The trailing remnants of the setting sun were all that remained now to light the quiet landscape below. Kurt could see only shadowy traces of trees and houses and the winding road leading from the Copper Valley to the tiny town; and only a series of faint glimmers where the river flowed through the Nickel Hills and into the Valley.

A soft breeze began to blow, and with it something strange began to happen inside the boy. Nickledown and all his friends, who were so real to him just moments ago, were taking on an illusory air, as though an elfin presence—perhaps the same one that tugged at his shirttails and coaxed him to stay that first day in the Meadow—was now preparing him to return to his own world.

Kurt pressed the book tight against his chest in preparation for entering the passage. Then realizing he might never see Notch again, he opened the volume one more time.

"I had to say goodbye again, Notch, since you'll be invisible when we get home."

"I'm glad you did," said the little worm. "But Kurt, there's something I think you ought to know. I believe there's yet another page to be read. I feel the letters. They're very close."

Kurt lifted Notch and turned the page; and just as the worm said, there was a new page written in *The Book of Light*. Kurt placed the booknotch on the spine of the book and read:

> *I planted a seed—*
> *A sprouted seed that flew in through the window—*
> *A tiny seed with a delicate stem.*
> *The words, "will understand" were written.*
> *I cherished the seed.*
>
> *A petal flew in through the window.*
> *From the seed had come a blossom.*
> *I cherished the petal.*
>
> *I looked up, and the air was full as snow of the petals*
> *Of many blossoms carried upon the wind from many places,*
> *Some far distant and hidden away.*
>
> *Blossoms were borne from places*
> *Where seeds had hitherto not been planted.*
>
> *Other petals fell upon me in blessing.*
>
> *I cherished them all.*

Kurt felt a sudden chill and noticed movement in the air around him. When he looked up, he saw clouds had formed above the mountain. It was beginning to snow.

The boy gently tucked Notch into the book for the last time and closed the cover. He pressed the book firmly against his chest again with his left arm, and with his right hand, took hold of Charlie's tail. "Let's go, boy," he said, checking his grip. "Goodbye, Polestar!" he shouted, as Charlie stepped into the opening, pulling Kurt in after him.

The guidelithes, led by Polestar, swarmed into the opening behind them, filling the space with a marvelous light. There was a sudden acceleration, and in what seemed an instant, Kurt and Charlie found themselves back beside the rocky cliff by the lake—back in Kurt's world—back home.

Kurt touched his face. He had no whiskers. The pack was still slung over his right shoulder, but the book was gone. He searched the ground around him, but the ancient volume was nowhere to be found. "Notch!" he cried. But there was no answer.

When the boy looked around, he saw his fishing pole lying on the ground where he dropped it. The can of worms was still in the shadow of the rock near the water's edge. "The polyglops!" he said, hurrying over to look in the can. Most of the worms were still inside, so he carried the can to a spot where the soil was rich and moist and emptied it ever so carefully.

Kurt's secret place looked much the same as it did when he climbed the boulder chasing Charlie. Only the weather was different. There was no sign of the storm except for a few lingering rain clouds drifting slowly toward the east.

The boy was sure this was the same day. "But how could all that time have passed in Whiskers and so little have passed here?" he asked himself. "Maybe none of it happened at all. Maybe I fell and hit my head when I climbed the boulder."

He noticed Charlie staring at something in the sky, and when he looked up, for an instant he thought he saw the Nimbus. The bird seemed to flash silver as it crossed the sun. "Parhelion!" he shouted, but no one answered. "Just a bird," he said to Charlie. "Let's go, boy." He patted Charlie on the back of his neck and realized the dog's collar was missing. "What happened to your collar, boy?" he asked, half expecting Charlie to answer. The dog wagged his tail and a little puff of sparkling dust settled slowly to the ground.

Out of curiosity, he checked the backpack. No Chunkie Chewies. He noticed the library book on the ground where he dropped it—near the scrub oak tree, now a pile of splintered rubble. Though the book was soaked, when he picked it up, it opened precisely to the page he had last been reading. He closed it again, ever so gently, and put it into his backpack.

A glint of light caught his eye. Raindrops clinging to a spider web between two branches of a pine tree caused the delicate lacework to glisten in the sun like fine silver. A shining trail left by a snail ran up the side of the same tree. "That one must not be afraid of heights," he said to Charlie.

The last remnants of the storm had drifted away by then, leaving in their stead a rainbow that materialized before Kurt's eyes. The boy looked at the rainbow for a moment and took the chain from around his neck and held the key in his hand. The key, the chain, and the clasp all shone with the fine patina of old silver.

Kurt looked up at the great bow. He wrapped his fingers around the key and smiled. "It's not a pot of gold that lies at the end of the rainbow, Charlie; it's the Land of Whiskers."

At last he understood. He and Charlie could go back anytime—anytime, that is, when a gentle rain falls at dawn and a flute plays and the air is filled with silver light. He would wait and listen for the call and watch for the open passage. And he would answer—if not the next time, then the time after that—or the time after that.

He reached down and picked up his fishing pole, and when he started walking toward home, he noticed an all-too-familiar quality to his gait. He was lame again. But somehow it didn't matter. He thought about Stinkle and Fraidy and Tattle and Notch. "You know, Charlie, it's not what you're *called*; it's what you *are* that counts. C'mon, boy," he said, hoisting the fishing pole up onto his shoulder, "I'm going back to school tomorrow. And right after school, we're going to buy you a new collar—a bright yellow one."

ℰPILOGUE

Thus it happened, just as told to me by the Nimbus.

When Kurt arrived home, his mother had not yet returned from her trip to the train station. But another was there waiting for the boy—someone he dearly loved and missed.

When Kurt's father drove the Troll from Whiskers years before, he was seized by the Troll's Vanguard and imprisoned behind the veil in the underground sea. In a vengeful attempt to spread a shadow of despair over the land, the Troll's legions deceived some into believing death had occurred in Whiskers. Even the Nimbus believed it was so.

But even then, light triumphed over darkness, for the tale of death failed to spread beyond the Far Regions.

Kurt's father never lost faith in the Legacy. He knew Kurt would come to Whiskers. When Kurt sealed the Troll in his tomb and defeated the power of darkness, the veil lifted. Kurt's father stepped through the archway, and in an instant, found himself back in his own world.

Perhaps you think the story ends here. Not so. As I said when I began this tale, I found *The Book* in the woods near the lake. What was I doing there? I was searching for my little dog. There had been rumblings all morning from an approaching storm, you see, and she, being afraid of thunder, had run into the woods. I found her huddled behind a large, gray boulder near a steep wall of rock. It was then I stumbled upon *The Book* and picked it up. I thumbed through it all the way to the last page, which was blank. As I turned the last page, another appeared, also blank, and yet another after that. There seemed no end to *The Book*. Indeed, every page seemed but a beginning. Then the Nimbus appeared, and the rest I have told you.

Oh! There's yet one other thing. The Nimbus told me this also:

> *The boy, in passing through the gate,*
> *Had sealed the Troll unto his fate,*
> *Nevermore to hear the knell*
> *And waken to the leaden bell.*
>
> *He'd held the flask within his hand*
> *And spread its fragrance on the Land*
> *And called to life the jubilant sprite*
> *And dressed her once again in light.*
>
> *So watch the air at dawn's first glow,*
> *When clouds have sent to earth below*
> *The precious pearls, the silver grain,*
> *The soft, the silent, silver rain,*
>
> *And elfin voices on the breeze*
> *Have whispered through the swaying trees*
> *And dried the drops and left behind*
> *The fairy dust of silver shine.*
>
> *For somewhere dancing in the light,*
> *Her silken gown the purest white,*
> *With rainbows shining in her hair,*
> *A sunbeam twirls upon the air.*

THE END

ORDER INFORMATION

To order additional copies of this book, please visit
www.redemption-press.com.
Also available on Amazon.com and BarnesandNoble.com
or by calling toll-free 1-844-2REDEEM.

CPSIA information can be obtained
at www.ICGtesting.com
Printed in the USA
BVHW061821060522
636307BV00010BA/677

9 781646 455218